D1516806

THE REIGN
OF THE STAVKA

Ray Little,

Please enjoy my literary
adventure.

9-29-95

THE REIGN OF THE STAVKA

Timothy Burton Anderson

G & D

Grossmont & Diehl
Publishers, Inc.

New York

Grossmont & Diehl Publishers, Inc.
244 Madison Avenue #700
New York, New York 10018

This novel is a work of fiction. The events described here are imaginary. The settings and characters are fictitious and not intended to represent specific places or living persons.

Copyright 1995 by Timothy Burton Anderson
All rights reserved. This book or parts thereof may not be reproduced in any form without permission.

Library of Congress Catalogue Card Number:
94-7416

ISBN 0-9644713-0-2

Manufactered in the United States of America

1 2 3 4 5 6 7 8 9 10

Book design by Wallace Brazzeal

This book is dedicated to

Vicki,

McKinna,

Auston,

and Preston

Carefully selecting his steps, Joe worked his way across the scattered debris in the direction of the individuals. Ron Duncansen followed close behind. As they reached the pair, Joe shined his flashlight in their direction. He noted what at first appeared to be the dark recesses or shadows around the eyes of the two men. Closer inspection revealed the unmistakable peculiarity that they both seemed to be wearing sunglasses. He approached from a distance of about ten feet and detected military-type uniforms, each of them wearing bloused pants with high boots and dark colored shirts. He focused on the berets they wore and noted that one of the two was carrying a military rifle. The forward facing hand grips, as well as the way it was slung over the man's shoulder, caused Joe to double check his vision, and then look back at Ron Duncansen. Ron shrugged. Joe leaned toward the men. "Who the hell are you?"

There was no answer. The two men seemed frozen where they stood in the ray of light, as if his flashlight possessed some hypnotic power. Even in his inexperience, Joe sensed the signals of some type of self-perceived culpability on the part of the two. They simply looked guilty. He demanded more vigorously, "What are you doing out here?" The silence persisted and Joe reached down and unlatched the leather strap across the holster of his wide grip 357 magnum police revolver. The two men still stood motionless. Joe was struggling with the thought of what to do next.

Presently, one of the men moved slightly by looking over his shoulder in the direction of the ranch. In the next moment, out of the darkness another man, clad in more civilian attire came forward, out of breath from his negotiation of the rugged boulder area to the crash site. "Hello - hello!" he called.

Joe redirected his flashlight. By then Ron Duncansen had joined him. "Are you with these two . . . guys?"

"Yes, these men are with me from . . . from the ranch. We heard the commotion and came to see if we could help. It's all very tragic."

"Did you see what happened?" Ron interjected.

"No, we didn't. We just came out here to unlock the gate. It looks like there's nothing we can do," he said firmly.

Joe responded almost to himself, "It looks like there's nothing any of us can do."

As if communicating in sign language to the deaf, the man gave indisputable hand signals for the two uniformed men to return to the ranch. They began to leave. The spokesman remained. "This is terrible, isn't it? We had no idea this could happen!"

Joe had left his notebook in the patrol car and was not yet prepared to start his report. The man began walking into the darkness as had the other two only moments earlier. "Hold up there, mister, where do you live in case I need to talk to you again? I need your name."

"Uh, I'm at the ranch. My name is Jim."

"Jim - what?" Joe demanded. The man ignored the question and disappeared into the unlit field in the direction of the ranch.

Although the confrontation with the strangers had seemed peculiar, Joe and Ron were overwhelmed with the immensity of the catastrophe and directed their attention to the task at hand. Their efforts continued on into the night. By midnight, the ambulance crew had hastened away to support better prospects of survival elsewhere. They had been replaced by Utah Department of Transportation crews who had set up powerful construction area lighting so that the grotesque work of recovering the dead could continue through the night. Joe also remained at the scene.

By the time he left at 4 a.m., he knew that the bodies were going to be extremely difficult to identify due to the puzzling fact that there were no purses, wallets or other identifying documents in the wreckage or found anywhere near the crash site.

Moscow, Russian Republic, Early September, 1992

He chuckled at the American term, "bean counting" as he studied the Western concomitant to his present occupation. What wasn't humorous, was the amount of time that Alexander Kutuzov had spent trying to push his hand-held calculator to its limits.

The task had been relatively simple; to confirm what appeared to be an absence of U.S. dollar currency funds in the general loan account at the Moscow headquarters of his employer - Toko Bank. Each attempt to

PROLOGUE

Bright light flashed in the night high upon the mesa, like brilliant crystals exploding, dancing, then dissipating into the crisp, callous cold of the desert midnight in early spring, 1993. From the distant vantage in the town below, debate had been ignited by the events of the evening past.

Some claimed a freak electrical storm, sort of a bizarre mutation of already unusual weather patterns riding the southwesterlies into the county. Others were certain they saw and heard more. Strange flying objects. UFO's maybe? Of course, the mesa had been used by Hollywood for everything from westerns to science fiction thrillers. It might have been a film shoot. The black smoke disbursing into the morning sky advanced the theory of a range fire to the fore. The moderate winter, allowing for dry sagebrush, lent credence to such conjecture.

The activities atop the flat sprawl of the Hurricane Mesa had always been a source of mystery and rumor to the sparsely distributed citizens dwelling in the washes and valleys in the desert expanse below. They knew that there was a runway and some buildings on the mesa. Whatever the phenomenon, most folks agreed that it had happened at the "Test Site," a post World War II derivative effectively passed on from cowboy grandparent to grandchild as an aberration of local lore - and caution.

After years of living in the long shadow of the massive mountain, speculation and rumor would suffice as the fullest practical extent of local inquiry. Would the dark secret, if there was one, be safely kept?

CHAPTER 1

Kolob Mountain Road, Southwestern, Utah, Early September, 1992

"Drive a little slower, honey, this road twists all over the place!" The woman expressed her concern to her husband as he guided the light-weight Toyota 4-door down the Kolob Mountain Road toward the small town of Virgin, Utah. It had been a long day with a visit to friends in Cedar City. The detour over Cedar Mountain to enjoy the spectacle of preautumnal colors and a little trout fishing had come as somewhat of an afterthought. Darkness had overpowered the massive red rock monoliths of the western reaches of Zion National Park as the car followed the narrow two lane road across Smith Flat to the snake-like switchbacks which descended to the Virgin River valley below.

It had been a successful day. The irrigation demands of eastern Washington County had reduced the level of the Kolob Reservoir, producing excellent fishing by depriving the cutthroat trout of remote spots in which to hide. But sundown had arrived and it was time to leave the mountain. It would be an even longer drive through the night, at least three hours to Las Vegas, once they rejoined Interstate 15. The trip could continue beyond Barstow if they were of a mind to travel late into the night. The ultimate destination was home near Sacramento.

The tight five mile per hour turns made the woman's stomach uneasy. She was five month's pregnant. She had attempted a conversation with her fourteen year old niece in the back seat to take her mind off the nausea, but the niece was dozing, unaffected by the erratic motion of the small car on the mountain road.

The Toyota finally encountered a straightaway, a relief of sorts. Still, with dark canyons on either side as the road ascended the spine of the mesa in a southerly direction, cautious driving was paramount. Figuring that any cause for gastric upset was now at an end, the woman finally began to relax.

Suddenly, scrub oak trees could be seen filling the beam of the car's headlights. The woman shrieked, "Watch out!" Her husband was already correcting hard to the right in an effort to deal with the loss of control. His action resulted in the fishtail motion causing the headlights to again frame the desert vegetation, this time on the left side of the road.

For a moment control seemed realized, but the car jerked violently once again, creating a more startling picture in the split second following. There were no trees, but only lights beaming off into the black void. And then the car was careening headlong into the dark sky, having been launched off the cliff into the gaping recesses of the canyon below like a child's toy accidentally dropped into a deep well. First impact occurred four hundred feet later.

There was time only for terrified gasps, but little more, as the auto did a complete flip in the air. It then impacted, rear end first, on jagged rock spindles designed by nature to mercilessly rip, maim and tear any wingless victim of gravity be it a pebble or a bus launched from atop the cliff.

The vehicle broke into three large pieces relegating its occupants to human projectiles as one smash after another made the violence of death only more absolute. The main torso of the car stopped rolling about forty feet inside the security gate on the gravel road leading to the remote canyon confines of the Sunset Canyon Ranch.

For a moment there was subtle movement in the part of the car where the woman passenger had been sitting. But along with all other life so often dependent upon the outcome of reflex, split second judgement and luck as well, the motion in her womb stirred slightly, then was still.

* * *

Washington County sheriff's deputy, Joe Wilson, had just completed a stolen property investigation in the town of Springdale at the mouth of Zion National Park when he received a call from the sheriff's dispatcher in the town of St. George some forty miles to the west. He knew the Sunset Canyon Ranch area well, having spent many days of his youth riding horses in the area, and even more importantly, accompanying friends to see the magnificent quarter horses being bred and trained for racing at the ranch. He noted an uneasiness deep in his gut as he made the turn at the town of Virgin to head northward up the Kolob Mountain Road. A deputy sheriff for only three months, he had already seen two major car wrecks. In both cases, the morbid reality of death had remained etched painfully in his mind.

Somehow the solitude at the scene of a serious car accident on a lonely country road seemed inconsistent with his perception of how such an event should be. On both prior occasions he had found himself sharing the stillness of a roadside disaster area with people who were either dead or nearly beyond help as they awaited the ambulance. There had been no sound other than muted groans of agony stifled by the cold desert wind. The wind seemed to deliver a chill even on the warmest of summer nights when death was present. He did not want to face it alone again.

It irritated him that the sheriff had put only one deputy on duty at a time in the east end of the county. To the twenty-one year old, the county sheriff's budget matters were insignificant. He had sidestepped college in favor of a patrol car - at least for awhile. At nine hundred dollars a month, he was one of the few young men in the county willing to work for less than minimum wage.

From the first report over the radio until his arrival at the Sunset Canyon Ranch security gate, almost twenty minutes had elapsed. He could see the flickering of flashing red and blue lights of emergency vehicles dancing on the canyon walls several miles ahead of him proclaiming an awful event.

On arrival it was evident that the county ambulance had preceded him by not more than five minutes. The knotting in his stomach intensified as he added the strength of his headlights to the fixed beams of the ambulance already focused on a spot at the base of the cliff. The main part of the wreckage was strangely still in contrast to the idling of the emergency vehicle engines. Several other cars with gawking passersby had gathered where Kolob Mountain Road joined the access road to the ranch. They too were shining lights into the crash area.

Debris was strewn across the lighted area and well beyond. Where the main wreckage had come to rest, it appeared that the top of the car had been entirely sheared off with seats and other interior parts spread in scattered clumps across the jagged rocks and sage brush. In the misty gray rays of headlights, it was difficult to tell vehicle parts from body parts.

The horrid scene notwithstanding, Joe tried to maintain a semblance of professional bearing as he searched for initial clues. Had there been a fire? Had more than one vehicle been involved? How many bodies were in the wreck? Within a few moments of this grim effort, he found himself so dizzy, he was afraid he would be ill. He retreated to the ambulance where the paramedics applied ammonia capsules. Within minutes, he was wandering back to the gory job that would consume the balance of his shift.

Suddenly, Joe thought he saw motion in the crash area. Adjusting his focus, he noted the paramedics were congregated near the ambulance. He instinctively checked the bystanders. They were still seventy-five to a hundred yards to the south along the Kolob Road and well clear of the crash area. Squinting, he could make out two figures wandering amid the wreckage casting giant stick-figured silhouettes against the canyon wall as they went.

''Are those your people, Ron?''

''Joe, they were at the gate when we got here.'' Ron Duncansen was a long-time pro, having served as a paramedic and ambulance driver for many years.

''Did you ask them what happened, or if they saw anything?''

''I tried to talk to 'em at the gate because at first they acted kinda' like they didn't wanta' let us in. It was really kind of weird, Joe,'' Ron said. ''In fact, none of 'em really said anything even though I called over to 'em a few times. Then another guy came up and opened the gate. He motioned for us to come in. It looks like they came from over at the ranch there.''

Ron was gesturing toward the dimly lit ranch house of the Sunset Canyon Ranch set back in the trees about a quarter mile across an open field at the mouth of a narrow side canyon.

obtain a balance on the bank's account with the Russian Ministry of Aviation had proven a herculean undertaking. It was a certainty that he would encounter severe difficulty in trying to elicit the assistance of other employees. Nevertheless, Nieca Gabrilyan, a part-time employee, had uncharacteristically remained after hours to lend assistance.

Alexander, sporting a lean, even youthful appearance on his six foot frame, was fifty-six years old. Grey strands were the exception rather than the rule in what was still largely a full head of hair with only a partially receding hairline near the part above his left eye. By Russian standards he was handsome, and at times, able to play a clever provocative smile to his advantage. It was the look of a pilot, or even better - a Cosmonaut, the most cherished of Russian images.

He was in his second full year with the bank following his early retirement with the Foreign Ministry. Government work over the years had largely confined him to the African theater doing work out of Russian embassies in Algeria, Morocco, and Angola. More than once he had been assigned to duties under the control of the Second Directorate of the KGB. He had never thought of himself as a spy and could not reconcile spending so much of his life gathering information on perceived enemies of the State. But the KGB had endeavored to press into service every Soviet national outside the boundaries of the Motherland, and Alexander had been no exception from the practice.

Nieca was a slender, well-designed thirty-six year old. Her blonde hair and blazing blue eyes gave a nordic look. Unlike the majority of Russian women, not the weather, food, nor the culture had yet ravaged her appearance. Alexander had noticed her and found himself stirred by her nearness. It was the first time since the untimely passing of his wife approximately six months after he joined the bank that he had sensed such emotions. Despite the attraction, Alexander had kept his feelings to himself. He assumed that he shared the same impulses with the rest of the men in the bank. From time to time he made a positive gesture with flowers from the market, but that was as far as his courage allowed him to go. In return, Nieca's wide and radiant smile, combined with a warm sense of being seemed a plentiful reward. He enjoyed being with her, and he often wondered if she had feelings for him.

The unsuccessful coup of August 1991 was no boon to the Russian banking industry. On the contrary, the Russian parliament in tandem with the Ministry of Finance of the Republic of Russia had passed regulations that further restricted the outflow of currency for projects in Western countries. This stifled the creative efforts of Russian entrepreneurs pioneering foreign trade opportunities that might bring much needed capital into the country. The international department of Toko Bank was placed in a position of having to retrench in its planning for what it initially had anticipated to be a bounteous opportunity of joining the real world of high finance.

The irony of stricter controls, after a supposedly more progressive noncommunist regime had taken over, filtrated into other areas of Russian bureaucracy. To a large extent, it was just one group of kings replacing another, accompanied by the simplistic adoration of much of the Western World.

Alexander wondered why, as a banker, he was still using a simple hand calculator while trying to track the whereabouts of significant funds of the Russian Ministry of Aviation. The Ministry had computers - and not just any computers. There were some four hundred thousand IBM compatible PC's in use throughout the former Soviet Union, some with 386 and 486 CPUs. Of that number, over three hundred thousand were owned and operated by defense related industries, the most prominent of which were the Ministries of Aviation and Aerospace. Russian software engineers and computer technicians had gone to extensive efforts to network the mass of PC's. This required hi-tech improvisation on a grand scale. The result was PC's being used for tasks beyond the expertise of Western computer engineers.

As Alexander and Nieca moved through dozens of volumes of account sheets stuffed into large manila folders, they discovered certain entries which read, "see computer printouts." This resulted in an immediate dead end, since the printouts were not kept in the bank, but across town at the Ministry of Aviation. Nevertheless, Alexander had been instructed to provide a report. He was fully cognizant of hints that he had received from superiors that a report favorable to the Ministry might be welcomed, given the reality that one of the principal subsidiaries of the Ministry of Aviation owned one third of the bank's entire stock. Troubled by this mandate, Alexander ventured that perhaps a pattern of withdrawals or wire transfers to other accounts might emerge that could at least give him some idea of where and how the funds were being used.

Ironies continued to strike him as he examined the foreign currency account of the Ministry of Aviation. He realized that next to photographs of children and family in one's wallet or purse, it was likely that the portrait of the American patriot, George Washington on the dollar bill, was most treasured in Russia. Dollars always spoke louder than rubles.

The currency account had to be funded by some foreign transaction. Something had to be sold by the Ministry of Aviation or its subsidiaries to someone with dollars, marks, yen, or some convertible foreign currency in order to put foreign currency in the account. Alexander reasoned that something of value would need to be given in order to cause the Ministry to take currency out of the account and wire it to another destination. In effect, Alexander was educating himself regarding the most fundamental aspects of the doctrine of consideration. Without the printouts from the Ministry of Aviation, he would have no success.

After giving his dilemma careful consideration, he decided to turn in a report which would frustrate his superiors as a sort of test. His prying inquisitive personality demanded it. In Russia it was the era of criticism and controversy. Alexander sensed there would be little recrimination. The report was simple and to the point. After scratching the essence of his thoughts on a note pad, he handed it to Nieca. Their hands touched. She smiled and read out loud:

To First Deputy Director, Toko Bank from Alexander Kutuzov:
Thank you for allowing me to inspect the Ministry of Aviation
accounts regarding possible missing currency funds. Unfortu-
nately, without computer printouts from the Ministry of Avi-
ation, which can explain such entries, I am unable to inform you
as to the full nature of such transactions.

"You are a fine thinker, Alexander Kutuzov," she said.

* * *

The next morning the First Deputy checked his correspondence. His attention was drawn to the impertinent memo from Deputy Kutuzov. He was not amused. He was angered. He pondered the subject of Kutuzov's son. A recent graduate of Moscow University's Institute for International Finance could well be overlooked for a possible position with Toko Bank because of the memo. His response was to pen a terse return memo to Kutuzov:

You should understand that it is not bank policy to inquire as to the nature of confidential defense-related expenditures. Your assignment was only to note their existence and not to seek backup documentation. It is not the position of this bank to inquire into State secrets and if a report on the Ministry of Aviation accounts is not submitted to me before 5:00 p.m. tomorrow, I will then take the matter up with the Bank Director and it will not be well for you.

Shortly after lunch, Alexander walked to Nieca's work area and showed her the First Deputy Director's response. She put her hand on his arm and he sat down beside her. "I am perplexed, Alex. You work so hard."

Alexander responded with a smile and said, "I've been here for two years, but these people still don't know Alexander Kutuzov." He was feeling close to Nieca and puffed up by his bravery. He felt it was time. "Would you join me at the music theater evening after next?"

"Yes," was the immediate reply.

Kutuzov, taken by surprise, decided that he had made more progress in one day than over the previous two years. Toko Bank's problems had only just begun.

CHAPTER 2

St. Petersburg - Moscow Highway, Early September, 1992

She cuddled the infant warmly in her arms then brought him to her breast for his morning meal. Gurgles and sweet sounds of a nestling baby warmly consumed the moment. Seldom had there been such contentment and sense of well being as she held the six week old baby close and simply allowed the passing time to take care of itself.

Presently, she could hear her four year old daughter begin to stretch and move in her bed across the hall as she arose from a long night's rest. Within moments, she felt a slight vibration caused by the thud of a child's feet reaching the floor from atop a thick mattress on a high bed frame. It was followed by the shuffle of tiny feet making their way across the hall toward the master bedroom.

The singing of birds nesting in the backyard trees afforded a wake-up call yielding a soft serenade accompanied by momentary strains from the downstairs television. Her six year old was also awake and probably engrossed in the Muppet Babies or Sesame Street. The radiant warmth of the southwest desert sun beaming through her easterly window added enjoyment to the perfect moment. Always so completely serene and happy. How could life be so good - how could it all be so pleasurable?

Suddenly she jerked forward. Something was wrong. Again, a jolt! In the next moment, she catapulted forward and struck something hard and cold. She found herself gazing into a strange darkness. It was then she felt the strong hand of her husband braced against her ribs as he spoke, "Careful, Gina, these gears are giving me trouble again!"

"Uh...what...where am I? Where are they. . .?"

"I think you're dreaming again, sweetheart," he spoke softly.

"Yes. . . I suppose I was." Gina squeezed her eyes closed and tried to cuddle back against the seat in the cab of the semi-trailer truck as it bounced along, intending to return to the land of her dreams. Tossing and turning for a few minutes, she resigned herself to being awake and felt the disappointment of reality. "Michael, where are we?"

"We're about five kilometers west of Kalpine."

"And where is that from Leningrad - I mean how far are we from St. Petersburg?"

"The way these highway signs are in Russia, it's hard to tell, sweetheart. But I can still see the lights of the city in the rear view mirror, reflecting off the clouds. So, I guess it's about thirty kilometers behind us."

Gina was now wide awake and attempting to make a full recovery from her sleep by looking in the mirror and putting on some make-up from her Merle Norman cosmetics compact in her purse. She checked her watch. It was 5:30 a.m. Her mind immediately went into the time-zone calculating mode to decide what time it was at various points across the world that were important to her. In Denmark, it is 3:30 a.m. She then allowed her mind to wander halfway around the world to the American Southwest where she estimated it was 11:30 at night. Those places were significant, far more significant than where she was at present - somewhere along the St. Petersburg to Moscow highway early on a late summer morning which, as far as she was concerned, was already winter.

Realizing that his wife had been awakened from a dream, he talked to her in English. The conversation could just as well have occurred in Danish inasmuch as the two shared their conversation time with one another equally in either language. Michael was Danish, having been born and bred in Copenhagen. He was the product of an uncharacteristically large family. With ten siblings, his family was nine above the children per couple average in his country.

The family was reasonably affluent by Danish standards, his father having operated several businesses over the years both within and outside of Denmark. This had allowed some travel for Michael, along with his father, to other countries of Europe. Another unique trait of the Christensen family was that in 1967 they had converted to the Church of Jesus Christ of Latter-Day Saints, also known as the Mormons. As members of a small congregation in Copenhagen, they experienced close ties to the church with its headquarters in Salt Lake City, Utah. When Michael had reached the age of nineteen years, an even more uncharacteristic event occurred as the church sent him on a proselyting mission to the state of Utah. Thus, a product of one of the church's most distant outposts was being sent to the heartland to teach the Gospel.

For Michael, this was a unique opportunity. Provincial Americans in Utah being taught Mormonism by a boy from Denmark raised eyebrows at every turn. His two year experience took him to many parts of Utah including the southwestern town of St. George. For him, St. George was an enjoyable assignment. It was the largest community in the red rock desert canyon country of the southwestern part of his mission.

Over the course of his mission, as in the case of all such foreign missionaries, he mastered the language. His distinguished accent bolstered his presentations with a certain degree of cultural flare and credibility. In some circles it conferred a sort of celebrity status.

Gina had observed Michael during church meetings. When his mission concluded, he qualified for a student visa and entered the local community college. She was pleased - attractions developed, they fell in love, and after a few months of courtship they were married.

Gina was sufficiently lucid now to realize it was likely they would celebrate an anniversary of their marriage somewhere on a secluded stretch of Russian highway. It would be another one of those events where the unusual overshadowed the celebration. How many girls from St. George, Utah get to enjoy their tenth anniversary in the cab of a semi-truck on the road to Moscow, she thought to herself. Lucky me.

The experience in Denmark was viewed as temporary duty only. She longed to return with her husband and children to the wide open spaces of the land of her upbringing. Denmark was not the place to raise a family. Michael had tasted life in America enough to be in full agreement.

Work as a salesman in the Danish Data Distributor computer store in Copenhagen had been a demanding but rewarding start for Michael as a young businessman. The market in Denmark for PC's was not large and finding buyers was an almost around-the-clock effort. Then, just as sales prospects were going from bad to bleak, a group of sailors from a Soviet freighter had come into the store and Michael made an effortless sale of one hundred computers. It took less than twenty minutes.

In the months that followed, Russian ships docking in Copenhagen became a unique sales opportunity for Michael. Soviet sailors were in his store weekly and he was unloading a considerable amount of inventory to them on a cash-and-carry basis. In less than three months, he became the top salesman in the company. Almost overnight he became a major player for sales of IBM PC's, components, and software products in Denmark. Recognizing his earnest willingness to learn, the company sent Michael to the Copenhagen Institute where he excelled, rapidly proving his brilliance in advanced computer studies. Soon his reputation preceded him among the several chain computer stores in the country. Michael Christensen was the guy who could run almost any hardware on the market from simple PC"s to ultra sophisticated Crays and teach the craft to other salesmen in well organized workshop style. Within months, he was spending as much time teaching as he was selling. Michael had become the whiz kid of the computer sales industry as deals of all sizes, domestic and military, national and international, began to materialize.

Yet, even with all of the success, the Danish market was small. Remembering well his first major sale, Michael became one of the early computer sales entrepreneurs looking eastward with an eye to opening up the almost infinite emerging free market of the rapidly transitioning Soviet Union.

"I wish we could somehow call home and check on the kids," Gina said.

"We're in Russia. That's just not possible," Michael responded, just as tired but kept awake by the challenge of driving the truck.

"I know that, but I worry about the kids. I'm worried about your parents - the kids are such a handful." She paused, then addressed her deeper concern, "I really don't like the idea of spreading our children out across the world. Here we are driving a semi across Russia, with three of our kids in Denmark and two of them back in St. George. It's just too uncertain. . . too. . ." she was grasping for some early morning conclusion, "too out-of-control. I feel like we don't have enough control over our lives. And, I hate relying on these Russians for anything."

"Well, this will be the last time I'm going to drive a truckload of computers from Copenhagen to Moscow. But you never know what they're going to come up with next."

"I don't trust them, Michael - not for anything. You know as well as I do that they don't do anything unless they can take advantage of us."

"I think you're right, sweetheart. But, I think they need me. There's been talk about setting up an office in the States. It's just talk. It would be hard to live in New York or L.A. - at least it's in the States. I think they gotta' keep me satisfied so that they have someone who'll front for them if they do decide to do something in America. It's pretty hard to find someone from the West who really understands them enough to work longer than a month or so. They're not easy people to work for."

"That's for sure," she agreed.

"We've come a long way with them. After those six months in Moscow last year - I mean, I think it was sort of baptism by fire. We surprised them by sticking it out. I know it was a hard thing for us to go through; sort of like going camping in a big city for six months. But I think it was a test of loyalty. And you know how the Russians are about loyalty. They won't do business with anybody they don't know extremely well. Ability and competence don't account for much. Kind of a strange way to do business, but then they're pretty strange people."

"It's all so iffy," Gina commented. "It's been that way ever since you've been working with them."

Michael changed the subject. "Should we stop and stretch? I'm not sure I still have a rear-end. It's been asleep for the last two hours. I guess I'm just not the long-haul trucker type."

Gina reached over and squeezed Michael's hand. "Thank goodness for that."

Hurricane, Utah, Early September, 1992

Had it been done according to the book, the accident report would have been written up and submitted in triplicate into the department logs prior to going off shift. Hanging around the repulsive accident scene at the Sunset Canyon Ranch until 4 a.m. had been quite enough. The demands of intense fatigue had superseded the need to report.

Sunday was his day off, but apprehension stirred by the events of the previous night plagued his consciousness. There was only one place to go; the sheriff's office to fill out the accident report rather than wait until Monday.

Budgeting constraints of the Washington County's sheriff's office had long since driven away secretarial help at the substation in the small town of Hurricane. The bare storefront office included little more than a desk, a security lock-up closet, and an emergency dispatch radio. The radio, however, was seldom in use because the main dispatch was in St. George, the county seat, some eighteen miles to the southwest.

As he sat alone pouring over the incident report form that required him to describe his special observations, he began filling in the essentials:

Reporting Officer: Joe Wilson
Date of incident: Sept. 3, 1992
Place: Kolob Road, Sunset Canyon Ranch
Time: Apx 2130 hrs.
Weather: Clear
Incident: One Toyota Tercel '89, traveling southbound on Kolob Mountain Road veered across the N. bound lane, and left the right-of-way to the East. Minimal shoulder. Car traveled some 400 ft. off cliff. All occupants dead at scene. Witnesses included resident at Sunset Canyon Ranch, person named "Jim" who heard the crash. Two other adult males at scene with Jim. No names given, will investigate further.
Observations:

*1) Three victims dead at scene. No first aid. Para-
medics at scene prior to R.O.
2) No identifying documents at scene. Could not find wallets, purses or valuables. Watches and rings likewise not on
bodies nor found at accident site. R.O. will proceed with daylight follow-up.
3) UDOT arrived with flood lights at 2345.
4) Recovery of victims and vehicle completed by 0400,
Sept. 24.*

Moscow, Russian Republic, Early September, 1992

The First Deputy took his job very seriously. Impertinent memos from subordinates were intolerable, an utter insult to his overt Russian pride. He had ample reason to be proud of his accomplishments. The Intersectorial Commercial Bank for the Development for Wholesale Trade, known as Toko Bank, had fared very well in its first two years. Emerging as one of the early positive outcomes of Peristroika, the bank had commenced operation with the declared authorized fund of 55.7 million rubles. By the end of the first year of operation, it had transacted 151 million rubles in business, showing a profit of 21 million. Profit was something to which Russians were not accustomed, and for the Russian who could successfully turn such a trade, the squalid demands of work became a pleasure. A profitable Russian bank was a puzzling anomaly.

During the brief period of time of the bank's existence, it had set up divisions and branch banks in several regions including Siberia, the Far East, and the Central Plain. The branch offices had been instituted in the cities of Leningrad, Vladivostok, Yuzhno-Sakalinska, Kuybyshev, and Denepropetroesk. Plans had been underway to increase the network of branch banks in future years. The bank's principal ownership consisted of a three-sided consortium including the Republic of Russia on the governmental side, AgroProm Bank, and Technoserv, a burgeoning state-owned business and subsidiary of the Ministry of Aviation on the other side.

The First Deputy was mulling over the documentation of the purchase of several brick plants by the Moscow-based amalgamation Dagomos. Even the Tetaev Motorworks in Yaroslav County had recently become a candidate for funding.

"It is beyond belief," the First Deputy Director muttered to himself, realizing that only a few years earlier winning such projects and charging interest would have been viewed as the most decadent of Western practices. But the Moscow-trained banker who had only read of commercial bank operations in the West but never seen them, was right in the middle of it all. He often advertised his management style as one based on the implementation of a Russian proverb, "Measure it twice, and cut once," to make sure the interests of all parties in a transaction were clearly respected.

In turn, respect had grown for the First Deputy among the elite. He was viewed as one of the bright spots in an otherwise dark void of commercial and business banking failures. More than once the President of Russia had consulted with the First Deputy on key financial and economic issues. He reveled in the parade of high-level economists and aparatchiks who made the trek to the bank from the Kremlin, each with a question which he could often answer. But the ongoing deficiencies of the Russian system could not be ignored. The First Deputy had studiously concluded that the lack of fundamental banking and finance knowledge on the part of the government officials was destined to drown the Motherland in a sea of incompetence unless a major refinance plan was quickly implemented.

As the senior member of the Russian Parliament, his banking successes kept him well in the favorable stead of the majority of Moscow's elite to whom profitable banking was worse than the mystery of the ages. Even though the Party had died a sudden death at the hands of Yeltsin and the reformers, the First Deputy's prominence and purpose had not suffered. On the contrary, all sides were well-suited to a supposed Western style banker trafficking among the highest levels of the Parliamentary leadership. His role with the Supreme Soviet, the forerunner to the new Parliament, and now the reputation of quick and significant investment banking successes had combined to catapult him into a position of stardom amidst the political and economic debate among various factions of the fledgling republic.

For all of his success, the First Deputy had certain forces working against him. The first was his health. Years of chain smoking had taken its toll - a flight of stairs was now a major obstacle. His burly, rounded features covered by thick brown hair made him the human equivalent of the Russian bear. But shortness of breath caused him to rasp and wheeze as he spoke. His gait was a slow, dragging process akin to a severely wounded bear at best. If wealth and success was to be his, it would need to be immediate. There was no time to wait around for reforms to take hold. Like a good capitalist, he wanted it all - and preferably while he was alive to enjoy it.

But he also knew that the days of Yeltsin were numbered. The secret meetings of the Parliament's Security Committee had become more frequent. The fact that the conclaves had been moved off the grounds of the Russian White House to a nondescript flat in the Cheremushki district was signal enough that something serious was brewing. But upon his admission to one of the sessions, he had learned even more than he had wanted to know. The old way would be restored, but in a new and better form. The words had been vague, but the resolve very clear and forceful. A plan was in place and at some point he would learn the details. In the interim however, he knew that a wise man could make a personal fortune.

As he viewed the report submitted to him by Alexander Kutuzov, he was offended by the impertinence, but delighted with the result. It made sense, he thought, to assign a minion with limited banking experience to officially audit the Aviation Ministry account. It assured that the Ministry's questionable holdings would be safe from disclosure, and that was important to the First Deputy. Once the obligatory audit had been performed, nothing out of the ordinary would be reported. The fact that questions might exist for more underlying documentary detail was insignificant. It would protect him for a short time at least.

His certainty about the impermanent nature of his success and his deduction that the bank would never survive the changes ahead controlled his actions. There was no such thing as fraud in a nation whose living generations had known only deceit. The First Deputy had no intention of going down with a sinking ship. His next move was to the telephone where he placed a long-distance call to a remote Far Eastern location.

CHAPTER 3

Sunset Canyon Ranch, Early September, 1992

A warm wind of late summer blew down the canyon through the Cottonwoods along the river and across the well-kept pasture. It created a sound of rushing water which gave way to a whistle around the eaves of the ranch house and pressed tree branches against windows with a grating sound amplified by the stillness of the night. Inside, the house was cold.

In an upstairs bedroom, Flora Jackson clutched at the stale smelling quilt to cover her nakedness. Despite the warmth it gave her, she trembled from the shock and horror of the last hours. As she pressed her thighs together, she could feel the moistness of the towel placed between her legs to help staunch the bleeding. A searing pain shot through her body as she moved nearer the edge of the bed, away from the wheezing, snoring old man now sleeping by her side. A slow trickle of blood oozed from the scratches he had made on her neck with his long, jagged fingernails. Her head pulsated from the trauma of her hair being yanked by him in a sort of perverted pleasure.

Nothing could ever blot from the mind of the fifteen year old girl the memory of the night just past. She cried softly in fear and agony, but lay still and rigid as the old man flung his bony, withered hand across her body. She was uncertain of his age. She did not know his name and he spoke a strange language she did not understand. But it had taken only moments for her to discover what he wanted.

Flora lay frozen, afraid of waking the old man and being subjected to still further degrading horrors. She closed her eyes and tried to escape by remembering the innocent beginnings of the previous day.

It had been a beautiful morning in the farming community of Red Rock City, Arizona. Flora had gone with her mother to the orchard. She was happy to be spending the day outdoors and looked forward to having a long talk with her mother, Hannah Jackson, away from the others. Usually, they worked in groups. Their conversations, though pleasant enough, tended to be guarded and stilted. The wives and daughters were careful what they said, lest they be summoned before the brethren to explain a ''recreant'' attitude.

Life in Red Rock City to the rest of the world was unique, but not to Flora. She had been taught that it was a place at the center of the world and that outside its boundaries existed only evil where no compromise could be made. Her parents had fled in earlier years to Red Rock City after having been excommunicated from the Mormon church for practicing polygamy. Life in Red Rock City had been dreary, but she learned to quiet the rebellious spirit within her and enjoy her lot. After all, it was such a beautiful place. The high red rock cliffs and cavernous mountain country was certainly a gift from God. As boring, bleak and mundane as she often found life to be, at age fifteen she still thought it the most beautiful place in all the world.

Flora's chestnut brown hair curled around her face and hung down her back. For a rare moment, it had been free of the clips and pins that usually bound it up into a tight, parochially prescribed bun, and it hung in natural loveliness almost to her waist. The other women had been quick to whisper their disapproval regarding the way her mother had allowed Flora to wear her hair. It was a sign of rebellion, rebellion that could not be tolerated.

As they had finally been able to move away from the others and find their own area in the field, Flora began to talk with her mother about things unmentionable in Red Rock City. She looked directly at her mother and asked, "What did you *really* think when father married Pauline?"

Flora remembered her mother turning away to hide the tears. Oblivious that her mother did not want to talk about Pauline, Flora had pressed the issue. "Mother, Pauline is two months younger than me. Yet, she is now the wife of...of.... my father and your husband. Doesn't that almost make you sick, Mother? Will I be given a husband also?"

Flora could remember an earlier response to the eager question, "You are only a child, my dear - your time will come. I hope that for you it is much better than what Pauline has...much better."

"What do you mean, Mother?" she had asked. "What do you mean, exactly?"

Again, she recalled her mother was unwilling to engage in formal discussion on the matter. "Your father...well he is...ah...we must do our duty but...." Her mother had been withdrawn and evasive, "but there are things I hope will be better for you...than they were, well,....for me."

"But Pauline, is my very best friend. I want the best for her too."

"Pauline is only a child, Flora," her mother had said.

"Well, she is old enough to have babies, and so am I. That's what the teachers at school and the brethren say. That as soon as we're old enough to have babies we should become wives," Flora spoke methodically.

She remembered her mother speaking only briefly and saying, "But you are also only a child, Flora."

She recalled her mother's furrowed brow in an effort to control her emotions as they had discussed between mother and daughter a very sensitive subject. She wanted to be like all the other girls in Red Rock City. At the same time, she had remembered thinking that she was only a little girl. Only four months earlier, she and Pauline had played together in the woods, carefree girls, making doll houses out of pine cones. Now Pauline was her father's new wife and already expecting a child. Flora winced at the thought of Pauline in her father's bed. She thought of it now as she listened to the guttural snoring of the stranger beside her.

Following the day's work, the station wagon had turned off the highway and slowed as it hit familiar jolts and bounced along the bumpy half mile lane leading to their house. Flora had asked to stop by Pauline's house to put the finishing touches on a quilt that they had started to tie off

earlier. Her mother had then dropped her off and Flora had happily made her way to one of her father's houses. Hannah's sister-wives were located in various homes and now one was the home of her best friend Pauline and two other sister-wives. It made Flora uneasy to think of Pauline a "sister-mother" or a "sister-wife." They all shared chores and helped with the children.

When she entered the house, her father sat with his arm around Pauline. No, we will not play with dolls ever again, Flora thought. Pauline was now pregnant. She stood inside the door, she felt unusually uncomfortable as her father stared at her, like a stranger appraising her looks.

"Come over here and sit down, Flora. You really do look tired. I suppose you have been working in the orchard today. I'm so glad the weather was nice. It was a cool day." She walked closer and he reached for her arm and pulled her down onto the couch opposite Pauline. "We're glad you finally got here - we've just been talking about you."

She looked at Pauline, "Do you think we can finish the quilt tonight, Pauline?"

"We won't worry about the quilt right now," her father interjected.

"Well, I'd really like to finish it. It's almost done." Flora tensed as she realized that she had disagreed with her father. She watched Pauline who seemed unusually distant. The bridge of understanding between the two friends had started to crumble after the marriage, with each trying to hold on to their childhood feelings. "I can come back another night if you're busy."

"Flora, stand up and let me look at you. I haven't seen you for days." The blustery, patronizing voice of her father boomed through the house like a sermon. Children and sister-wives came in and out of the room. No one seemed to pay attention to what he had to say. "My, but you are growing up, Flora - why, I've watched you shoot up before my very eyes. It makes me proud to see you develop into a full grown woman. The Lord blesses young spirits like yours who enter adulthood, keeping His commandments and living a righteous life. Pauline and I have talked about that often lately, now that she is with child. As a bearer of the priesthood and an obedient servant of our Prophet, I now share the burden of planning for Pauline's exaltation. When her heart seems heavy, I must remind her of her calling and her place. Isn't that true, Pauline?''

The young wife had answered and stood up, busying herself at the quilt on the frame on one side of the room, ''I've been growing in spirit. . .'' The reply was like a recorded message.

Her father's sermonizing had made Flora uneasy. She did not like being the center of attention. Realizing her father was making pious statements for others to hear, she suspected a motive.

Approximately one hour later, when dinner was set, she recalled her father appearing at the table wearing his suit. This meant he was going to a meeting somewhere. Many meetings were held in the homes of members to discuss loyalty, sacrifice, and doctrine. The dogmatic repetition kept cult members in tune with the expectations of the Prophet. She had hoped that the meeting would not be at his home lest she be caught having to sit through a long and boring sermon by one of the community brethren. As he negotiated his way through a long and incantatious prayer, he included one phrase that caught her attention. ''This day, Lord, bless thy daughter Flora with the wisdom of thy spirit, to be obedient and put her trust in her father.''

As the prayer had ended, she had felt the cautious glances of the others. Her father had continued to converse only with her, ignoring the other children. His tone was somewhat apologetic as he cross-examined her through the course of the meal.

Finally, dessert was served, proper appreciation was expressed and the children were excused to study their scriptures.

There had been an uneasy silence for a few moments, broken finally by her father. He cleared his throat and looked directly at her. ''My dear daughter,'' he began.

He's using his church voice, Flora thought to herself.

He continued, ''It was not by accident that you happened by here tonight. It was the Lord's doing. He sent you here for your special mission to undertake a certain challenge in this life. You will join me in a very important test of your faith. This very night, you will have the opportunity to prove your true devotion to our leader. It will be wonderful and good for you if you pass the test. If you do not, however, awful and terrible will be your lot in life - your survival in the eternities is at stake.''

As he had rambled, she remembered feeling the blood draining from her face. Her heart had begun to pound so hard that she scarcely heard the words of her father. She had looked down at her dress and smoothed it with her clenched fists. The words had gone on and on. This was a meeting night alright, she had thought to herself, and somehow it would involve a test of her faith. Fear crept into Flora's very soul. A fear she had never before known.

Eventually, at her father's insistence, they had left his home accompanied by one of his wives who was second only to Flora's mother in seniority. With little discussion, they drove off into the evening. After a silent hour in the car, they stopped in front of a high fence with a locked gate which bore the words "Sunset Canyon Ranch" across the top. It had seemed like such a beautiful name.

They had driven to a sprawling ranch house set back in the trees. She and her sister-mother were invited in; her father had remained outside talking to the old man who now lay beside her. She had walked up the stairs into a small room and her sister-mother, without allowing conversation or explanation, had helped her undress, bathe and dress in night clothing that was totally foreign to anything she had ever seen or felt before. She was then assisted in applying make-up, perfume, also unlike anything used or applied back in Red Rock City. The sister-mother then smiled, kissed her on the forehead and simply said, "Remember, you must be obedient. Your salvation in this life and the next is at stake. Do exactly as you are told." She then gathered Flora's work clothes and left the room without a backward glance.

Within the next few minutes, the old man was at the door. He entered - Flora did as she was told.

It had been a gruesome and terrifying experience. As she lay in the dark, breathing in painful but silent gasps, Flora wondered if there would be life beyond this moment. She listened for other sounds beyond the room. The only sound she could hear were bare branches scratching against the window pane. Did I pass the test, Dear God - did I pass the test?

St. Petersburg - Moscow Highway, Early September, 1992

It was the most remarkable nose Michael had ever seen. Captain Petrovski, fresh off the deck of a less-than-fresh Soviet coal ship, had waddled into the computer store for the third time asking questions by grunting and pointing in a manner which was completely consistent with his unkept and grotesque look. The ripped holes in the armpits of his sea captain's jacket and strange hat, pushed forward and scrunched against his skull exposing the bald part of the back of his head, caused him to appear as a profusely overweight version of the cartoon character, Popeye.

Michael was amused but tactfully kept his distance. The old man sported a broad array of body odors and was likewise a tactician. He conversed at an offensive point blank range. This allowed a periodic spray of saliva and whatever else might be trafficking through his mouth and between his toothless gums to project in the direction of his hapless victim. By the third visit, Michael had become quick afoot and astute at maneuvering himself into position to carry on discussions with the man at a safe distance. With the wide sales-counter between him and the Captain, Michael enjoyed a certain degree of success.

The Captain had become enamored with all of the computer equipment for sale inside the store. He had docked his aging coal ship in the Langelinje Dock area of Copenhagen for the purpose of better scavenging for other more non-tech goods, such as bulk food items. After one visit to Michael's store however, he found it preferable to spend his time watching words and images bounce across the monitor on the computers in the store.

By the third visit, he had arrived with sufficient Danish money to cause Michael to risk entering the man's danger zone to discuss a possible sale. By the end of the visit, the smell of money was almost as thick as Captain Petrovski's putrid odor as he made it clear through sign language and a degree of broken Danish, that he intended to purchase one hundred computers. When Michael could see the Russian was serious about consummating a deal, he realized the magnitude of the sale would enable him to immediately reach his sales goal for the year.

In response to the good fortune of the old Captain's visit, Michael had accepted an invitation to visit the Soviet coal ship. The ship, some three hundred feet in length, had several giant openings where the coal was loaded into the hold through huge sliding doors across the top of the deck. With very little explanation, the Captain beckoned Michael to follow and they worked their way down to his cabin in the aft of the ship immediately below the control room. Michael was overcome by the strong stench that could only be described as a mix between stale and rancid tobacco, sour feet and sweat. The old man picked up an ancient telephone and ordered a meal and drinks for the both of them.

As they waited it was not difficult to strike up a conversation, even with the captain's limited skill at the Danish language. The walls of the cabin were covered with newspaper and magazine pictures from nude women to portraits of Christ. The yellowing of the paper due to years of exposure seemed to color coordinate well with the bulkhead rust that had long ago replaced any semblance of paint. The naked women needed little explanation, but some of the other pictures were masterpieces of memorabilia. Michael was drawn to a picture of the American President Kennedy and the famous Russian Cosmonaut, Yuri Gagarin.

"He is alive," the captain explained gruffly between snorts and spits, pointing at the picture.

Michael looked carefully at the four year old paper and could see it was another one of those Bild Zeitung or National Enquirer-type rags that still had Hitler alive and doing well in a Swedish health clinic or Elvis working for the FBI against the mob. "What makes you think so? Didn't Yuri Gagarin die in a plane crash or something back in the sixties?" Michael asked, wanting to humor the old fellow.

"The Hero of Soviet Union... not dead. He is seen in Russia... he hide."

"Why does he hide?"

"He like Kennedy...they try to kill."

"Who tries to kill?" Michael was intrigued.

"Not know... but I hear rumors... and newspaper say." He pointed to the picture as his principal reckoning point inferring that if it was in print, it must be true.

It was not a new concept. Michael knew that practically every third elderly grandmother in Denmark, Germany and France still had an embroidered memento of the young American President's visit to Europe back in 1963 hanging on a wall somewhere. Kennedy had become an overnight symbol of hope. For the Russians it had been no different, except for the face. As the American's greatest token of its time had been a charismatic messenger of diplomacy, so had the Russian's greatest memory been a Cosmonaut who was first to orbit the earth. It made sense to Michael to assume that the old captain, like so many of the older generation, had taken comfort in the best parts of the past. He chose to avoid further discussion. There was a look in the crusty old man's eyes that signaled to Michael that what appeared as rotting newspapers on the walls to Michael, might be a shrine to the old sailor.

Shortly, a steward appeared at the cabin door carrying a tray of food consisting of a unfamiliar type of breaded meat, canned peas that must have been ten years old and a dish composed of red and white cabbage in vinegar. The requisite caviar was piled on a separate plate.

Michael could hardly keep from gagging and tried to limit his portion to meat and potatoes since the other parts of the meal were, in his mind, clearly not fit for human consumption. But the worst was the chicken. It looked like the remnants of a bad road kill. Michael took one bite, choked down a Coca-Cola and asked if he could have a tour of the ship.

Suddenly, Michael found himself blinking his eyes and momentarily shaking his head to fight off the drowsiness.

"What's wrong, Michael - honey, are you awake?"

Michael, realizing that he was parked along the roadside, grabbed the door handle of the blue Volvo truck and rolled the window down allowing the rush of cold air to awaken him. "I was thinking about the Captain again."

"Just think, if it wasn't for that wonderful guy, we wouldn't be on this road tonight...You really know how to pick your Russians." Gina was willing to apportion the blame.

"Yeah... good ol' Petrovski and his one hundred computers. I was wondering what ever became of him.

"How far do we have to go before we get to Moscow?" Gina changed the subject. She often found herself wishing that her husband had never met the sea captain.

Michael checked the map and estimated their position. "I think we have a pretty good chance of getting there by mid-morning. That is, if we stay at it and don't pull over to do any more sleeping."

He started the engine. The truck continued the journey in the direction of the eastern sky which was already beginning to display its pallet of early morning colors in broad array across the distant horizon.

Hurricane, Utah, Early September, 1992

It was almost noon and Joe Wilson had already driven the entire length of the Hurricane main drag for the seventh time in three hours. Its strategic proximity to Zion National Park kept the restaurants full of tourists at lunch time. Joe had busied himself trying to meet the sheriff's expectations of a new traffic ticket quota. Several surprised out-of-towners had departed the community a little lighter in the checkbook. Yet, Joe knew he was still destined to incur the wrath of the sheriff. Over half of his citations had been written as warnings only. The sheriff hated warnings, but for Joe's part, he hated ruining vacations.

In his trips past the Chevron on the north end of town, he had perfected his ability to ignore the piled heap of wreckage to the rear of the gas station. No one had claimed the car - it would soon be sold for scrap. Joe had mentioned its existence during a telephone call to the bereaved relatives of the man who had perished in the crash. Dental matches had allowed the bodies to be claimed, but neither relatives nor insurers had any interest in claiming the car for salvage value. Looking the other way helped a little, but not much.

Suddenly his attention was drawn to an old mechanic standing near the curb waiving at Joe to stop. Joe pulled over and rolled down his window catching first a blast of the still ninety-plus degree dry temperature.

"Deputy, there's somthin' you gotta see... look'a this!" The man positioned between his fingers a small piece of mangled grey metal less than a half inch in length.

Joe gazed at it momentarily. The mechanic smiled and awaited a congratulatory comment. "So what is it?" Joe asked.

"Don't ya know a bullet when you see one deputy? Don't they teach ya anything these days?" He handed it to Joe who inspected it closely.

"And what's so special about this bullet?"

"I got it out of the wrecked car yonder."

Joe abruptly stepped out of the cruiser and walked toward the wreck he had avoided since the completion of his investigation. "Show me where you found it."

The mechanic was delighted to give Joe a tour of the scrap pile. "I was jest goin' through this stuff and came upon this here wheel." The man raised a black wheel rim from the ground. "It was imbedded in the aluminum side of the rim ... layin' sideways like this." He slipped the bullet back into the slot in the rim of the wheel like a tooth set in the jawbone of a skull.

Joe forgot about lunch as he spent the rest of his shift sifting piece by piece through the disjointed remnants of the ill-fated Toyota, searching for cipherable clues to corroborate the old mechanic's find. For the remainder of the day, tourists traveled citation-free down Main Street in Hurricane, Utah.

Moscow, Early September, 1992

"If this goes on much longer I think our teeth are going to fall out," Gina spoke loudly over the noise as the semi-truck rumbled through the Baumana section of Moscow, along the Stromynka Prospekt toward their destination on the southeast edge of Moscow's Middle Ring. It had been a rough three and a half days and both were looking forward to a bath or a shower and worried that this might be difficult to find.

"I hope they have someone there to unload all this computer stuff," Michael said. "The last time I was here, it took almost as long to unload the trucks as it did to haul it from Denmark."

"That's the very thing we don't need. If it's going to take long, then please get me to the hotel before you have to unload. I'm so tired I think I might drop the second I get out of this truck."

"I'll see what I can do," Michael was concerned over Gina's exhausted state. Yet, he knew from experience that as he arrived at the Technoserv offices, his Russian employers would show little concern for either him or his wife.

It was a bizarre and different world, as Michael observed the buildings suffering from years of neglect with crumbling stucco surrounded by yards with no grass but only dirt piles and clumps of weeds. Despite his many years in working with Russians and residing for a portion of the time in Moscow, he still found it difficult to fathom the contrast between his Danish homeland and the urban wasteland of the Russian metropolis. He then guided the truck off the busy Stromynka Prospekt onto the less traveled Pervomeskya and drove approximately three miles to the intersection with Parkovaya Street, the location of the Technoserv offices.

Gina stayed in the truck and Michael walked up the scarred stairs requesting permission for entry from the militia guardsman posted at the door. The same beat-up carpet still covered the floor, and the elevator - as usual - was not working. He waved at the old woman sitting behind the counter near the elevator as she recognized him immediately. It was her job to run the elevator. She had nothing to do but wave. He dragged himself up the stairs to the third floor offices of Boris Yarov.

Yarov, a portly, thick-eyebrowed man of fifty-five years of age, sat relaxed at his chair with his feet up on the dark green government-styled steel desk. He sported a full head of black hair with almost gorilla-like fur bedecking the rest of his body. It protruded out from between the top and next highest button on his shirt. He saw Michael out of the corner of his eye, smiled and waved, and then continued his telephone conversation.

The look was one that Michael recognized. It really irritated him. Yarov was a first-class jerk in any culture, Michael thought. All he wanted was someone to help him to unload the truck so he could go to the hotel, get some sleep and deal with his Russian counterparts tomorrow.

As he spoke on the phone, Yarov stood up and peering through a glass window beckoned the attention of a Russian less than half Yarov's age. He looked at the interpreter and fired a few short Russian comments. "How was your trip, Michael?" the translator asked.

As Michael tried to give an answer, he was interrupted by the translator. "Yarov wants to know where the equipment is and why it has taken so long to get it here."

This day is only going to get worse, Michael thought to himself. "We tried to get it here as fast as we could, Yarov, but many of the components you asked for have been difficult to get. The order called for power converters and cables that would really work. It would be useless until you have those things. They're little things, but they're very important."

Yarov rattled off more Russian to the translator. "Yarov wants you to get it up here right now."

"I need some people to haul it up here, Yarov. I'm worn out, and I need to get my wife to the hotel. She's very tired from the trip."

"Yarov says you can worry about those things when the equipment is up here and fully inspected." The translator was rolling his eyes as he looked at Michael. It was clear that along with many Technoserv employees he hated Yarov, too. "I can only give you one man. That's all I can spare." The translator again spoke after Yarov's demands had been made.

Michael pointed to a group of four Technoserv employees languishing at unkempt computer stations in the large foyer along the hallway outside of Yarov's office. "What about them? They can help." His throat was dry from fatigue. Words were rough and hard to speak.

Yarov continued a discussion on the telephone, sat down, spun around on the swivel chair and turned his back to Michael and the interpreter. After another two minutes he swung around on the noisy chair, covered the mouthpiece, and spoke in Russian. The interpreter then spoke, "He says he can't afford to take any of the other people off the job at present, but he did say that I should help you."

From time to time, Michael had taken a stand on various business issues with the Technoserv people. Whenever he dug in his heels, it took a considerable amount of time, but usually he would prevail. At this point, he realized he didn't have the time, since he knew it would be classic Russian business to spend more time talking about who might carry the computer equipment up the stairs than it would be to actually undertake and complete the task. He stormed out the door and signaled for the interpreter to follow.

Three and a half hours later, the final box had been carted up the stairs and set in the hallway outside Yarov's office. Gina helped carry some of the lighter boxes, until she no longer had any strength.

Just as he and the interpreter had completed unloading the cargo at the upstairs offices of Technoserv, a disheveled man wearing a scraggly blue uniform, sporting wide, red shoulder boards, turned up and announced himself to be the Commerce Inspector. Michael could not understand what the fuss was all about as a rather heated exchange took place between the Inspector and Yarov which led to the uniformed man storming out of the office. It was explained to Michael that, since the cargo had been brought into the country in a sealed load, it could not be accepted by Technoserv until a cargo import stamp could be obtained through the Ministry of Imports.

"So what does this mean?" Michael demanded. "You told me before we came that you would arrange for the inspection to take place here!"

"I'm sorry, Michael. There's nothing I can tell you - it's the law." Yarov was apologetic.

"Who do I have to see? Where do I have to go to get this ridiculous matter settled?"

Yarov unloaded a boisterous barrage at the interpreter before Michael had fully completed his comment. Michael suspected that Yarov knew some English.

"Mr. Yarov says, that according to the Commerce Inspector you cannot obtain an import stamp unless the full load is inspected inside the truck."

"You mean I have to. . ."

The interpreter interrupted, "Yes. . .the truck must be reloaded."

"You've got to be kidding!" Michael threw his hands in the air in disgust.

"No, that is the only solution," the interpreter stated.

"Yes, zat is true, T-R-U-E." Yarov injected in broken English.

Michael lost patience, looked around the room once more and then pointed his finger firmly at Yarov and heatedly shouted, "Then you or your boys will reload the truck!" Without waiting for a reply, Michael stormed out of the office and down the stairs.

As Yarov confirmed the interpretation, he pounded his fist on the table, then glared up at the interpreter and bellowed, "That foreigner has a lot to learn!"

Michael and Gina left the rig parked in front of the Technoserv office building then took a cab to the Hotel Kosmos to get some sleep.

CHAPTER 4

Ozero Khanka Trestle, Far Eastern Russia, Early September, 1992

Dimitri Sarabrov, square shouldered and solid as a rock, stood erect on the high wind-blown ridge as he peered through his field glasses at the long stretch of railroad below. With perfect predatory vision, he followed the tracks as they snaked across the plain below, and then became straight just before the approach to the trestle that bridged a four hundred foot deep gorge almost directly in front of his position.

The radio crackled with the hiss of static. A radioman kneeling nearby handed him a telephone. "Captain Major, the charges are now in place."

"Please evacuate the bridge as soon as possible," he spoke calmly.

"We'll be out of here in ten minutes, Sir."

"Very good." The Captain Major handed the phone back to the radioman and again looked off into the mountains beyond the flat, treeless steppes to detect any sign of the expected train. Seeing none, he continued to view the beautiful sunset to the west. His thoughts turned to a name carved deep in his heart, Yelana. It must be daytime at the home of my beloved Yelana in Moscow, he thought to himself. He was increasingly haunted by the prospect that he might never see her again.

When the 23rd Spetsnaz Company first slipped across the Sino-Soviet border, it had moved undetected through Manchuria until reaching the sprawling Chinese provincial capital of Jiamusi. At that point, the contingent appeared at the front gate of a police station, much to the startled surprise of the sleepy People's Militia guard. It was an event that at any other time in history would have provoked a major international incident between the two super powers. But the date had been August 25th, 1991 as the coup to unseat Gorbachev from power in Moscow had failed. To the one hundred-fifteen men, including nine officers and eleven ensigns, all was lost in the beloved Motherland they had left behind. The logical choice for the 23rd was to defect to the only viable Communist power remaining in the world.

The proud Black Berets had found it embarrassing and demeaning to surrender their weapons to the Chinese. The offense was tempered, at least slightly, as they learned that over 3,500 of their countrymen had done the same, rather than remain in Russia where the coup of the hard-liners had failed to save the cause. Their lot was to bivouac in a kaserne for the better part of a year as their surprised Chinese hosts attempted to determine what to do with their long-term visitors. In time, they had been turned out to farm camps in the country. To the Spetsnaz troopers accustomed to treatment reserved for the elite of the armed forces of the Soviet Union, it had taken on the air of a prison.

Captain Major Sarabrov had initiated his career in the 207th Motor Regiment assigned to the Red Army's famed 24th Division. His earliest action had been in Czechoslovakia as he and his fellow soldiers had entered the country to crush the ongoing rebellion by anti-communists and fascists in 1968. Only eighteen years old at the time, he had been spirited. He remembered kissing the famed battle flag of the 24th Division which had been recovered from a remote World War II grave discovered in 1963 near Minsk. As the story went, a young soldier had wrapped himself in the flag as he died. The Germans tossed his body, flag and all, in a mass grave. The flag had become the spiritual icon of the Soviet warrior. Inspired far beyond his youthful years, Sarabrov had participated in quelling the uprising which included shooting many unarmed protesters in the streets of the Prague Spring rebellion.

Only two years after the campaign to liberate Czechoslovakia, the KGB First Directorate had formed the elite Spetsnaz detachments. By good fortune, Sarabrov was selected from many thousands of volunteers who sought a new and better opportunity to advance themselves in this super-secret branch of the military. There was no disappointment as he found extraordinary joy as a Spetsnaz trooper. He advanced rapidly through the ranks, even becoming a member of the Central Army Sportsman's Club in Moscow. A most memorable benefit of the job had included serving as an assistant coach to the USSR wrestling team at the Olympics in Montreal Canada in 1976. The advantages of Spetsnaz status were varied, including training as a sportsman in many areas with the use of weapons for hunting, fencing, as well as judo. It was a good life and he had everything a strapping young Soviet officer would desire, including women at his slightest request. The Soviet Army treated its elite Spetsnaz troopers very well, and Dimitri Sarabrov had made the most of his unique situation.

And now he found himself preparing to attack the Trans-Siberian Railroad on the Far Eastern Front which he had at one time taken an oath to protect. In his mind, however, there was nothing left to defend. The Motherland was dead. Yet, as the last rays of the setting sun encrypted themselves into the horizon, he passed the moment with a heavy heart.

Moscow, Russian Republic, Early September, 1992

The Vladivostok Enterprise Zone in the Far East had been a hot topic at Toko Bank. The bank was one of only three banks branched into Russia's single major port city on the Pacific Ocean. Peristroika had resulted in the loosening of restrictions on State-owned businesses, and efforts by the Russian Republic were now underway to create free trade or enterprise zones in certain border areas of the Republic that would encourage joint ventures with Western companies. Although the effort had been attempted to some degree in Western Russia, there seemed to be a greater interest shown in the Far East by Japanese, Korean, and American entrepreneurs who were frothing at the mouth to get their hands on some of the vast natural resources of Eastern Siberia.

To the American oil men, the tape measure had already been run across many globes in the posh corporate board rooms of New York, London, Tokyo and Berlin, disclosing that the oil fields on the eastern slope of the Khrebet Sikhote Alin mountains were only one hundred miles farther away from the port of Los Angeles than Prudhoe Bay, Alaska. With no expensive pipeline and a relatively decent port from which to ship, it was a good place to have oil. As a deep water port, Vladivostok would serve that purpose well.

Alexander Kutuzov's purpose for being in the meeting was to provide information as to availability of bank funds for funding the Vladivostok branch bank in its efforts to be a major player in the new economic trade zone. The zone would be opening within the next two years and already foreign oil men were exploring the Russian outback to locate the most convenient spots to bring oil to the surface.

"Marriott Hotels and Hyatt Hotels, both American chains, have just announced plans to study the building of facilities in Vladivostok," the chairman of the committee was explaining with delight.

"What about McDonald's? Are we going to get a McDonald's there, too?" another member asked. Everyone laughed.

"Are we going to fund the Coca-Cola bottling facility there?" another commented. Everyone laughed again.

The chairman retorted, "That will depend on what the water's like. I haven't been there since we opened the branch a year and a half ago. The water was very bad then and I assume it still is now - so everyone will want to drink Coca-Cola." The laughter continued.

"What I'm concerned about," another participant interjected, "is whether they have good quality vodka. You know there's been some question about that."

The First Deputy then set a more serious tone, and began to discuss various aspects of staffing the bank in its Vladivostok office in anticipation of major commerce in the area. He then turned to Alexander Kutuzov and asked the question, "What are the plans for funding that office? Has the audit and planning department made adequate plans for funding?" Alexander gazed around the room, then responded, "Mr. Director, I can only respond to that question in confidence."

"You're in good company, my friend. You forget the KGB has lost its power. There's no one here that we cannot trust with the information on currency transfers."

"Thank you, Sir," Alexander responded. "We carried out your orders to ship three hundred thousand dollars, U.S., and two and one half million rubles by government train last Monday.   It should be there sometime   today or tomorrow. The branch should then have sufficient funds to meet its needs for the foreseeable future."

"Good work, Kutuzov. Very good work," the Chairman spoke with a resolute smile. *Kutuzov was a fool. He loved Kutuzov.*

CHAPTER 5

Ozero Khanka Trestle, Far Eastern Russia, Early September, 1992

Sarabrov's most trusted sergeant was a Tartar named Bantor. The sergeant's position was atop a rocky bluff about four hundred yards south of the trestle spanning a deep gorge along the tracks leading to Vladivostok. His job would be to lay down over ten rounds per minute of flat trajectory fire at the armored escort train which would likely precede the government postal train by several hundred yards. His Playma DZK-B 122 millimeter anti-armor rocket launcher was an old, but reliable weapon.

Doing as much damage as possible, and diverting some of the government train's protection, his effort was intended to allow the main attack to occur north of the gorge against the government postal train itself. He would fire all of his rockets and then abandon the launcher and disappear with the four men under his command into the mountains to the southwest to gather at the predesignated rallying point with the Captain Major and the remainder of the force.

To Sarabrov, it was a military operation of a strange sort. The orders had come in an unconventional format. Following the long period in detainment under the supposed orders of the Governor of the Manchurian Province of Hegang, their Chinese hosts suddenly arrived at the compound with trucks containing all of the weapons which the Spetsnaz unit had initially carried into China. Soon thereafter, Sarabrov received a visit from a Chinese man who spoke respectable Russian. The man, claiming to be from Hong Kong, had produced a pouch of the exact type used by Soviet Army battlefield command couriers on Spetsnaz assignment only. The pouch contained specific orders in secret Spetsnaz codes. The communication had afforded the Captain Major new hope that the Communist Party of the Soviet Union was still alive, and that he and his men might ultimately be used for the purposes for which they had been expertly trained.

For the Captain Major, the strategy of an interdiction action on the plain east of Ozero Khanka, the large inland sea between China and Russia north of Vladivostok, was by no means a novelty. As early as 1904, the order of battle for the capture of Vladivostok had been well-simplified; merely cut off the Trans-Siberian railroad access and the force with the superior Navy would control the port. During the Russo-Japanese War, the Japanese were partially successful in their effort at the latter, but the railroad, over time, held together as a successful route for resupplying the Vladivostok garrison. The Captain Major had unknowingly selected the same spot for ambush as had warriors on so many occasions over the past two centuries.

The Captain Major was lured from his contemplation by the shrill whistle of the distant locomotive. Using a Far Eastern Command defense map, he calculated that the train had just made its way through the small town of Lesozavodsk and that it would slow only once more to meet the legal requirement of a safe transit through the village at Sibertsevo. It would then follow an almost straight course to the north side of the trestle.

One hundred fifteen men of the 23rd were deployed into four sections. Only four men, along with the Sergeant Major Bantor, would remain on the south side of the gorge. Further up the track, two groups were stationed along the west side of the rails approximately four hundred yards apart. On the east side of the north-south railroad line, at the crest of the hill, he stationed his third unit armed with the M21 and RPG-90 shoulder-fired antitank missiles. They would, hopefully, be fired over open sights at almost point-blank range. With any luck, the entire incident would be ended very quickly.

It took another hour for the lead locomotive to wander down the track toward the ambush sight. Consistent with his expectations, the Captain Major received reports from his scouts up the line that an armed locomotive with two gun cars and mine-detonating fixtures was leading the government train by approximately one kilometer. The radio again crackled as the advance scouts reported the turrets on the escort train mounted with 73 millimeter twin automatic guns. The Captain Major considered the information carefully and continued to prepare by moving from his position on the ridge down to a makeshift bunker. The point from which the attack would be directed had been constructed only hours before on the southwestern hillside about forty feet above the tracks and only one hundred feet north of the trestle spanning the gorge. From here, although the event would be loud and confusing, he knew he could control most aspects of the battle.

Arizona Strip, Early September, 1992

On the other side of the globe it was daytime.

"This is St. George area-wide dispatch, One-X-Four. Proceed to Cinder Pit off State 59. See the man at Cinder Pit, south of Big Pine Junction, near mile-post number thirty-nine. Man reports two DP's. Do you copy? Over."

Deputy Joe Wilson picked up the microphone, "Affirmative. Have you called the medical examiner?"

"Affirmative, he's on his way."

Another routine day for deputy sheriff Joe Wilson was being interrupted by an unsettling and, to him, nauseating scene. It had been only a week since the nightmarish car-over-the-cliff incident on the Kolob Road. Since that time, Joe had handled only minor traffic accidents. Other than a few first aid calls in the town of Hurricane, things had been relatively quiet.

It took him approximately twenty minutes to drive from the point of the call at the Hurricane City Industrial Park up to the mesa, then eastward across the flat country known as the Arizona Strip to the Big Pine Junction turnoff. From there, he traveled southward along a well-maintained dirt road toward a cinder cone protruding above the desert plain to an elevation of about two hundred feet. Over the years, the hill had been quartered by excavators in need of the volcanic cinders for road construction. As he drove up, he noted several cars at the base of the hill, including a Travel-All with a boat attached. Wilson got out of his car and approached a group of men standing near the west side of the pit. He recognized Ron Duncansen, the EMT whom he had not seen since the Kolob accident.

"Joe, I heard the call on the radio. I was on my way back from Lake Powell...down there with the underwater rescue boys from Page." He pointed, "Looks like we got two dead guys here and from what I can see, they could'a just died yesterday."

Joe pulled out his notebook and started walking toward a fresh pile of dirt and cinders. "So, who called up?" Joe asked.

"I did." Hod Foremaster, long time rancher signaled with his hand.

Joe had known Hod for as long as he could remember. Hod and his family had run cattle on the BLM allotment for years. Joe walked to where he could see the outline of two persons still clothed, lying on their faces in blood-soaked dirt. They were slightly decomposed in a grave approximately two feet below the surface. "Hell, Hod, how did you find this mess?"

"Not me that did it...was them dogs." Hod had the drawl of the consummate cowboy. "They been see'n coyotes digg'n over here every damn time we gone by since yesterday. A couple o' times, the dogs jumped out of the truck and chased the coyotes off. Finally, I followed 'em up here to see what the hell was goin' on. Thought coyotes had taken down one of my beefers. They had dug down and pulled what you see over there outta' that cinder mix. One hell of a thing to happen around here, Joe."

"Yea, you can say that again." Joe lowered himself onto his haunches and looked closer. He picked up a stick and poked gently at the back of one of the bodies.

"I've already looked at them fairly close," Duncansen volunteered. "This is an execution, Joe. Just look at those hands. I think the coyotes pulled one hand loose, but...look at the other guy, he's got rope around his wrists and tied to the back part of his belt. Looks to me like somebody executed these dudes. Joe, you don't want to see the other side of those heads. They've been blown from nostril to noggin. Their teeth've been blown right off the dental charts. Looks like a shotgun blast to the back of the head in each case."

"Hod, when was it your dogs first started chasing over here?" Joe asked.

"The best I can figure, Joe, is maybe yesterday mornin'. I just don't stop here normally - don't have anything to do with this hill. You know the cinder pit ain't even on my allotment. My place starts about another mile up the road."

"Have you seen anybody around here that would be suspicious in the past while?"

"Nope, can't say I have," Hod responded. "I see the polygs out here once in awhile. They're the only ones I know of that use this cinder pit. You know how they are...think they can make gold out of it. They've been in trouble with the BLM over this stuff before. Only I haven't seen 'em for a couple of years, at least as far as workin' the hill goes. Take a look at the pit, don't look like anybody's been over there. There ain't been nothing moved outta' here for three or four years."

"You see any spent cartridges or anything out here?" Joe asked.

"Oh, there's a lot of twenty-two stuff around here. Just kids out shootin'." Hod commented. "I seen people at the start of every huntin' season sightin' in their deer rifles. I can't remember see'n any out here this year though."

"Well, maybe it's still a little bit early," Joe responded. Joe then began to wander around the site walking in a slow circle. He paused near the bodies, working his way through the area hoping he might find a spent cartridge or any other evidence that may have been left at the scene. He looked closely for tire tracks.

About twenty minutes later, Al Bonsack, the part-time southern Utah representative of the State Medical Examiners office arrived. He spent a few minutes with his equipment and gloved hands at the scene. Joe had about finished his search for evidence in the area and went back to where the examiner was stooped over the bodies.

"Joe, this is clearly a murder. Execution... gangland, done by pros."

"Do you think it could it have been the polygs?" Joe heard rumors of violence among the polygamist cults in the area.

"No, I don't think so, Joe." Al sounded certain. "I haven't heard of any trouble over in Red Rock City for quite awhile. Usually, you know, rumors get started and least we kinda' hear about it before it gets too serious. The last time I saw this, it was traced to a Mafia hit from professionals out of Vegas. Nope, this wasn't the polygs doing."

Ozero Khanka Trestle, Far Eastern Russia, Early September, 1992

The ETA at the bridge was fifteen minutes. The hubs on the wheels of Sergeant Bantor's motorless gun carriage were already locked as he jammed the modified system in place against the rock escarpment. His firing position placed him some fifty feet above the track and several hundred yards south of the bridge. The tactical instructions were simple: destroy if possible the escort locomotive which would likely precede the government postal train by approximately one kilometer. Worried about the massive steel with which the Trans-Continental locomotives were built, he knew that his timing must be perfect and his aim true. There was a slight fever in his trigger finger as his conscience told him that he would be aiming his sights for the first time at his fellow countrymen. The thought was only fleeting. He was a Tartar and assumed that he would only be killing Russians.

From his earpiece the spotters reported the train's progress to the Captain Major. An ensign and two sergeants under his command reported both an escort train with three cars and the government mail train to have passed through the switch yards at Sibirtsevo only ten minutes earlier. Sarabrov checked his watch and noted that it should be within his range soon. He responded through his mouthpiece a "go ahead" order.

Within one minute an ensign and two sergeants walked through the unguarded door of the small rail yard switching station at Sibirtsevo, seven miles north along the rail line. An elderly rail worker turned only quickly enough to perceive the flash of something coming at him from the direction of the door. In the next fraction of a second, a wide-blade, ten inch Khasahki knife, having been hurled across the room, entered his body between his collar bone and windpipe, partially severing his head. Blood spurted in all directions. The man recoiled into the chair near his desk, then rolled onto the floor.

With quiet and deliberate dispatch, the ensign approached the switching console in front of a large glass window which overlooked the small, dimly lit rail yard. He took stock of the twelve long levers running almost the entire height of the wall from the ceiling to the floor. Grabbing the eleventh lever, the ensign pulled it down, jamming it against the floor as he locked it in place by rotating his foot against a steel connector rod that protruded from the baseboard area. He and the two sergeants then took up positions around the building to protect against the possibility that anyone might attempt to undo their work.

The Captain Major received a tap on the shoulder from the radioman. To avoid distraction as he listened to the sound of the oncoming train in measuring both time and distance, he refused the telephone and merely nodded in approval at the positive news that the switching station at Sibirtsevo was now under control. He made one final check with the lieutenant stationed across from him on the east side of the track. A signal from his sergeants, each stationed with their men at various positions along the west side of the track, told him all was ready.

He knew his sergeants would perform well. They had enjoyed an impeccable record in Afghanistan. The pending ambush would be relatively mild compared with many of the encounters they had endured with the Mujhadin.

The train whistle was now clearly discernable to each of the one hundred fifteen men concealed quietly in the deserted darkness along the train route. The whistle meant that the train was approaching the last road crossing before the slight jog up the hill to cross the river running from the eastern coastal mountains into the inland sea, Ozero Khanka.

The bright light of the locomotive began shining and bouncing off the rocks on either side of the track as it reached the curve one half mile north of the northern-most position of the ambush. Shrieking in intensity, the large iron hulk of the lead escort locomotive filled the cut between the two embankments as it rolled down the rails. The vibration shook the ground where the Captain Major's men were crouching in their foxholes and behind rocks, ready to spring into action on the first order.

Across the bridge, Sergeant Bantor, behind the DKZ-B anti-tank rocket launcher, was standing erect. He and his four men were positioned and eager to open fire. They assumed that the light of the locomotive would not shine high enough to disclose their position on top of the bluff, particularly since it would be directed in a straightaway fashion as the locomotive crossed the bridge. In the next seconds the locomotive had passed the cut and was now moving across the two hundred foot expanse of the bridge. Sergeant Bantor took careful aim and waited for the mammoth machine to clear the trestle along with the two armored gun cars which bore the sobering likeness of modified T-54 tanks on rails. He held his hand up to give the nonverbal signal to open fire.

Two things happened simultaneously. First, a towering fireball erupted followed by numerous secondary explosions in the space where the bridge had been. And second, even before the fireball's plume climbed to the apex of its expansion, the sergeant dropped his hand causing his men to fire the anti-tank rockets in an almost point-blank flat trajectory at the locomotive and gun cars. Within the first thirty seconds he had pumped five 122 millimeter rockets into the steel plates of the railroad cars. The locomotive jolted from the successive impacts, but still remained on the track. The turrets on each of the respective gun cars began whirling around in circles, their shocked and frightened gunners uncertain where to fire or even what to do.

A look of terror filled the face of the engineer as he found himself on the front end of a train traveling thirty-five miles an hour with less than one thousand yards to stop before reaching the inferno of where the bridge had once been. He immediately jammed the steel wheels in reverse causing sparks and fire as he found himself, along with the engine, sliding downhill toward a certain end to his life. The train responded well to his command and began to slow and finally came to an agonizing stop with less than fifty yards to go.

The commander of the postal guard gripped the engineer's shoulder

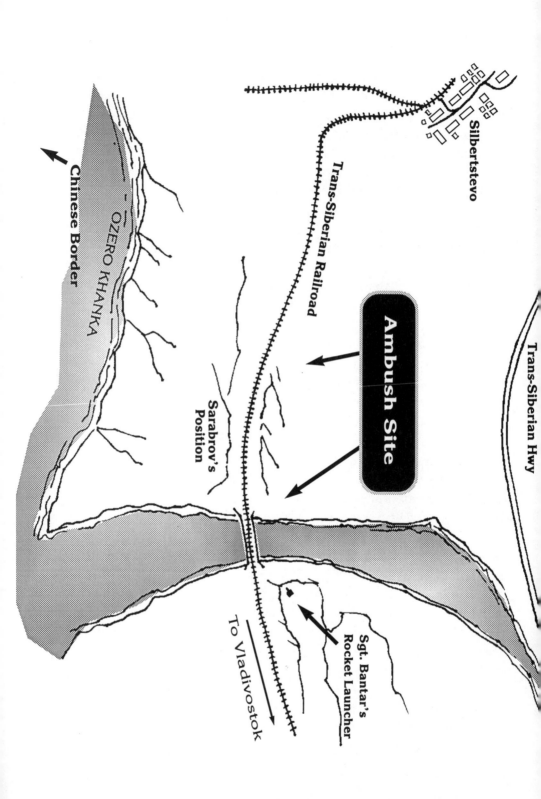

and demanded to know what in the hell was happening. As the engineer searched for an answer, a ricocheting Playma rocket from the battle across the ravine shot through the air like a flaming spear on the tracks in front of him. At that point, the commander barked an order to the men in another gun car three cars back to start selecting the targets and open fire.

The Captain Major had hoped that the postal guard would exit the train and run forward to the lead locomotive to try to ferret out the origin of the battle that was raging on the south side of the ravine between the escort train and Sergeant Bantor's unit. His expectation did not materialize as the commander of the postal guard clutched the train's intercom and screamed at his forty-three men to grab their weapons and defend the train from within.

The Captain Major gave the prearranged signal which reported into the headset of each Spetsnaz trooper. In quick rejoinder, the distinct swish of ten Mukha anti-tank rocket launchers were heard almost in unison resulting in huge explosions in and around the engine and its fuel car. The engineer and the cool-headed postal guard commander were immediately killed.

The gun turret on the fifth car back whirled around and responded by unloading its vicious 73 millimeter rounds from its automatic gun into the embankment near the Captain Major from the point where the rockets had been fired. At the rate of one round every two seconds, trenches were being transformed into graves for several of the Captain Major's men. The postal guard was apparently not willing to simply roll over and be killed as the Captain Major had hoped.

His task was complicated by the fact that he was under strict orders not to destroy or derail the vault cars which had been strategically placed both before and after the gun car in fifth position. He knew that one single rocket into the gun car would probably ignite the ammunition and scatter the vault cars and their contents across the countryside.

On the south side of the ravine, things were going equally badly for the sergeant. As quickly as the first shot was fired, he recognized that he had not properly estimated the angle of entry of his anti-tank rockets. Although the locomotive had been entirely incapacitated, the rockets were bouncing off the armor of the gun cars and ricocheting into the ravine. On the fortunate side, however, the 73 millimeter automatic cannon on the first gun car had been damaged by one of the first rockets and was not firing at all. The second one, however, was with each shot working its way up the hill, attempting to accurately find its range to silence the attack. Bantor knew that he had only a few seconds before he and his men would be clearly in jeopardy. Trying to resolve the standoff with the surviving gun car, he immediately dispatched one of his troopers with plastic explosives and sent two others down the hill, each armed with Mhuka anti-tank rocket launchers, to try to get a ninety-degree angle shot directly into the side of the gun car.

Inside the turret of the second gun car, five terrified postal guards were doing their best to respond to the situation. Two of them continued to load the magazines while a third rotated the turret and squinted through its sights trying to locate the source of the fire on the hill approximately three hundred yards to the south. The fourth and fifth men moved around in the car peering out of the gun ports by sliding back the iron slit covers to determine, if possible, other locations of the attackers.

A fierce explosion flung Sergeant Bantor away from his position at the sighting scope of his rocket launcher. The 73 millimeter gun from the escort train had found its target and within the next second the Spetsnaz sergeant sprawled awkwardly against the frozen earth with his torso above his head. There was no feeling in his foot, all sensation had left his foot, which unbeknown to him, was some thirty feet away on the crest of the hill.

On the north side of the gorge, a lull had developed as the gun car on the postal train ceased firing. The Captain Major assumed that ammunition was running low and that he could soon be in a position to demand surrender of the train's defenders.

It was time now for psychological warfare. Seizing his bullhorn, Sarabrov commanded the occupants of the train to surrender, then waited impatiently for a response. There was only silence. He again announced, "I demand that everyone in the train come out without your weapons. If you refuse, you will all be killed!"

"What do you want of us?" a terrified voice shrieked from a gun port on the armored gun car.

The Captain Major responded, "Surrender the train and you will all live. Your position is hopeless and unless you surrender now, you will all die!"

The silence lasted for another half minute. The Captain Major again triggered the bullhorn. ''What is your response? Must we start firing again?''

''We are considering your proposition!'' the nervous voice responded.

Sarabrov checked his watch and then yelled back, ''I will give you three minutes to decide. Three minutes, and no longer!''

The call came again, ''What do you want of us?''

''Three minutes. . . and that's all. No more negotiations!''

Vladivostok, Far Eastern Russia, Early September, 1992

The telephone rang in the kitchen of Andrea Ziyetski. At 11:30 p.m., he had been asleep for over an hour and was uncertain how many times it had rung before he reached it from his bedroom. His fatigue was replaced by the rapid flow of adrenalin as the watch officer in the operations room at the Vladivostok headquarters of the KGB's newest creation, the Federation Security Agency, reported that large explosions had been seen by an Aeroflot pilot on final approached to the Vladivostok airport. He placed the event approximately forty kilometers north of the city on the highway leading to Khabarovsk. The pilot had admitted that his estimation could have been off by several kilometers since he could not clearly discern the size or the scope of the explosions or how close they were to the Chinese border.

Andrea ordered that a KGB border patrol team be dispatched to the area immediately. Inasmuch as he lived on the north side of the city, he arranged for an armed ground patrol to move northward on the highway so that he could meet them at a designated intersection.

As he returned to his bedroom to dress, his wife was sitting up visibly disturbed, aware that something was awry. He threw on his clothes, grabbed his PPS52 state factory built submachine gun and ran out the door without a further word to his wife or his two children who were likewise awakened by the commotion.

Andrea reached the intersection before the three BMP-1 wheeled version infantry combat vehicles. As he waited, he listened on his hand-held radio to reports from truck drivers who now were discussing the puzzling explosion on the Trans-Siberian Railroad several kilometers west of the highway. Andrea calculated his least fear against his greatest fear. The least was that of a train wreck. His greatest fear was the possibility of a repeat of the 1969 Chinese surprise attack along the Ussuri River in which thousands of KGB frontier troops had been killed by both the Chinese and the sub-zero Siberian winter. Fortunately, this time, it was a summer night. Unfortunately, the Ussuri River flowed into the Ozero Khanka which was in the immediate region of the reported explosions.

Andrea had avoided Afghanistan and had spent a good portion of his twenty KGB years on rather comfortable assignments in the Yalta command area. Unlike the remote assignments of so many of the KGB Border Forces, this had allowed him to live with his family. Whether his abrupt assignment to Vladivostok had been a promotion and reward or banishment and punishment, was inconclusive. Ziyetski, who had just a few years earlier enjoyed the warm environs of the Black Sea town of Foros, now feared that he was about to discover the true nature of his assignment to the Far East.

On August 18, 1991 as Commander of all Crimean Border Guards, Ziyetski began receiving reports of unusual events at the huge family compound housing President Gorbachev and his family on summer holiday across the bay. A communications break at the compound had been followed by the failure of the six-channel radio set-up operated by the KGB at the Presidential Dacha. He knew it was more than coincidence, particularly as new security forces from a command other than his own were reported operating in the presidential compound itself.

At that point, he had feared that the Gorbachev family was in trouble. By the next morning, he had decided on a course of action. He issued an order to his troops stating that their primary mission was to protect the President and his family at the President's Dacha - as well as the Constitution of the USSR. Moreover, his units would not accept orders from the Extraordinary State Emergency Committee that had taken control of the country in the late evening hours of the previous day. He had worked out a plan to bring an armed seaborne Marine unit ashore to defend Gorbachev, if possible. He soon realized that his unit's capability was limited as it was discovered that the draft of the picket boats was too deep to allow docking at the compound. He and his men stood by, ready to swim his troops ashore if violence erupted. But without further information as to what was actually happening at the compound and no clear evidence of shooting on the grounds, he was worried that the appearance of an armed force in addition to those already in place at the Dacha would only exacerbate the situation.

To his consternation, on the day after the coup ended, President Gorbachev himself claimed that the local KGB had been in league with the coup plotters and had blocked his escape by sea. The President's statement was completely unfounded, but it was sufficient to cause Ziyetski to be relieved of his command and to appear in Moscow before the Coup Investigative Committee. After relating the events of the seven days in August, the committee concluded that Gorbachev had, in fact, been subjected to the misinformation by his captors and was not at any time blockaded by Ziyetski's force as he had thought. The decision had come as warm vindication to the KGB Colonel, but its significance to his career had been quickly cooled by an immediate transfer to far off Vladivostok.

The warm winds of the Crimean Shore were a mere memory as he waited impatiently in the frigid air and dark night for his men to arrive.

Ozero Khanka Trestle, Far Eastern Russia, Early September, 1992

Captain Major Sarabrov's watch showed only fifteen seconds remaining. He again spoke sharply through the bullhorn, "What is your response?"

A chorus of voices responded, almost in unison, "We surrender! Please do not shoot!"

In the course of the next five minutes, train workers, postal guards, and a few passengers who had survived the attack, were herded out of the

train and forced to lay face down on the east side of the tracks. The Spetsnaz troopers swarmed through the train searching for any remaining defenders. There were none. Moments later the Captain Major and his troopers withdrew to the opposite side of the train and took up positions with the train between themselves and their captives.

Taking careful aim, a lieutenant on the eastern bluff, who, along with his men had not fired any shots thus far in the battle, opened fire with their Kalashnikov rifles murdering the entire group of persons below.

The Spetsnaz troopers then took charge of the train. They waited only minutes before a sole locomotive appeared from the north and unceremoniously hitched itself to the caboose. During the wait, the Captain Major had his dead and wounded comrades loaded on the train. He scanned the gorge in an effort to locate Sergeant Bantor and his team who had mounted the attack on the far side of the ravine. The smoke was thick and he could see nothing. Attempts to contact the men by radio likewise failed. When the destroyed mail train locomotive was finally unhitched with the use of a small plastic explosive, Sarabrov could wait no longer. He climbed aboard the train as it began steaming north toward the switch yard that his men controlled at Sibirtsevo. Upon arrival, the train with its captive cars was switched onto a seldom used ten mile stretch of track which led westward to the Chinese border.

Northern Virginia, Early September, 1992

"Sir, check this out." The duty technician at the secret National Reconnaissance Organization complex in Vint Hill, Virgina called the shift supervisor to his station. Together, they read the data as it poured out over the Samsung monitor in the Raw Data Analysis Center.

"So what do you think?" the supervisor asked.

The technician responded, "Well, it's clearly a RAWDAT transmission. TDRS caught a weak, but still significant heat impulse just north of Vladivostok."

The supervisor scratched his head. The TDRS (Tracking and Data Relay Satellite No. 4) had been in space since the second week in August, 1992, having been placed in a semi-stationary orbit by the space shuttle Atlantis in its maiden voyage. The satellite had been positioned over the missile fields of mid-Siberia and Khazakistan. It detected the distant eastern blip as an afterthought. "So, what have they got in that part of the world?"

"Well, certainly no ICBM's. They do have land based anti-ship missiles and a lot of Navy out there. But if there'd been a mobile train launch we would've picked it up," the technician spoke confidently.

"All this tells us is that we have an explosion - right?" the supervisor asked.

"That's right, Sir, but a big enough one to get the Spy in the Sky's attention."

Momentarily, another technician behind them and across the room pushed across the slick floor on the wheels of his rotating chair, hanging onto his earphones in the process. "Now, this is something!" he exclaimed in a startled voice. "Sir, ya gotta look at this!"

The Watch Officer walked to another screen to see a readout from a report that had just come in from an electronic emissions monitoring station run jointly by the U.S. and Japanese in the coastal mountain range on the west side of Hokkaido near Soporo, Japan. "They've turned on a major part of their defense network out there, Sir," the analyst spoke with excitement. "It looks like everybody but the Navy has its ears up and there are definitely forces on the move."

With both pieces of data now firmly in mind, the supervisor pulled out a clipboard which allowed for eight electronic carbon copies of anything he might write. He jotted down his most immediate conclusion:

Possible hostile Sino-Soviet action near Ussuri River frontier disputed zone. Significant detonation near Trans-Siberian Rail line north of Vladivostok and significant Russian military activity near border.

"Yep, looks like Christmas in the east end of Russia town! " The technician spoke in a Texas drawl to match his Tony Llamas. Pressing a button on the clipboard he immediately transmitted his notes by code to the Situation Room in the basement of the White House; to the World Wide Military Operation Command and Control Center located at the Pentagon, five hundred feet below the Potomac River; to Pacific Command headquarters at Pearl Harbor, Hawaii; to North American Defense Command (NORAD) deep inside Cheyenne Mountain near Colorado Springs and to the ready room of the CIA in Langley, Virginia. Remaining transmissions would be used internally for upgrade and downgrade analysis. He turned to another technician in the same room who had been observing the action, but professionally avoiding any involvement. ''See what you can get out of China - this could be big!''

CHAPTER 6

Vladivostok, Far Eastern Russia, Early September, 1992

It was well after midnight when the column of BMP 1 infantry combat vehicles rumbled up to the intersection where KGB Colonel Andrea Ziyetski was waiting. Before climbing into the smaller command car at the front of the convoy, he walked to the rear of the column and inquired of each vehicle commander as to whether he had a full complement of ammunition. A crisp affirmative response was signaled by each. The small KGB border guard force then moved rapidly north beyond the outskirts of Vladivostok.

Andrea checked with his lieutenant who was examining terrain and area maps in the back seat of the command car. "So, what is the status at this moment?"

"Sir, a truck driver with the State security net radio was willing to report the fire but not willing to stop. He said it sounded like Afghanistan and he was not going to take any chances. He also refused to give his commerce transportation number. I guess he didn't want to get involved."

Andrea thought to himself that there was a time when that would have been an imprisonable offense. Since the transition, however, no one seemed to want to get involved in anything. He then responded to the lieutenant, "I want to get the name of the trucker. If this turns out to be a train accident and he failed to stop and render assistance, I'll have his license, at the very least!"

"Yes, Sir, I'll see that it's done, Sir."

"What is the FEC (Far Eastern Command) doing?"

"They're waiting to hear from us, Sir. They want us to check the situation out first."

Andrea glanced at his watch and then looked at the map and realized that it would be another half an hour before they would reach the site. He picked up the radio-telephone, keyed it into the FEC command and control frequency, "This is Colonel Ziyetski, KGB unit 4." As he waited for the response from the operation control center at the naval base in Vladivostok, he again quickly examined his situation in terms of the sketchy information at hand. At the very worst, he and his small unit of thirty men in four vehicles could run into several thousand Chinese infantrymen and be wiped out in less than a minute. The train wreck idea was much more appealing. Major rescue efforts would need to be undertaken. Deciding to cover both possibilities, he continued, "I would like two gun ships and two rescue helicopters to rendezvous with us at the Zivag River-Ozero Khanka trestle in one half hour. They are instructed to await my orders from the ground before going in. At this point we do not, I repeat, we do not know whether this is a railway accident or a hostile event!"

As they rolled up the highway, Andrea opened the round porthole atop the steel command car. He stood erect and peered through his field glasses looking at a flickering glow on the hillside about five miles to the northwest. From his vantage point, he directed the group off the main highway in the direction of the railway access service road. While twisting around to look back toward the city, he could see the distant lights in the sky of navy helicopters working their way up the valley from the ocean front in his direction. He felt the lieutenant tugging at his arm and he quickly slid back into the command car slamming closed the hatch above.

"Sir, additional information - a real problem!" The lieutenant handed the telephone to Andrea, who pressed it quickly to his ear.

"This is KGB Unit 12. I'm at the switch yard house at Sibirtsevo. I found a dead rail worker - he's been murdered. Clearly Khasakhi knife wounds.   Looks like a professional type hit.   Can't find any other disturbance, Sir!''

"What's your force size?'' Andrea asked.

"I've got five BPM1's and fifty-five men. Half ammo though. We weren't prepared for this. It happened too fast!''

"What do you think it is, Lieutenant?''

"It's hostile action, Sir. We're already in a defensive position around the rail yard. Soon as I saw this old man, I deployed for a fight.''

"Good move. What I'd like you to do now is keep two of your BPM's at the rail yard and move down the access road toward the explosion site with the other three. But if you run into any hostile problems, drop back to the rail yard and hold until you hear further from me. I've got air support on its way. ''

"Yes, Sir.''

With the report from Border KGB Unit 12 in hand, Colonel Ziyetski took no chances. He called the operations center at FEC and provided the coded signal for serious hostile action. This alerted the entire defense network of the Far Eastern Command from Vladivostok along the Chinese border to a point 1500 miles to the west at Irtkusk, on the shores of Lake Baykal. KGB border troops were mustered from their barracks and moved to combat positions. Likewise, the Trans-Siberian Railroad Postal Guard moved its four thousand troops in the region onto Alert Status. Colonel Ziyetski was not going to wait another twenty minutes before he reached the site to confirm his worst fears.

Moscow, Russian Republic, Early September, 1992

The beds at Hotel Kosmos were almost as hard as Russian bread, but, at least they were beds. It was a major improvement over the cab seat in the semi. But there was no heat despite the fact that it was a cold, gray day in which the temperature had not exceeded fifty-five degrees.

In Moscow, late summer was not always late summer. By decree, the heat was turned on in the city on a bureaucracy-specified day in September. The decision was controlled by the calendar and not by weather conditions. Thus, Gina could not get warm despite two additional down comforters from the hall-lady who catered to the needs of hotel guests.

Shortly after they began to doze, the phone rang, startling Michael but scarcely rousing Gina. Michael grabbed the phone. The rings were slow, meaning that it was a local call. Rings in rapid succession would have meant an international call - and a problem at home.

He was informed that the truck at Technoserv had been reloaded, but that he would need to attend to the all-important issue of obtaining an import permit himself. Irritated, but pleased that at least something had been done, Michael dressed and made his way down to the awaiting Technoserv car that would take him back to his truck.

It was 2 p.m. by the time Michael was ready to leave Technoserv with the reloaded semi. Along with his interpreter, he rolled into the chilly, grey afternoon and worked his way up the narrow streets for approximately twenty minutes before arriving at a building housing the Head Administration Office of State Customs Inspectors.

According to the interpreter, the Ministry was a large, square, five story building in the middle of the dilapidated part of the city at 1A Komsomolskaya Place, approximately one block north of Paveletsiy Station. Michael wondered whether or not he was getting accurate information. He could not see a parking lot large enough to accommodate his or any other truck. He recalled numerous semi-trucks along the highway, braving their way into Moscow from Europe, and assumed that he was not alone in the need to obtain an import permit.

The interpreter inquired inside the building and returned. He instructed Michael to back his truck approximately one hundred feet up a narrow, cobblestone alley. Michael complied. Although he had some experience in truck driving, none had been on the scale of this Russia trip and he hoped that he would never have to repeat the experience. On at least two occasions during the tense effort, he scraped the side of his truck on the wall of the buildings. He could only imagine what the rental company in Copenhagen was going to charge for the damage.

Upon being told to halt, he got out of the truck. Before him stood an officious looking man wearing a blue tattered uniform with red shoulder-boards and a broad, circular hat similar to that of the Commerce official who had protested the unloading of the truck at Technoserv the previous day. The man poured over his clipboard, writing license plate numbers and recording other identifying characteristics of the vehicle. He paced up and down the alley next to the truck, examining it closely like a gestapo officer in an old American war movie. At the rear of the truck, next to the gate on the trailer, he began conversing with the interpreter.

"This man says it's the seal on the back of your truck. You see, Mr. Christensen," the interpreter continued, "he says that since the seal on the back of the truck is broken that means he cannot give a certification stamp for this load. He is worried that you have sold some of the equipment out of the back of the truck on the black market as you traveled to Moscow from St. Petersburg. He says it's in violation of Council of Ministers Decree No. 203 on Measures for State Regulation of Foreign Economic Relations. He says he intends to report it."

Michael felt his blood beginning to boil once again. It was another one of thousands of laws put in place by the Soviet Council of Ministers back in the USSR days, only to be adopted by Yeltsin's Russian Republic. Michael wondered if there were any laws passed by the Communists that the new government hadn't adopted. He had spent the last four years working with the Russians, who it seemed, consistenly had a rule to stop anything from being accomplished. Always a roadblock no matter what you do, he angrily thought to himself. He questioned how such a country could survive. The answer was simple - it didn't have a chance. In his frustration, he glanced into a window along the alley and saw a small oil lamp burning in the darkened recesses of a tiny apartment inside the huge, gray building. It makes sense, he thought to himself, the reliability of getting electricity into that apartment is probably so low that the poor people have no choice but to burn oil. He was reminded of the continuing condition in Russia that the left hand was always oblivious to the activities of the right hand.

It was time to try to work out a solution. Michael spoke to his interpreter, "Ask him what he thinks I should do. I've backed this truck all the way up this alley and torn it up in the process. What does this brilliant bureaucrat think I'm supposed to do now?"

It was clear to Michael that the interpreter was being reasonably judicious in his phrase by phrase interpretation of Michael's comments. "He says that you have to take the truck out to the Customs Office and get your import stamp there."

"And what's wrong with this place?" Michael demanded an answer.

"It is the Head Administrative Office of Customs Inspectors as opposed to the Customs Office. This man says there's a difference!"

"And where is this Customs Office?"

The response again infuriated Michael. "It's out in Butova, on the way to Vnukovo Airport. He says you will see many trucks out there."

Michael paused. He remembered that he was in Russia, the land of the bribe and the home of the fee. "Ask him what he really wants. Can he give me the stamp if I give him money?" Michael watched the conversation between the interpreter and the official. In most countries, a public employee would be shocked at such a request, but Michael knew that this official was posturing for money. He would not have spent the amount of time dealing with the truck in the alley looking for every violation he could conjure up, unless he knew there was something in it for him.

"The officer wants to know what kind of money you have."

Michael was beyond being perturbed. He might as well be getting mugged and robbed in the back streets of Copenhagen. But in this case, the muggers wore uniforms. "Tell him I've got dollars."

"He says, you pay him fifty dollars."

"And then I get the stamp?" Michael asked.

There was a pause and the interpreter worked on getting the explanation straight. "No, he says that for fifty dollars, he will not report the unsealed load to the Customs Ministry. He says this is part of his job, but he will overlook it if you pay him fifty dollars."

Michael shook his head, waved his arm at the official in disgust and walked back up to the cab of the truck and called to the interpreter to hurry. In the next minute they were slowly working their way out of the alley in the direction of the street. Just as they reached the alley, however, a policeman or a State Militiaman - Michael never could tell the difference- appeared in front of the truck and commanded him to halt. He stepped up to the cab and yelled in Russian, which was quickly interpreted, that the

Ministry's use fee for the alley had not been paid. "Well, how much is it?" Michael yelled both at the policeman and the interpreter.

"Fifty dollars," came back the reply.

Michael again put his hands up to his head in total disgust, then reached in his wallet and hung a fifty dollar bill out the cab window. He then sarcastically called, "Don't I get a receipt?"

The policeman was gone as quickly as he had appeared. Michael pulled out into the street without a receipt.

*   *   *

It was 4:30 in the afternoon and time for Yarov to engage in his daily feed. In a country where food was scarce and many were hungry, one could not tell that Yarov was suffering at all. On the contrary, he was a survivor within the protective insulation of a bureaucracy that had weathered the storm of the reform movement.

Yarov had done very well to assure that a significant portion of the scarce resources were made available to his subdivision of the Aviation Ministry. Almost daily, he would send a group of the most subordinate employees in the office to scour the markets for bread, fresh vegetables, and sometimes even meat. Often, when the best purchase could be located, he would send his most trusted employees who would show up at the store with dollars.

Yarov and his chief lieutenants were fed first. The scraps and leftovers were made available to the computer programmers, software engineers, and other support employees. It allowed for most employees to take home food at least one day per week. This was a significant benefit of working for Yarov.

Since feeding himself was never far from his mind, he instructed his driver to take him to Festivalnyy Detskiy Park where he would make his purchase; at an outdoor farmer's market. It was located one block north of the Olympia Penta Hotel on Frifonovskoya, and a good place to go unnoticed.

Upon arrival, he ordered his driver to make the purchase for him. As his driver was occupied with the task, Yarov wandered in the direction of a fountain where a beheaded statue of Lenin still stood. He amused himself with the thought that it had been over two years since the official beheading and no one seemed to know what new head should be put on top of the strangely headless torso. It reminds me of my country, he thought to himself as he sat on a wooden park bench.

Within five minutes Yarov was not alone. Taking a seat next to him was the First Deputy of Toko Bank. Each of the men carefully surveyed the park to see who might recognize them. Yarov then opened a newspaper and the First Deputy did likewise.

"So, what have you heard?" Yarov asked while staring directly at the newspaper.

"Nothing has arrived at the Vladivostok branch," the First Deputy whispered.

"When should it have arrived?"

"More than twelve hours ago," was the reply.

There was a brief pause as both men continued to feign the reading of their respective newspapers.

"So, is it done, or isn't it?" Yarov inquired.

"The branch manager reports a lot of helicopters and troops on the move around the port. Sirens went off at the naval base in the night. He says the post office will not say what's happened to the train."

"So, is it done, or isn't it?" Yarov demanded again in a gruff tone.

"All I can tell you, Yarov, is that the train did not arrive. That is all we know and perhaps all we will know for several days!" The comment evoked a certain nervous tension which was immediately recognized by Yarov. He chose to ask no further questions. Yarov spotted his driver still waiting in the line in the market. He stood and marched over to the driver and pulled him out of the line. For the first day in many, Yarov was not hungry.

* * *

By the time Michael had navigated his way through traffic and reached the Ministry of Customs Office complex near Vnukovo Airport it was already 5:00 p.m. As described, there were many trucks, and all positioned in the proverbial line which seemed to dominate every aspect of Russian commerce. Michael knew that he would be confronted with the issue of the broken seal on the back of the truck at some point. The fact that it had in actuality broken open due to the excessive bouncing and rattling caused by the poorly maintained Russian highways would likely be viewed as an inadequate excuse. Rather than make excuses, Michael decided that it would be best to tell the truth and try to work the matter out.

Delivery of the computer equipment was the paramount issue. Upon notification of delivery, he would call the office in Copenhagen and a sizable portion of Technoserv prepayment to the Danish arm of the company would be credited to the Danish account. It would be good for the company and make Michael's trip worthwhile - so long as nothing else went wrong.

It was striking to Michael that with all of the trucks waiting in line, they were still outnumbered by men and women in the blue customs inspector uniforms. The officials seemed to be swarming over a truck randomly selected, and then walking up the line five or six trucks before selecting another target for inspection.

Eventually, they reached Michael's truck and examined its every inch. Again, each had his or her own officious clipboard, and was busily jotting comments. Several other officers simply stood and watched from a distance, but still moved with the team of officials as they meandered up the line and stopped at his truck. Apparently suspecting Michael's purpose for remaining in the truck, they asked him to climb out of the vehicle and stand back to watch the proceedings.

After completing their search, the entire group gathered around Michael and the interpreter and began firing questions. "Where did you get the computers?" asked one. Before Michael could answer, another asked, "Where are you going with these goods? Are you aware of the penalty for having brought goods into the country in an unsealed trailer?"

Michael attempted to answer through his interpreter, but each time, before the interpreter could make any comment, the rapid-fire interrogation continued as the Russian inspectors attempted to find every possible problem with the truck. Another inspector continued the inquisition regarding the overall weight of the vehicle. Michael was amused, as it occurred to him that given the condition of the Russian roads, the weight of vehicles could hardly be a factor. The inspectors finished their work, and informed Michael that they would be back later to deal with him and moved on.

By 7:00 p.m., the sun was lowering in the sky and the evening was getting cold. Michael and the interpreter remained in the truck having moved not more than ten spaces in a line of almost twenty vehicles. By 7:30, the line started to move more rapidly. Finally, reaching the fee area, Michael pulled his up to the station, climbed out and went inside to face his accusers, who consisted of a group of seven, blue uniformed officials, clipboards in hand, sitting shoulder to shoulder on an old, tattered couch. Michael walked across the musty, cigarette smoke-filled room to the counter and handed the official the initial application. The official spoke to the interpreter, ''That will be fifty dollars.''

Michael quickly pulled out the fifty dollars from his wallet, handed it to the official. The term ''fifty dollars'' had a certain ring to it. The official then looked beyond Michael and commanded, ''Next!''

Michael was stunned by the anti-climax of it all. ''Don't I get a permit or something?''

''No paper... we have number on truck. You..okay.'' The bureaucrat did his best in broken English.

Michael was amazed at the development. He pivoted on his heel, gazed at the interpreter, and rolled his eyes in disbelief. They both automatically looked over at the gathering of inspectors sitting on the sofa. Although the uniforms were the same, neither Michael nor the interpreter recognized a single face. Apparently the earlier examiners had gone off-shift and had not bothered to pass their findings onto any of their replacements. Without further delay, Michael and the interpreter climbed into the cab and drove the two hours back into the Technoserv office.

It was midnight by the time the two had unloaded the contents of the semi. Totally exhausted and with muscles that had long since ceased to cooperate, Michael collapsed into the bed at Hotel Kosmos. The mattress was like one large brick, but Michael didn't notice.

*   *   *

The concert at the Chamber Music Theater on Leningvadsky Prospect had been a beautiful event. The only drawback, according to Alexander Kutuzov, was that the concert itself elicited the attention of both himself and Nieca to the stage, rather than to one another. He found himself becoming even more struck by her charm as they walked out of the theater, her arm ringed within his. The theater is wonderful, he thought, but times like this - to actually talk to such a beautiful woman and have her respond in kind is rare. If nothing further between us develops, the relationship, even to this point, has been far more than I could ever hope for - but, please, don't let it stop now.

As they rode toward the apartment in a taxi through the bustling Koptevo district, she spoke of her girlhood. He earnestly listened, realizing that the days of her childhood were so different from his. He had grown up in the war years, and she in the sixties when there was, by Soviet standards, seeming abundance and prosperity.

As she spoke, he wondered to himself why such an uncommonly beautiful woman had not been channeled into the aparatchik class as a mistress, or even a wife of one of the prominent leaders. It was truly a realization of a dream that someone as attractive, graceful, and accomplished as she would take an interest in him. The intense physical awareness that she created within him was, for Alexander, unprecedented. He would savor the moment and enjoy the friendship, or whatever it might become.

The apartment was located not far from the Shelepikha Bridge on the west bank of the Moscow River. It wore the look of upper-middle class. There were three rooms in addition to the kitchen and bathroom. Two of the rooms were regularly outfitted as bedrooms. This allowed for Nieca's mother to have a room for herself, an unusual luxury by Moscow standards. The decorative accessories throughout the home caused him to assume that Nieca had sources of income beyond her meager salary at Toko Bank.

On this evening however, her room had been set up as if it was a dining room. Returning from the theater, she placed candles on the table and produced some bread and rare cheese and caviar that her mother had picked up after waiting hours in line at the market the day before. Her mother had also prepared some borscht for the late dinner. It pleased him as he observed the effort to which Nieca had gone to make the evening special.

As they sat in the candlelight, Nieca continued to talk in annimated fashion about the days in the countryside with her family and summers with other children at a children's resort in Latvia. Just watching and listening made Alexander lightheaded. He wondered to himself about the effect of an even closer encounter. Carefully scanning the room at the various pictures and mementos of the family, he commented, "I don't see any pictures of your former husband here."

"I like to forget him. He ran off at a time when I needed him the most. He was a soldier, you know - always into something. When he disappeared in Afghanistan, we were already estranged from one another. I have never considered myself a war widow. But the pension does help." She stared off toward the window that looked across the city from the fourteenth floor of the high-rise. He sensed he had touched on a subject that would be wise not to pursue further.

"The First Deputy was in a particularly jovial mood at the Vladivostok trade zone committee meeting today." He tactfully changed the subject and lightened the conversation.

"How so?"

"We spent more time holding our ribs from laughter than we did talking serious business. It was a fairly short meeting. I think the First Deputy just wanted to make sure that at least as far as I was concerned, the currency shipment had been made. They were amused by the news that two American hotel chains are considering projects in Vladivostok. You know how that is, once the American hotels go in, then American dollars and Japanese yen start to flow like the Volga. It's the type of news that makes bankers happy."

"And so, the currency shipment was made?" she asked, redirecting him to his earlier point.

"Oh, yes, I sent it late last week by government postal train."

"Why did you not use Aeroflot?"

"I had been specifically asked by the First Deputy to use the government postal train. It is much cheaper and also much safer. We've had dollars disappear with Aeroflot before. This was just too much money to send any other way. And what the First Deputy asks for, he usually gets."

"You are right about that," she agreed.

"But on the audit we're doing, that's a different matter." Alexander leaned back in an apparent effort to show off his cleverness. "I've got a friend at the Aviation Ministry who can access the computer printouts we need for a real audit. Things have changed in Russia, and once the First Deputy sees that we can document all the underlying expenditures for which those accounts are used, I think he'll appreciate the fact that we have them. After all, with such large withdrawals taking place, we have to report the disposition of these funds. The Government banking regulations require it, and I don't think we should be overlooking the expenditures by one of our largest customers, should we?"

"Well, you know, Alexander, that the Ministry of Aviation owns almost one third of the stock of Toko Bank."

"I know that. That's all the more reason for bank management to know where the funds are going. We must comply with the banking laws."

The subject then changed to other matters - from family to gossip around the office. By late evening Alexander excused himself and walked to the door. Just before leaving Nieca squeezed his hand and said, "Thank you." The squeeze was quite enough. He found himself light-headed again. Amazing, he thought to himself, how could I be so affected by this person? He wished her "goodnight," made his way the street and walked several blocks to the subway that took him across the city in the direction of his apartment complex.

Red Rock City, Arizona, Early September, 1992

Flora's mother, Hannah Jackson, had been waiting impatiently for the better part of the afternoon and now well into the evening. Her husband had been on a business trip in Phoenix, Arizona for the past three days. Earlier that morning in a telephone conversation with a sister-wife in Mesa, she learned that Flora did not make the trip.

Hannah had searched frantically throughout the Red Rock City community, contacting first each of the sister-wives and then friends and neighbors inquiring as to Flora's whereabouts. No one came forward with any information. Hannah did sense a certain sanctimonious tone that told her she was to understand that it was not her place to inquire regarding the whereabouts of her own daughter. With each frenzied call, she found herself becoming more frantic. Something has happened to Flora, she thought to herself, and I am sure that Fred knows!

When Hannah slept, she dreamed that demons were trying to destroy her and pull Flora from her grasp. She awakened tired and longed for sleep to block out the reality of her life with Fred over the past few months - ever since he married Pauline. Only fifteen, she thought sadly. His pandering comments regarding his own daughter's beauty rang in her ears. Incest was not routine among the polygamists nor was it a rarity. From time to time, such a relationship, viewed as illicit to the rest of the world, would be ratified and even condoned by pious religious leaders within the community. There were no other leaders or city fathers of note, but only sectarian superiors who controlled every aspect affecting the citizenry within the town. The Mayor and five members of the City Council were polygamists, each a feeble old man with five or more wives. Likewise, the majority of school teachers in the schools were from polygamist families. The area, including the right to live upon the land throughout the town of Red Rock City, was virtually controlled by the leaders of one fundamentalist cult. Those who expressed dissention would find themselves on the outside, at the very least.

Hannah had lived her whole life with the well-grounded doctrine that the young women should submit themselves in every respect to the dictates of the male religious leaders. Accordingly, she had engaged in an unfailing and tireless effort to raise Flora within the faith and avoided acting upon any rebellious thoughts which sometimes had invaded her mind. It was only appropriate that she should exercise unquestioning faith, for Hannah herself had been a daughter of one of the principal founders of the movement in Red Rock City. She had observed her father on many occasions speaking in front of large gatherings with devoted and loyal followers hanging on his every word. She had always considered him to be a wonderful man. When the time had come for her to be placed in marriage, although a mere seventeen years of age, her father had taken her aside and asked her who she would like to marry. She responded by selecting Fred, only twenty-one. Her father had then called the young man into his office and explained that his new wife would be Hannah.

Hannah's marital opportunity had been an exception because she, unlike most other women of the community, had been given a choice. All had progressed seemingly well, that is until Fred decided to choose other wives. Over the course of the years, Hannah had become calloused to Fred's continual boyish hunt for new women to court. But when his eyes zeroed in on his niece, Pauline, a mere child at fifteen - to Hannah, it was evil. Yet, there was nothing she could do. Within a month prior to Fred's announcement of the marriage to Pauline, the brethren had approved the incestuous relationship of a prominent community member who had, a year earlier, adopted his fourteen year old niece then taken her to wife having consummated the relationship, as many had said, long before the formalities of the religious plural marriage. It all seemed so terribly corrupt to Hannah. Her greatest disappointment, however, was that she had always assumed that somehow for her sweet little Flora, betrothal and marriage would come about as an exception to the rules as it had in Hannah's life. But now, she feared that Fred had given her away in marriage since Hannah had not been invited to the wedding.

* * *

The large four-door Lincoln Continental Towncar made its way up the dirt driveway to the partially finished home just after sundown. Fred had spread his five wives around the country with three in Red Rock City, one in Salt Lake City, and one in Mesa, Arizona. His businesses were conveniently arranged at each of those locations so that he would not go without his needs being properly serviced and being given the attention which he, as a member of the brethren overseeing the fundamentalist church, was entitled. The home was only partially finished. It was something he would get to someday, but for now there were more pressing matters with which to deal.

"Where is Flora?" Hannah snapped without deference, as Fred walked up the rickety outdoor steps to the front door, his suitcase in hand.

"Woman, I'll talk to you later - I've been traveling all day. I need some dinner and I hope to hell it's ready!"

"You filthy son-of-a-bitch!" She screamed at him loud enough to be heard at one of the farm houses across the street. "You tell me what you've done with my daughter! I thought you took her with you! She's gone! What have you done with Flora?"

The balding, late middle-aged man whose wrinkled face belied his years, brushed past Hannah, walked into the home and hauled his suitcase into a back bedroom.

Hannah stood at the door still enraged and then began to cry uncontrollably. Collapsing at the door, she kneeled on the floor and whimpered as Fred unloaded the contents of his suitcase and began hanging shirts in the closet. "Just tell me *anything*, Fred. All I want to know, is where my daughter is and that she is alright. Please," she begged, "please, just give me some hope. She is my whole life - she is all I have! You have your other wives, your other children, your businesses. You come and go whenever you want. But all I have is Flora! Please...please tell me where she is, so I can talk to her!"

"I don't have to tell you anything!" Fred spoke. "But I will tell you an arrangement has been made with the approval of the brethren. You'll be notified as to what that arrangement is when the brethren are good and ready. It is not your place to ask, and it's not *my* place to have to inform you as to what decisions are made at the direction of our prophet.

You know that - your father was one of them.''

"I'm hurting so bad! Try to understand, Fred. I just want my little girl to be here with me! If you've done a marriage without me knowing about it, tell me - tell me. Can I call her on the phone so I know she's alright?''

Putting his empty suitcase in the closet, Fred stepped past Hannah and walked back up the hall into the kitchen. A producer of only one child, she had been awarded poorer living accommodations. The home was small with two cramped bedrooms. An unrelated younger couple had rented the partially finished basement. Fred noted that no dinner was awaiting him. "It looks like you're becomin' a might unglued, Hannah. You know the will of the Lord. And one of the first principles of the Gospel is that you don't question the actions of his servants. I tell you again - Flora is fine. So, just let it rest!''

"Well, I can't! Fred, I'm going to call the police.''

Fred smiled, "You really are a silly woman, Hannah. Here, let me hand you the telephone so you can call *my* nephew, the town marshal. Or maybe you'd like to call *my* cousin, his deputy. Do you seriously think any of them are gonna question the actions of the brethren?''

Hannah looked at her husband for a long moment, then stood up, smoothed her skirt and walked to the cupboard.

"I'm hungry now, not later. So you just forget about me tonight. I have other wives in this town and I'm sure any one of them will be a lot more interestin' than you. So I'll come back tomorrow, and I hope to hell by then you've pulled yourself together. A little pray'n wouldn't hurt you none neither.'' Fred walked out the door without a backward glance.

Hannah pressed her shaking body against the wall, then slid to the floor. She was filled with a prescience of something terrible. Oh, Flora - Flora - where are you?

CHAPTER 7

Ozero Khanka Trestle, Far Eastern Russia, Early September, 1992

The early morning sun was thawing the light frost that coated the hilltops even in the summer in eastern Russia. Four Mil Mi-24 Hind "F" battle helicopters, with their generators emitting a monotone whine much like the emergency broadcast tone of American television, sat otherwise inactive in the flat area on a meadow, west of the tracks. The spot was only two hundred yards from the foxhole where the Captain Major had concealed himself the night before as his Spetsnaz company had carried out its deadly mission. Colonel Ziyetski had set up a command and investigation center on the west side of the wrecked train and several hundred yards to the north along the service access road. It was a good location for the crowd of high ranking investigation officials to congregate and mull over the mysterious events of the past night. Another compelling reason - the wind was blowing the stench of the dead in the other direction.

Despite a long night with minimal sleep, Ziyetski was not overly tired. He had been guzzling, thick as tar, Russian coffee through much of the night. Within the last hour, a KGB Field Kitchen unit had arrived with enough warm food for the three hundred or so men who were now combing the area for clues.

The KGB Crime Laboratory, which also included police officers from Vladivostok, had reached the scene and was commencing a gory corpse by corpse analysis. The lieutenant of KGB Border Unit 12, who had first discovered the murdered switch yard worker in Sibirtsevo to the north, had, under orders of Colonel Ziyetski, moved his unit along the remote rail line to the west in the direction of the Chinese border. Due to the poor condition of the road, members of KGB Unit 12 were frequently leaving their vehicles and cautiously proceeding on foot as they examine the rugged mountain terrain along the shores of Ozero Kankha, and on to the Chinese border.

As each item of evidence was recorded, it was brought into Colonel Ziyetski's field tent for various teams of experts to analyze. This gave him input as he started his preliminary report. Nervous calls from the FEC command center had been received during the day asking whether or not there had been a Chinese incursion into Soviet territory. From what the Colonel could see, the myriad of facts led only to confusion and uncertainty. The obvious facts before him were the destroyed escort train and fifty-eight dead railway employees and passengers. More cryptic was the burned out hulk of the steam engine and three coal and barracks cars of the government postal train with the baffling absence of two vault cars, two armored gun cars and a caboose. An emergency message had already been sent westward to railway guard units along the Siberian Railway to be alert and to check all remote sidings and switchyard areas.

Ziyetski hoped to hear soon from the lieutenant and his fifty-five men who were closing in the Chinese border to the west. He considered Border Unit 12 to be his best bet for new evidence. The helicopters had completed their search. There was no sign of the train along the rail line. The search had gone as far into China as the aerial observers could view without violating Chinese airspace. It was incredible that five massive railway cars could simply disappear with the only remaining trace being the wrecked engine, the coal cars and the fifty-eight dead.

The ballistics team brought in hard proof that the choice of the attackers had been limited to Soviet and East Bloc weaponry only. No evidence of Chinese made anti-tank weapons was showing up among the fragments that were being gathered by the dozen soldiers with metal detectors searching the embankment on the east side of the burned out postal service engine. This evidence was helpful, but not overly significant since Soviet and East Bloc ammunition had flooded world arms markets for years at the instigation and design of the country's former leaders. Whether showing up in mini-wars in Indonesia, Philippines, South America or Africa, the war supplies provided by the Soviets were readily available everywhere.

As Ziyetski mentally diagrammed the scene, he concluded that the gunners in the 73 millimeter turreted guns on the train had not given up easily, but had mounted a fierce defense. Unexploded rounds were found imbedded in the earth all along the ridge on the west side of the tracks. Not only had earth been displaced and cratered, but large rocks had been flung in some cases, a quarter of a mile by the high explosives of the intense automatic cannon fire.

Having run out of adrenalin, Ziyetski was finally starting to give way to the fatigue of the long night and full day without sleep. Suddenly he was revitalized by a report over the field telephone from KGB troopers on the south side of the destroyed bridge, "We've got a live one in here Colonel! Need blow torches down here immediately! He's trapped underneath the gun car!"

The Colonel quickly left the tent and ran full stride south along the track. He could see a group of soldiers gathering next to the gun car which was tipped up on its side on the mangled rails on the south side of the deep gorge. As he considered his options in reaching the scene, he determined there was no time to wait for the helicopter. Climbing down along the rock spines and ridges into the ravine, Ziyetski worked his way through the twisted wreckage of the collapsed bridge. The iron was still hot in places from the fire, blistering his hands slightly as he progressed.

His staff, unenthralled about the route he had chosen, followed cautiously. The Colonel clambered up the other side, swinging through pieces of wrecked metal like a seasoned gymnast, and finally was hoisted up the ledge on the south side by a rope as his soldiers pulled him to the top. He ran to a point where he could see a young man grimacing with pain in the dark recesses of the railroad ties and the mass of the twenty ton railroad gun car. "I want him out of here, alive!" the Colonel barked in a terse command.

"We're trying as fast as we can!" a sergeant responded.

Colonel Ziyetski could see that the sergeant was doing his best at supervising the rescue and did not need interference - not even from his CO. It had been a long night, and now a long day. He would not push his men unreasonably.

As the rescue proceeded, it became obvious that with no crane available, the best approach would be to try to use the helicopters. Within a half hour, two of the massive Mil Mi-24 battle helicopters were hovering at different altitudes to avoid becoming entangled in one another's rotors with their cables attached to straps around secure parts of the gun car. On the sergeant's signal, the helicopters struggled upward against the weight of the car. A corpsman had already injected the trapped postal guard with morphine. The injured man was largely unaware of the massive effort around him. As the helicopter pilots labored above, the car finally began to move slightly. With only inches to spare a KGB Border trooper crawled into the narrow space and pulled the trapped young man to safety.

He was unconscious. The Colonel's questioning would have to wait. In the next few minutes the injured man was loaded aboard one of the battle helicopters and rushed down the valley to the FEC Naval Hospital at Vladivostok.

Moscow, Russian Republic, Early September, 1992

The aging, dirty and poorly maintained Moscow city bus limped over the cobblestones, potholes, and cable car lines and jerked to a stop. The cargo of hardened Muscovites was ejected out of the two doors like toothpaste being squeezed from a tube. Once on the sidewalk and safely clear of the bus, each began to straighten his or her clothing, brushing off hair and other residue resulting from the human log jam. Though it was morning, most of the persons were stone-faced and tired-eyed as they dispersed in various directions for the day's activities.

Unaffected by it all, however, was Alexander Kutuzov. He, for the first time in many years, noticed the sound of birds, the smell of flowers, and the smiles of children on their way to school. He pondered his life and wondered how it was that he could be so content and joyful when everyone else seemed so sad and downtrodden. It was not beyond his perception that in the middle of some of the worst conditions to exist in Russia in his memory, including the war years, there was still time to reap fulfillment from a sense of discovery of new beginnings.

It occurred to him that, perhaps for the first time, he understood how his parents might have felt as they found each another, fell in love, and were married in the middle of the purges, upheaval, and distress of the mid-1930's. In their time, the entire country was in a state of chaos. People were dying from exposure to the cold and from lack of food that had rotted in the field at harvest time. Fear was the order of the day. He remembered his father telling him that they had spent much of their time trying to gain information so they could avoid being caught in the dragnets as supposed "enemies of the State," or being mistaken for someone else, whose fate had been predetermined by Stalin, his evil KGB Chief, Beria or their henchmen.

Things have not changed much, he thought to himself. Now the Motherland had broken up in many pieces. Danger seemed to lurk at all crossroads. Strangely, it all seemed inconsequential. No matter what he did or where he went, he sensed the surging power of Nieca's presence in his mind. It was a much different love than he had known with the mother of his son. They had enjoyed a good and meaningful marriage. But the strain of the long years of absence in Africa and elsewhere with the Foreign Ministry of the USSR had clearly impacted the relationship for the worse.

Only once, when he had suffered a severely broken leg in a car accident in Morocco, did the government allow his wife to travel outside of the Soviet Union to see him. While under the care of French doctors in Marrakesh, their entire range of activity was limited to sitting at the hospital room while he healed. Even then, despite Alexander's Party allegiance, the KGB Station Chief in Morocco had his men maintain a close watch on the Kutuzovs, while both husband and wife were out of the Soviet Union at the same time.

To his misfortune, at the very moment he had reached the level of seniority where he could come home to Moscow, his wife had become ill and died. It had all seemed like a bad dream - one from which he earnestly wanted to be awakened. With Nieca in his life, he was waking up at last.

His route to work required a detour. With the computer center for the Aviation Ministry located at Technoserv, only ten blocks from Toko Bank, he decided to pay a visit to an old friend. Entering the service door of the large nondescript building, his intention was to avoid the building guards. Still, he had to show the pass in his pocket-size red I.D. book to a soldier.

"Well, how is the most brave, heroic, courageous, outstanding, farsighted, intelligent, and idiotic banker in Moscow?" Leonid "Leni" Artimoshkin greeted his guest with a broad smile as Alexander walked through the door.

"What I want to know is how is the most conniving, secretive, conspiring, slimy, clever, aggressive, and basically good guy of a software engineer in Moscow doing?" Alexander replied as the two engaged each other in a friendly Russian bear hug.

"But you entered through the back door, my friend Alexanderovitch," Leni observed. "That must mean you are here for some sinister reason, does it not?"

"Not necessarily, Leonidovitch, I just didn't want to ruin an otherwise wonderful day by having to converse with Yarov's goons at the main entrance downstairs."

"Very well said, but some say that I am a Yarov goon."

"Some may say that, but I know better. You're as much a Yarov goon as I am Felix Dzerzhinskiy's son."

"I see that you're here on a mission," Artimoshkin observed. "This is more than just a social visit isn't it?"

"Can we speak in confidence here?" Alexander inquired with an air of seriousness.

"Yes, there are no bugs here. This room is my shop, and these computers are my computers. I don't think they worry about me anymore. They've got bigger problems. Yarov's inspectors come in here once a week and check serial numbers on the machines to make sure that nothing's being sold out the back door. That's about the extent of it. It used to be a major shake down. Now it's really nothing."

"So how's business otherwise?"

"It really isn't too bad except there's nothing to do here. You can only play so many computer games and live to tell about it. You ought to see how great I am with the Mig 31 Foxhound," Leni pointed with excitement to his 486 IBM clone. He changed his mood quickly as he explained, "We haven't had an aircraft design order come through this department for eight months. Not even an airframe retrofit. They have me back to copying Russian language accounting software packages made in London. Sort of the chief thief. So. . . that's me. So what've you got?"

"Leni, remember how I told you that they weren't taking me seriously at the bank? They didn't really think much of an ex-foreign service guy being dropped into the accounting department at the most progressive bank in town."

"Yeah, I remember that."

"I think I'm being put to the test. They've given me an assignment to audit a number of major accounts with the bank - including the Ministry of Aviation. I think they've given it to me in hopes that I will stumble and fall, and then they can railroad me out of the bank."

"Sound's normal. Why am I not surprised? Come now, Alexanderovich, tell me something new!" Leni had perfected the art of Russian sarcasm.

"But if I can perform an audit that is credible and accurate, then not only will it secure me a much stronger position with the bank, but if it turns up what I think, the First Deputy will be forced to leave me alone. I have important reasons to keep this job. I'm fifty-six years old. I've got good years left. I don't want to end up as a night watchman at the bank's motor pool or some demeaning thing like that. I've got to stay where I am!"

Leni could see the discussion was going to lead to a request. As one of the most competent software engineers in the Aviation Ministry as well as one of the most closely watched before the coup, he was always cautious when asked to do favors for anyone. But to Leni, Alexander was not just anyone. He was the godfather of his two school aged sons. He was one of only a few that attended the secret christening of one of the Artimoshkin babies many years before as the parents had sought to incur the blessings of a Christian God upon their family. Leni had, in turn, attended as chief mourner at the funeral of Alexander's wife. They were that close. "So what do you want me to do?"

"I need you to access the Dark Accounts, and get me a printout of the expenditures," Alexander responded.

Leni sat quietly for a moment looking around the room as if the answer was written somewhere on the wall. "The Dark Accounts! That's very high level. Although, as far as I know, we're not designing anything, those are State secrets."

"I only need the accounts for Toko Bank," Alexander was persistent. "And I only need them for accounting purposes. I want to provide an audit to the Board of Directors that proves that large withdrawals are being made for expenditures that may not exist."

"Well, you know, Alexander, everyone cheats. I don't think the Ministry is any different. They make up invoices and send them in for payment and the invoices are set up so that neither the KGB nor anyone else can confirm whether or not they are legitimate."

"I know that, and that's exactly why I need the information. I want to catch the First Deputy at his game. Once he knows I've got something on him, my job will be secure forever."

"Sound's like the Russian way of doing business to me!" Leni inserted. "No leverage - no job."

"Toko Bank is a legitimate, viable - almost a Western-style - banking business. It has a chance to earn a profit and pay its employees so they can live well." Kutusov was attempting to add altruistic meaning to his request. "It's not an evil thing to earn a good living. In all my years in the Foreign Service, I saw the Americans, the Germans, the British, the Arabs, and those who worked hard, living well. I think someday, we will live well, too. But I need that information."

Leni stood up, stretched and pensively walked across the room. He was quietly thinking. "What if I tell you that's information that I just cannot get my hands on?"

"Then you'd be lying to the godfather of your sons."

The silence continued as Leni again continued to move about the room. And then he looked up and communicated a wry smile in the direction of his old friend, "You say Toko Bank only, is that right, Alexanderovitch?"

"That's exactly right," Alexander spoke in a warm, but resolute tone. He could detect that his friend was reluctant but possibly willing.

"Then you shall have it before the end of the day tomorrow."

The two men shook hands and again engaged in a Russian hug of a much less jovial nature than had earlier occurred. Alexander made his way back down the stairs and out onto the street. He found comfort in a brisk gait up Novikova Boulevard in the direction of the Toko Bank headquarters - and Nieca.

Washington D.C., Early September, 1992

Vice Admiral Richard Moody stared at the huge electronic map of the world, confident that he had already made all the obligatory moves. As the operations chief at the Worldwide Command and Control Center at the Pentagon, he had evaluated the download of information regarding activities in the Far East from various electronic sources. He had rerouted TDRS-4 spy satellite in order to get a better picture of the area. The initial transmission and report of a massive heat signature was now over twenty-four hours old. The Vice Admiral was preparing a follow-up briefing to be presented to key national security personnel and possibly the President, regarding the corresponding military activity in East Asia at their morning briefings.

One of the tools at his disposal, in use for the first time, was a simple AT&T telephone call placed to his counterpart in the underground control center known as Shermoto Station, some four levels below Red Square, next to the Kremlin in Moscow. The secretive KGB lair had been constructed during the metropolitan subway system upgrade in the sixties, but was walled off from and was unknown to the hundreds of thousands of passengers who passed through the station each day. Times had certainly changed as the Vice Admiral was able to simply dial a number on a dedicated line and have his interpreter, over a speaker phone, ask the obvious question, "What is going on near the Ussuri River?"

The response had been equally unique. Rather than receiving the anticipated Russian verbosity designed to protect any breach of pride or deflect accurate suspicions for security reasons, the response was a frank, "I wish I knew. If you have any information at all, please let me know."

The Vice Admiral immediately began feeding information by telefax and electronic mail directly to the Kremlin. With the completion of the transmissions, the Russians in Shermoto Station expressed their sincere gratitude and appreciation.

The underlying American concern was that the People's Republic of China was, in some fashion, resurrecting its objection to strategic lands held by the Russians near the Ussuri River frontier since the early 1930's. But satellite photos confirmed that there was no major Chinese military movement in the area. The Vice Admiral was certain of this. He knew that the relatively unsophisticated Chinese forces had no reasonable ability to avoid satellite detection. Obviously, a military incursion as deep as ten miles inside of Russia would have to have been supported by significant logistical resources, such as masses of trucks, tanks or supply trains on the railroad. None had shown on the many hundreds of photographs now being relayed back to the Pentagon from outer space.

Presently, the telephone rang and the interpreter was active again as the simultaneously interpreted words of the Soviet General in Moscow were printed across the screen. "We think we have encountered a criminal event of immense proportions. The Federation Security Agency (KGB) in Vladivostok reports what appears to be the hijacking of a train. We cannot find part of the train and we have almost sixty dead, all murdered at the scene. The KGB office in Vladivostok has requested that we ask of your government the assistance of your advanced FBI mobile crime laboratory."

The Vice Admiral issued orders to his communications technician, "Call the White House. I need to talk to the President's Chief of Staff immediately."

Ozero Khanka Trestle, Far Eastern Russia, Early September, 1992

It had been almost a full day before the blood hounds arrived at the crime scene. This did not surprise Colonel Ziyetski, but it did discourage him. He knew that to use dogs effectively, they must be on the scene while scents were still fresh. This was particularly important in the case of a pool of blood which was found near the scattered remnants of the Playma anti-tank rocket launcher on the hill south of the gorge. The coagulated blood was assumed to have been that of the gunner.

Not far uphill from the blood, a left boot with the gory remnants of a foot still in it had been recovered. This launched searchers on the morbid hunt to find the individual to whom the foot had belonged. The local KGB crime lab conducted tissue tests against the pool of blood to see if any could be matched. More basic, however, was the need to follow the clear trail of blood which went across the track, up the embankment to the west, and off into the field and foothill country beyond. KGB border patrol units and helicopters had been dispatched in that direction, but no additional evidence had turned up.

As Ziyetski replayed the events of the previous day in his mind, the most perplexing detail was the underlying issue of motive. From information provided by the government postal service the postal freight logs showed that the train had been just that - a mail train. The only freight of value in the vault cars was three hundred thousand U.S. dollars and one and a half million rubles earmarked for the Toko Bank branch in Vladivostok. He had quickly determined that at even a liberal government exchange rate, there was less than four hundred thousand U.S. dollars total value in the vaults. By his estimate, there had to have been at least one hundred attackers. It seemed like a relatively small amount of money to be the focus of a military operation large enough to kill fifty-eight people. It was much more of a mystery than he was accustomed to dealing with - he knew he needed help.

The process of ferreting out crucial facts in even small criminal investigations had been a problem for the KGB in Vladivostok. They had requested assistance from the national crime lab of the Federation Security Agency in Moscow, but were informed that the Agency was currently being reorganized and would not be available. At that point, the Colonel had strongly suggested that if the KGB's top experts would not help, perhaps they should ask the Americans for assistance. To his favorable surprise, his superiors in Moscow consented to make the request. Their rapid acquiescence added to the intrigue, but there was only time for one mystery at a time. He would greatly welcome the American help.

Moscow, Russian Republic, Early September, 1992

Still fatigued by the long truck trip and the frustrating battle with the Moscow bureaucracy only days earlier, Michael arrived at the Technoserv offices at approximately 9:30 a.m. His Danish-driven habit was to get to work early and not allow the day to get away from him. It annoyed him that his work ethic was not shared at Technoserv. By mid-morning, the lower level employees were drawn to work by hunger as they began wandering in to see what food had been gathered by Yarov's daily scavenger-hunters. Consistent with tradition and proper etiquette, upper management would not arrive until after the lower echelons were well in place. Michael prepared himself for the many self-serving platitudes that would be spewed about by Yarov and his management as to how hard they worked.

"Michael, it's good to see that you survived yesterday's ordeal. You know that those sorts of things happen in Russia."

"All too well," was Michael's response through the interpreter.

"Well, let's put that behind us. I think we need to talk about your relationship with Technoserv." Michael watched Yarov's eyebrows dance like dueling caterpillars as he talked. "We have been considering a presence in the United States. We feel that this may be something you can help us with. Would you be interested?"

The approach was classic Russian, Michael thought to himself. They think that I will jump at the general idea before they fill in the details.

I have no intention of becoming just another Yarov goon. "Where in America do you plan on locating?"

Yarov was disturbed. He had expected more enthusiasm. "Does it matter, Michael? Are you not interested?"

"The United States is a big country."

Yarov looked at his watch and then called his driver. "We will go to Star City." The command was not interpreted. "Michael, let's go for a short trip. I would like to show you something that will help you engender a little more zeal for our plans."

As they drove off into the forested area to the southeast of the city, Michael's thoughts moved through the years of effort he had put into the Danish-Soviet joint venture. But he knew that with the completion of one of his most important deliveries of computers, his role would change. Whether he could abide the Russians any further was a serious question. Perhaps this was the time to make a clean break.

After leaving the city on the Moscow Ring Road and then turning East onto Strenenka U1, the car reached police roadblocks intended to keep the public and all other unauthorized persons from traveling further down the wide boulevard. Guards signaled with respect as they waived the car through the checkpoints. Presently, they arrived at the security gate of what appeared to be one of the secret military installations sequestered away from public view and access in one of the restricted zones that ringed Moscow.

Yarov spoke, his arrogance was unmistakable. "I will take you on a tour of one of our facilities. This will be interesting, for today I will show you things that few Westerners have ever seen. I thought it would be well for you to see Star City."

"Isn't Star City off-limits for foreign nationals?"

"Yes it is. But from time to time we have allowed foreign guests here, and since I supply it with all of its computers they let me bring whomever I want. You know, rank has its privileges."

Within the half hour they arrived at a modern, hi-tech commercial center with long warehouses and other buildings. Michael's first impression was that the buildings were clean, well-built, and took on the polished appearance of the most contemporary industrial areas that he'd seen in Europe and the United States. In place of mounds of dirt, weeds and unmowed grass, he could see well-trimmed hedges and manicured lawns. The unkempt and trashy scenes sometimes hidden, but always present for the prying eye elsewhere in Moscow, were nowhere to be seen. Michael concluded that this was, indeed, an extraordinary place.

The car pulled up to a building which appeared to be the headquarters. As they entered, smartly-dressed guards snapped to attention and saluted Yarov as if he were in uniform. "Now, let me show you what we've got, Michael. I take great pride in this place."

They walked through an office area to the other side of the building and climbed into a small golf cart-type vehicle and proceeded across a sparsely occupied parking lot to an industrial-sized blue door, against a large yellow corrugated steel warehouse. The door lifted and they drove inside. Yarov pulled the cart next to a handrail where they looked down into a circular tank of water, which by Michael's estimation, was easily sixty feet in diameter. The underwater areas were illuminated by powerful lights built into the walls. Michael could see motion under the water.

"This is our zero gravity tank, Michael," Yarov began to explain. "If you will come down these stairs with me, we'll look inside so you can get a better idea what we're doing." They walked down a set of stairs to a platform where they viewed the tank from a window built into the side of the tank. Michael could see men clad in clothing similar to spacesuits with cylindrical air tanks on their backpacks.

"This is where we practice operating in zero gravity," Yarov explained. "It is what you call extravehicular activity, meaning that these young men inside are Cosmonauts who someday will be conducting spacewalks. We can closely simulate a spacewalk by controlling the environment in this tank. It may not be absolute zero gravity, but it comes very close, particularly since we have built small ballast tanks into the spacesuits which offset the tendency of the Cosmonaut to sink to the bottom. It is great fun. Perhaps you would like to give it a try, eh?" He winked at Michael.

After a time, they again climbed the stairs and went outside to a massive rectangular structure about two blocks to the north. As the group entered, Michael found himself looking up inside another two-level cylindrical structure. There were people in white Cosmonaut suits surrounding him and from inside their helmets they nodded respectful acknowledgement to Yarov. Each seemed to be busily engaged in a particular task.

"Now, this is something I know you will really enjoy." Yarov pointed to a female Cosmonaut who was working her way out of the pressure suit and into what was very little clothing at all. She smiled at the group then looked directly at Michael while removing her clothes entirely. After stepping into a narrow six foot glass capsule which was attached in the lower room, a male counterpart walked to the side of the capsule, pushed a button, and Michael was surprised to see jets of water shooting from the top and the bottom of the tubular compartment with equal strength. The water was apparently being sucked out from both ends almost as fast as it was being injected into the capsule. The woman inside caught his attention even more. He found himself momentarily mesmerized by her incredible body. He had never seen such stunning perfection.

Within two minutes the process was discontinued and the woman provacatively dried herself off with a towel. She spent considerable time drying her long flowing red hair, while she, in her nakedness remained exposed to full view. She seemed to totally disregard the fact that the men were watching the entire event with intense interest. She put on her spacesuit, turned and smiled at the group and continued on to her next task which was of less interest to the onlookers. Yarov explained that she was modifying a small kitchen table with tiny holes which were to be used for recovering food crumbs that would otherwise loosely float around in the space capsule under zero gravity conditions.

Michael felt a certain degree of disgust. He recognized the typical Russian ploy. They wanted to entertain him, to tease him as a precursor to a favor. He had been around Russians long enough to know that seventy years of supposed egalitarian Communist doctrine had still left women in the vortex of male domination. Females were still relegated to the status of the used and abused. Much of the street system of Moscow had been built on their strong backs. So why not use them as cheap pre-negotiation entertainment at Star City as well?

"So, as you can see, Michael, this entire facility is a mock up of the Mir space station which is presently orbiting the earth. You should understand that the three Cosmonauts which you observed in the space station are undertaking the very same activities as the three Cosmonauts aboard the Mir. We simulate all activities one hour before they are actually performed in outer space in order to forestall any problems. So, I hope you understand the matter with the young lady was not to appeal to your erogenous instincts, but as a highly trained professional at work.''

Michael didn't respond. He knew Yarov was merely trying to justify the tasteless scene which had appeared to fail in its intended affect.

At mid-day, Yarov took Michael to lunch at the officer's club. Michael was impressed with the exquisite service and the decent taste of the Russian food - it was a pleasant surprise. It was clear to Michael that this part of the military was not sharing the food shortages with the rest of the country. Fresh vegetables, watermelon and even tangerines and oranges were included with the meal. He surmised that those were items which could not be found on more than a dozen other tables in the entire city of fourteen million. He commented, ''Your people eat very well. This is several steps above the Technoserv cafeteria.''

''Yes, that is certainly true,'' Yarov responded. ''We take very good care of our people here. Star City is indeed a very unique place.''

Throughout the afternoon, the tour of the base took him to an area in which he was able to view the original sister to the Sputnik whose circumnavigation of the earth opened space for exploration in 1957. He was treated to the demonstration of a remote-control Venetian lander which simulated one of Russia's greatest space accomplishments. Actual x-ray fluoroscopic analysis of dirt and rock samples from the Venetian surface were picked up and tested by the Soviet Venus probe, Venery 13 in October of 1981. For almost an hour, he was in the seat of a Mig 29 Fulcrum flight simulator which gave him the ride of a lifetime, including repeated crash landings.

By late afternoon, the tour had made its way through the apartment areas, schools, and meticulously maintained soccer stadium and track and field facilities. ''As you can see, this is a good life for these people,'' Yarov editorialized. ''And it's good for Russians, Ukrainians, and people elsewhere in our new Commonwealth. In the Ukraine the tables are plentiful, just like they are here. I know that you have spent most of your time in Moscow and you suffer the same frustration of so many of my countrymen. But this is a big land and as you can see, even this close to Moscow, life in Russia can be very good. There are many positive things happening right here at Star City.''

As the sun began to descend, the group drove in the direction of a building with a circular dome. The building was positioned within a half mile of the launch facility that Michael had toured earlier in the day.

"Please now, let's move on. I would like to show you something very special.'' Michael was led into an austere but spacious room with an old wooden desk in the center. On a stage to one side of the room, was a large, full wall-size map of the world, dimly illuminated by display lights built into the ceiling.

"This, Michael, is a very special room. In fact, I would say it is a sacred room,'' Yarov spoke reverently. "Before each voyage into outer space, the Cosmonaut will enter into this room and meditate for approximately one hour. Great and wondrous things have happened here which motivate the heroic pursuit of the universe by our Cosmonauts. Some may call it an initiation. The fraternity of Cosmonauts holds an exceptionally venerated station in our culture. This room,'' he paused for emphasis, "it is the place of focus for that relationship. We, Russians, were meant to explore the universe, and great sacrifices, by us and our entire nation, have been directed to that end. In other lands, such as in America, or in your Denmark, the extent of the sacrifice cannot be clearly understood because those are lands of plenty. But in Russia the sacrifice is very great as we enter into a new age of dominion over the universe.''

Michael was moved by the words, but still harbored suspicions. He was hearing Russians exulting themselves - a sort of common cultural aberration. But there was no explanation for the moisture in Yarov's eyes. Even that surprised Michael.

"Come, sit in the place of the hero.'' Yarov moved back one chair at the desk and offered the other to Michael. As they sat down he continued, "Never has a non-Russian occupied that chair. In fact, few foreigners have ever seen this room. Very few Russians know of its existence. It is the ultimate hall of honor and valor for our people. We invited you here to see this for a very specific reason.''

Michael was preparing to hear the sales pitch.

From the side door, a steward wheeled in a scale model of what appeared to be a building complex of some kind.

Yarov sat back in silence while Michael carefully examined it. The model included a dome in one part and an overpass across a public road leading to an imposing building with columns and spinnerets. All features were distinctively Russian. "Well, what do you think?" Yarov asked.

"It's very interesting, " Michael responded.

Yarov reached forward, flipped a switch, and a crisp beam of light shot out of a circular point on the top of the scale model, projecting a distinct pillar of light streaming to the ceiling like a bright florescent tube.

Although impressed by the scale model and all the gadgetry, Michael was more intrigued by Yarov's reverence for the model itself. Even if it was intended as Star City's latest construction project, it still seemed to Michael that Yarov was being overly dramatic in his presentation of the project. It was a side of Yarov he had never seen.

"This, my young friend, is the Russia Center. It is destined to be a showcase for the greatest achievements of Russian Space exploration and will be seen by people from all parts of the world. It will be our foremost opportunity to share our vision of the universe, a sacred shrine to showcase the accomplishments of our greatest heros. This pillar of light will someday reach out into the universe from deep inside the Russia Center complex. There will be displays and exhibits for children, adults, tourists, and everyone who wishes to know more about the many great things we have accomplished and which heretofore have been largely maintained in secrecy. In fact, it will change the mistaken view that the world has of Russia, the Commonwealth, and its many peoples. As visitors are drawn in and educated there, they will go away with a different feeling for our Motherland. It will erase misconceptions and bring people together in the cause of the exploration of the unknown."

Yarov's religious-like fervor left Michael perplexed. I've been brought all the way to Star City, given the V.I.P. tour, and ushered into the Cosmonaut's inner sanctum, so that I can be shown a scale model of a museum! The entire event was suddenly changing from interesting to weird. Michael was getting more uneasy. What does this have to do with me, he again asked himself. Maybe, Yarov thinks I have money. "It really does appear to be an incredible project," Michael courteously commented. "Does this mean that you are going to open up Star City as a museum or something?"

"No, Michael, not at all. This is why we want to talk to you. We have carefully studied all of the places in the world where the Russia Center could best be located. It is desirous that it be constructed in a place where international tourists regularly travel. Yet, we do not want it to be overshadowed by other major attractions that could minimize its significance.''

Michael was thinking to himself that Odessa on the Black Sea might be a good location. People would likely travel there in droves, once the problems of the former Soviet Union were straightened out. The arid climate and miles of beachfront would compete well with the French Riviera or the Gold Coast.

''In fact, we plan to place it on the edge of what is the third largest tourism crescent in the entire world. And we desire to locate it in a place which is readily identifiable by tourists from all over the world.''

Michael wondered why the sales pitch was taking so long. He could not think of any serious international tourism area in Russia. ''So, if you're not going to put this project at Star City, and if you're going to attract all these tourists, where do you intend to construct the Russia Center?'' Michael asked.

''As I told you,'' Yarov's voice was inflecting self-perceived cleverness. ''In a place that every international traveler would know. . . between Las Vegas - everyone knows where Las Vegas is - and the Grand Canyon - everyone knows where the Grand Canyon is - namely, right in the city of St. George in the southwestern corner of the state of Utah. You are familiar with St. George are you not?''

Michael scratched his head and wondered if he had just heard what he thought he had heard. Just when he thought he had the Russians figured out, they totally surprised him. ''Wait a minute, you mean that you intend to build this huge museum in the United States instead of Russia?''

''That's exactly what we mean,'' Yarov was pontificating. ''That's why we need you, Michael. You have lived in St. George. Your wife is from that city.''

''This sounds very . . . it's clearly beyond anything I expected!'' Michael was still struggling for words. ''But you know, St. George is just a small town. It has about forty-five thousand people on a wet day.'' Yarov looked to the translator for an interpretation of the idiom. The translator shrugged and gave no answer. '' This sounds like a very interesting project, but are you sure that you want to do it in St. George?... I mean, uh, I would love to see something big like this come to St. George, but ... do you really think it has a chance there?" Michael was speaking with guarded excitement.

"This is not a precipitous decision. We know what's there. We have studied the matter very carefully and we know that each year over twenty-five million tourists travel to what is known as the Golden Triangle with Los Angeles, San Francisco, and Las Vegas, at each point of the angles. Immediately adjacent to the Las Vegas part of the Golden Triangle, is what the Americans call the Grand Circle of the National Parks. You have the Grand Canyon, Monument Valley, Lake Powell, Bryce Canyon, Zions, Arches, Natural Bridges and other beautiful National Parks spread all over that area. People from all over the United States and millions from Germany and Japan travel there each year. Our studies show that they are normally highly educated travelers who are not merely going to Las Vegas to gamble or sit on a beach somewhere and get suntans. An important aspect of the plan is that everyone traveling into the Grand Circle must first go through St. George.

"The interstate highway goes right through the area. The city is a thriving resort town with many golf courses, swimming pools, tennis courts, and other resort amenities. Further, there are no large minority populations. There's no community of Poles, or Vietnamese, or Chinese in the region. This causes us to feel that we would have a unique opportunity to set up our own Russia Center near where millions of tourists travel, but not be swallowed up by the casinos of Las Vegas or the Disneyland's of California, or other ethnic groups that are more formidably established in America already."

Michael felt himself being progressively convinced as Yarov continued his narrative. Somehow, it made more sense than anything he had ever heard from a Russian. He was surprised and to a degree overcome by what appeared to be the competent and thorough planning. It was inconsistent with anything he had seen or experienced in all of his years at Technoserv.

"So, what do you want me to do?"

Yarov smiled, "You are tired of Russia, are you not, Michael?" Yarov knew that most foreigners quickly grew weary of Russia.

Michael nodded in the affirmative.

"Technoserv is a computer related company. You will set up a subsidiary in America which will ostensibly operate as such. In reality, you will be laying the ground work for the Russia Center."

Michael again looked at the scale model on the table. What had initially appeared to be a half-baked presentation was now taking on new significance.

"So, what do we do from here?" Michael asked.

"You will report for work tomorrow as the new Executive Director of the Russia Center. We will need you to return to America as soon as possible. The resources of Star City will be available to back this important project. You will be paid well. You must make your decision immediately. As for me, I shall take a vacation to the Caucuses beginning tomorrow."

Yarov stood up and ushered the group out of the room. Michael could hardly conceal his enthusiasm. *And to think that all this started when I sold a computer to that smelly old Russian sea captain.*

As he was driven back to the hotel in a staff car from Star City, his mind wandered through a review of the day's events. His normally cynical opinion of Russians was on hold. Michael was delighted, confused and surprised by all that he had just seen and was anxious to try and explain it all to Gina.

CHAPTER 8

Manchuria, Mid September, 1992

Captain Major Sarabrov glanced through the open door of the freight car as the train chugged slowly through the hill country in the direction of the sprawling Manchurian industrial center of Harbin. Glad to be alive, he sniffed the air and reflected on the attack he had directed several days earlier. A discernable pain lingered as he thought of his troopers who had fallen - their remains having been placed in a deep grave just inside the Manchurian border. It occurred to him that the traditional delivery of the fallen troopers' black beret to their families back in Russia would never happen. They were forever relegated to the status of unknown soldier whose fate would be the subject of eternal speculation. That is, he thought for a fleeting moment, until the Motherland could be rescued at the hands of the STAVKA. His mind wandered into a day dream of the illusory shadow power that he had sworn to serve. With a deep and almost divine sense of the mission of the devout Communist, he was secure in his personal testimony that the future of the Motherland rested in the guiding hands of a mysterious few whom he was dedicated to serve, to the death, if necessary. The STAVKA, as they were known, like the holy spirit to the most devout priest, would deliver up salvation to the world. So it was, as with the STAVKA who delivered tangible orders to Captain Major Sarabrov, the performance of blind faith would endow the allegiant with its rewards.

As he leaned down, his hair blowing in the wind, he found himself admiring the dispatch with which the entire operation had been performed. The train was Chinese. The railroad gauges were different in China, the Chinese train being slightly larger. It was a strategy conceived by the Chinese as their Russian neighbor to the north had become an enemy. It assured that the size of the railroad track would not accommodate the invader's trains.

Chinese ingenuity had overcome every obstacle as the Captain Major looked back at the flatbeds covered with huge canvases where the two vault cars of the Trans-Siberian Railroad were now riding as mere railroad cargo. Although he had not been present as the transfer was made, it did not appear the vault cars had been opened or disturbed.

Another matter of concern was the whereabouts of Sergeant Bantor and four men assigned to operate the DKZ-B anti-tank weapon at the south side of the railroad bridge. Having withdrawn from the area of the train, Sarabrov was uncertain as to whether Bantor's group had survived or if any might have fallen into enemy hands. He was particularly worried by the possibility that the dead or wounded in the group may not have been carried away from the area by their comrades. If such was the case, he knew there would be repercussions. His orders had been express and specific that he was to leave absolutely no trace of Spetsnaz troopers at the scene.

The STAVKA would be unforgiving if any major mistakes were made. As he gazed off into the Manchurian summer, he hoped that what he had always been taught - that is, that the STAVKA had influence everywhere, would also apply in China. It was possible that the only hope for survival for himself and his men, would be the STAVKA's ability to extricate them from China.

It was not difficult, nor unusual, to be largely uninformed as to what the next moment, day, or month, might bring. Spetsnaz Alpha Group members had been trained to be patient while awaiting orders. Uncommon discipline required spending long hours, months and even years in the throes of uncertainty. Sarabrov hoped that when they reached Harbin he would receive word of their next assignment, so they could avoid languishing at the pleasure of their Chinese hosts any longer than necessary.

Moscow, Russian Republic, Mid September, 1992

"This is for you, Alexander. Our evening together last week was very enjoyable for me and I hope for you also." Nieca's face was glowing as she put the small package in his hand.

"Oh, there was no need." He was almost tongue-tied in her presence, but her warm smile managed to put him at ease.

She took his hand, "Open it - right now, so I can watch."

He walked to his desk and fumbled with the coarse wrapping paper until he could open the box. He pulled out a stylish tie tack that sported the design of two hearts, one overlapping the other.

"It is so nice. I mean, I...I...thank you."

"I picked silver because I think it suits you. Please, wear it always. Unlike most men here, you always wear a tie. I admire that. I admire you for many reasons, Alexander."

Her words echoed in his head. He could feel her nearness and smell her light perfume. I am too old to be this capricious, he thought as he looked at the shiny hearts in the box.

Alexander was brought back to reality by a secretary informing him that the First Deputy wanted to meet with him immediately. He reluctantly put thoughts of Nieca on hold and walked to the bank's executive office.

"So, Kutuzov, you do not consider the audit to be complete, is that correct?"

"Yes, Mr. First Deputy," Kutuzov had almost said the word, Comrade. He was not yet accustomed to addressing persons without the requisite party imperative. "I really do think there's more to do. My guesses are certainly not adequate for your needs."

The First Deputy paused and then glared contemptuously at Kutuzov. "What *are* my needs then, Mr. Kutuzov?"

Sensing the First Deputy's extreme derision, Kutuzov was caught off guard but he still ventured a somewhat hesitant response, "I assume your needs, Mr. First Deputy - at least in this regard - are audit reports of good quality with accurate information as to assets and liabilities so that the bank can fully be informed as to its true condition."

"That may be true," the First Deputy was recanting his position slightly, "but don't you think the work you have done is adequate?"

"No, Sir, not at all. There must be a debit in the account to match every withdrawal. Inasmuch as the account is that of a government entity, the law requires spot checking of the actual expenditure manifests also be done. So that's what I'm doing. It's particularly important since the Ministry of Aviation owns part of the bank. You wouldn't want the Ministry to take money out of the bank without your knowledge, would you, Com. . ." Kutuzov had slipped again, "would you?"

The First Deputy paused, seeing that his subordinate was expressing himself reasonably well on a very key issue. He could not dispute Kutuzov's position. "I must tell you Mr. Kutuzov, there are some very sensitive national security matters with which this bank is involved. Coming from the Foreign Service, I assume you know how important that is." He had chosen to acquiesce rather than make a direct response.

"I do appreciate your conscientiousness in attempting to provide us with the best information you can find. Although I suggest to you that some detail is highly confidential. I would informally tell you that if you will be so kind as to complete your audit and accept the Aviation Ministry detail as it is indicated on the bank's records only, then the national security issues will be adequately protected. If, however, you persist, it will probably be necessary for us to put a person with a true security clearance in the audit position and move you to a different department."

With that statement Kutuzov was dismissed. As he retreated from the First Deputy's office, he was confused yet determined not to allow the First Deputy's criticism to ruin his day. After all, he would see Nieca in a moment. Her work station was only two desks away from his. He determined it would be best to put off the Ministry of Aviation audit until he could talk to Artimoshkin and sort the issues out more clearly in his mind.

Vladivostok, Far Eastern Russia, Mid September, 1992

The young man had been placed on the upper floor of the Far Eastern Command Hospital in Vladivostok in an area reserved for only the most prominent patients. It served the aristocracy of the Far Eastern Command well and was one of the few advantages for those at the Pacific coast outpost.

For the moment, the postal train guard fighting for his life was not concerned about his lavishly appointed hospital suite. Numerous attempts had been made to bring the young soldier out of his coma. Colonel Ziyetski waited impatiently for an interview, hoping that the soldier had seen his attackers. From his investigation he had concluded that the battle at the Ozero Khanka trestle had lasted almost forty-five minutes from start to finish. This, Ziyetski thought, should have allowed a survivor ample time to reach a number of conclusions as to what had actually happened. The injured soldier, however, remained mentally dormant. The Colonel's hope for a star witness was still on hold.

The Colonel had only recently returned from his base camp at the site of the massacre. Earlier in the day, Ziyetski had met with a team of FBI agents that had arrived from the United States together with dogs and sophisticated equipment. Comprised of twenty-one members, the team had required two C141 Star Lifters which had appeared as an anomalous specter of East-West cooperation on the tarmac at the naval military air base in Vladivostok.

Ziyetski's entire regiment had been pressed into service to comb the mountain area near the border. The blood hounds that had ranged off into the foothills had come up empty-pawed and were soon to be taken out of service. They had started late, and were unable to pick up further scents from a cold trail. Yet, Ziyetski knew that whoever belonged to the foot which had been found in the paratrooper's boot on the hill south of the trestle could not have gone far. He had either been buried in a shallow grave in the hill country, or had been carried into one of the nearby villages for care. With the latter possibility as a strong consideration, a door-to-door search was still underway by the KGB border troops in the villages of Novokachalinsk, and Kamen Rybslov. He determined that the apparent escape on foot could not have taken the injured attacker further than about ten miles from the site of the battle. And even at that, he surmised, it would be a very long and painful walk for the soldier or his comrades under such conditions. No other vehicle tracks had been seen in the area. Still, speculation continued to occupy the investigators regarding the location of the rest of the train. It had disappeared without a trace.

Moscow, Russian Republic, Mid September, 1992

The meeting had been prearranged at the request of Leni Artimoshkin. The two men walked down the Parkovaya Street, at a nondescript location some two blocks east of the Technoserv offices. The city was just awakening to the strong smell of thick smoke billowing out of the industrial stacks of the Chukhlinka State Steel Works on the opposite side of Petrovskiy Park to the southwest and hanging low over this part of Moscow.

"How did you get this?" Alexander Kutuzov demanded anxiously, looking at the papers that Leni had brought to their meeting.

"It would be better if you didn't know, Alexanderovitch," Leni spoke kindly to his friend.

"But Leni, these printouts show huge expenditures. I have never heard of such projects before."

"Well, that may not be unusual. All kinds of things are going on in this country that none of us know about," Artimoshkin responded.

"That is true, but I really think that when I compare this to the Aviation Ministry's account at the bank, things will not add up. The expenditures are very large. It is truly incredible, but again, it is not far from what I expected."

As they walked, they continued to pour over the printout. Alexander carried with him a copy of a bank ledger attempting to make the comparison, and at the same time avoid tripping over major cracks in the sidewalk. "Here, for example, is a very good one. On the bank ledger for this account, you can see a payout of three million rubles. It was done for this project ... look here... TTI. But when we look at the printout there is nothing that supports the invoice to the bank. The invoice was for three million rubles. But on the printout, the TTI expenditure was only one million rubles."

"Isn't that fraud, Alexander?"

"It's the old trick that we have lived with for many years. You submit a false invoice so you can spend the difference. How do you think I survived on Foreign Service wages all those years?"

"This is a huge amount of money, Alex!"

"Don't be surprised if it's the way Yarov lives so high off Technoserv," Kutusov remarked.

"But you know how Yarov is, anything is possible with him. I seriously doubt that he has any conscience in these things. I've known him for too long."

"Now, look at this one," Alexander continued, "here is a twelve million ruble payout from the Toko Bank...it's called," he concentrated on the name, "the Zion Plan."

Artimoshkin interrupted, "What do you think that is?"

"I don't know. Maybe some resettlement of Jews to Israel or something. But look over here," Alexander again directed his finger to the appropriate line on the printout being carried by Leni. "There are absolutely no expenditures. It just shows under the expenditure category one big zero. So the bank's paid out twelve million rubles, and yet there's no underlying list of expenditures inside the ministry."

"And so, let's see," Leni was learning fast, "who was the check made out to by the bank?" He ran his finger down the list of entries on the banks ledger. "Look at this, Technoserv - Yarov. That's all under the Zion Plan."

"Well, it means that Yarov was given a check for twelve million rubles," Alexander responded trying not to show his sense of alarm to passersby. "What do you think he did with it?"

Leni scratched his head in confusion, "That's the strange part of this. On the printouts, I found several of these entries. The Zion Plan which shows up on your bank ledger just shows up with a code number over here on the Aviation Ministry printout. But look at these others.'' Leni was pointing to what he had found to be a corresponding pattern between the two ledgers. ''Here is the Zion Plan, then turn several pages over and we find the Caucus Station Plan. Maybe there are some more, but it looks like...well, just a whole bunch of plans of some kind.''

The two men stopped and were now stooping over a small wooden bench along the wide sidewalk next to an old building. Alexander was continuing his intense perusal of the documents. ''Is there any way that we can determine what the expenditures are within each of these so-called plans? If there is some plan going on and money is being put into it, how do we find out how the money is being parceled out? Do you think Yarov is putting it into his own pocket?''

''I think that is doubtful,'' Artimoshkin responded. ''Yarov may cheat on his expense account, but the penalty for embezzlement of State money is still death. If we can see what's happening here, then so can the KGB.''

''Can you get at those other accounts Leni? It might tell the story of what's really happening here.''

''The problem is, to get within those plans I would have to figure out the access codes. I have no idea what they might be. Those could just as easily be words or phrases, and they don't have to be in cyrillic. It's impossible for me to unscramble. This could be the end of the line, my friend, as far as trying to chase anything down on these computers is concerned. Why don't you just ask the First Deputy why there is so much money going into the Zion Plan? Maybe he will tell you.''

''I would need to know more about it before I would approach him. He has warned me about violating national security already. I guess this is one of those times,'' Kutuzov responded. ''He's already looking for a pretext to get me. Maybe there's enough here to at least make him leave me alone. I'll have to think about it.''

'' All I can tell you is what I have found.'' Artimoshkin was very hesitant. ''I've probably gone about as far as I can with this. On second thought, maybe you'd best not approach the First Deputy. If it really is a big secret deal then what's to stop him having you hauled down to Dzerzinski Square for interrogation. It still happens you know. A few people still disappear every month. I don't think it's worth the risk.''

"I understand, Leonideovich. I'll see what else I can do. At least you have helped me get started. But I can't let that bank just fail. If it fails, I'm gone with it. And for the first time in a very long time, I have some very good reasons to make a success of myself."

"So, you're becoming a Yankee capitalist?" Leni laughed.

"No, Leni, something much better than that."

"And what might that be?"

Kutusov smiled gently, "I wish I could tell you - Yarov isn't the only person left in Moscow with a few secrets."

Harbin - Shanghai Railroad, Mid September, 1992

The crisp and cool mornings of the Manchurian high plains had given way to balmy, humid and sticky warmth as the train slowly made its way along the coastal plains of central China. Captain Major Sarabrov was now relaxed as he gazed across the green panorama of rice paddies that blended into the horizon. All had gone well since passing back through Harbin.

There had been only one tense moment when the Chinese military commander at the Harbin Kaserne informed the Captain Major that the Russians would need to surrender all of their weapons to the Chinese once again. As quickly as he had contested the commandant's request, the Chinese officer had produced the same leather pouch which unmistakenly bore all of the unique stamps of STAVKA high command. The Spetsnaz Company communications sergeant quickly deciphered the code on the magnetic tape from the pouch which informed the Captain Major that weapons would no longer be necessary. The message had also congratulated him further on a job effectively done. From that point forward, Sarabrov's soldierly instincts told him all would be well. He had done his duty - the most paramount of his concerns.

He wondered what the 23rd Spetsnaz Company would do without weapons. He hoped the battle for the train would not be the last action he would see. But whatever the job, he sensed in his heart a burning destiny to serve the Motherland forever, and unto death if necessary. Not only was he gratified by the STAVKA's congratulatory message, but also by the parting salutation, "Stand-by for further orders."

Now that there was time to think and ponder, as well as hope for the future, he found himself reveling in those thoughts which are only available to the living. His heart was heavy as recent history had changed his relationship with his homeland forever. He could not suppress the yearning for his beloved Yelana. So many years had passed that he sometimes wondered if she still thought of him. At such moments, he hoped that she was somewhere back in Moscow longing equally for him.

Caucus Mountains, Former Georgia SSR, Mid September, 1992

The flickering fire in the fireplace was the only light in the otherwise darkened room. Two figures sat, still and sullen, gazing into the dwindling flames. The only sound was the soft whistling of night wind through the mountain pines.

Presently, one figure, an elderly man, stood up and walked to the broad window which ran to the apex of the high ceiling. From his Dacha he looked out to the southwest at the broad black expanse of the valley far below. The flicker of lights were only sporadic in the distance and little activity could be seen in the town of Svanathia at a distance of approximately ten miles. The air was clear, there were no clouds or smog. The mountain retreat was situated at a strategic lookout on the western slope of the Caucuses, an area known only to a few of the indigenous Georgian mountain people, and to the most elite of the former Soviet Union.

Approximately one mile down the hill in all directions, existed a three hundred yard wide no-mans-land much like a moat to a castle. Patrolled continually by a detachment of a Spetsnaz regiment, the Dacha was virtually inaccessible on the ground from any direction. A maze of guard dogs, electronic surveillance and other detection devices were spread across the hillside. No one, except those specially invited, had ever gained access to the Dacha.

Opposite the fireplace, the light danced across the face of a golden bust of Lenin. The old man turned from the window and observed the sculpture, noting the smooth, proud forehead, high cheekbones and noble nose. To him, the face seemed eternal, casting an endless gaze through the thick log walls of the Dacha and across the hills, plains and the world beyond. The man could not help but note Lenin's resolute expression - almost an anachronism in this time when the Motherland could no longer comprehend the meaning of such words. "It is good," he spoke softly, "that Vladimir Illiavich Lenin is dead. This is far more than even he could withstand."

"Do you really think so?" the younger man asked.

The man at the window paused. His voice was aggrieved, but nevertheless clear and certain, "The Motherland is in need of rebirth, Comrade. There is no question that she is in need. Much like a woman who has starved herself to a point where even food would not save her, she is thin, she is emaciated, she must now be fed through the veins by radical measures. Her virtual survival lies singularly in our hands. We are all that is left of the STAVKA."

"That is true Chairman Andropov," the younger man spoke, his eyes still focused on the bust of Lenin. "Yes, Mr. Chairman that is very true."

The older man leaned back in his chair. "I thought you would agree, my famous young Cosmonaut, you always do."

CHAPTER 9

Hurricane, Utah, Early October, 1992

For Joe Wilson, growing up in the canyon country of southwestern Utah had been both a blessing as well as a curse. From his earliest days he could remember long hikes and hunting trips far off into the remote reaches of the desert high country. The spectacular colored sandstone terraces, mesas and monoliths had been his childhood playground. It was the land of the Hollywood western, the movie producer's dream, where they had made the John Waynes, Gary Coopers, Robert Redfords and Clint Eastwoods of the world famous and rich.

At some point he had become aware of the curse of it all which was spawned largely by the fact that the town of Hurricane was at least almost a two day trip from anywhere else. The point had been made even more profoundly over time as Joe had worked during the summer in the national parks and met tourists from all points of the compass.

At the end of his senior year of high school, he had his chance to travel with the graduating class on the obligatory trip to Disneyland and see what California had to offer. In truth, it had intimidated him, too many people, too much noise. Thus, confused as to how a young man with marginal grades and limited means could afford any further education, Joe decided to stay home and get a job. Within a year, the deputy sheriff position had become available as the previous officer had moved on to another job with a larger city. Joe considered it to be a stepping stone, one that would look good on a resume, although he still avoided the mental discomfort that the thought of someday leaving town created.

His high school sweetheart had already moved away for college. She had promised to write and remain true to Joe. But from the day she left for school, Joe never heard from her again. Her family reported that she was doing a lot of dating and seldom had time to write to them either. Joe knew that it was really just their polite way of saying they were relieved she was not spending time with him anymore. She was the only girl he had ever kissed and he was now discovering the loneliness that often accompanies the process of growing up.

The best method of dealing with the situation was to bury himself in his work, an attribute that the sheriff, much to Joe's distress, did not seem to fully appreciate. In his extra time, Joe had tried to investigate cases, assuming the role of detective. This seemed entirely appropriate in a county where the sheriff's department did not have a detective on staff. But the sheriff had made it clear that Joe was to write tickets and respond to emergency calls. He didn't want a young deputy out drumming up evidence against the citizens who might take offense to the activities of the sheriff's office when they walked into the voting booth.

"One-X-Four, One-X-One wants to talk to you on the telephone. How far are you from the Hurricane office?" The dispatcher's voice inflections told Joe that he was in trouble with the sheriff again.

"I'll be there in two - tell him ta' hang on." Joe headed for the Hurricane sheriff's office, unlocked the door and picked up the phone which had apparently been ringing for several minutes. The sheriff was his usual ill-tempered self. "Wilson here," he tried to sound calm.

"Wilson, what makes you think you can spend this county's money on a whim? What's this bill for three hundred dollars from the State Crime Lab?" The sheriff sounded on the verge of losing control, an event that occurred with unpredictable regularity.

Joe searched his mind for an answer and then suddenly remembered the incident of the bullet in the wheel. "Well Sheriff, I got a bullet out of the wheel of that Kolob wreck. You weren't in town so I sent it up... I thought they did that stuff for free."

"Hell, they do it for free when it's a part of a criminal investigation. But there ain't one on that car accident and you know it!... You moonlighting as a damn insurance adjuster or somethin?"

Joe resented the accusation but could see the sheriff's point. "No, nothin' like that. But it was a bullet, and a big one Sheriff. Shouldn't we open a criminal case... somebody shot at that car."

"Whether we do a case or not is not *your* decision. But you need to get something real straight, you don't go sending stuff to the crime lab without my permission and especially don't send nothin' if we haven't opened a case - I'm taking this bill outa' your paycheck! Maybe it'll teach you a lesson! So don't you go worrying about no case. You just see if you can get the procedures straight so it doesn't cost *you* any more money!"

There was a long pause in the conversation. Joe was toying with the thought of resigning. But he realized that bullet or no bullet, the sheriff was probably right on this one, a little contrition might be appropriate. He took a deep breath and decided not to enflame the situation. "Sorry, Sheriff. I guess I wasn't aware of just how it works."

"Well, just think real clear before you act, boy. At least this wasn't some situation where your life was on the line."

Joe noted the lack of sincerity on the part of the sheriff. "So, Sheriff, if I'm paying for the report, what does it say?"

"This is why there ain't gonna' be no case. Them state boys are up in the night. It says '.337 caliber specialty round for a Soviet State factory made Tokarev Assault rifle.' "

"What's that?"

"I dunno, I think those boys at the state are spoofing us. There ain't no such stuff being fired around here or within ten thousand miles of here."

"So, you're not going to open a case?"

"Joe, what I really think all the fluff is about, is that a fishing line weight from the tackle box in that Toyota got jammed up in the wheel area from the force of the impact. Those dudes at state don't wanta' admit that they can't identify everything in the world. They've been wrong before. To them everything is a bullet... Remember, those people in the car, they were fishing up at the reservoir just before the crash." The sheriff paused, confident in his analysis, "Unless we got some real strong evidence, I'm not gonna spend money chasin' wild hunches based on an antique Russian bullet. So, you get back to work and forget about it."

Joe wasn't fully satisfied with the sheriff's position, but he was glad to terminate the conversation. Joe returned to patrol and dutifully angered a score of out-of-state tourists through the course of the afternoon as they passed through town at five over the speed limit.

Moscow, Russian Republic, Early October, 1992

Moscow is a crowded city. Perhaps the difficulty in finding seclusion is one of the reasons for a declining birth rate. In the summer nights the parks are crowded. Consequently, the darker and more secluded portions of the public parks become the spawning ground for many of the city's children. Such is preferable to the confines of overcrowded apartments littered with mothers and fathers-in-law and children usually all present and compacted into cramped rooms.

"On the first audit, I gave in to the First Deputy. I almost feel ashamed for doing so," Alexander remorsefully related his perceived failure of his first assignment at the bank to Nieca as they strolled in Gorki Park across Krymskiy Boulevard from the Central House of Artists after attending the rock opera "Juno and Avos." The deafening music was still ringing in Alexander's ears causing him to wonder if he had suffered permanent hearing loss. He tried to camouflage the considerable sacrifice he had just made to bridge the generation gap by talking business rather than paying any compliments to the ghastly musical.

"I have no idea if the First Deputy is dishonest, everyone seems to be dishonest these days. But we are, after all, a bank. We must take great care of the accounts or the bank will close." He paused, then looked at Nieca to carry out his real intent, "If the bank were to close...we would seldom see each other. I cannot tell you, dearest Nieca, how that would pain me."

She took his hand and looked into his eyes and with gathering tears said, "I have much the same worry." After a pause, she continued, "You must do what you feel is right. If the First Deputy or his friends are stealing money from the bank, then someone must disclose it."

"But that's part of the problem," he continued. "It is extremely difficult for me to understand exactly what's going on. It's like knowing that you're sick, but not understanding the nature of the disease. I'm not an accountant. I'm just retired Foreign Service. I know about passports, visas, and arranging for shipments of aid from the Soviet Union to our allies, or at least those that used to be our allies. But I'm having trouble getting a handle on this problem."

"Well, how will you do it? What is your plan?" she asked.

"I took some steps during the last audit to try to figure things out and I'm getting some help from a computer friend of mine. Maybe that will help."

"Oh, that would be wonderful," she said with an air of encouragement.

"It's something that I have to do. I am also worried that when the State Bank Chartering Commission renews the charter and reviews my audits, they will find grave disparity, then I, myself, might be in trouble. It would be terrible if the First Deputy were stealing from the bank and the authorities viewed me as being in complicity with him."

"I hadn't thought of it that way," she responded. "That is a serious concern. I will support you, Alexander, in whatever you decide to do." She turned and faced him.

He took her in his arms and kissed her. Even after anticipating this moment for so long, the reality was far better than the dream. Her response was like nothing he had ever experienced.

Vladivostok, Far Eastern Russia, Early October, 1992

Colonel Ziyetski was enjoying his first evening at home with the family for almost a month. The train massacre and hijacking had consumed his time almost without pause since the urgent call in the middle of the night. He had grown distant from the family as he found himself sitting in the den of their large apartment sifting through piles of documents and still mystified as to what actually happened on the Trans-Siberian Railroad. The young postal guard at Vladivostok FEC Hospital had briefly regained consciousness two weeks earlier. The Colonel was summoned, but before he made it to the hospital, the young man had slipped back into the coma.

The American FBI had been enthusiastic and willing to help, but had provided little additional information that he and his KGB investigators had not likewise obtained on their own. It was disappointingly clear to him that the Americans suffered from a major information gap when it came to an understanding of Russians and the logic and procedures by which Russian railroads were operated. The FBI had been helpful in one respect, and that was the identification of the origins of the mysterious bloody boot. Not only were the Americans able to determine how it had been constructed but also found the location of the manufacturer.

The rubber on the sole of the boot was of a type only available in Vietnam. The manufacturing facility that used the unique rubber was not located within the Commonwealth. It was traced to the "Statschuenvereign," a defunct shoe manufacturing facility in the former East Berlin. The Americans concluded that the boot would have to have been manufactured prior to the fall of the Berlin Wall since shortly thereafter, the supply of boots to the Soviet Red Army by the Germans was discontinued. It was further pointed out that the boots were of the highest quality German manufacture, issued only to the most elite of the Soviet military. Much poorer quality boots, manufactured in Russia, were issued to general infantry and other Red Army forces.

The pressure was beginning to mount. The Admiral at FEC had demanded a full report with a prioritized list of suspected wrongdoers in the train hijacking. Colonel Ziyetski was well past his deadline and needed to prepare the report as soon as possible or allow his office to face major criticism from headquarters FEC. Being as politically correct as possible in these times of change was important. Thus, he decided to list his theories regarding the train attack and hope that by the time they were circulated at headquarters FEC, he would be prepared to defend them. Leaning forward at the desk, he put pen to paper and listed his suspicions:

Priority No. 1: Insurgent action by well-armed anti-government terrorists in need of money to support their cause.

Priority No. 2: Military incursion by highly-trained members of Chinese Peoples' Liberation Army to probe the defenses and response of Commonwealth forces near Ussuri River disputed borders.

He looked at the two options he had written down on the paper and felt almost satisfied that they were defensible. The points seemed logical, reasonably calculated and less than controversial. But with the information he had in hand, he needed to make one more supposition. Knowing that he would raise serious concern up and down the levels of Russian military authority, he nevertheless wrote:

Priority No. 3: Attack by highly-trained Spetsnaz unit upon orders from some command level within the country and perhaps within the Federal Republic of Russia Armed Forces itself.

The Colonel felt a degree of relief, having finally written the words that he had harbored in his mind for several days. He knew that Spetsnaz forces acted only on orders from superiors. Although many things had changed in the Motherland over the past several years, there was no doubt in his mind that the Spetsnaz remained highly disciplined and active. Both the KGB investigators and the FBI alike had agreed that the boot and the foot that had been severed from the soldier's leg were a perfect fit. The FBI had supplied a 360 degree computerized diagram of the exterior of the foot showing the callouses, as well as the indentations in the leather and the rubber sole. The boot had been worn by its owner regularly over a three year period. A pathologist's dissection of the foot had shown it to be extremely muscular and well-developed and without question, not that of a Chinaman or any of the tribes of the Eastern Plateau or Siberian Steppes.

It would be difficult responding to the FEC's questions about a motive for the wholesale slaughter of the train's occupants. Yet, he knew that the Spetsnaz was thoroughly capable of carrying out such a murderous atrocity without hesitation.   There were others whom he suspected of facilitating such terrorism, but the efficiency of the killing, together with the boot, at least allowed for reasonable suspicion that the Spetsnaz should be a principal suspect. He would submit the report and await the response from FEC which he anticipated would be filled with shock and indignation at his suggestion that the military might have perpetrated the act.

Moscow, Republic of Russia, Late October, 1992

The two men sat in the park again reading newspapers and watching pigeons scrap for crumbs on the cobblestones near the playgrounds which had been vacated by the children as evening approached. In contrast to their earlier meeting, they were now wearing heavy coats. The Moscow air was frigid. Yarov wore earmuffs and removed them only long enough to participate in the conversation.

The First Deputy had been reluctant to meet with Yarov outside official contacts between the bank and its investors. The Moscow office of the KGB had been investigating acts of fraud and corruption among public, banking and other government officials. Dishonesty was rampant and the new KGB was attempting to expose the debauchery wherever possible. At the behest of Yeltsin, there was particular interest in the business and political activities of prominent opposition members of Parliament.

Commercial banking was a new experience for even the most sophisticated of Russian businessmen. Among the KGB ranks were very few persons trained to identify the symptoms of bank or economic fraud. They were again resorting to the most rudimentary technology by electronic eavesdropping and otherwise maintaining surveillance on bank officials wherever possible in order to obtain incriminating statements and other evidence which might lead to successful prosecutions. The presence of the First Deputy of Toko Bank and a parliamentarian in private conversation with the head of Technoserv, a one third shareholder in the bank, would have been a conversation of intense interest to the KGB. Both men knew it, and endeavored to be as discreet as possible in making their way to the park.

"So, you wanted this meeting," the First Deputy spoke. "What's on your mind - it had better be important."

"You needn't get overly exercised my dear First Deputy," Yarov responded. "I haven't been followed today. And I assume that unless you are absolutely stupid, you came here with the same precautions."

"Of course I did. But let's make it quick, precautions or not it seems that no matter how big this city gets, it's always a small one when you're trying to be discreet."

"I do have a distinct problem," Yarov continued. "We at Star City are about to receive the first installment of a two hundred million dollar payment for the January Baychaunus space shot. It's a satellite, a Western communications satellite. It's a very good arrangement through one of our private companies. It will revitalize our space program. And, the profits go to the STAVKA so your bank will not have to keep making donations. But there is a problem."

"So, tell me." The First Deputy was gruff.

"We will receive the check tomorrow. But we must have twenty five million dollars transferred to the international account of the Western company at Gossbank by the following day to shore up our side of the financing or we will lose the deal."

"Why do you come to me?" The First Deputy was becoming nervous. "Use some of the billions you got from the train."

"We don't have it yet. It is still in a laundering mode in Hong Kong. We need more money from your bank."

The First Deputy did not speak. He stood up and gazed across the park in a vacant stare. After a moment, Yarov worked his rotund frame to its feet and placed himself face to face with the First Deputy. "There is no time. We must have the money day after tomorrow."

"Will your people reimburse the twenty-five million plus interest as soon as the train money is useable?"

"There are no guarantees." Yarov spoke sternly.

"And if I refuse?"

"My good friend... or silly friend... I'm not certain which - nobody refuses the STAVKA...nobody."

The stark comment chilled the First Deputy. The sub-zero temperature suddenly seemed warm compared to Yarov's demand. He started to shake, his speech assuming a drunkard's slur, "I would never turn down the STAVKA, but I am *finished* with the bank if I do this thing. I will probably go to prison."

"You are the only one who can help. The STAVKA is relying on you." Yarov was focused.

"You just don't *know* what you are asking. This is terrible."

"Will you or will you not facilitate the transfer? I must have an unequivocal answer." Yarov's impatience was beginning to show.

The First Deputy started to cough. He then remedied the problem by lighting up another of his many daily cigarettes. "I need some time... just a little time."

"Time is not ours. You are the only person in the whole of the Motherland who can help us with this matter. I am also told that if you cannot commit to me now... at this moment, then you must present yourself at the Cosmonaut's Room of Honor tomorrow night at 2200. You will receive a telephone contact from the STAVKA."

"Will they kill me?"

"I don't know. They are relying on you."

"But Yarov, I have done all I can at the bank short of walking myself to the gallows. There is no money left to turn over to the STAVKA." The First Deputy continued to tremble.

"I suggest strongly, my dear First Deputy, that you be there. Perhaps you can somehow work it out with the STAVKA. Good day." Yarov turned and walked across the park, disappearing into the crowd. The First Deputy crumpled to the bench where he pondered his future for another hour in the freezing Moscow evening.

CHAPTER 10

Caucus Mountains, Late October, 1992

On the eighth day of creation God gave the land to many peoples of the earth. When he had finished, he started home and met the Georgians sitting at a table along the roadside. God said, ''While I was dividing up the world, you just sat here, eating and drinking wine. Now there is no land left for you.''

''That may be so,'' replied one of the Georgians, ''but while you were busy, we didn't forget you. We drank many toasts to you, thanking you for such a beautiful world.''

''That's more than anyone else did,'' said God. ''And so I am going to give you the last little corner of the world - the part that I was saving for myself because it is so much like Paradise.'' Or, so the story goes, thought Lado Deniken to himself as he surveyed the broad expanse of the mountain range from the balcony of the militia barracks in the town of Svanathia. To the northwest, at a distance of about thirty miles, he could see the striking outline of the magnificent Mount Elbrus almost in the shape of a bear's tooth. It reached 18,500 feet into the sky. According to the myth, Zeus, the King of the Gods, chained the warrior Prometheus to a rock on the mountainside after he stole the secret of fire and brought it to mankind. Thus, one of the greatest of Greek legends, known even to many children in the Western world, was supposed to have taken place on a high mountain in the country of Georgia-Transcaucasia, formerly the Georgia Socialist Soviet Republic, tucked neatly along the far eastern shores of the Black Sea.

Svanathia was a most serene and beautiful setting, sandwiched in the foothill valleys along the southern slopes of the Caucus Mountains. The name Svanathia means "shelter" or "refuge." According to local legend, fugitives fled to Svanathia to escape the authorities. The steep mountains around Svanathia made it accessible only to those traveling by foot. In the winter months, snow cut off the land completely from the outside world. Any bounty hunter or policeman who made his way into the valley in pursuit of a fugitive would have to face proud Svan warriors who recognized no authority but their own and who pledged that they would rather fight and die than turn over a fugitive.

Although the Georgian Military Highway had been constructed across the Caucasus from Russia on the north to the Georgian capital of Tbilisi, passing through Svanathia in the process, the people of the area were still largely independent and unaffected by the outside world. Lado Deniken was no exception. He had grown up learning that accommodating the Russians was simply a way of doing business. Anything beyond that, particularly friendship or association of any kind with a Russian, would result in severe criticism. Castigation would not only come from his own people, but also from any other ethnic groups in the area that likewise harbored a major distaste for their neighbors to the north.

Lado was a ruggedly handsome man in his early fifties, with a broad sun-beaten face and square jaw. He was still able to out-drink the younger fellows as well as best them in performing the traditional Fundruki dance during the festival time of year. It was his good looks, his careful choice of marrying into the family of a prominent farmer in the Svanathian Valley as well as his keen understanding and manipulation of the Blat system that had provided a relatively comfortable living since his teenage years.

His father-in-law was wise. He had skillfully developed a sincere adherence to the Georgian adage, "It may be a disgrace to be rich in a Socialist country, but in Georgia it's also a disgrace to be poor." With this approach in mind he had amassed great wealth and had assured that his sons-in-law would find good work farming the ancient vineyards of the plush valley.

Living under Communist rule had not been easy. But when the Second World War ended, Lado, as a teenager, had come to realize that bending rules within the system often engendered very positive results. Blat was the term designated throughout the country as the special method of patronage and favors used to circumvent the rules and regulations of the Soviet-imposed economic system. In particular, Blat meant obtaining jobs or other benefits based upon performance, personal favors and exerting influence, rather than by merit. Often it extended to outright fraud, threat and coercion.

Lado had become an expert at black market trading. One of his earlier ventures was privately growing flowers and shipping suitcases full of bright yellow daffodils north to Moscow on airliners. On the other end, the money was always good. The Muscovites would pay top ruble, and at times, top American dollar for the beautiful Georgian mountain flowers.

Growing up as a young boy had been joyful and largely without challenge. But even his keen Blat abilities were inadequate to protect him from being impressed into the Red Army for a one year tour of duty, at age eighteen. To make matters worse, the one year was extended to eighteen months because he had fallen out of favor with a certain sergeant in basic training and was placed in a training division. Much of his time was spent at hard labor. He remembered counting the days through the latter part of 1963 in anticipation of the day that he could finally leave the dreary Salinisky Military Farm north of Minsk and return to his beloved homeland in Georgia. A poor excuse for a soldier, he had never thought of himself as a Russian. He considered the entire arrangement as a form of slavery impressed on his people years before he was born.

Much had changed, however, since the days of living off the Blat system. Along with his prominence, Lado was now experiencing responsibility that he had not dealt with before. With the crumbling of the Soviet presence in Eastern Europe, and particularly in the Georgian corner of southeastern Europe, he was counted among the founders of the

Transcaucasian Militia, a para-military force dedicated to eradicating all remaining vestiges of the Soviet presence in Georgia.

Lado's year and a half in the Russian Army, along with his unique abilities within the Blat system, had qualified him well. He had been elevated to the part-time position of District Military Commissar. The job included responsibility over the military affairs of Svanathia and its satellite communities throughout the river valley.

His forces were regularly gaining strength. As the Red Army bases in Georgia began to close, Soviet soldiers found themselves streaming northward to an uncertain future, and at the same time practically tripping over each other in the stampede to sell arms and equipment to Georgian black marketeers. At the end of every underground black market trail was a Transcaucasian District Militia Commissar. The proof of the system's efficiency was in the grain warehouses on his father-in-law's farm where weapons were now being stored in large quantities.

As a fifty-three year old, Lado was by Georgian standards, only a spry middle-ager. His father had lived to the age of one hundred fourteen, and his wife's father was still happily fathering children at the age of seventy-five. In the land of the Abkhazian mountain people, quality life well past one hundred years of age was expected. Like the Svan warriors of the earlier century who had been reported to have lived even longer, Lado planned a long life for himself - that is, unless a Russian bullet changed his plans.

The Security Commissar of the parliament in Tbilisi had gathered each of the district Commissars together and commissioned a surveillance and mild harassment policy against all Red Army troops remaining in the region. This meant tracking the license plates and other identifying numbers on vehicles and aircraft, siphoning gas out of the tanks of parked vehicles, and even more aggressive harassment like slashing tires from time to time. No direct confrontation was ordered, only passive harassment. It was hoped that through this effort, the message would swell through the ranks of the occupying force that the time to go home was long overdue.

Lado, however, had been given a particular assignment which took on a much more ominous prospect than those of his associates. On the mountain ridges to the north and to the west in the direction of the great

Mount Elbrus, a secret Soviet military installation had been operating for many years. It showed no signs of abandonment or evacuation despite the breakup of the Soviet Union and the advent of Georgian independence. He could recall as a young boy freely wandering the mountains while herding sheep with his father. Following the war, however, a large part of the high ridge and plateau had been cordoned off by Soviet troops. Even larger areas of the southern and western slopes of the Caucasus had been transformed into a military exclusionary zone. Guard towers had been erected to oversee the wide-open, clear-cut strips of forest with mines, barb wire, and dogs, as well as guards who had, on more than one occasion, shot and killed animals and sometimes people who strayed into the area.

It was in 1984 that the first leather-jacketed and black beret-clad soldiers were seen in the area. They had increased in numbers during the course of the Afghan War and were regularly observed driving through Svanathian villages in their BMP troop carriers.

Over the course of the last several months, Lado and his militia, now numbering some seven thousand throughout the valley, had observed an increase in activity of aircraft coming and going onto the airfield that had been constructed by the foreigners on the high mountain plateau. From time to time, he was able to position observers near the peaks of the mountains above the base, who, through their binoculars, were able to read tail numbers, count personnel and identify types of equipment. In more recent times, however, Soviet truck traffic along the Georgian Military Highway had reduced. It was also notable that regular Soviet Army troops were seldom, if ever, seen in the area, having been replaced in significant numbers by the feared black-bereted Spetsnaz troopers.

It was getting late in the day as Lado pensively gazed into the mountain heights above the town and could, with the naked eye, locate many of the antennas and look-out towers which signaled the ominous perimeter of the secret military base. He pulled a piece of paper out of his pocket and read it once, then read it again. Looking down toward the river valley he imagined the beauty of the seashore along the Black Sea beyond the mountains. He then walked into the staff room and faced his twelve most trusted commanders who sat quietly around a table waiting for him. "I have an announcement. It is to be kept in utmost secrecy. You know I love all of you as brothers, but if anyone divulges this information, he will die." The group sat motionless, awaiting Lado's next words. "With approval of the new President in Tbilisi and the Security Commissar, we have been requested to commence the process which will ultimately lead to the attack and occupation of the Spetsnaz base on the plateau. This is not an order to attack now. As you know, this is something we could not do at present. It is an order for us to very quietly and surely begin taking up our positions so that we may be able to do this thing, as this order says, very soon."

As each member of the group repeated the oath of secrecy, in the solemnity of the occasion, an additional word fell from the lips of each mouth. *"Steffan,"* Lado spoke quietly upon his turn. He reached into his pocket, pulled out a small leather folder, opened it and looked at the picture of his son who would forever be nineteen years of age. *"Steffan,"* he spoke again as his face paled and his eyes darkened. The men filed out and Lado stood alone in the room. He made no effort to hold back the tears.

Hong Kong, Late October, 1992

Leaning over from the bed, he pushed the button and watched the heavy drapes draw back in two directions, exposing the large glass window. He pushed another button on the console and the sheers automatically drew back to an incredible breathtaking view of the broad expanse of the Hong Kong Harbor below.

Captain Major Sarabrov had not seen sheers before. The ornate heavy curtains were only slightly familiar. He had been impressed by the marble stone finish and glass decor in the bathrooms. A room on the seventeenth floor of the majestic Marriott Hotel at Pacific Place in Hong Kong was a vast improvement over the confines of the Chinese freight car which the 23rd Spetsnaz Company had called home for several weeks. As the stay at the rail yard in Shenzhen had almost reached an unbearable state, a Chinese businessman from Hong Kong representing himself as a Mr. H. I. Hui, had arrived and provided good food and fine clothing for the entire unit. A different train had taken them and the captured vault cars, without inspection of any kind, past the Hong Kong authorities, and into the sprawling seaport late at night. Buses then carried the men to the hotel. He was informed by Mr. Hui that the vault cars would be attended to by a major Hong Kong bank.

Billeting in the luxury of one of Asia's most extravagant hotels still presented certain challenges for Sarabrov. His English-speaking ensign was busily consuming every fact of informational or strategic value in the newspapers and reducing them to cyrillic for Sarabrov to read. Communications among the members of the unit were likewise difficult because the 23rd was dispersed into rooms at various locations throughout the thirty-seven story, three thousand room hotel. It had taken them almost a day since arrival to discover that they could contact each other by merely dialing room numbers on the telephone. But as quickly as they did so, they assumed that all telephones were subject to electronic bugging as was the case in all Moscow hotels.

No mustering point had yet been found where all ninty-three men could meet for conventional military briefings. To deal with the problem, Sarabrov appointed his communications ensign to concoct a code that could be spoken over the telephone for simple and necessary communications. None of the group harbored any doubt as to the possibility that the American owners of the hotel were actively trying to discover the true identities of their Russian guests.

For the present, the group was registered at the hotel as a delegation of the State Sports Committee for the Republic of Russia. For any of the group engaged in conversation, their respective expertise in many sports including judo, skydiving, karate, Greco-Roman wrestling, or boxing served as a perfect cover. Each could expertly discuss at least one such sport. It was a helpful deception, one which lent them ample opportunity to spend a considerable amount of the day in the spacious sports and fitness center at the Marriott without attracting undue suspicion.

Sarabrov viewed the spectacular scene from his window with great interest. Looking northward across the expanse of the Hong Kong Bay at the mouth of the Pearl River with the city of Kowloon on the other side, he discovered himself marveling at the seemingly systematic organization of the community around him. Everything was in motion like a huge moving picture, helicopters in the sky, ships sailing in all directions up and down the river, and automobiles literally jamming the roads as they competed for every inch of space. The most shocking reality was the fact that everyone seemed to be going somewhere, or even more mysterious - everyone had somewhere to go.

His thoughts were interrupted as his ensign in charge of reconnaissance operations reported to him with a dozen different maps of the Hong Kong area under his arm. "These people are very naive," the ensign said as he opened the maps. "There is no sense of security in Hong Kong, Captain Major Sarabrov, Sir! Just look at these maps. I have a map of every harbor facility! And look at this one - it is a 'Restaurant Guide to Hong Kong.' It shows almost every strategic lookout point in the mountains above Hong Kong. And look at this one. This is a map on 'Tours of the Harbor.' This shows where each of the British navy shipyards are as well as the configuration and length of each pier."

"They think they are invincible," the Captain Major laughed cynically. "The British have always thought that their flag has some special power - that it can scare away millions of Chinese or keep our tanks in Europe from invading. The British have always been naive. I think the Hong Kong has become too British in its thinking. In 1997, this entire area will fall easily to the control of the Peoples' Liberation Army. And you can bet that every tactical commander of the PRC in southern China has these and other maps in hand and already knows his objective...that is why you will not find a map of Moscow in Moscow."

"How would you like me to use these maps, Sir?" the ensign inquired.

"We will stick to our normal procedure. We are in a foreign country. We begin tomorrow our strategic reconnaissance patrols. We will try to map the appropriate ten block squares for the nuclear target acquisition exercise."

"But Captain Major," the ensign spoke, "we have nowhere to submit our reports - what will we do with them?" The ensign was surprised at his commander's decision. It meant a lot of work, and Hong Kong was already being treated by many of the soldiers as a place for well-deserved rest and relaxation.

"How is it that we have been placed in this luxurious setting? This is the best proof I know of that the STAVKA is alive and well... and taking good care of us."

"Yes, Sir!" The ensign was immediately cooperative.

As he walked to the door, Sarabrov made a final comment. "I certainly do not want to be without surveillance reports when we are required to account for our activities in Hong Kong. You will personally conduct the first reconnaissance patrol in the morning. I want accurate maps using the dark ink on the transparent overlays."

As the ensign walked out of the room, Sarabrov again gazed out across the scene before him. These people are so simple-minded and defenseless. I could probably destroy half the city with my unit alone. I need orders. When, he asked himself, will I again hear from STAVKA?

St. George, Utah, Late October, 1992

Michael and Gina were rapidly getting settled into St. George, Utah. By all measures, it was a dream come true. The older children were in school and Michael was busily attending to the demands of setting up his new office in the southwest desert resort city.

Upon arrival, Michael had followed the instructions given him. He sought out the most exclusive office building in the area, and rented a suite of offices in a building known as Tabernacle Tower, named for its location on Tabernacle Street, one of St. George's business thoroughfares. The three story building was a remake of an old turn-of-the-century train station.

The first test of the new relationship, as far as Michael was concerned, had been to see if the money, which had been promised by Yarov, would appear. Although he had not dwelt heavily on the issue, Michael harbored a nagging suspicion that somehow when he arrived in St. George, he would receive a fax from Yarov explaining that the deal was off. It just seemed like the Russian thing to do.

To his pleasant surprise, however, not only was the initially promised one hundred seventy thousand dollars wired to the new company's bank account at the St. George branch of Zion First National Bank, but two days later, an additional five hundred thousand dollars arrived in the account.   Each deposit came by direct wire from the International Department at Toko Bank in Moscow.   The ease with which the money arrived from Russia astounded him. It was a well-defined departure from the bumbling which Michael had anticipated in this unusual relationship.

Initially, the plan had been to set up a Utah corporation that would be owned ninety percent by Technoserv and ten percent by Michael himself. The Russians faxed a resolution of the Board of Directors of the new company named Transcontinental Trading, Inc. and a list of equipment to be obtained. The Board consisted of Yarov as chairman and two individuals whose names Michael did not recognize. One was a man and the other a woman. The list of equipment read like a computer hack's Christmas list including Cray II supercomputers which Michael knew he could not send due to Department of Commerce prohibitions on export of strategic items. It didn't surprise him that the Russians would at least ask.

As the weeks continued, Michael was run ragged by the non-stop listing of items to be acquired and shipped back to Technoserv in Moscow. The jubilation and enthusiasm he had felt with the company's start-up in St. George had quickly given way to the frustration of trying to keep up with all the expedited orders for shipment to Russia. It seemed strange to Michael that there was no mention of the Russia Center in the correspondence. He wondered if the Russia Center idea, which he understood to be the main purpose of his move to St. George, had been abandoned.

By the third week, the problems had become even more intense. Michael could not keep pace with Yarov's demands. He was also receiving shopping lists from members of other departments at Technoserv via the electronic mail. Everything from shoes to cigarettes, from nylon stockings to Levi jeans were being requested. Michael was asked to review American computer catalogs and magazines and send publications which met certain specifications to Russia. The Russians planned to translate parts of the magazines and prepared Russian language inserts for the purpose of marketing the magazines to computer users in Russia. At even the slightest delay, he would receive terse electronic transmissions from Yarov himself criticizing him for an apparent dereliction of duty. He was exasperated and overwhelmed. Being a "gofer" for the huge Russian Aviation and Aerospace industry in the United States was quickly becoming a thirty-six hour a day job.

Michael still felt that the job might work well, that is, so long as the Russians stayed in Russia. But Michael knew that it was only a matter of time before they would be coming to St. George and, for better or worse, he would have to be their host.

Michael's conception of Russia seemed to be in a state of continual evolution. It had seemed like such a vacant, frigid and harsh land. After a few weeks in the U.S. again, he chided himself for ever having lived in Russia. Only a fool would have taken his family there to live, he thought to himself. Despite the electronic mail and daily telephone conversations, in the warmth of the desert Utah sun, Moscow was not just eight thousand miles away, it was more like eight light-years.

Moscow, Russian Republic, Late October, 1992

The dark gray ILYUSHIN 76II Soviet transport plane made its final approach and crept out of the night sky like a ghost onto the runway at Star City. Although often active with test and training flights in the daytime, the runways at Star City, with the exception of the security guards nearby, were deserted and generally unused at night. The runway lights, nevertheless, could be turned on for emergency night test flights or special visitors - such as the four-engine Soviet short-field takeoff and landing jet, with no tail numbers or insignia.

The First Deputy was seated in the Cosmonaut's chair in the Room of Honor that had been shown to Michael Christensen during his Star City visit. The man was frightened, sweat poured from his forehead. His effort at removing money from the coffers of the State banks had been so easy when the Party had been in power. Such moves had garnered status and influence beyond his dreams. But now, he demeaned himself by sneaking around in the night, or holding secret meetings with Yarov in the parks of Moscow, or covertly gathering with members of Parliament at the clandestine flat just to do what had been theretofore the normal business of State. The slight pain in his chest momentarily broke his train of thought, reminding him that he needed medical treatment that a bankrupt Russia could no longer provide.

It was now well after 2200 hours and the expected call had not materialized. Having been to the base on several occasions, and being well-acquainted with the security situation there, the First Deputy pushed a buzzer on the telephone to see if the communication might have been mistakenly sent to another location. There was no response. This surprised him. The duty officer was always on station. To be absent would invite immediate court martial.

Momentarily astonished at the development, the First Deputy picked up the phone again and attempted to contact the base security station to request that the duty officer be located and ordered to report to him immediately. Strangely, the phone at the security station was not answered. How could this happen, especially while he awaited such an important communication? He allowed the phone to ring for twenty rings then slammed down the receiver and stormed to the main door of the Cosmonaut's Room of Honor, loudly calling for a member of the night guard who was always posted nearby. Again, his calls went unanswered. He was startled to hear his own voice echoing down the circular hall of the half-museum, half-office complex. The guard was not at his post either.

Fear of the unknown knotted in his stomach. He staggered into the hall and ran the length of the circular path until it reached the front door leading outside of the building. There, he grabbed the handle with a ferocious push, and at the same moment, his body lunged against the immovable steel frame as its reinforced steel wire and mesh window refused to give way. The door was locked. It suddenly occurred to him that he could not exit the building. Frantically lurching further down the circular hall to another door, he realized that escape from the building was now the smart order to follow.

Reaching the exit on the opposite side of the circular building, he again found himself grabbing at a locked door. Out of fear, futility and irritation, he yelled out, "I order that whoever is playing this ridiculous game, respond to me immediately! This is a courtmartial offense - I am awaiting an important call and cannot be toyed with in this manner!''

When he looked out the window, even the guard station across the parking lot was empty. A confusing rush of anticipation and dread whirled within him. His heart pounded, launching projectiles of pain through his neck that collided violently against the top of his skull. He sensed a weakness and vulnerability not felt in many years. The First Deputy became still. He deduced that it would be wiser to walk deliberately and quietly through the building to whatever awaited him.

Suddenly, as he passed one of the four doors leading up the steps into the wooden floored Cosmonaut's Room of Honor, the First Deputy heard what sounded like the rustling of paper. Stopping, he listened more carefully and crept quietly to the door, crawling up the steps to enable himself to see undetected into the room from a sniper's view. He reached the edge of the open doorway. A man was sitting in the Chairman's seat behind the wooden desk turning the pages of the Cosmonaut's Yearbook that was routinely located in the lower left hand drawer. The First Deputy continued to stare for about thirty seconds. He could not believe what he saw. He absently wiped the sweat from his eyes as the rapid pace of his heartbeat continued. The face that he was seeing was an image his brain would not allow him to comprehend. The face was still youthful, only slightly aged. But it was him...unbelievable! How could it be?

The man at the desk straightened himself back in the seat and spoke with a rich timbered voice which stoutly reverberated across the room. ''Mr. First Deputy, please come forward and sit in the chair of heroes.''

From his concealment near the doorway, the First Deputy stumbled into the room unable to believe his eyes. He straightened up and looked again, trying to clear his vision and then look again. He stuttered as he spoke, ''Aren't you ... aren't you Yuri Gagarin?''

The man stood up from behind the desk and spoke with royal and dignified flair. ''Yes, I'm Yuri Gagarin. Please sit down.'' He again beckoned to the First Deputy.

The First Deputy was sweating profusely, shaking as he unsteadily walked forward. He sat down, not taking his eyes off his host for even a second. ''But...you are dead! You died in an airplane crash in the Ukraine in 1968! The whole nation... the world mourned your death.''

"Well, if that were true, First Deputy, then I am resurrected from the dead! But as you know, when I went into space back in '61, I did not see God nor did I see any angels, and, as you can see, I am here, Yuri Gagarin in the flesh."

"It really is you," the First Deputy was completely humbled and speaking in still quivering tones. "It's the same smile that moved our nation. You made us all so proud. We named our children 'Yuri'... after you."

The First Deputy was both confounded and awestruck, yet as he came to the realization that he was not dreaming, exhilaration took over. "Where have you been, Comrade Gagarin? If you did not die in the crash, then where have you been - why have I not seen you before?"

Gagarin stood up slowly and walked to the huge map of the world with Russia and the City of Moscow at its center. "I have moved on to a higher calling in service of the State. As you look at this map, do you not wish that the Motherland could always be the center of the world and the universe?"

"Yes, that is the desire. It was declared as a goal by the Party."

"So, you have not forgotten the Party, Comrade First Deputy," Gagarin noted, "That is a very good thing. The Motherland is changing and there is a great deal of work to do. And it is only through men like you that the Motherland will fulfill her destiny."

"So, what should I do?" The First Deputy inquired meekly as if caught in a mystical spell.

"As you know, the Baychaunus satellite launch program here at Star City will only succeed if there is some funding from Russian sources as well. You must produce twenty-five million dollars for a payment to the Westerners by tomorrow.

There was a brief pause. The euphoria of the moment suffered a slight setback. "Yarov asked for that, but I have arranged for all the funds possible...tens of billions."

"We need more."

"There is no more of the bank's money that I can transfer."

"Comrade," Gagarin's inflection was decidedly patronizing, "It's not the bank's money...it belongs to the Motherland...and the STAVKA is her steward!"

The First Deputy felt a tightening in his chest. The pain was always there, but at times like this the pain was sharp, penetrating into his extremities. "It will take time. The Trans-Siberian train shipment took almost a year to arrange."

"We have no time - it must be tomorrow!"

"You don't understand, this time the State inspectors would find out. I would be arrested, and fraud on the State brings the death penalty!"

"Tell me about death, Comrade. We know your situation very well. Your physician has told us that you are dying. You are in need of medical procedures not available in this country."

"Is there something you can do for me?" The First Deputy felt a rush within as if his own heart knew that it was the subject of the conversation.

"We can give you life."

Tears began to fill the First Deputy's eyes. "How can you do this?"

"We have the medical facilities and the expertise to provide to you...surgery and even a new heart if necessary. We will take care of you if you will perform the transfer tomorrow."

"The KGB... they will be after me."

"How soon?"

"It may take months, but they will discover the loss...it would only be a matter of time."

"We could have you out of here before that - to our special medical facility."

The First Deputy was still guarded in his gratitude, and uncertain whether to heed his suspicions. But he had done business in the Soviet Union long enough to know that it was wise to trust no one, not even the nation's greatest hero. "How do I know...that I will be taken care of as you say?" He feared that he would again anger Gagarin.

The famous Cosmonaut reached into his pocket and then extended his open hand, "This is something with which I would never part. You give it to me when we meet again."

The item needed no introduction as the First Deputy felt the cold metal of Gagarin's Hero of the Soviet Union medal pressed into his hand. He examined the medal momentarily, then looked up, realizing that the seemingly impossible interview was coming to a close. "I am so overwhelmed to see that you are really alive. There have been so many rumors, sightings over the years since your death...but always dismissed as lunatic nonsense. Will you soon announce your return?''

"Some day soon... and you are to tell no one of this meeting. But this much I will tell you - I will return and stand as a solid comrade of the Parliament against the forces of Yeltsin and the reformers. The people will rise up as a new Soviet Union is restored. Yeltsin will have no power."

"This is all too incredible and wonderful!" The First Deputy was overwhelmed.

"Please obtain the funds. They are needed to preserve our space program. It is the single greatest accomplishment of the Motherland since the revolution of 1917... When I return, not only you, but the rest of the world will see me as I am. And the medal, you can give it back to me before the Parliament and before the world. The Motherland will know you have served her well..." Gagarin's voice converted from warm to cold and demanding, "Comrade First Deputy, do your duty, get the money!"

The First Deputy allowed the dangerous implications of his assignment to surrender to a chance for life and hopefully a part in the powerful force that had been so often rumored to be in control of the Motherland. A living Yuri Gagarin was overwhelming proof of its existence.

Gagarin stood, walked toward the First Deputy and shook his hand. The grip was firm and certain. "You are still so young, Comrade Gagarin."

"I am rather young by certain standards and I intend to be here for many years to come. In due time we will all reinherit the Motherland in all of its glory."

There was a slight disturbance at the door to Gagarin's right. The First Deputy turned to see two black beret and leather jacket-clad Spetsnaz troopers standing in the doorway. The First Deputy had always hated the Spetsnaz, but in this setting, it somehow gave new meaning, hope and pride to him as a resident of an otherwise downtrodden, broken and disjointed land.

"Farewell, Comrade." Gagarin saluted and walked crisply across the wooden floor and through the door with the attending Spetsnaz guard.

The First Deputy retook his position in the chair of honor. He closed his eyes for a few moments to sort his thoughts. After several minutes, he picked up the phone.

"This is the duty officer. I am at your disposal, Mr. First Deputy, what may I do for you?"

CHAPTER 11

Washington D. C., Early November, 1992

Stony Chapman was a chameleon. Fifteen years ago his head was routinely ringed in a cloud of smoke. By 1992, he jogged eight miles a day. He was once promiscuous, but with the advent of AIDS, he rededicated himself to monogamy. Stony was initially a staunch hawk looking for opportunities to hang liberals at every turn. In more recent times he had been branded by the press as a moderate. With all these attributes, Stony Chapman was the ideal United States Congressman from the Sooner state of Oklahoma.

In early years, his fraternity buddies from Stillwater had positioned themselves well within the savings and loan industry as it expanded beyond its traditional role of home finance into large commercial and industrial projects often intended as tax shelters for the rich. Stony, on the other hand, focused on politics rather than banking. It turned out to be a good decision, for some twenty years later as a member of the House Banking Committee, he had presided over the burial processions of many of his former friends' careers.

The world had changed, yet Stony had remained astute at making all the right moves at the most expedient, correct and judicious moment. As a result, the House of Representatives seat for the Sixth District of Oklahoma, taking in much of the northern part of Oklahoma City as well as the prominent suburb of Edmond, had been his and his alone for over two decades. As one of the most powerful Republican Congressmen on Capitol Hill, Stony Chapman had a hand in virtually everything that moved in the halls of Congress.

His wife had watched him change. She appreciated the distinct metamorphosis in his habits that had created a better person than the man she had originally married. She often thought to herself that this was a unique claim than most women could not make about their prominent husbands. Time had a positive effect on Stony Chapman with perhaps the advent of grandchildren being the most reflective and inspiring reality of his life.

His family had grown over the years, and as much as he loved and cherished his three daughters, he alway had always yearned for a son. Unenthusiastic at first about his respective three sons-in-law, as each had come on the scene and enticed a daughter into marriage over Stony's objections, he was beginning to warm up to them. Maybe it was because he could see his own reflection in the faces of his grandchildren. Perhaps it was his chameleon instinct to change with the times. Whatever the reasons, he had developed a sense of loyalty to his family that superseded even his commitment to the job as a U.S. Congressman.

Most pieces of significant legislation could only find their way through the House of Representatives by being passed politely through Stony Chapman's door, an accomplishment that no other Republican in the Democratic controlled house could claim. He relished the power and enjoyed a certain conceit that served as a very adequate self-defense when necessary. Even the Presidents of the United States were known to pause for courage from time to time before approaching Stony Chapman on a critical issue.

Such was the case as Congressman Chapman sat in his office having returned briefly from the House Chamber to await a prearranged call from the President-elect of the United States. It was the first such call, but given Stony's prominence, it would not be the last. But this one was important. The incoming president was already clearing his plans with key leaders of the House and Senate in order to insure the broadest support possible on a controversial piece of social legislation to be presented during his first one hundred days in office.

The proposed bill attempted a new approach at the subject of abortion. It would allow abortion as an act of conscience, protected under the Free Exercise Clause of the First Amendment. The language had been carefully crafted into a bill which had survived earlier debate. The bill, known as "The Women's Religious Freedom of Conscience Act," was simple and to the point:

> **Any woman who determines as an act of conscience that abortion is the correct choice for her personal, spiritual, or social welfare, is hereby permitted to make such a choice and is entitled to the protection of the Free Exercise clause of the First Amendment regardless of whether such decision is motivated by organized or non-organized religious belief and/or secular or sectarian purpose.**

For years Stony Chapman had been ambivalent on abortion. He had judiciously avoided being dragged into the controversy and had watched the demise of other senators and congressmen by the dozen, who had, to their regret, ventured too close to the fire pit of such a hot topic. Yet recently, he found himself more personally affected by the subject, as his middle daughter, Jan, who had been unable to bear children, had without success tried to adopt. The anguish the congressman and his wife felt, as they had seen one promised adoption after another fall through, had been heartbreaking. If only their daughter could have just one baby, they often thought to themselves, all would be well.

From a political and party perspective, Chapman knew he could not step far from the party center without incurring major criticism. An alliance with the new young Democrat in the White House might be a gamble. But Stony also knew that siding with the President could, as he had so often done, extract a favor in return.

The state of Oklahoma was experiencing a severe economic crisis. Having finally weathered the storm of a long difficult recession caused by the closing down of much of the oil field servicing companies, followed by the savings and loan fiascos of the 1980's, the state was still hurting. Just as the economic problems seemed to be working themselves out, the entire country lapsed into a moderate recession which had translated into severe difficulties for his home district.

The end of the Cold War had been no help. Tinker Air Force Base had already laid off a thousand civilian workers. Another setback had recently arisen with the threatened closing of the General Motors parts manufacturing plant along Interstate 35 between Oklahoma City and Edmond, with its forty-two hundred workers. With another three thousand employees in support facilities located in the adjacent industrial park, a major economic disaster was in the making.

Stony had dedicated much of his time as a congressman to budgetary legislation. His primary agenda at the moment was budget reform, although he still had a variety of other pet finance and revenue-related projects. In each case it had translated into opportunities for the award of defense contracts and other Pork Barrels within the boundaries of his congressional district. In spite of all his efforts, the problem could not be solved in Washington so long as the principal culprit was in Tokyo.

The secretary buzzed, and the congressman's ego was comfortably massaged by the word, "Congressman Chapman, the President-elect is on the line."

He squared his shoulders, leaned back in his swivel chair, placed his cowboy boot-clad feet on his desk, reached over to his credenza and picked up the phone. "Mr. President-elect, what a delight to hear from you!"

Vladivostok, Far Eastern Russia, Early November, 1992

It was reminiscent of an earlier call as the phone rang in Colonel Ziyetski's apartment. Despite the 2:00 a.m. hour, it took only a moment for him to clear his head and listen. His duty officer who had been carefully monitoring incoming intelligence information was calling with important news. An agent had given him a message that required the Colonel's immediate attention. It could not wait until morning, nor could he risk a telephone conversation. Hoping it would shed some light on the train massacre, he dressed, loaded his PPS 52 sub-machine gun, climbed into his private car and headed for the parking lot at the Vladivostok North soccer stadium.

It was a good place to meet, one which could be kept under surveillance by a small team of KGB troopers as they looked for agents from other departments of Russian government or military, or possibly even operatives from foreign powers. The four-man grayish KGB truck was first to arrive. The exact place for the discussions had been prearranged. Concealment was good at night, particularly where pine trees bushed out onto the pavement. The vehicle parked - the occupants remained inside.

Soon, Colonel Ziyetski's car circled once to double check security in the area, then stopped. "Lieutenant, what do you have?" The Colonel knew his well-trained adjutant would only disturb him at such an hour for a most important reason.

From the window the lieutenant spoke, "Colonel, I fear we have uncovered a very significant and worrisome development."

Ziyetski knew without further inquiry that the matter involved the Trans-Siberian rail line attack of a month earlier. He and his men had spent every moment since the incident attempting to break the case.

"Sir, I have with me, KGB Corporal Smirna. He has something important to tell you."

The vehicle windows were inches from one another. "Sir," the corporal began, "I was, this evening, about an hour ago, at the bar in the Zarya Vostoka in the Vavilova Street. There were three orderlies from the naval hospital who were drunk and speaking softly, but most clearly to each other. I was at my post, listening. Those men have often spoken of military matters while off duty. I have heard it before. But today... I mean tonight, they spoke of a startling thing."

"Tell me, trooper, what was it?"

"They also spoke of the Trans-Siberian rail guard - he is under their care. They bragged about how they drugged him whenever he would come awake. One said it was a good way to keep his mouth shut. The other suggested that after almost two months of this treatment, he is sure to die at any time.''

Details followed and the conversation continued well into the early morning hours. It was indeed sufficient reason for the lieutenant to have awakened the Colonel.

Reston, Virginia, Early November, 1992

Stony Chapman reclined in the overstuffed chair in the study of his Reston, Virginia home. It had been a week since his discussion with the incoming President and he was under pressure to formulate a response. The President's subtle appeal had been unconvincing. He agreed with the underlying logic, but was also aware of the strenuous effort by the Democratic Party to improve the status of abortion rights throughout the country. Such legislation had been viewed as necessary by its proponents in light of the recent decisions by the United States Supreme Court allowing states to require parental and spousal consent and other regulation that leaned in the conservative anti-abortion direction. But Chapman would need time. In any good deal, especially where he was being asked to cross party lines, he would need something more. It was the Stony Chapman way of doing things.

As Chapman pondered possible concessions from the White House, his thoughts drifted to his daughter, Jan, and her difficult circumstances. Not only had she experienced fertility problems, but her husband's business was in trouble. More than once, Jan had approached her parents in tears expressing her fear that Jim would lose his business.

Jim Burrows had enjoyed a certain degree of success in the development of computerized visualization software for the Macintosh. Apple's Macintosh Computer had long since established itself as the leading platform for graphics designers and illustrators, particularly in the area of three-dimensional modeling and rendering. Taking advantage of a niche in the market, Jim founded the company, Oki-Soft in the garage of his rented home. Within a year, it employed twelve people and was enjoying over one and a half million dollars of gross revenues. All seemed to be going well until the competition closed the gap. Suddenly, architects, designers and artists began purchasing from the established competition elsewhere in the country.

Recognizing that the envelope of opportunity for a software company was rather small, Burrows began looking for new approaches for the exploitation of his products. He realized that to rely solely on the Macintosh would be commercial suicide. Common sense dictated that the quickest and most effective route to resolve the matter would be to successfully engineer his graphics package for IBM PC and compatible. This would open Oki-Soft to a substantially larger market and certainly save the company.

Saving the company was an absolute necessity. Jim had borrowed heavily from friends and relatives, not the least of which was his prominent father-in-law, Congressman Chapman. To fail under the present circumstances was simply not acceptable. To accomplish the conversion to the new platforms, he would need substantial investors. He knew that he would have to obtain an investment in excess of one million dollars to survive. Yet, to give up more than forty-nine percent of the stock of the company would require him to expose its desperate condition to the new stockholder who would justifiably remove him from the management of the business.

Over the course of the previous two-month period, Jim had advertised in the various software magazines for a joint venture partner. He had also contacted an investment company for the purpose of preparing a private offering. The problem however, was that the cost of the private offering would be high while the prospect of actually finding an investor would be low. Thus, he turned to the only remaining possibility, the foreign investor market.

The phone on the table next to him rang. "Daddy, I have good news - really good news! Oh, I guess, good news and bad news!"

"Well, sweetheart, what is it?" Jan's voice was buoyant and positive, something he had not heard for far too long.

"I have been accepted into the in-vitro fertilization program down at Tulsa. Even though they say it could be very difficult - they think they found a way. I mean, isn't that wonderful?''

The excitement in her voice lifted his spirits. ''How soon do you start?''

There was a slight pause. ''Well, I guess getting in the program is the good news, Daddy.'' The jubilant bubble of the moment was threatening to pop. ''It's not a routine procedure.'' She paused again and her voice quivered. ''You know Jim and I don't have health insurance, Daddy. I don' t think health insurance would cover it anyway. The hospital wants - well, they have to have a deposit of twenty-five thousand dollars to start. Please help me, Daddy.'' Her voice broke.

Stony's response was as it had always been. ''Don't worry, sweetheart, we'll take care of it.''

Caucus Mountains, Early November, 1992

Raw and violent independence was characteristic of the Georgians. Like the Azerbaijanies, Armenians and the other tribes and races of the Transcaucasian area, the Georgians had their own way of resolving disputes. It had normally been efficiently expressed outside the all-seeing eye of the Communist authorities. But now the Russians were off the streets and out of the country, save the remnant military installations with their high fences. The local joke was that the fences were now used to keep Russians in rather than keep the Georgians out. The single exception was the mysterious stronghold on the ridge above the Svanathian Valley which was avoided by even the most intrepid of mountain warriors.

Ledo Deniken had always resented the existence of the Russian base above the Potolemei Ridge and the fact the Svan were prohibited from herding their sheep across the mountain plateau. If, in fact, a supposed Commonwealth of Independent States had been formed, then why was there a Russian base right in the middle of the most beautiful hunting and grazing ground in the entire country of Georgia? He often posed the question to both himself and his fellow clansmen. Most often the answers came in the form of profane descriptions of what the Georgian mountain warrior would do with a Russian soldier should he get the chance.

In more sobering moments, courageous boasting gave way to tongue biting silence as they watched the troops from the base drive through the villages in the valley on their way east to Tbilisi, or west to the resorts on the Black Sea. The soldiers wore the feared black berets and the black jackets. Even to the bravest Georgian, the word, "Spetsnaz" struck fear and trepidation into his heart. It was a word that often meant death at the hands of the most brutal and barbarous men-at-arms ever created by the Soviet Chieftains in Moscow.

Deniken had gathered a considerable amount of intelligence regarding the Spetsnaz base. He knew it was called Caucus Station One, and that it was a high priority to the group that resided there. From his surveillance of the defenses at the base, he was certain that its defenders were prepared to stand and fight. Seldom were his patrols able to work their way closer than a mile from the perimeter fence. The area was heavily mined and there seemed to be electronic censors everywhere. More than once, they had spooked mountain goats into the area near the base fences only to set off land mines or automatically aimed spring-operated machine guns.

Deniken had acquired twelve 130 millimeter M-46 field guns which, with a great deal of effort, had been hauled to the flat top of the hill adjacent to the lush Kartalinian Forest. Then, over a two week period, in an effort to make an initial show of strength, he had moved two companies of infantrymen totaling three hundred men to the hilltop position to join the artillerymen there. It was just close enough to be provocative. But at four miles from the nearest point of the base perimeter, it was far enough away to require a substantial effort on the part of the base's defenders to do anything about it.

Within a month, he looked forward to delivering a terse letter to the commander of the base, informing him that all ground routes to the base had been cut off and demanding immediate surrender of the facility to the independent nation of Georgia. Harboring no illusions that the commander would consent, Deniken was prepared to launch a ground assault with five thousand men from the sheep camps along the Potolemei Ridge northward against the perimeter of the base with the plan of overrunning the airfield on the first day of battle. He had chosen the Potolemei Ridge as one of the few locations so he could position troops where they would not be fighting uphill. He knew, however, that the area was heavily mined and well-defended. For this reason, he would need tanks. According to the commander of the National Guard in Tbilisi, within the next three weeks, two dozen old but durable T72 Main Battle tanks from the partially closed Red Army Base on the Turkish border near Batumi, would be delivered in Svanathia.

Earlier in the week, he had moved BMT Infantry personnel carriers up to the sheep camp for the purpose of holding the position against any preemptive effort by the base's defenders to control the strategic Potolemei Ridge. Soon, he would move a vanguard of one thousand infantrymen onto the ridge. Despite the deep snow, he would have them dig extensive trench lines for the purpose of establishing a defensible position from which he could launch offensive operations.

Washington D. C., Mid November, 1992

Heavy drinking was one aspect of Stony Chapman's life that he had been unable to put behind him. To create some emotional solace, he had gone public with the problem during the mid-eighties when it became fashionable for politicians to air their lesser qualities to the voters and the press at a strategically opportune moment. There had seemed to be a sort of sanctuary from criticism of a public figure's "dirty laundry" so long as it came from his mouth first, well ahead of the investigative reporter's pen. It seemed that the perceived vice, as far as the public was concerned, was not the personal indiscretion itself, but the attempt to conceal. Thus, Stony Chapman surrendered the privacy of his alcoholism in 1987, and despite two subsequent drunk-driving convictions, his re-election was never impacted by such an improvident faux pas.

As he sat at his desk on a Friday afternoon in the Cannon House Office Building, he began to prematurely wash his concerns away with a bottle of scotch whiskey. He had spent the better part of the day reviewing various drafts of a bill which he had authored. In an effort to counter the problems of the impending joblessness at the auto parts plant in Oklahoma, he had decided to target the culprit causing the unfortunate closings.

Several weeks earlier he had commissioned research to focus in on a number of issues, including the right of major corporations to arbitrarily shut down plants in a manner that would impact large numbers of workers. He had also requested an investigation into the impact of Japanese auto industry competition on such plants.

The research resulted in seemingly deadend solutions. The Labor Relations Act already consuming five volumes of the United States Code, would be difficult to amend. To put pressure on the Big Three Auto makers to abide by any further regulation would be almost impossible. Not only did they substantially "own" a large number of congressmen and senators, but further employment laws would be so narrowly trimmed by the time it reached the House floor, that it would have little, if any, impact on the jobless situation in his district.

The Japanese problem was similar in nature. The President had already spent a considerable amount of time cajoling, threatening and negotiating with the Japanese to reduce imports in order to avoid a major congressional backlash. The Japanese had come to the table prepared and had mounted a public relations campaign through the American divisions of their various major automobile companies throughout the United States. This coincidentally corresponded with a minor reduction in imports from Japan. American public opinion had been molded effectively by the Japanese effort and it was clear that major anti-import legislation against Japan would be difficult.

The Japanese were already well-entrenched. Chapman's staff reported numerous Toyota, Mazda, Nissan and Subaru dealerships in his district. A substantial reduction in imports might create the loss of more jobs by Americans working for Japanese-owned companies throughout Oklahoma and the world. It was clear that promoting restrictions on Japanese imports was too fraught with uncertainty. For a politician, it was a predicament wherein the cure would be more painful than the disease.

The previous evening, he had been handed another solution sheet by his staff which he considered to be a blockbuster. Referred to as "Aid for Gold," it focused on the fact that according to the most recent CIA estimates, the former Soviet Union had within its vaults over four hundred billion dollars of refined ingots and bullion gold. In addition, the report cited the fact that from 1970 to 1985, the Soviet Union had maintained its position as second only to South Africa in production of gold and diamonds. Archaic recovery methods had not hindered the vast deposits of gold into State bank vaults.

By world standards, even maintaining a reserve of four hundred billion, U.S. gold in government vaults was not substantial. Many other nations enjoyed much larger reserves. Given the present crisis in the former Soviet Union, however, gold seemed to be one of the few remaining assets which could be easily liquidated to facilitate aid from the United States. The legislative proposal would simply require that a price be placed on each shipment of aid sent by the United States to Russia and paid for C.O.D. This would create a sort of "cash and carry" arrangement for aid to the former Soviet Union.

The staff reported that such an arrangement would benefit a large number of Oklahoma firms, farmers and other agriculturally related interests. The farm belt was already involved in providing the types of supply and food stuffs that were essential for the Russian aid program. Rather than requiring the United States Government to go further into debt through minimum price programs and in making conservative allocations for large purchase orders of goods to be supplied to the former Soviet Union, liberal orders at market prices could be filled which would benefit all of the "breadbasket" states of which Oklahoma was a principal member.

Even in his inebriated state, it seemed like a good idea to Stony Chapman. He would pursue his contacts to find a strong Senate sponsor, preferably a Republican, to avoid having the bill get bogged down in partisan politics.

The euphoria of a possible solution to the joblessness issue helped, but did not carry the day. The congressman found himself pouring more drinks and pondering further his most important concern - how he would pay for the expensive in-vitro fertilization surgery that awaited his daughter. In earlier years, he would have contacted one of his loyal supporters and "manufactured" a loan. The congressman, however, had long since exhausted his Pork Barrel credit opportunities and had placed himself under the watchful eye of a financial manager. He had relied on the manager to extricate him from his financial troubles and other personal embarrassments in the public arena of the mid 1980's. He continued to rack his brain in an effort to reach a solution.

The alcohol and his mind converged to come up with a foggy strategy. He would attach a rider to the upcoming annual Head Start Program funding legislation. The Head Start appropriation totaled 1.6 billion dollars. Good - the perfect solution. He would present a rider at the last moment, as an amendment on the House floor to provide a three million dollar research grant for the Tulsa University Medical Center's infertility program. Brilliant, he thought to himself. As he considered the matter further, his enthusiasm jousted with the alcoholic mist of his mind. He decided that a donation directly to the infertility program would be too obvious. Even a rookie reporter could get to the bottom of that, he thought. At least a general donation to the university would be possible.

But the surgery was needed now and the Head Start bill would not hit the House floor for another ten days. With mounting frustration he contacted his secretary and asked her to get the head administrator of the Tulsa University Medical Research Center on the phone immediately. His devoted secretary knew from the slur of his voice, that it was not one of her boss's better days. She also knew that he had functioned quite successfully under much worse conditions. Under such conditions she would stop short of putting a call through to the White House or any member of the House or Senate leadership but a doctor in Tulsa was no problem.

Presently the speaker crackled, "Congressman, Dr. David Houston is on the line."

"Dr. Houston, I'm not certain that we've ever met. But I do appreciate the chance to speak with you for a moment."

"Well, it's an honor," Houston responded in his hard Oklahoma drawl. "What can I do for you, Congressman Chapman?"

"I've got two problems and they both involve your institution. The first problem is that my daughter has been accepted into the in-vitro fertilization program at UTMC. It is a very important matter to her and is of course of utmost importance to me. I've been told that the deposit to get this work started is twenty-five thousand dollars. As soon as it's paid she can begin treatment. There is nothing in the world I would like more than for her to give birth to a child." He paused, then proceeded with caution. "The next thing is, I am trying to find a way to attach as a rider to the upcoming Head Start Appropriations Bill a research grant to your institution in the amount of three million dollars. All you would need to do is quickly prepare a grant application, have it to me by the end of next week, and I would do my best to push it through. I'm rather certain I can get it done."

"Well, that's mighty thoughtful of you, Congressman. I'm sorry to hear about your daughter and ...well, I'm not sure what you are getting at, but those in-vitro procedures do get expensive. So what are you saying? Are you saying that the two are somehow connected?"

"You bet your rear end that they are," the congressman blustered, his voice taking on an obstinate edge. "You get my daughter in the program. Her name is Jan Burrows, and do it this next week. And I will do my very best to get you that grant by the time the legislation hits the floor two weeks from now."

After a slight pause, the administrator spoke. "Well, I'm not sure I understand, Congressman. I'm not sure I can make that type of commitment."

"Well, if you can't do that kind of a deal, then how about you just wait until I get this legislation done so you know that the grant's in the pipeline and admit her into the program two weeks from now."

The administrator was still restrained in his response but then mustered the courage to respond. "Congressman, if you are really trying to bribe this institution, we have nothing further to talk about. We greatly appreciate any efforts you and your colleagues make on behalf of Tulsa University, and especially the Medical Center, but there is no way we can waive your daughter's medical retainer in exchange for your efforts on a research grant."

There was no pause, no lack of resolve in the congressman's voice. "If that is the case, Dr. Houston, we can assume that this conversation did not take place."

"That would be best. As far as I'm concerned, we did *not* have this conversation," Houston responded.

There was a click on the other end. Chapman tensed, then pounded his desk with the ferocity of an enraged mafia Don as the sweat rolled off his forehead. Fortunately, the other party to the phone call could not see his beleaguered condition.

Moscow, Russian Republic, Mid November, 1992

In Moscow, Nieca and Alexander joined one another for lunch at the Toko Bank cafeteria. Nieca routinely brought her lunch from home, but Alexander had taken the time to wait in line for the bowl of borscht along with a small piece of bread that would constitute his lunch for the day. He joined her at a table in the corner, away from the main group of employees.

Since their first date in September, she had learned to read Alexander well. He would lean a certain way and run his left hand through his partially graying hair. She watched him do it now, almost a dozen times while standing in line across the room.

As he approached and placed his plate on the table, she inquired, "So, Alexander, tell me what is wrong. I can see that you are distressed."

"I apologize, Nieca, is it so obvious?"

"Yes, it is. Tell me what's wrong.," she asked quietly. "Does it have something to do with me?"

"Yes and no." He could see she considered his response to be unsettling. "The First Deputy called me into his office this morning. After the conversation, I had to leave the building. I walked out on the streets for a time."

She leaned forward and touched his cheek. "Well, what could be so terrible? Is maybe ...the bank closing?"

"No, it's not that. But he has ordered me to go to the Vladivostok Branch."

Nieca gasped in surprise. "Oh, Alexander, how long would it be?"

"Only three weeks. At least, that's what he told me. He said it would be temporary, an internal audit at the branch. I knew I'd have to do it sometime. It's just - well, I have a feeling he's trying to get me out of Moscow.''

''Why do you say that - why do you think he's trying to get you out of Moscow?''

''Well, it's more of the same. I have seen records of the Aviation Ministry account that, at least on paper, cause me to believe that money is being channeled into projects for which there is no underlying documentation. Some of them are foreign. And I even found ... well, I probably shouldn't bore you with all this.''

She shook her head and her deep blue eyes looked directly into his. ''No, please tell me. I'm interested.''

He felt warm and reassured. With the exception of disclosing the involvement of his good friend Leni, he told her everything he knew regarding his investigation of the undocumented disbursements. He assumed she had no understanding of its significance but it felt good to have a sounding board. She listened intently, following every word. As he spoke, she reached for his hand and held it close to her breast. He could feel her heartbeat and imagined other sensations.

''The most disturbing part of this whole thing, Nieca, is that I will not see you for at least three weeks.''

''This disturbs me also,'' Nieca responded. ''It is a painful thought. I cannot bear to think about it, Alexander.''

He paused, leaned toward her, but clasped his hands together under the table so that she would not see them tremble. ''What if...'' The words stuck in his throat. ''What if we were to...?''

''Go ahead and say it, Alexander.''

''What if we were to be married upon my return?'' he whispered.

Nieca stood and put her hands gently on his shoulders. Alexander rose, his eyes not leaving hers for an instant. He moved toward her, feeling like an awkward boy. He was almost embarrassed by the passion of their kiss - more embarrassed still, when the tie tac she had given him caught a thread on her blouse as they drew apart.

Nieca released the thread and carefully adjusted the tac. ''It seems we are not meant to be separated,'' she said with a mischievous grin. ''You must wear the tie tac always, my Alexander.''

''This will make my stay in Vladivostok much more tolerable.''

"And we will have our wedding as soon as you return. I can make all the arrangements!" She spoke like a charmed school girl.

They left the cafeteria, hand in hand. Such a public display of affection made Alexander a little uncomfortable. Even so, he had to admit that he was *very* pleased at the unexpected turn that his life had taken.

CHAPTER 12

St. George, Utah, Mid November, 1992

The time difference between Moscow and St. George, Utah created an exasperating problem for Michael. At one o'clock in the morning Utah time, it was eight o'clock a.m. in Moscow. As usual, by three or four in the morning, Michael's telephone was ringing off the hook with one demand after another from wide-eyed Russians completely oblivious to Michael's inconvenience. To work for Russians, you had to work Moscow shifts. That's just the way it was despite the eight thousand miles of global surface in between.

Yarov had suddenly focused on the Russia Center. An irksome memo demanding progress on the Russia Center project had been sent to Michael. It had intimated that Yarov was less than satisfied with Michael's efforts. But the worst part of the message was the announcement of Yarov's intention to hold a Board of Director's meeting in St. George for the new company. It served as a clear signal to Michael that the much appreciated autonomy of his new job would soon come to an end.

Yarov also asked Michael to obtain new multi-entry visas for himself, a woman by the name of Raissa Kovacs and the interpreter. This meant they would be entitled to travel in and out of the United States at leisure during the six month life of the visa. Closely scrutinized, such visas were not always granted.

To Michael, the woman Raissa Kovacs, was a new name. He knew of no such person at Technoserv. It seemed odd for her to be on the Board of Directors of Transcontinental Trading, Inc. since Michael knew that Yarov only used people for such positions who were part of his inner circle.

Planning for the Russia Center had slowed considerably. Michael's effort to merely keep pace with the constant demands from Technoserv for a steady supply of computer equipment had occupied most of his time. It was clear to him from the caustic comments in the electronic mail letter that the Russians had no idea what it would take to actually plan, design and construct the Russia Center. For Michael's part, he too, was confused, having never been involved in a construction project before. Suddenly being thrown into what could be a thirty to fifty million dollar undertaking, seemed overwhelming. He concluded that by Russian standards, it was not unusual to try something uncertain and unproven.

The Russia Center was a constant concern. A few days earlier, Michael had received a report from the local architect that at least conceptual drawings would be available when the Russian delegation arrived in ten days. The principal worry, however, was that Yarov and his group expected complete renderings and even a scale model. Michael knew that the Russians had no concept of the time and effort required to deal with such a mammoth project. He was also concerned about the possibility of making a total fool out of himself by pitching the idea of a multi-million dollar project in downtown St. George to conservative city fathers only to find that the Russians were unwilling to stay the course.

The plan called for a five story hotel to be built on the main street of a town whose highest building at present was only four stories. The hotel was to be situated where a group of dilapidated shops currently stood in the downtown historical district of St. George. From the front of the hotel, an ornate overpass structure with hanging gardens was to be constructed that would lead to the Russia Center itself on a four-lane, downtown street. The Russia Center would include over eighty thousand square feet of museum exhibits and retail space consuming the better part of a city block. The plans also included office facilities for TTI and other

Russian companies.

Michael confidentially determined the price of the various parcels of real estate in the downtown area. He then sent a message to Yarov suggesting that it would cost approximately two and a half million dollars to acquire property in the redevelopment district area. As he awaited a response to his suggestion, he received a call the following day from the bank. He was informed that a two and a half million dollar wire had just been credited to the TTI account. Michael's hopes were bolstered. He was feeding his family and doing a fair job of it. Not bad for a computer salesman from Denmark, he thought to himself. But then he returned to the frustration. Being prepared for the Yarov visit meant around-the-clock work on the Russian Center project. With the arrival of the money, he knew that Yarov expected immediate results while having little or no understanding of the immensity of the task.

Washington D. C., Late November, 1992

The Tuesday morning edition of the Washington Post was the first paper to break the story. It was indeed a blockbuster for Washington insiders and political scientists. The headline read: **STONY AND THE PRESIDENT-ELECT JOIN FORCES ON ABORTION AND RUSSIAN AID.** The front page of the Post included a news report from the evening before as well as an inset feature setting forth the particulars as to how, the President-elect, at a press conference, had proclaimed the existence of the unlikely alliance.

Both men were all smiles as they announced that the President-elect would receive support that would allow him to breathe easier on what he considered a critical piece of his new social legislation agenda to be let loose on the floors of congress in the first one hundred days of the upcoming session. It would assure passage for any Democratic abortion legislation targeted at circumvention of the conservative-minded Supreme Court. The President-elect chose careful words to express his gratitude to the Republican Congressman from Oklahoma and to avoid offending the current President of the United States that he had defeated just three weeks earlier.

It was then Stony Chapman's turn to explain what the President-elect had given him in return. "This is an historic day for our Nation and especially for the people of the farm belt states including my state of Oklahoma." He imparted his friendly southern drawl into the microphone in front of the reporters and extensive television audience. "My staff has confirmed what had been suspected by both the CIA and the Department of State for many years. Specifically, the former Soviet Union has reserves of gold bullion in excess of three hundred billion dollars. A request to confirm this amount through the offices of the Republic of Russia here in Washington or any of the other Commonwealth States, has been entirely rebuffed. In some ways, I feel like we're still dealing with the old Soviet Union on this issue. One thing is clear, our nation and much of the Western World is propping up the economy of the former Soviet Union at a current cost of approximately four billion dollars per month.

"I will therefore propose a bill in January which I feel insures bipartisan support and the optimum prospect of success in both Houses of Congress, that every American relief shipment sent to the former Soviet Union which carrys goods supplied by any of your tax dollars, should receive 'gold on the barrel head.' Thus, arrangements should be made for return flights with Russian gold bullion sufficient to pay for the goods carried by each aircraft. We would require a value to be agreed upon in the United States, before the aircraft leaves the ground, and the gold bullion would be made available and loaded at the airport on what you might call, a 'gold and carry basis.' The same will apply to ships. This should cure the problem of default on U.S. loans by Russia. This bill will be known as 'Gold for Aid.' We are long overdue in dealing with this matter.

"The net affect of this bill should be felt immediately. First, in my state and throughout the midwest, large amounts of farm goods can be made available for shipment to Russia. The problem is the meager prices being paid at present, particularly where they're being purchased by the U.S. government for donation to the Commonwealth of Independent States. If anything, it continues to drive prices down. If, however, direct payment in gold can be made to the United States, then the fair value of the goods can be established, and more importantly, farmers and other manufacturers of goods earmarked for the Commonwealth States will be encouraged to produce at market levels rather than artificial aid levels.''

Chapman continued. ''I realize that there are many who feel we are unfairly taking advantage of the former Soviet Union. As I see Americans lose their jobs due to events in other parts of the world, and when there is another part of the world that can provide cash on the barrel head in the form of gold, then there is no reason why the Commonwealth States should not be required to liquidate their assets to pay for our efforts first, and then let us look at a true aid situation when we finally reach that point.''

The news report quoted only portions of the President-elect's remarks, but zeroed in on his key compromise: *"As you know, I am not in favor of building barriers in a time of crisis. We've spent many years trying to tear down the walls and iron curtains that have divided nations. Nevertheless, I feel that Congressman Chapman's approach is one which the American people will support. I will stand with him if he is able to rally the type of support necessary among his congressional associates. All should understand that this is not a bill in the traditional sense, but a resolution which is nonbinding. As part of the agreement, I will support the resolution and impose the appropriate administrative and presidential directives to conform the resolution for legal implementation if the House and Senate respond favorably. Furthermore, I am very encouraged by the broad step which Congressman Chapman has taken, admittedly a long way from the heart of his own party, to support the abortion legislation."*

By mid-afternoon, the major news organizations throughout the United States and across the world were bracing for the fireworks on the international front.

At the former Soviet Embassy, the Ambassador from the Russian Republic had already made a firm and unequivocal statement, ''The Russian people have suffered greatly for the past seventy years under the arm of totalitarianism. We hoped that had ended when the flag of Russia was raised above the Kremlin. Now we see that there are those in America who have gained the attention of even the incoming President of the United States, who seek to strike our Motherland where it hurts the most and at Her most vulnerable moment. On behalf of my country, I can only deliver a warning that this act by the United States Congress and the President will be viewed as a seriously counterproductive development in relations between our two spheres.''

Tuesday, both Tass and Investia were again sounding like the official organ of the Communist Party and the Red Army respectively as they announced what was tantamount to a declaration of economic war by the United States on the people of Russia. ''The American people only want to take and not really give,'' was the comment by a Russian shopkeeper being interviewed on the NBC Today Show.

But the legislation clearly seemed to appeal to the American middle class. Beneath the surface, most Americans had harbored a feeling that it made little sense to hurt so much at home while trying to feed a part of the world that was only poor because it had for seventy years intentionally been following the road to economic suicide.

Stony Chapman had struck a chord with middle-America that harmonized with a positive political future far beyond his dreams. He was in the national limelight, at the height of his power. It was the Stony Chapman way of doing business.

Caucus Station, Late November, 1992

Even Colonel Aniamov, the commander of the Spetsnaz regiment assigned to the defense of the Dacha on the high mountain base in former Soviet Georgia was forbidden from speaking directly to the members of the STAVKA. The only direct communication was through a coterie of stern-looking aides who served as intermediaries on pertinent issues. The protocol had changed little over the course of the twenty years of the base's existence.

Like other members of the special Spetsnaz regiment, the Colonel had no wife and family. The resorts along the eastern shores of the Black Sea were designed to compensate for any disadvantages of bachelorhood. Base officials routinely supplied the exclusive resorts with the most seductive Greek and Turkish women. It was a good life, he concluded, far better than that which most Russians were now experiencing under the new and experimental Yeltsin Russia.

But the secrets of Caucus Station were absolute. The base was as much a place of confinement for most of its occupants as it was a retreat. Coming and going was not easy as the suffocating process of surveillance and tracking of all base personnel was a standard practice. None of the employees resided outside of the installation and support personnel such as cooks, physicians and the like were routinely flown in from other Spetsnaz bases in the Commonwealth. It was a unique and closed society. As a matter of official policy, the only way out was death.

On one occasion, early in his assignment at the base, Aniamov had been allowed to enter the restricted area near the Dacha. It was a massive log building, hidden by an overgrowth of trees with a sprawling lawn area on the downhill side that afforded a wide-open western exposure to the valley below. He was almost certain that he had seen Yuri Andropov, the former President of the Soviet Union sitting on the sun deck near a pool. It made no sense, he knew that Andropov had died in 1984. How was it possible? Yet, his observant military mind told him that the man looked exactly like Andropov. Indeed, it reconfirmed to him that, if in fact it was the former Chairman, this was undoubtedly the most secret military installation in the world.

But within the last month, he had been permitted access to meetings that had totally challenged his sense of reality. Andropov had not materialized, but even a greater hero of the past, the famed Cosmonaut, Yuri Gagarin, had nonchalantly walked into the base command center asking for information regarding the security situation. The Spetsnaz troopers on duty, confounded beyond belief, had almost lost their soldierly decorum. For his part, Gagarin merely observed dryly, ''You men look like you've just seen a ghost,'' and then summarily announced that he would be assuming all communications between the base defensive unit and the STAVKA. He then proceeded as if he had been a daily fixture over the past twenty years. No one dared venture the obvious question as to where the national legend had been since the supposed fatal plane crash in 1968. Rumors had flourished for years of a possible coverup. Reports that the national hero was still alive were frequent. But the sightings were normally dismissed as incredulous and fanciful. His face continued to loom as large as life in the conscience of the Russian people.

Aniamov was prepared to make his presentation to Gagarin as the famed Cosmonaut walked into the room. The Colonel and his team snapped to attention. Gagarin, a lean-built man, had retained the electrifying smile which combined with his achievements in space, had etched his name in world history. He was a sharp interrogator who clearly listened to each answer.

After preliminary discussions, Colonel Anaimov commenced his presentation. "Comrade General Gagarin, as you can see, I have provided for you a written update of conditions as they currently exist. I would like to go through some detail with you if I could, Sir?"

"The detail I have, Comrade Colonel," Gagarin noted. "I have seen every draft of your report since it was first presented to the print shop. We review everything that is copied or printed there. Your report has been of major concern to me. But for the benefit of others, please touch upon the major points. How much more time do we have at Caucus Station?"

"As you know by the report, Sir, indigenous forces in the Svanathian Valley have been gathering strength. These are mainly former National Guardsmen who are loosely aligned with the government in Tbilisi. Until approximately three months ago, we were experiencing very little negative contact with indigenous forces," the Colonel continued with his report. "But we now know that activity is being accelerated, and that it has the tacit support of the central government in Tbilisi. If you will recall, approximately six months ago a newspaper in Tbilisi called for the removal of this base from Georgian soil. We did eliminate both the author of that article as well as the publisher and his entire family. We have seen no further discussion of the subject in the Georgian newspapers. However, when our vehicles leave the base they are being routinely vandalized. We are shadowed wherever we go in the Svanathian Valley and we have been required to shut down two of our four resorts on the Black Sea. The helicopters from Caucus Station are usually followed by private aircraft. Thus, when we fly our people to the resorts, the Georgians know they are from Caucus Station. I can tell you now, Sir, we cannot defend the resorts. Our security there is minimal and I would strongly advise against any overt endeavor to actually defend perimeters on the Black Sea."

"Yes, the resorts are a problem," Gagarin responded, "although my principal concern is Caucus Station One. What are we really looking at as far as time is concerned?''

"Sir, I currently have a force of two thousand eight hundred men. That is a small number to defend a ten mile perimeter. Despite the small number, our complement of helicopters and tanks still makes us the most potent military force in the Trans-Caucus region. I must say in all earnestness, that if indigenous forces can muster as many as twenty thousand armed and trained soldiers, and if full scale hostilities were to ensue, it would be difficult to defend the full perimeter for more than two weeks. We would need to withdraw into more defensible positions.''

"In your opinion Colonel, how long could we hold enough of the base so we can still evacuate safely?''

"With the food and ammunition stocks maintained at full level, and with the impossibility of access of any large force from the northwest due to the steep mountain terrain, we could hold for... I would estimate a month, maybe even two. You understand, I am assuming that our opposition would be entirely Georgian Militia, and not better trained or fully equipped military units.''

"Yes, I understand that,'' Gagarin responded. "So, when do you expect this siege to actually begin?''

"We have seen patrols of armed National Guardsmen and Militia on the Potolemei Ridge at the sheepherder camps. Two weeks ago, they brought six BMP 4 infantry vehicles up the road and stopped within two miles of our perimeter. I chose not to use the general area alarm because the force was only about fifty men. But I did bring two of our tanks across to that side of the plateau and stationed a full Spetsnaz company there for a week.''

"Was there ever any contact?''

"No direct contact. On the third day we infiltrated the force at the sheepherder camp and determined that this unit was insufficiently armed to be a threat. But it did represent the presence of at least a thousand infantrymen who were bold enough to come up the ridge in risk of the consequences.''

"What is the buildup we have noted on the ridges in the Kartalinian Forest?''

"That development is troublesome in a different way. There is a militiaman by the name of Lado Deniken who is leading the contingent in the Svanathian Valley. He has stirred up a great deal of opposition to our base. His group is actually positioning a battery of 130 millimeter field guns on the ridge across the reaches of the Kartalinian Forest. We're uncertain as to how efficiently they can operate the guns. It may be more for show than anything else.''

"And if you dislodge them from the hill?''

"I would need at least eight hundred men. We would need to work our way through the forest to the west of the perimeter down along a very steep slope and then attack upward against the defenders. I would obviously support such an effort with our Mi-24's from the air. I could not effectively take the hill without experiencing at least twenty to thirty dead and wounded.''

"But you could not hold it?''

"No, it is not defensible. It is simply too far from the base perimeter.''

"So your recommendation is that we evacuate?''

"Yes, Comrade Gagarin, it is only a matter of time. Sir, we can decisively win all of the early battles. We have water, we have food and we have ammunition. But unless a subsequent plan is devised to successfully retake control of the entire State of Georgia, we will ultimately have to leave this place. I would like to be more positive. But I must give you my honest conclusions. You understand, however, General Gagarin, that the Spetsnaz brotherhood is prepared to fight to the very last man and follow whatever orders the STAVKA gives us.'' The Colonel's report was grim.

Yuri Gagarin was slow in response to the pessimistic report of the trusted Spetsnaz Colonel. He wandered over to the map and looked closely at each of the locations that had been described in the briefing. Caucus Station had been the perfect location for many years. Since the supposed airplane crash in which Gagarin had reportedly perished, Caucus Station had been his home. The thought of leaving the security of the mountain haunted him. He had become accustomed to the beautiful Dacha mansion hidden in the trees near the western edge of the plateau. To the west on a flatter surface, but still high on the plateau, were the four barracks buildings together with the STAVKA Command and Control Center where he had gone to work every day with the exception of the few trips off the plateau to the resorts. On rare occasions he had ventured, incognito, away from the base and into Moscow itself. To the west of the barracks, and built into the mountain, were two deep tunnels in which ammunition and food stocks were located. Each tunnel ran over a half a mile into the mountain and included facilities from workshops to shooting ranges. Even luxurious sleeping quarters and a special medical surgery facility were deep inside the mountain. It had been the nuclear war retreat for the STAVKA, an impregnable bastion in the event of world holocaust, but now ironically vulnerable to poorly armed Georgians.

Across the plateau to the east on an open flat area was the airfield. High on the ridge, the communications towers, satellite dishes and other devices were carefully positioned to gather such information the STAVKA deemed important. Adjacent to the airfield stood five large hangars in which the Mil Mi-24 helicopters were housed with their Gatling guns, anti-tank missiles and chemical warhead delivery systems on the ready.

On the eastern edge of the plateau, a road snaked its way up the mile-high ridge from the Georgian military highway which accessed the valley below. Local residents had long since ceased using the road. The most compelling reason for its non-use was the ominous sign near a major intersection of the highway which read, **"HALT! DO NOT PROCEED FURTHER! PERSONS COMING WITHIN 4 KILOMETERS OF THE MILITARY PERIMETERS WHICH ARE ACCESSED BY THIS ROAD WILL BE SHOT."**

As the meeting with Gagarin was reaching its conclusion in the safe confines of the Command Center, one of Lado Deniken's men was defiantly taking an axe to the notorious sign. "We'll see who shoots who!" The Svan Warrior was preparing for war.

Vladivostok, Far Eastern Russia, Late November, 1992

The Vladivostok branch of Toko Bank was located in the old business district not far from the harbor. Colonel Ziyetski arrived at the bank and was immediately introduced to Alexander Kutuzov. Following the usual pleasantries, it was apparent to the Colonel that Kutuzov was seemingly sincere in his efforts as an auditor. Ziyetski's knowledge of bank auditing was nonexistent, so he questioned Kutuzov extensively to at least get some idea of what Kutusov was doing in Vladivostok.

Eventually the discussion reached the point where Ziyetski felt comfortable raising the subject of the Trans-Siberian rail shipment. Neither the bank nor any public place was suitable for discussing the matter. He invited Kutuzov to go for a drive.

With the Colonel driving, and Kutuzov in the front seat, a scribe sat in the back seat taking careful notes in shorthand. Kutuzov was at ease having dealt with KGB officers often during the course of his Foreign Service experience. To him, this policeman seemed to have a trustworthy and considerate approach in seeking answers to his questions. It impressed him.

"So, it was you who actually ordered the cash shipments to the Toko Bank branch in Vladivostok, is that correct?" the Colonel asked.

"Yes, it was. And now I wished that I hadn't."

"You don't really believe that the train was attacked just to get at such a small amount of cash do you?" Ziyetski asked.

"No, I don't believe that either. But perhaps someone thought there was more cash being sent. I mean, it was only three hundred thousand U.S. dollars, and four hundred thousand rubles. But it's possible that someone at the bank was mistakenly convinced that larger amounts of cash were in transit."

Ziyetski continued to probe. "To whom did you make the order?"

"To the cashier. He's the only person who can order the physical transfer of cash. Once I received instructions from the bank's First Deputy, I contacted the cashier."

"Do you ever ship gold to Vladivostok?"

"Certainly not. With the breakup of Gosbank USSR, the gold stocks were redistributed among the banks. But that's mainly for safe keeping. The gold belongs, at this point, to the Russian Republic, and in some cases, other commonwealth states. As far as I know, the various Commonwealth of Independent States leaders have made every effort to keep the gold totally under lock and key. They don't want rocks showing up to replace currency on the streets of Moscow. It's bad enough the way it is," he mused.

"But is it possible?" the Colonel asked. "Is it possible that someone else in the bank could order a shipment of gold to come in this direction - I mean without your knowledge and maybe even without the cashier knowing about it?"

"I cannot imagine it. I can see no reason why gold would be shipped in this direction. There's no market, no purpose and no use for it at the Vladivostok branch," Kutuzov responded.

"But there had to be something of great value in those train cars, Mr. Kutuzov. And whatever it was, it was in the vaults. Why else would they take only the vault cars? They killed every possible witness. If it wasn't gold, then it was something else of extremely great value. But you still don't see any possibility that it could have been gold?"

"Colonel Ziyetski, I certainly am not the last word on banking in Russia. But I do know how the branch bank and the branches of other banks in Vladivostok operate. They're small and their needs are very limited. Other than cash to cover certain operations from time to time, minimal rubles and currency are sent here. This could change, however," he added. "There is talk of an enterprise zone that could require considerable Western investment in Vladivostok. Still, the need for gold would make no sense at this time."

The two men continued their discussion for another hour as they drove around the city of Vladivostok.

CHAPTER 13

Hong Kong, Late November, 1992

The "hurry up and wait" of military life had been the rule, rather than the exception for Captain Major Sarabrov's entire career. Residency in the exquisite confines of the Hong Kong Marriott Hotel for six weeks had been an anomaly that he would not soon forget. A telephone call had been received from a source which had provided the proper codes to his communication ensign. The message was simple and could be trusted, "Be at the Hong Kong - Kowloon Ferry for the 8:30 p.m. crossing of the harbor on the Hong Kong Island side. Further information would be given at that point."

Initially, he had separated the company into small groups. But it was becoming increasingly clear that some members were becoming less committed in maintaining the strict physical discipline required of a Spetsnaz trooper. He knew it was only a matter of time before the soft, easy life and vices of Hong Kong would tempt some of his soldiers away from the principal focus of their duties to the Motherland. Thus, he hoped for a new and less enticing base of operation - and sooner rather than later.

The troopers busied themselves preparing their target overlays for the Rocket Forces of the Soviet Union. Having read the translations of the English language newspapers, Sarabrov questioned whether or not the Rocket Forces were even still in place. His concern had been relieved as he read an article in one of the Hong Kong papers reporting that U.S. government officials were still concerned about the fact that the former Soviet Union had not ceased all of its nuclear weapons production. And in Scandinavia, the Swedes were again dropping depth charges in the Baltic to bring a mysterious intruder within their national waters to the surface. The Captain Major took this as a signal that in spite of all the changes, the underlying force to whom he was dedicated was still in power.

What you see in Russia is seldom what you really get. This is something the West will never understand, he thought.

Sarabrov and his two lieutenants took the elevator two floors below the hotel lobby level where it opened up into a posh underground shopping and restaurant area at Pacific Place. They exited, walked east through the shopping mall and then took the long escalators which led them to a sky walk leading northward across the crowded Queens Way Express Road, one of Hong Kong's principal thoroughfares. This put them in the lower floors of the imposing Hong Kong and Shanghai Banking Corporation Building. They turned north inside the shopping mall, took another elevated sky walk across Cotton Tree Drive into the massive glass and steel structure some eighty stories high housing the Bank of Hong Kong. From there they entered elevators again to the street level which opened up on the north side facing the park adjacent to the old Territorial Courts Building.

The two story Courts Building, a provincial 19th century structure, sat awkwardly out of place amidst the eighty to ninety story high-rise structures on all sides of the square. Surrounding the colonial building was a magnificent park with lush greenery and a myriad of sidewalks and pathways. On this block, the group split up and worked their way across the park and regrouped at Edinburgh Place in front of the stately City Hall two blocks to the northeast and near the front gate of the ferry. At that point, they assumed that they were safe from any possible surveillance. They worked their way past the General Post Office and across the parking lot to purchase their tickets for the Hong Kong-Kowloon Ferry. There was still half an hour before the 8:30 meeting. The men sat quietly on the green benches beneath the covered portion of the ferry pier. They carefully watched the people who had just embarked on one of the eleven-minute crossings of the busy strait for the fifty-sixth time on that particular day.

After several minutes, Sarabrov picked out the ferry from the vast parade of lights skating in all directions on the water. Even at night, barges, san pans, large freighters, tugs and tourist boats were fighting for space at the mouth of the Pearl River. Most were traveling up or down the river in an easterly or westerly direction. The ferry, however, moving north to south, could be easily sighted at a long distance by Sarabrov's military eyes as the one set of boat lights without any significant lateral motion.

The wide blue and white two story ferry arrived. A large number of people, mostly Chinese intermixed with a few Caucasian tourists, exited the boat onto the long pier and crowded into the walkway headed towards the Hong Kong shore. Sarabrov and his group walked cautiously through the turnstiles and up the stairs onto the upper deck. Other people were also taking their places on the hundreds of wooden chairs situated across the boat deck. Sarabrov, noting that the majority of the passengers preferred to be forward, moved aft to a more secluded spot. They waited, and within five minutes, the ferry was underway.

As the ferry approached the completion of its journey on the Kowloon side of the river, Sarabrov wondered if he had perhaps missed his contact. He was also worried that the meeting may have been waived off at the last minute due to some detection by enemy forces. The boat pulled into the berth and people began to disembark, oblivious to the nervous Russians still sitting in the aft deck chairs.

When the boat was almost empty, Sarabrov watched as a young Chinese man approached the group. He walked forward and bowed slightly and spoke. "Sarabrov, please come with me."

Sarabrov looked at his interpreter, who simply nodded and stated to Sarabrov, "We must follow."

Without further discussion, the men exited the pier area and walked quickly up side streets. After some eight blocks they arrived at the Night Market situated along the full expanse of Hankow Road, running north-south in the middle of the Kowloon District. The area was illuminated brilliantly by millions of neon bulbs. Makeshift shops had been set up in the middle of the street in an area closed off to traffic.

Even Sarabrov was amazed at the extensive business activity and the endless types of gadgetry, clothing, toys and food available. But he remained focused. His job was to keep track of the small Chinese man who moved intently through the crowd. It was not easy. He assumed that security problems had arisen which required such extraordinary efforts in making contact. The meeting, he had thought, would be on the ferry, but now, having walked another mile, he was uncertain where he and his men were being taken.

Working their way through various street shops in the Night Market, they reached a dimly lit point on the north end of the street. Along the west side of the road, he could see small lanterns on tables spaced every twenty yards next to the buildings. Chinese folk music emanated from a contingent of musicians situated in the yards of the buildings to the east.

Suddenly, the young man stopped and walked toward one of the tables. Seated was a man in a broad-brimmed hat. The guide spoke again, ''You sit - have fortune told.'' Without further comment, he walked off, disappearing into the crowd.

The four Russians cautiously surveyed the entire scene again, then sat down in the four chairs surrounding the table. The fortune teller raised the brim of his hat and stared directly at Sarabrov.

''Mr. Hui!'' He was looking into the face of the man that had been their principal contact while in Hong Kong, but whom they had not seen for more than a week. Mr. Hui's absence had been unnerving even to Sarabrov.

''I have orders.'' He reached under the table and produced the weathered Spetsnaz communication's pouch.

The sight of the old leather satchel immediately warmed Sarabrov's heart as he knew that no one could have had access to the Spetsnaz pouches unless they had direct contact with leaders at the highest levels of the Red Army. He anticipated good news.

In the next moment, Hui pulled a piece of paper from his pocket, held it to the light and began reading. ''You are hereby ordered to have your men at the International Airport at 0800 hours on November 28th to travel to a new destination. All travel documents are in the pouch, including airline tickets for all ninety-three of your men. You will fly by Cathay Pacific Airlines to Mexico City. Your contact there will be a man named

Jim. He will give you further instructions and will be in possession of identifying codes.''

Hui then put the paper in the pouch, closed the zipper and latched the leather straps at the buckle and handed it to Sarabrov, ''Good luck to you, Mr. Sarabrov. It has been a pleasure having you in Hong Kong, but it is surely time that you go. One can only hide ninety-three Russian soldiers in Hong Kong for so long before people start to ask questions. Be careful as you travel back tonight. I would suggest that you do not take the ferry. It would be better for you to take the underground. It will get you back to the hotel more quickly, and it is unlikely they are watching it this time of night. But one never knows, so be careful.'' He then smiled, ''And that, gentlemen, is your fortune.''

Caucus Mountains, Late November, 1992

The morning had come early for Lado Deniken. His oft-repeated nightmare allowed for limited sleep. The dream had taken him back to the fateful morning some ten years earlier when he had climbed the mountains into the dense Kartalinian Forest at the beckoning of sheepherders working in the area. There, lying inside an area with the words **"BEWARE OF MINES"** on a placard tacked to a tree, was the body of his young nineteen year old son, Steffan. It appeared as though a gaping hole had been blown in his chest as he had stumbled onto a land mine. The boy had been missing for days. Although most members of the Svanathian leadership drew heavily on the deaths of their respective sons in Afghanistan as the catalyst for their nationalistic stand, Lado's commitment was simple. He had lost his son to the foreigners on the mountain before his son could even have taken his chances in Afghanistan. It had continued as a devastating memory and one that could only be vindicated by finally driving the foreigners out of the land and taking as many of their lives as possible in the process.

Sufficiently awake to now consider the methodology, he reevaluated his military position as he had done every morning for the past year. The artillery battery was firmly in place on the Kartalinian Ridge. He hoped that the Russians on the base would attempt to move against the battery. He knew he could not hold the hill in the face of an infantry attack supported by helicopter gunships. But equally, the same strategy would rebound on the defenders of the base should they decide to extend their perimeter out to the Kartalinian Ridge. The snowy winter in Svanathia had not deterred the vigilance of his one thousand men already on the Potolomei Ridge base camp from which the ground attack would begin.

It was another morning over the land of Svanathia. Yet, despite all the changes in recent times, Lado Deniken and many of his countrymen were still occupied by the ancient task of trying to figure out how they would rid their land of the invaders from the North. He picked up his field glasses and caught the metallic glimmer of the morning sun reflecting off a guard tower two miles up the mountain from where he stood. My Steffan was the strongest and smartest of the young sheepherders. He knew the Kartalinian Forest in both day and night. But for the foreigners on the mountain, I would still have my son with me and my life would be entirely different than it is now. He again peered through his field glasses at the mountain, as he had for so many years, always in anticipation that something would appear that might resolve some of his most solemn and painful questions.

Caucus Station, Late November, 1992

Yuri Andropov had spent the better part of the morning hours with two adolescent females from Turkey. It had been a feast of habitual pleasures for him - totally frightening for them. For the parents of the children in the Black Sea Port City of Sinop, there was now sufficient money to purchase their dreams. The daughters would eventually be returned to the harsh and rugged lifestyle of the Turkish fishermen and their families and in time, the experience with the old man in the Caucuses would subordinate itself to other more pressing hardships.

With an aide at his side, Andropov made his way from the recreational rooms of the Dacha, across the back lawn to the traditional Nordic Russian bath house which had been constructed for the pleasure of the Dacha's prominent residents. Although the air temperature was cold and the walk across the partially cleared paths slightly treacherous, Andropov handled the task with little difficulty. In fact, his steps were often brisk and carefully selected. For a man nearly eighty years of age, he was unusually adept on his feet.

In the life of Yuri Andropov, there were no equals. Andropov had enjoyed a stint as President of the Soviet Union from 1982 to 1984. For twenty years prior to his presidency, he had been Chief of the KGB and a dominant member of the Politburo. Intent on avoiding further hardship, he had moved on to the STAVKA level at the earliest opportunity. He was particularly enthused about the idea of longevity practices, largely perfected by STAVKA doctors and researchers, and availed only to the most deserving. It furnished a strong incentive for an old man to replace his political position atop a declining empire in favor of the best form of a fountain of youth that Soviet tax dollars could buy.

Reaching the bathhouse, he opened the door only to find his long-time comrade Boris Yarov already lounging leisurely in the water. Andropov removed his robe exposing the long thick purple scar from the top of his chest to the middle of his belly, evidencing extensive open-heart surgery.

Significant advances in longevity studies through the Soviet Academy of Science in Moscow and the Moscow Biological Research Institute had been moved underground as one of the major assets of the Motherland that would not be shared with the West despite the supposed new relationship. Gene splicing and brain matter implants from renowned deceased Soviet scientists and artists had been attempted by the KGB in earlier years to pursue every possible theory for extension and regeneration of life. More recently, however, a more systematic and natural approach had been developed by STAVKA experts in Soviet Georgia. The STAVKA based its approach on the perfection of human growth hormones as well as the study of the "Dolgozhiteli," Georgian mountain people who survived regularly in good health, often well into their one hundred tenth to one hundred twentieth years. Andropov had become the most prominent beneficiary of the research, a truth unknown to anyone other than STAVKA doctors, who were sworn to secrecy under threat of immediate death should they ever default in their commitments.

"So, how was your morning, Comrade Chairman?" Yarov asked.

"It was not bad. Actually, I don't think the Koran could have described a better state of paradise. It was truly a land of milk and honey this morning."

Yarov laughed. He was well aware of the code of the STAVKA which was intended to provide all of the benefits of the good life to those who had reached the untouchable caste.

"I am still troubled by our decision on the First Deputy," Yarov commented. "I can' t accept the prospect of bringing him here for a transplant."

Andropov responded, "He did get the money for us. Without him, we wouldn't have billions in the Hong Kong banks. His help has been significant."

"I don't dispute that in the slightest. But to get a heart - we don't have a lot of them laying around you know."

"Can't we just pick up another shepherd boy down in the valley?" Andropov suggested.

"It's not that easy. Gagarin says that the Spetsnaz are being followed and harassed. It's a lot harder to operate in Georgia now."

"Well, at least we'll run him through the tests. If there is no heart, there is no heart - he'll just have to die." Andropov chose not to trouble himself further with concerns over a lowly bureaucrat the likes of the First Deputy. He changed the subject and attempted a joke, "We could bring Yeltsin in."

Yarov laughed, "Sure, and we might as well open up STAVKA membership to taxi drivers in Moscow!"

"But what if he succeeds?" Andropov was worried. "The Congress of Peoples' Deputies can only hold him off for so long. They are not as strong as before, not by any measure."

"Very true, Mr. Chairman, but he needs the money from the West. He'll milk it as long as he can... However, when we bring Gagarin back, the Parliament will have no problem with Yeltsin.''

The mention of Yuri Gagarin induced more sobering inflections, Andropov paused and then spoke, ''The doctors say that Gagarin will need a heart soon.''

''The future of the Motherland bears on his shoulders,'' Yarov echoed the thoughts of his prominent mentor.

''I was seventy-five when I got mine. I hoped they could wait.''

''The technology was way behind then. The doctors say that the prime time is before the body deteriorates...while all of the other organs are still functioning well. Gagarin may live... who knows...it could be for another eighty years.''

''How old is the young Cosmonaut now?'' Andropov was too old to estimate age.

''He's almost sixty.''

''That amazes me. It seems like just yesterday that he was launched into space for the first time. Those were glorious years.''

''We will see those years again, Comrade - I am certain.'' Yarov was reassuring.

''Yes, the plan is going well. It appears as though there is no end to the Western money pouring into the Motherland. We default on wheat and grain purchases and they still send money. The Germans and the Japanese are drooling all over us to compete to see who can out-contribute the United States. And they are, in reality, getting absolutely nothing in return.''

Yarov laughed as Andropov continued. ''They don't get land because we don't sell land. They don't get money because we don't have any. They waive billions of dollars of interest on loans at the G-7 meetings. We couldn't have done this well if we had somehow captured the entirety of the United States without firing a shot. What more could we ask for?'' Yeltsin may be a dupe, but the real fools are the Western leaders. This grand illusion is brilliant, even if I did think it up myself.''

''There is one problem.'' Yarov was hesitant to speak in the wake of Andropov's boasting. ''The STAVKA staff has given me reports of a new bill which will be introduced in the United States Congress in January. It demands payment in gold bullion from the Republic of Russia treasury for all aid coming from the United States. You can be certain that if the

United States commences this practice, that the Japanese and the Germans won't be far behind. If we refuse to pay them in gold, they will probably want to start taking land."

"And when did this come about?" Andropov was suddenly alarmed.

"I received the report yesterday. I think you were occupied with a young lady from Bulgaria at the time."

"What's been the response from Moscow?" Andropov asked.

"Well, at least they're not lying down on the issue. In fact, almost every state in the Commonwealth has been belligerent in its response. They are attacking the sincerity of the aid and suggesting that it is no more than pretext to gain control over the former Soviet Union. It's Cold War rhetoric and so far it looks like surprisingly good stuff. Yesterday, a pair of Tupulov Bears flew all the way from a base in the Ukraine to the Alaskan Coast where the American Air Force had to intercept and escort them out of U.S. airspace. It was a good sign of displeasure."

"That could be a problem. If the Americans were to start calling on gold reserves, it could be a serious problem. I'm sure the Russian treasury has no knowledge that we have removed over half of its gold bullion and safely deposited it in Hong Kong banks. And it's not something they will discover unless ..."

"That's right," Yarov interrupted, "unless they have to start accounting for the gold to foreign governments. That would stop foreign aid very quickly, and of course the whole restoration plan would be in jeopardy. We've *got* to put a stop to this American legislation."

Vladivostok, Far Eastern Russia, Late November, 1992

Colonel Ziyetski had attempted to obtain permission from Moscow to act. As quickly as he had received the intelligence regarding the drugging of the sole survivor of the train attack, he had passed the discovery on to the Federation Security Agency headquarters in Moscow with recommendations that the man be placed in KGB protection. But the weekend had intervened, and he had merely received a request for more information. In the meantime, Ziyetski had infiltrated the hospital with his people to find that the drugging was getting worse. The KGB doctor assigned to Ziyetski concluded that if the man were not quickly taken off the current drug, he would very likely sink to a vegetative-state within a week.

Determining that there was no more time to lose, he decided to act without orders and risk incurring the wrath of the KGB in Moscow. If the young man was being pumped full of drugs to cause a coma, he would soon be useless to their investigation.

The Far Eastern Command Headquarters area was located in a compound surrounded by a ten-foot block wall. The extensive combination of barbed wire and guard towers at various points along the wall, gave the appearance of either a fortress or a prison, depending on one's perspective. Directly inside the front gate was a large parking lot to accommodate parades as well as cars. Beyond that was the sprawling Fleet Headquarters building of the Pacific Naval Fleet.

Immediately to the east of the building stood a three story barracks building which served as the Fleet Hospital. Containing over four hundred beds, it was the largest medical facility in eastern Russia. At the far end of the third floor, a special ward dedicated to serving the higher ranking members of the Far Eastern Command, including Army, Navy and Air Force personnel and their families was tucked away, out of sight from the average Russian.

It was in a room in this ward where the young railroad guard, Corporal Sokof had slept, drifting in and out of consciousness, since his commitment there as the sole survivor of the Trans-Siberian train massacre. With this location in mind, Colonel Ziyetski moved two squads of KGB Border Troops into place approximately one block from the main gate. Upon his signal, the group rolled up to the gate with their troop-carrier vans, showed their passes and gained immediate access. In order to interdict any communications from the main gate to other security forces on the base, the second van, upon being waived through, stopped.

Three KGB men climbed out of the back of the van, entered the guard shack and ordered the military policeman at gunpoint to make no communications regarding the KGB's presence on the post. The three

KGB Border Guard troopers remained in the shack to make certain that their demand was not violated.

It took less than a minute to reach the hospital from the main gate. The Colonel and his four team members moved briskly into the hospital, flashing their KGB badges wherever necessary to obtain cooperation from guards and hospital personnel. Avoiding the elevators, they climbed the stairs to the special ward and young Sokof's room.

The doctor on duty in the ward was summoned to Sokof's bedside by the Colonel. Shortly thereafter, the group was joined by a KGB physician who had earlier infiltrated into the hospital. The doctor had been requested by the Colonel to make his way to the special ward at the opportune moment. Quickly, the KGB doctor reviewed the medication chart and confirmed the suspicion that powerful drugs were being used to prohibit the patient's return to full consciousness. For Ziyetski, it was sufficient evidence to continue with the plan. The physician detached the intravenous tubes from the patient. The KGB team then loaded Sokof onto a stretcher, and in the next minute rapidly carried him out to a waiting KGB van.

The whole operation had taken less than seven minutes. The group evacuated the hospital area and by the time the KGB's venture onto the base was communicated to the duty officer of Fleet Headquarters of the Far Eastern Command, the patient and his accompanying KGB entourage were within two minutes of the large steel door at the rear of Vladivostok KGB Center. A medical team, with a clinic especially prepared for the occasion, was waiting for Sokof.

Hurricane, Utah, Late November, 1992

By late Fall, life had evolved to a general state of malaise for Joe Wilson. He was developing a reputation of being the deputy with the "bad attitude." Rumors were circulating that he would be gone by the first of the year. Joe knew that it would take a hard sell for the sheriff to get a new man for the job. But next year, at the local high school graduation, there might be another small-town sucker roped into the trap by the television-inspired glamour of a badge, a car, and a gun. For Joe, the attraction had lasted about one week.

It was past time to move on, but relocating took money, and Joe was still short on cash. He had become aware of a job opening at a batch plant nearby and decided that he would look into the possibility of working there at least part time in order to save enough money to move elsewhere. Joe realized that there was minimal excitement in driving a cement truck, but the hours and the pay were likely to make up the difference. The best part would be knowing that he wouldn't have to deal with any more gruesome accidents. He didn't think the speeders would miss him, either.

Clearly the worst part of the current circumstances was the loneliness. Joe could not ignore the ever increasing urges to have some fun, some companionship. Yet, in the town of Hurricane, there was no one to date. For the local deputy at age twenty-one, to show up at the high school dance as anything but a policeman to keep the peace, would make him the laughing stock of the community. The net result was that Joe found himself drawing away from people into a protective shell and taking his own troubles with him.

As Joe stopped in at the Hurricane substation, he noted a small envelope shoved under the door. He opened it up and read the contents.

Dear Sheriff's Department,

My name is Hannah Jackson. My daughter, Flora, who is 15 years old has been taken away from me by the people here in Red Rock City. They have taken her against her will and will not tell me where. She may have been forced into a marriage without my permission, but I strongly doubt that she has. The authorities here wil not help. I fear that I will never see her again unless someone helps. Can you please at least force my husband or the Brethren in the town to tell me what has happened to my daughter. I don't

*know if their acts are criminal. Because I do not
know the law. But they are certainly wrong and
I fear terribly for my daughter. She is all I have.
My situation is desperate. Please help me. And
Please help soon.*

*Respectfully,
Hannah Jackson*

*P.S. In case you are concerned, I live on the Utah side
of the border and am therefore within the county.*

Joe reread the note. It was easy to detect the call for help in the
woman's note. It momentarily worried him. But in the next second, he
dismissed the concern with the same logic as any local southern Utahn
would - just another polyg problem that's none of our business. In his
current frame of mind, he quickly concluded that it was not his mountain
to climb. He couldn't do anything without the sheriff's permission,
anyway. Without further thought, he put the note in the sheriff's correspondence basket and turned and walked back to his car. He'd get a response
from the sheriff soon enough if there was any work to do on the matter.

As he returned to patrol on the streets of Hurricane for the
remainder of the afternoon, Joe spent his time planning his future - a future
that did not include a badge, a car, or a gun. But he would try to do his best
to make sure that it involved a social life.

CHAPTER 14

Washington D.C., Early December, 1992

The view from the upper right hand side at the top of the steps of the Lincoln Memorial was spectacular. The reflecting pool, Washington Monument and United States Capital building beyond, portrayed an awesome image of stability, beauty and order. As he stood there, taking in the scene while experiencing the chilled air of impending winter, Congressman Stony Chapman was only marginally affected by the panorama before him. As a youngster, trips to Washington had been often capped with a visit to the Lincoln Memorial. More recently, following long years of personal trials, complications and distresses resulting from his career as a congressman, he was no longer easily affected by its sentimental trappings.

Approximately two hours earlier he had been contacted by a respected associate at the Washington office of the European Bank for Reconstruction and Development, a subsidiary of the World Bank. He was told simply to go to the Lincoln Memorial and wait at the top of the steps on the south side. He would be contacted by someone who had very important information for him. Inasmuch as he was reasonably well-acquainted with the banker, he was satisfied that the request was safe as well as a worthwhile use of his time. Accordingly, he had left the Hill early at approximately 4:30 p.m. and was now standing in the semi-dusk at the designated location.

Presently, he saw a man in a brown trench coat at the bottom of the long wide stairway, stop, look up, pause again and then begin walking deliberately up the stairs in his direction. The man was wearing a hat with a wide brim which was slightly uncharacteristic of Washington style. He approached the congressman. Chapman could see that the man was Asian and probably in his mid-fifties.

"You are Congressman Stonewall Chapman, is that correct?" the man asked.

"Yes, that's me. I'm here, as requested. So, how about letting me in on the secret." Chapman was asserting his personality in order to gain the upper hand on the conversation, a tactic that usually proved successful in any negotiation.

"Mr. Congressman Chapman," the Asian began, "I have a serious matter to discuss with you. It involves some very significant issues. I hope you will listen closely. There are several things I have been told about you. First, your son-in-law, Mr. James Burrows, owns Oki-Soft, a small software company in Edmond, Oklahoma. The company, as you know, is in financial trouble at the moment and is in immediate need of substantial equity capital."

The congressman nodded in the affirmative, but said nothing.

"I also understand that you are deeply in debt personally and your daughter is in urgent need of funding for surgery in Oklahoma - surgery related to fertility, I believe."

Chapman was getting hot under the collar. It offended him that a complete stranger could know so much about his personal affairs. "How the hell do you know all this?" he asked tersely.

"Mr. Congressman Chapman, you either listen to me or continue to live with problems that will go unresolved. I'm here to tell you the following - I am authorized by undisclosed principals to see to it that a two million dollar investment is made to purchase forty-nine percent of the shares of Oki-Soft before the end of next week. I realize your son-in-law has been requesting approximately one to one and a half million dollars. My principals are prepared to pay two million dollars. It will provide sufficient funds for your son-in-law's company, enough to satisfy your daughter's concerns and likewise pay off all of her husband's indebtedness to you.''

Chapman sensed a cold but definite sensation of greed and relief taking charge. The thought of resolving the financial strains under which he had lived for decades, and particularly at this most crucial time, gave him great comfort. Of course he knew there was a hitch. ''Nobody gives something for nothing. Not here, not anywhere. So what's the real story, Mr. ....ah, what did you say your name was?''

''I choose not to give you my name, Sir. I will tell you this. What you must do, is withdraw your sponsorship of the 'Gold for Aid' legislation which you plan to introduce in Congress next week. It's as simple as that. You withdraw the support and you, your son-in-law, and your daughter receive what you each most urgently need.''

''How do I know this just isn't some kind of scam? For all I know, you're with the Justice Department, are wired and have cameras pointed right at me. I've dealt with flakes before. If I were a betting man, I would assume that you are one of them!'' Chapman spoke forcefully, but without a tone of outright rejection.

''You are free to think that. It is not an unexpected observation. I would suggest, however, that you pay close attention to your son-in-law over the next week. He will be contacted and offered the opportunity of his lifetime. Whether or not the deal goes through is entirely up to you, Mr. Congressman. The first signal we can expect from you is that you delay the filing of the 'Gold for Aid' bill, I think you call it. If it is delayed, then the initial investment will be made. If, within five days of the initial delay, you proceed to withdraw your support of the bill altogether, then the remainder of the investment totaling two million dollars will be made. What your son-in-law chooses to do with you in the matter is entirely between you and him. There is no direct payment of any kind being made to you. Do not expect one. So, Mr. Congressman, govern yourself accordingly. This is not a set-up, but a legitimate business deal which has certain policy considerations in mind. You can rest assured, there are no cameras.''

Without further discussion, the Asian walked down the stairs, turned left, and disappeared into the crowd near the entrance to the

Vietnam War Memorial.

The congressman struggled within himself, pondering the pain of his daughter's dilemma and his own severe debt problems as well. It was clear that his daughter had one window of opportunity to resolve her infertility problems. There was no end of the earth to which he would not go for his daughter. He had often thought that if it were just a kidney or some other vital organ, he would happily donate his own in order to improve his child's life. This time, it was beyond his control, that is, unless he could produce the funds necessary to resolve the matter.

Over the next few minutes, he wandered back into the hall of the Lincoln Memorial. He observed the sixteenth President as a group of pigeons unceremoniously landed and launched into flight from the statue's head. He then walked to the north side of the hall, stood back, and for once, with a stretch of the neck, took the time to read, in entirety, Lincoln's Second Inaugural Address, magnificently carved across the fifty foot high granite facade.

St. George, Utah, Early December, 1992

With the immediacy of the arrival of the TTI Board of Directors on his mind, Michael determined that he would make every effort to set aside his presuppositions regarding Yarov and his group and endeavor to make their stay a pleasant one. At this point, TTI was all he had as far as business opportunities were concerned. It only made sense to put the best foot forward and avoid perpetuating the problems that had often arisen in Moscow.

In the United States, it was clear to Michael that if he performed well, Yarov needed him more than he needed Yarov. Without him and TTI firmly implanted, Yarov would have a hard time extending Technoserv's business to the United States.

Meetings had been scheduled with the mayor of St. George, as well as the City Council, to discuss the Russia Center concept. Michael had engaged various professionals to obtain option contracts on certain parcels of land needed for the Russia Center. He was hopeful that in the course of meetings with the city, the public officials would recognize the advantage of committing the land at a reasonably low cost for such a far-reaching project. The prospect of bringing literally hundreds of thousands of visitors into the downtown St. George, Utah area each year would be a business boon to the city of incomparable proportions. In private discussions, he had already laid the groundwork in developing relationships necessary to gain the cooperation of the city to move the project forward. However, the face to face meeting between the City Council and the Russians was the real test. He could not fully mitigate his fear that the Russians would somehow blow the opportunity.

Although he had been instructed to arrange for the rental of a black Mercedes for Yarov, Michael had been unable to do so. In St. George, there was not a single Mercedes available for lease. The best he could do was arrange for a new Lincoln Towncar that, from Michael's perspective, was still finer than anything that Yarov had probably ever seen. He dismissed his concerns assuming that no one would notice.

The situation was balanced in his favor as he assumed that he would be under much less stress working on his home turf than had been the case in Moscow where the Russians were free to play their irritating games. The remarkable natural beauty of the area and the opportunity to show it off would hopefully lay a relaxed common ground for the group and allow for a favorable impression of his operation of TTI.

The St. George airport sat high upon a plateau above the city. During the Second World War it had been used as a practice landing platform for aircraft carrier pilots. Although the runway had been significantly expanded since that time, to pilots, young and old, it was generally known as the Aircraft Carrier. Michael awaited the arrival of the Board of Directors mid-morning on an early December day. The group had planned to arrive on a Sky West Airlines flight from Las Vegas, following their Trans-Continental flight from Moscow to Los Angeles via New York. He knew they would be fatigued from jet lag. It was his intention to get them to the hotel as quickly as possible so they could catch some sleep.

The thirty-nine passenger Skywest Airlines Brasilia settled down on the runway and taxied up to the terminal. As passengers exited the airplane, Michael saw Yarov with his dark bushy eyebrows against his red forehead. He looked around and smelled the air. It was clear to Michael that Yarov was pleased. Then suddenly, Michael's jaw went slack with surprise as he noticed the woman accompanying Yarov. The red flowing hair was the instant giveaway. It was the Cosmonaut of Star City whom he had seen taking a shower in the Mir space station simulator.

As the group walked through the entry gate, Yarov recognized Michael. "We are here. It is as beautiful as you say," Yarov spoke with a broad smile, showing off the vault of gold holding his teeth together.

As for the woman, Michael sensed her predatory blue eyes fixed upon him in blatant Russian-style, like lasers, as he awaited introduction.

The interpreter interceded. "This is Raissa Kovac. She is a member of the Board of Directors and in charge of accounting for the company."

"I am pleased to meet you." Michael shook her hand. Even the touch of her hand made him nervous. He decided it best to be up front with his observation, "I believe I know you from somewhere. Didn't I see you working at Star City?"

She smiled and appeared to blush slightly. "Oh, yes, that was me. Just doing my duty. In fact you may have seen all of me that day." She spoke in slow, but credible English without an interpreter. Michael did not respond.

The interpreter was a nondescript business type. He would have passed for an accountant in almost any setting in the United States except for the fact that he projected a slight body odor that Michael knew would only get worse as the visit continued. The Russian tradition of bathing only once once per week would not hold in St. George, and especially in an effort to impress the mayor and the city council. Michael had already placed extra soap in conspicuous places at the hotel rooms. He hoped strong hints would catch on.

The woman got into the passenger seat next to him. As they traveled towards the Hilton, Michael was still very aware of her proximity to him. The others were in the back seat gazing out the window at the unusual black rock of the airport mesa. They relaxed into the comfort of the plush seats, apparently fatigued from jet lag. But the woman looked at him, and then fidgeted with the ash tray. Michael had adjusted to the fact that most Russian bureaucrats were smokers. She seemed to fail in her search. He looked at her and smiled, wondering what her purpose in St. George could possibly be. The interpreter dozed in the back seat.

Apparently deciding not to smoke, she eased her hand instead onto Michael's leg, resting it lightly on his thigh just above the knee. He froze momentarily, then reached down, lifted her hand and placed it firmly back in her lap in a manner that would be interpreted in any language as a rejection. Feeling a little foolish, Michael awakened the interpreter with a loud, awkward comment regarding the contrast of the weather in Russia to that of St. George. He continued to make small talk through the interpreter, acting as a sort of tour guide in the future home of the new Russia Center. The woman asked no questions. She simply stared at him.

At the hotel, he watched his guests search their rooms. It was a Russian ritual - always looking for electronic bugs. Michael went back to the office while the Russians got some sleep.

Mexico City, Early December, 1992

As the commercial airliner carrying the clandestine Spetsnaz Alpha Group touched down at Juarez International Airport in Mexico City, Captain Major Sarabrov was less than content with the situation. Although removal from the circumstances in Hong Kong had been welcomed, it occurred to him that there was now the vast expanse of the Pacific Ocean between him and Yelana. For some reason, he had in his own mind that if the very worst happened, he could always apply his ingenuity to somehow make his way back to Moscow on foot. Now, only through reliance upon the considerable efforts of a pilot or ship's captain, could he ever make it back to the Motherland and more importantly to the woman he loved. The dependence upon others to get what he wanted made the Spetsnaz officer nervous and insecure.

He found himself rehabilitating his thought processes. He knew he was not the only man of the ninety-three members of the 23rd Spetsnaz Company whose heart was heavy over absence from loved ones at home. He had hoped that someday they would all be able to fulfill their dreams and return to the Motherland. At present, however, they were soldiers, fulfilling their duty in the midst of a conflict with blurred battle lines and even less discernable enemies.

In the baggage claim area, various groups of men congregated in numbers of six or less as required by their training. Presently, a member of one of the groups walked up the hall to Sarabrov. "Sir, there is a Russian who says his name is Jim who wishes to speak with you. He is standing with the men of Fire Team C."

Sarabrov approached the man. He had expected someone either Mexican or Spanish. He was wrong. The man with the generic code name "Jim" was Russian. Sarabrov recognized him immediately as a superior officer, but there was no saluting as all men were in civilian garb and in enemy territory.

Jim's reputation had proceeded him. He was known by other names such as the "Killer of Kabul." For a period of three years from 1981 to 1983, the Russian had lived under a different name and had supervised the internment and execution of the majority of Mujahadin sympathizers in the Afghan Capital. He had finally been pulled out of Afghanistan at the request of Russia's own Afghan allies. Now, he was operating under the name "Jim" - a new name befitting a different assignment.

Captain Major Sarabrov knew it would be of no value to make small talk. "Comrade, we are the 23rd Spetsnaz Company. We are here at your disposal."

"I have buses available as soon as you complete your baggage pick up. We will travel north tonight. I hope the troopers had plenty of sleep on the airplane. It will be much less comfortable sleeping on the buses," Jim was polite but direct. His fierce gaze was unnerving to Sarabrov.

Within twenty minutes the baggage had been loaded into the two chartered tour buses. They drove off into the darkness, and were soon on a lonely road leading north out of the Mexico City sprawl.

St. George, Utah, Early December, 1992

His last words to the interpreter after he delivered the Lincoln Towncar to the St. George Hilton were that a meeting was scheduled with the mayor and the city council of the City of St. George at 10:00 a.m. the following day. It was now 11:30 a.m., one and one-half hours after the designated meeting time. The Mayor and the City Council had arrived at the TTI offices punctually and had courteously waited for forty-five minutes. Initially, Michael telephoned Yarov and was told they would be there shortly. After waiting another half hour, with still no Russians in sight, Michael again telephoned and there was no answer. He then waited an additional fifteen minutes, at which time several of the councilmen had other pressing business matters and left. The mayor had left as well. All Michael could do was be apologetic.

Finally, at 11:40 a.m., the black Lincoln Towncar pulled into the office building parking lot. Michael's efforts to put his best foot forward and avoid problems with the Russians were already being pushed to the limit. "Where were you? We were meeting with the Mayor and City Council regarding the Russia Center at ten o'clock!" Michael was almost shouting at Yarov.

"And how did the meeting go?" Yarov responded through the interpreter. He was evading any responsibility.

"There was no meeting without you. The whole purpose for this meeting was to introduce you to the City Council and the Mayor. Without their cooperation, there will be no Russia Center!" Michael spoke angrily.

Yarov listened intently to the interpreter's words and then responded in his boisterous Russian which needed no interpretation. "Of course, Michael, we had to have breakfast. We always have breakfast before we start a hard working day. We came here as soon as we finished eating. You need not be disturbed - I'm sure you can call the mayor and he can have his City Council people come here right away."

"They were here waiting for you at ten! They are all busy people and could not wait any longer - I am sure they cannot be available at your beck and call!" Michael was exasperated.

It was clear that the interpreter was having problems with the term "beck and call," but the point hit its target. "Who are these people? They should be happy that we are here in their city. How often do they have the opportunity to enjoy Russian guests?"

Michael could see that Yarov, in his arrogance, had the idea that the key to the city awaited him by just showing up. And therein lay his supreme task - to protect the Russians from themselves as they met with city officials and other Americans. It would be difficult for the Russians to reckon with the fact that the caste system, so prevalent in Russia, simply did not have an identical twin in the United States. Yarov was still of the mind that the entire world revolved around Moscow, and that Americans would hang on every word of the mysterious Russians if they would but travel to the United States to speak to them.

While Yarov, Raissa and the other board members gathered in the small conference room at TTI, Michael telephoned the mayor and attempted to arrange for a meeting in the place of the one that had not occurred. The mayor was gracious and offered to attempt to try and bring the group back together later in the day.

As Michael entered the conference room, Yarov and his board members were huddled at one corner of the table carrying on a serious conversation in Russian. The interpreter was sitting some distance away, apparently not invited to the confab. Understanding only a few words, Michael was still able to sense that they were clearly unhappy about something.

"Now, let us begin in our meeting with you, Michael," Yarov declared through the interpreter. "We have serious problems with your performance. You have not followed instructions. That car, a Lincoln. It is a nice car, but it is not a Mercedes as I had asked. Why did you not do as you were asked?"

"There are some instructions, Yarov, that are very hard to follow. To get a Mercedes for you to drive in St. George, I would have to go to Las Vegas, one hundred miles from here and pay three times the cost of the Lincoln. I realize it's your money, but I assume you want me to be careful in spending it."

"But I said Mercedes...black Mercedes!" was the retort as Yarov pounded his fist on the table like Kruschev at the U.N.

Michael returned the fire, "I find this so crazy! You complain about a Lincoln instead of a Mercedes as if you ever really knew the difference between the two! Yet in Russia you drive an old beat up wreck of a Volga. Why do you even care?"

Yarov was steaming with anger over Michael's impertinence. He raised his finger and pointed it directly at Michael, shouting in Russian. The simultaneous interpretation was not far behind. "We are not in Russia! What we decide ...or how we choose to spend the company's money here in America is our business - it is your duty to do as you are told! It is not to question!"

Michael could see the vein pulsating in Yarov's forehead, bulging with the redness of rage. Taking a deep breath, he chose to try to calm the situation rather than make it worse. It was a little early in the visit to let everything fall apart. "I will see what I can do to find a Mercedes. I was running out of time and perhaps there's some other way. If you need a car from Las Vegas, I will try to get one for you. Is that alright?"

"You must try, and try very hard!" was the response from Yarov as he sat back and folded his arms in a Napoleonic fashion and continued, "Now, we would like to know what you have done on the Russia Center. This matter is very important to us." Yarov was direct.

Michael avoided asking why the group had missed its morning meeting with the city officials if the Russia Center was such a high priority. Nevertheless, he dutifully unrolled the large plans he had received from the architect depicting a stylish and well-developed design of a multi-level Air and Space Museum bordered by retail shops and an additional art exhibit area connected to a magnificent five-star hotel facility.

The three Russians took several minutes examining the multicolored plans and drawings very closely. They continued to point out various features to one another and spoke and commented in Russian. The interpreter did not bother to translate any of the discussion.

Michael sat patiently, wondering whether or not the comments were pleasing or merely additional criticism. Finally, Yarov turned to Michael.

"There is one problem."

"What's that?" Michael asked, awaiting the next major confrontation.

"We see no place in these drawings for a Russian restaurant. It must have a Russian restaurant so all can enjoy the best of Russian cuisine."

Michael was relieved. The concern over additional space for a restaurant was the least of his worries. "Well, I'm sure we can work that out. It would require only a small space."

"Then we will send you a Russian cook right away. You will have him work in another restaurant in St. George until people here in the city like his food. He will then become a famous chef and have many customers. That would make a restaurant do very well, do you not think?"

To Michael, the issue of a Russian restaurant was about as nonsensical as the Mercedes. The food in Moscow would destroy even the most forgiving of Western taste buds, and he could not imagine supervising a Russian cook trying to get a job somewhere in the St. George area. It was a completely impractical idea, but he decided this was not the time to pull the rug out from under Yarov's euphoria..

"And we would have a place here for people to buy Russian toys, stuffed animals and dolls," Raissa spoke, pointing to the plan.

Again, Michael was totally dumbfounded. Here he was pitching a fifty million dollar project to the group of people who would be instrumental in its funding, and they busied themselves talking about Russian short-order cooks and toy curio shops. He was bewildered by their lack of focus.

Momentarily, an argument seemed to develop between Yarov and his assistant. Raissa was on the sidelines interjecting only periodic comments. They battled back and forth with impressive gesticulation. Raissa fixed her gaze on Michael. It led him to wonder again about her true purpose in coming to St. George. He wondered if Yarov was intending to try to use her to influence Michael in some fashion. The interpreter seemed to have been elbowed out of the dispute as well. Michael asked him why they were arguing.

"It's the cook. Yarov has a cousin that is a cook. The assistant has a mother he says is very good. They're arguing over who should be the cook."

"Tell them that we have much bigger things to worry about right now than who's going to be the cook once this thing is finished."

The interpreter's interruption was viewed as an insult and the three turned and glared as if Michael and the interpreter were unwelcome outsiders in a purely family dispute.

Yarov sat back in his chair and again folded his flabby arms. He abruptly changed the subject to other business, "Now, there is another matter, Michael, to which you should attend immediately. Specifically, you will be informed that I have had wired from our bank in Moscow a total of two million dollars. This amount should be used by you to purchase forty-nine percent of the stock of a software company in Oklahoma. The name is Oki-Soft and it is located at the address I have written on this paper." He slid a card across the table to Michael.

Michael looked at a business card which showed the name of James E. Burrows, Oki-Soft, Edmond, Oklahoma. He was puzzled. "Why do you want to purchase part of a software company in Oklahoma?"

"It is because we are in the computer business and consider this purchase to be to our benefit," Yarov responded.

"Well, what type of software does this company produce - I mean, what do they sell? Do you know anything about the company's debt structure, net worth or placement in the software market?"

Yarov looked at Raissa and shrugged his shoulders as if it were her responsibility to answer the question. She responded with a blank stare. He then continued, "That is not for you to concern yourself, Michael."

Michael responded, "I realize that, but I'm not certain you understand what is involved in acquiring another company in the United States. You have to make certain that it has sales which can give you income. You also have to carefully investigate the management of the company to make sure that if you do invest in the company, the management will work hard to make a return on your investment. You could lose all your money."

There was a pause as the three huddled at the end of the table and quietly conversed. When they completed their consultation, Yarov spoke in an automated tone. "We have reason to know that it's very good for us. That is all we can say."

Michael carefully watched the eye contact among the three while he was speaking. He could see they were reacting nervously and likely had little, if any, answer to his specific questions.

"It is as simple as this, Michael," Yarov stood, his finger stabbing invisible holes in the air as his jowls turned an interesting shade of red.

"You will be prepared to send the checks and purchase the stock of Oki-Soft when I tell you! I am the chairman of the board of this company and if you refuse to do exactly as you are told on this matter, then you will be fired! That is the order that I give, and it is a fact that you should understand!"

"Well, it's your money," Michael commented shrugging off Yarov's final comment as if he hadn't heard it, and then retreated from the subject altogether in his continuing confusion about the true intentions of this group. He looked at Raissa. She was impassively gazing out the window.

"We are pleased with what you have done in the computer business," Yarov spoke in conciliatory tones, accepting Michael's cue to change the subject. "We are greatly appreciative of the equipment that you have purchased and sent to Moscow. It is being used effectively and your heroic efforts have not gone unnoticed. I hope that if we have disagreements on a few minor details, you will nevertheless understand our need for solidarity on all matters."

Michael could see that Yarov had intentions of bringing the meeting to a close. He loathed the word solidarity. It sounded decidedly Bolshevik.

"I am hopeful that we can meet later today with the mayor of the city of St. George and his councilmen. I will then leave the interpreter here with you for a few days. We will travel for a well-deserved holiday to see the National Parks. I am told by you and others that they are quite spectacular. We'll be gone for three days and return on the fourth. I am hopeful by that time you will have arranged for a Mercedes automobile and completed each of the other tasks which we have assigned to you as well."

Michael found himself deliciously anticipating the moment when he would put them on the plane and send them back to Moscow.

Vladivostok, Far Eastern Russia, Early December, 1992

In the frigid streets of Vladivostok in far eastern Russia, the situation was heated. It did not surprise Colonel Ziyetski that by the time he was able to reach the KGB Center in Moscow, his superiors already knew the details of his aggressive move against the FEC. The Far Eastern Command's communications links into Moscow were superior to that of the KGB, thus Ziyetski's handling of the situation had been substantially exaggerated by early prejudicial reports of the FEC.

Edvard Dombrayov had been appointed Associate Director of the new Federation Security Agency for the Russian Republic when Gorbachev handed over the reins of power to Yeltsin on Christmas Day, 1991. Although he had risen through the ranks of the Communist-controlled KGB, he had never been an operative in the feared First Directorate. This gave him a sanitized reputation since he had never quelled internal political dissent through harassment and assassination of citizens. His job, like that of Colonel Ziyetski, had been that of a soldier protecting the borders of the country. He had been the right person to elevate out of the mid-level officer corps and place in a position of high responsibility. Yeltsin had subsequently benefited greatly from Dombrayov's astute combination of skills as a soldier, bureaucrat, and politician.

Based on good fortune, as well as political influence through his family, Dombreyov had been transferred to Leningrad and later spent a portion of his career in Latvia and Lithuania dealing with national security maritime issues. In August of 1991, when Leningrad's KGB Chief had issued orders for the Border KGB troops to subordinate themselves to the control of the First Directorate and prepare to move on pro-Yeltsin demonstrators, he refused. His example was followed by some three thousand Border KGB troops in the region. Within hours the word spread to the Leningrad Navy base and the paratrooper academy in Ryazan.

His actions became quickly known to Anatoly Sobchak, Mayor of Leningrad who had also led a high risk pro-Yeltsin demonstration at Palace Square before the allegiance of the KGB and military in the region had been clarified. By August 24, 1991, the head of the KGB in Leningrad had been arrested and was replaced by the daring young Edvard Dombrayov. From that point forward, his career was assured.

As the reports came in from the Vladivostok office by direct courier and from Supreme Headquarters of the Russian Republic Army ten blocks away, Dombrayov found himself playing the role of politician as much as policeman. He worried that Colonel Ziyetski may have already over-stepped his bounds by forcibly entering the Far Eastern Command Headquarters area and seizing a patient from the military hospital. In the new Russia, the KGB was not supposed to do this sort of thing.

At the same time, he felt grave concern from the report he was holding. Colonel Ziyetski had obviously done his homework and Dombrayov could not ignore the blatant inferences that could be drawn from the evidence. The prospect of internal involvement, especially by the Spetsnaz, sent chills down Edvard's spine. Even at his level in the Russian Federation hierarchy, he was unable to determine *who* actually controlled some of the secret Alpha Group battalions of the Spetsnaz. In his discussions with Yeltsin, the President often bragged that all was in order with respect to the feared enforcers of the traditional Communist order. Yet, from time to time, he received intelligence of the excesses taken by small, obscure Spetsnaz units in various parts of the country, acting independently. The incidents were rare, but the Trans-Siberian Railroad massacre had been too serious to ignore. If, in fact, the suspicions were correct, it could lead to an explosive result forestalling any peaceful resolution within the fragile new Russian state. The specter of major civil war continually loomed on the horizon and was squarely in the minds of high level Russian bureaucrats. Edvard was no exception.

Entering the office, the aide indicated to Dombrayov that a clear telephone line had been arranged for a conference with Colonel Ziyetski. Dombrayov picked up the telephone and after few pleasantries, plunged into the critical issues. "I have received a very sternly-worded complaint from the Supreme Command Headquarters indicating that you have committed a military act against the FEC in Vladivostok. What, in the hell, are you doing?"

"Sir," Colonel Ziyetski was prepared for a strong cross examina-tion. "As we speak, the young man we extracted from the naval hospital is being brought out of his comatose condition. Our physician is certain that it was drug-induced. We think that he has information that the Far Eastern Command would prefer we not know. Sokof was the only survivor from the Trans-Siberian Train massacre."

"I understand that," Dombrayov spoke with a sense of irritation. "But we cannot allow the KGB to go around strong-arming people, as if Joseph Stalin was still calling the shots! You have been instructed time and time again, Colonel, to be diplomatic in resolving these problems."

"You have seen my letter. My people made several visits but saw him in a continually comatose condition. Our own KGB physician was barred from reviewing his records. For me, this was cause enough. We think it collectively shows that evidence is being withheld by the FEC. Why else would the FEC pursue this strategy unless they were trying to hide FEC involvement in the massacre?"

"I'm not so certain that it is as compelling as you claim," Dombreyov responded.

Ziyetski cut him off. "Consider this. It's not in the report. The American FBI has provided strong evidence that the detached foot belonged to a Spetsnaz Alpha Group trooper. It was definitely Russian and not Chinese."

There was a pause in the tense discussion. Ziyetski decided to make his move. "And so, Sir, instead of backing off, I'm asking you for permission to have military warrants issued in Moscow for the investigative detention of the Admiral and the Chief Staff Officers of the Far Eastern Command."

"You must be out of your mind, Ziyetski!" Dombrayov yelled into the telephone. "In the first place, there are so many problems in the country that at this point there is no way that Yeltsin will allow us to arrest the leaders of one of our military fronts. Secondly, we still have a border to protect and a nation to defend. Without the Admiral and his staff in place, the command and control structure in that region would certainly be vulnerable."

"Well, he could be replaced!"

"Colonel, you are dreaming...If this turns into a war between the KGB and the Red Army, there is still plenty of red in the Red Army. The KGB will lose. Maybe you've forgotten, but there's no party to back us up. No KGB political officer in every unit. We can't forget the political realities that face the President...and those realities are bigger than anything either you or I can understand. So, I'm ordering you to back off and leave the Far Eastern Command alone! I sympathize with your situation, and you may be correct in your analysis of the evidence, but before I can give you further permission, I need something more.''

Colonel Ziyetski was disappointed by the response, but said, ''I understand, Sir, and I will do what you wish. What about the young man we retrieved from the hospital - what of him? They are demanding that we return him. I can assure you, that if we do, he will never be seen again.''

''I'm going to inform the Admiral that we will freeze our investigation in Vladivostok. We will neither move forward nor backwards. Do not turn the corporal over to the FEC. Let's see if this thing can settle down - that is, until the other side makes a wrong move. If they do, then perhaps we will have more to take to Yeltsin.''

The two men completed their telephone conversation. Colonel Ziyetski was satisfied that he had at least won half the battle. He would not be required to return the train guard.

Edvard Dombrayov, however, faced a more difficult problem. He was well aware that the rumors of forces far more powerful than President Yeltsin were at work in the land. He considered himself a patriot, but he was in no position to start a fight that he could not win.

CHAPTER 15

Washington D. C., Early December, 1992

The Dow Jones average fell eighty-six points and was still sliding when the computers automatically took over to slow the run on panic stock selling. The news had been devastating. Just as economists had projected the arrival of some positive growth and stabilization that might end the recession, it was announced that the highly touted "Gold for Aid" bill would be abandoned before the congress would have a chance to vote on it. Stony Chapman, the bill's architect and chief sponsor, had gathered the Capitol Hill press corps in his office and, without warning, backed out of his commitments with the President-elect who would surely suffer an embarassing setback even before officially taking office. Chapman declared that he was not only withdrawing his sponsorship of the "Gold for Aid" resolution, but was also taking a strong position in opposition, should anyone else act as sponsor. Many suspected that he had been part of a Republican political ambush to punish the new President for his aggressive pre-inauguration activity.

Chapman stated his reasoning before the cameras and microphones, *"Ladies and Gentlemen, you'll have to understand, I am doing*

*this with an understanding of the perilous course upon which it takes me.
I am convinced, after studying the issue very closely, that creating
additional problems for the people of the former Soviet Union at this time
simply is not in our best interests. I have read the cables, the letters, the
editorials and the speeches of the many leaders in Russia who are offended
by this bill. Upon closer examination, I have to admit that they are correct.
If we are truly a peace loving people, then it is not our place to, in effect,
seep the wealth, or the little bit that is remaining, out of the Eastern World
and into our own coffers. It would create an affront to those concerned
that we could not soon rectify. It may even create a type of instability in
that part of the world that could lead to civil war. I am thus rescinding
my agreement with the President-elect. I will no longer support his
position on abortion and I will no longer support the 'Gold for Aid'
legislation. That is all I have to say and I will not answer any questions.''*

As cameras flashed, the congressman left the lobby where the press
had gathered and worked his way down the back stairs to the health club
in the basement.

At his home in a southern state, the President-elect had been called
downstairs by his press secretary to watch the news report on CNN. Not
only was he extremely disturbed by Chapman's announcement, but also
offended by the fact that not even the courtesy of a phone call from the
congressman had preceded the press conference. The combative tenor of
the congressman's statement, suggesting that the President-elect had
somehow chosen to use the legislation to exact international dominance
was ill-conceived and a outright lie. He looked closely at the television to
see if the congressman was sober.

The President-elect's former campaign manager and chief advisor
watched with equal concern. One never given to reigning in his comments
regardless of whom the recipient thereof might be, he fumed, ''Mr.
President, you've been set up, spit upon, beat up and thrown out in the junk
pile on this one! You've just been turned into a warmonger by the
congressman from Oklahoma and you don't even have a key to the White
House in your pocket yet! Do you want me to get this screwball on the
phone?''

''No, I think we're dealing with a crazy man here. I need some time to think about it,'' the President-elect was still confused.

Sierra Madre Oriental Wilderness, Mexico, Early December, 1992

The box lunches provided to the 23rd Spetsnaz Troopers inside the four Mexican tour buses were not appetizing. The sharp taste and burning sensation on the tongue had caused more than one of the soldiers to repeat the Spetsnaz tactical rule, ''Trust no one.'' Some assumed that the group's demise would be at the hands of a sinister Mexican cook rather than a weapon of war.

Well after midnight, the two buses reached a remote air strip in the expanse of sand hills on the western edge of the Sierra Madre Oriental Wilderness near the small village of Rio Verde. There, the buses took refuge inside an airplane hangar. The men were finally able to get out, stretch, walk and hope they would never do battle with such gut-wrenching food again.

The soldiers bivouacked for the remainder of the night inside the hangar. They were feeling a sense of subdued exhilaration at the idea of seeing some kind of action in the near future. The very clandestine nature of their trip to Mexico had whetted their appetites for action. Sitting around, even in a Five-star hotel, had become tedious.

Strict instructions had been laid down by Jim to avoid leaving the building for any reason. He had informed the group that this was a highly confidential mission upon which they were now embarked, and that even the slightest mistake could disclose their whereabouts to the Americans.

''The Americans?'' Captain Major Sarabrov asked, somewhat with a start and even a more intense interest. He took Jim aside and asked him point blank, ''If we are going to be dealing with Americans, we need weapons. We also need equipment, but most of all we need to have an idea where we are going!''

Jim, who had barked out orders to the bus driver in perfect Spanish was now resorting to his native Russian tongue to talk to his countrymen.

"I can help you with two of your concerns, but not the third. First, there will be an aircraft arriving at nightfall and it will have the weapons necessary to accommodate your entire company.

"On the second issue, we will be flying you to a location where even more equipment is already in place. Your efforts over the next few months to further supply and equip the base will be part of your task. You will have the weapons and equipment that you need."

"That's nice to hear, very nice to hear!" Sarabrov commented. He relaxed with the thought that he would once again have his hand around the grip of a Kalashnikov rifle, the State factory's finest creation.

"As far as destination is concerned, that is quite another matter. Be prepared for anything," Jim instructed.

The November day was uneventful as the Spetsnaz troopers recovered from the encounter with the superior force of beans and rice that had largely incapacitated them the night before. They were relieved that there would be no work just to keep them occupied such as the reconnaissance patrols, mapping or physical training that they had encountered in Hong Kong..

Few of the men had any notion as to where they might be. In the mind of a Spetsnaz trooper, his location on the globe was significantly subordinate to his overriding need for target acquisition and fire-plotting distance. Each had been trained to live within a world over which he had extensive control - a world that was usually limited to anything within the sight and distance of his weaponry. The lack of equipment left the soldiers with an anxious feeling of vulnerability. Each trooper had learned to live with his sophisticated assault rifle or machine gun as if it were just another body appendage and was very glad to again feel his weapon in his hands.

Nightfall came early as it had in Hong Kong. Both the British Colony and the particular part of Mexico in which the Spetsnaz company was now located were roughly on the same global parallel. Shortly after sunset, the keen hearing of the men picked up the sound of a jet on approach to the remote airstrip. It took little effort to recognize the engines of the Ilyushin 76 which announced the arrival of the mid-size short field take off and landing transport, once the pride of the Soviet State aircraft factories. The plane touched down lightly on the runway and used only a small portion before stopping.

It took less than a minute for the four engine aircraft to taxi to the hangar and shut down its engines to generator mode only. Sarabrov ordered the men to move into the aircraft and take up their standard positions on the paratroop benches which lined each side of the cargo bay.

The most pleasing sight of all, however, was the tightly packed cargo pallet positioned against the bulkhead bearing the visible printed indication of the weapons and equipment it contained. Upon closer examination, they were delighted to find that they were in the company of a plentiful supply of assault rifles, grenade launchers and other weaponry supplied from a Red Army prepositioned stock in Cuba.

Last to climb on board the aircraft were Jim and Captain Major Sarabrov. They inspected the troops and were satisfied that all were tightly buckled into position.

Jim then addressed the group, "Comrades, and you should understand that I am one of you - I carry the rank of Major General in the Red Army and have been a Spetsnaz for twenty years since its founding. I know that your journey has been arduous and you have spent almost three years away from the Rodina. I assure you that there is a marvelous purpose in all of this and that unprecedented events will soon be unfolding for the benefit of our Motherland. Each of you is a warrior at the very forefront of a glorious revolution. You should know that all is going well and according to plan. As the most elite, you will soon be participating in events that will lead to changes unparalleled in the history of the world. *You* will be the fortunate few who will stand at the heart of these final moments." With these comments, he looked intently at the Spetsnaz soldiers, each in turn, then sat abruptly on the bench.

The invigoration of being once again inside a Soviet transport plane eventually diminished in favor of sleep. The box lunches again given to the troopers were this time definitely not Mexican.

After approximately four hours of flight the Captain Major was suddenly awakened to the jolt and gastric tingle indicating the plane's sharp descent. The fact was made even more obvious by the shaking and vibration. Several other troopers awakened and gathered near the small portholes. The Captain Major was anxious about the fact that he could not hear the vibration of wind rushing past the landing gear, and it was clear that despite the rapid descent, the plane was not slowing. Assuming, as all passengers do, that the pilot was clearly in control, he buried his concern in the nervous gaze through the small window near his seat.

The aircraft broke out of a cloud cover. Like glittering jewels against a soft velvet background, the glimmer of small villages lit the dark expanse below. The massive shadows of nearby mountains injected a frightening reality into his thoughts as he realized the aircraft was very low and skimming the rocky ridges, hedges and trees as it sped along at almost four hundred fifty miles per hour.

Although the descent had ended, the shaking continued. The Captain Major glanced back at Jim and saw that he was unlatched from the canvas paratroopers bench and reclined comfortably against a large equipment bag on the floor of the cargo bay. He could not tell if Jim was awake, but it was clear that Jim was unconcerned by the turbulence.

The aircraft vibrated and continued to bounce, gaining altitude and then again descending. As he looked out the window and saw the shadows in the dark canyon walls and high rock monoliths, the moon seemed to skip along behind the peaks. Suddenly, the plane began to twist, turning hard first to the right, flying straight, then jerking left as it bounced through the night sky. This pattern was repeated at intervals until, finally, it proceeded without a turn for several minutes

The Captain Major checked his watch and noted that seven and a quarter hours had elapsed since take off. The plane suddenly lifted up and ascended to an altitude of several thousand feet. The pilot slowly throttled the engines back - the aircraft slowed. Mechanical sounds of a descending landing gear together and lowering flaps intensified the rush of air. It was clear that the plane was on its final approach to landing. In the next moment, the blue lights of a taxiway could be seen rushing by. The nose of the aircraft lifted slightly and the aircraft settled delicately on the runway. It rolled less than a thousand feet before stopping.

The aircraft taxied to a small area of buildings surrounding a large hangar for the IL76 near the edge of the airport tarmac. The rear portion of the plane opened and a ramp emerged from the cargo bay to the concrete below.

All troopers remained inside. The Captain Major walked out in the company of his communication ensign and two armed paratroopers who had quickly unpacked their weapons in the plane. Jim followed them out as the engine of the aircraft shut down. The four men were standing in virtual darkness - the runway lights had been turned off. As Sarabrov's eyes adjusted to the darkness, he looked out across the airfield toward a barely discernable horizon. They were located on what appeared to be a high, treeless plateau. The sparse vegetation afforded a view across a broad valley in the direction which seemed to be the southwest. Even further in the distance, the glow of city lights danced off the intermittent clouds. The air was crisp, but not freezing and he could see no snow on the ground. Was he still in Mexico? He was not sure. "Comrade, where are we?"

"Captain Major Sarabrov," Jim spoke like a tour guide, "welcome to Zion Station."

For the four man crew, the furtive flight into the United States from Mexico had become increasingly routine. The ECM operator had perfected the approach to the largely undefended sky over Fort Huachuka in southern Arizona. With a confirmation of high intensity radio emissions from the Electronic Counter Measures disc mounted like a huge flat saucer atop the Ilyushin's fuselage, he was able to replicate the effects of the aurora borealis on the radar screens of the few Air Force RAPCON operators at Davis-Monthan and Luke Air Force bases. The same effect appeared on the sprinkling of Federal Drug Enforcement Administration radar installations along the border. The display of the mysterious anomaly was quickly blamed by air traffic controllers upon atmospheric interference or meteor showers, which, by the ECM operator's careful flight schedule coordination, conformed exactly with the meteorological calendar.

To assure against more rudimentary forms of detection such as infrequent, but possible patrol aircraft or ground observers, the flight operations were carefully timed to occur only at night. Some eighty miles before the U.S. border the pilot would drop the aircraft to ground-hugging altitude and follow a route preprogrammed into the Ilyushin's inertial guidance and low altitude terrain avoidance system. The flight had traveled through the remote southwest desert canyons and dry river washes, avoiding all centers of population and even incidental farms or ranches.

The automated terrain-following altitude control system had been perfected years earlier for the Tupolev Tu95 "Bear" bomber to allow it to penetrate U.S. defenses after launch from Nicaraguan bases in time of nuclear war. As Soviet surrogates in the region had fallen one by one, the southern approach strategy for the Soviet Nuclear Air Fleet had been scrapped in favor of the more traditional polar approach. With the thaw in U.S.-Soviet relations and the Eastern capitulation that followed, many of the bombers had been scrapped as well. But the plan to slip an Ilyushin safely into the U.S. had worked well as a singular beneficiary of years of Soviet military planning. As the pilots prepared to rest at the end of a long day that had begun in Cuba, not even the specially trained Spetsnaz flight crew fully understood the true significance of their effort.

St. George, Utah, Early December, 1992

The meeting with the city officials in St. George had gone well. The Russians had put on their best diplomatic faces for the meeting with the mayor and the city council. For that, Michael was grateful. He was even more appreciative of the fact that the Russians were now gone on their vacation to the National Parks for four days. This brief respite would allow him to move forward on the Russia Center without interference by Russians.

A shiny, black Mercedes had been sitting in the parking lot for two days. Yarov had used it only briefly. The daily rate was drawing against the TTI account. But again, Michael thought, it was their money, and he decided he would refrain from confronting them on their poorer business decisions.

About midday, he received a phone call from Yarov at the hotel. "We have had a wonderful time traveling in your National Parks. This is indeed a beautiful place. Someday I will need to take you to the Caucasus, Michael." He sounded jovial and relaxed. "They are even more beautiful."

Michael was delighted to see that the parks which had a positive effect on millions of people each year also affected Yarov.

"We will be leaving for meetings with associates in San Jose, California."

"What about this Mercedes? It's been here for two days. I assume you'll want to take it with you," Michael asked.

"No, we will not need it. You can take it back."

"What? You said I should take it back?" Michael could not believe what he was hearing.

The Russian interpreter responded, "While we do appreciate your efforts, please take it back and see if you can get a refund."

"On another matter, Michael," the interpreter began as he translated simultaneously. "You are instructed to proceed immediately to purchase the forty-nine percent interest of the company in Oklahoma. Do not delay. I want it done immediately. You must send me a copy of the bank wire no later than Friday of next week. Do you understand?"

"Like I said, Yarov, it's your money."

"And one final matter," the interpreter fired out Yarov's words as quickly as he spoke them, "on the transfer of the computer components to Technoserv in Moscow, I note that of the various computer items that you have been purchasing in the Salt Lake City area, you have required that they be first sent to St. George then repackaged and Federal Expressed to Moscow. That is an unnecessary step. I will assign you two persons to handle the gathering and shipment of those items in Salt Lake City. I will provide that information to you as soon as I get back to Moscow. You will need to send us visa applications for a woman and her husband to come to Salt Lake City to take care of this."

"So is that all?" Michael asked.

"That is all, and we will stay in touch."

Michael was both mystified and relieved. The group would not be returning to his office. Airing out the office from the smell of Yarov's new board member would be unnecessary.

It seemed strange that they had come all the way from Russia to only be present for business for just one and a half days. The group had spent more time touring the national parks than on official work at the TTI offices. And now, they were moving on to meet with Russians elsewhere in the country.

He remembered his oft-repeated and patently insincere statement,

"You ought to drop by and see me if you're ever in the area." Regardless of where the comment might be made, the Russian could very possibly show up on your door step, suitcase in hand, intending a lengthy stay. He expected that Yarov and company were in the process of calling upon a few "old friends" who might be surprised by their visit.

Vladivostok, Far Eastern Russia, Mid December, 1992

From the gate guards at the KGB Headquarters in Vladivostok the hourly report was of increased military traffic on the two main streets which circumnavigated the bastion. The fact of heightened tension with certain elements of the Far Eastern Command had already been communicated to all KGB units in the Far Eastern Region. Leaves had been canceled and the defensive contingent on the building grounds of the Vladivostok KGB had been considerably beefed up.

Inside was quite another story. External threats had given way to an intriguing rendition of frightening facts from the mouth of the young man who had been unable to speak for months. "I heard him over the loud speaker. There was a lull in the fighting. On a bull horn, he gave us only so many minutes. I was already pinned underneath the train. I was still conscious...and able to hear everything. The orders were clearly those of a Soviet military officer. It was the type of voice I heard in training...the type of voice I have been taught to obey. There's no question in my mind that he was not a foreigner. It was clear that he was a Russian!"

Colonel Ziyetski and his key interrogation assistant along with the KGB physician stood pensively listening to the explanation which further confirmed their suspicions.

Corporal Sokof continued, "In Moscow, when they put the train together, we joked as we saw the armored trucks drive up to the vault cars. The train cars were loaded with the assistance of small cranes apparently put in place for a special purpose. The armored trucks had been very low on their tires. As their loads were put into each of the vault cars on the train, we knew it was something important. Then, after we began to pull, the train was very sluggish. Very heavy weight had been placed in the vault cars. No, it couldn't have just been paper money, but we couldn't see what was being transported from the armored truck to the train vault car. They placed canvasses between the two. It was all very secretive and many armored trucks came. So I wasn't totally surprised when...when the shooting started."

The Colonel was not reluctant about continuing to refine his original hunch. It made sense to him that one of the first theories he had discussed with KGB investigators was that there must have been gold on the train. The question of where it went and how to find it had been entirely another matter, but it made sense that it would have been transported somewhere else away from eastern Russia. Still, the obstruction on the part of the FEC was becoming more apparent.

Now the Colonel had a credible witness. Was the gold being stashed on the base in Vladivostok? Where was the missing link - the body of the trooper whose foot was blown off? All of these questions, were solid support for a full-blown investigation of the Far Eastern Command.

Ziyetski contacted his communications center and requested that a call be placed once again to the Federation Security Agency headquarters in Moscow. He wanted to talk directly to Dombrayov. He hoped to again meet with Alexander Kutuzov who had returned to Moscow after spending several weeks at the Toko bank Vladivostok branch and try to confirm a suspicion that perhaps even the Moscow KGB may be reluctant to investigate - whether hundreds of billions of rubbles in gold had been removed from the National vaults in Moscow and transported east on the Trans-Siberian Railroad. With that one final fact in place, the investigation would expand from charges of obstruction of KGB investigation to mass murder, high treason and perhaps the largest theft in the history of the world. Ziyetski was determined. He hoped that his superiors, when faced with the hard and compelling facts, would be equally willing to deal with the problem.

Red Rock City, Arizona, Mid December, 1992

"You worn out old rag!" the polygamist Fred Jackson screamed at Hannah with fanatical conviction as he stormed into the house. His cousin, the town marshall, and Fred's nephew, the Mojave County Arizona deputy Sheriff were both following close behind. He slapped her across the face as he continued his tirade. "What in the hell has gotten into you? How dare you embarrass me in front of the brethren! What makes you think you have any rights?"

Hannah reeled from the blow and backed into the living room, "What are you talking about?"

" 'Cause in your stupidity, woman, you're bitin' the hand that feeds you!"

"What are you talking about?" she asked defensively.

"Look at this. You know damn good 'n well what you've done!" Fred held up a copy of the handwritten note which had appeared under the door of deputy sheriff Joe Wilson's precinct offices several weeks earlier. "You really think that runnin' to the gentiles is gonna make any difference? That's somethin' that a godless whore would do. I'm ashamed of you, but hell, nothin' you do surprises me! The gall of you - you make me sick!"

"All I want is my baby! I want her, I want to talk to her, I want to know where she is!"

"She's not your baby. She's my daughter. I'm the patriarch! You are merely the handmaiden!" Fred was making an effort to sound biblical, "I have placed her as the brethren have seen fit and approved. That is all you need to know!"

Hannah began to cry uncontrollably, sat down and curled up in a fetal position on the sofa. "What was it? Was it because I told her she could let her hair down the day we were working in the orchard - is it that, Fred? It was my fault. Don't punish Flora. She is *all* I have!"

"And it's all you ever gave!" he retorted. Fred resented Hannah because she had only produced one child for him. Even worse, sometimes in the presence of others, she had maintained that she had selected him rather than the marriage having come about through the mysterious hand of the brethren. He felt it demeaned his manhood, his religious position and signaled insubordination. A marriage not quite made in heaven did not settle well in polygamist dogma.

"Who was your little messenger, Hannah? The deputy and the town marshall want to know. You haven't been out of town. So who's your little helper - who *was* it?"

"What good will it do you if I tell you? You'll just make someone else's life miserable!"

"My dear wife," he said sarcastically, "we've got rules here. The kingdom of God is built upon rules and the brethren do not take kindly to people who sneak around and break 'em! And that's what you're doing. You let the devil run your life!"

Hannah replaced her sobs with anger. She rose to her feet defiantly. "Is it the devil that makes my heart ache wanting to know where you have taken my Flora? Do you *really* think it's God that has decided that I should be separated from the only person in this world who loves or cares about me?"

"That's just the type of devil-speak reasoning that you have been warned against in our church meet'ns. You're tryin' to turn my words around and use 'em against me. With your attitude, you will burn in hell!"

"Fred, I *am* in hell...and as far as I can tell, you're the devil himself!"

Fred had expected the presence of his nephew and cousin to frustrate his wife's defiance. Instead, amid the tears, she was standing her own ground with obstinate courage. He knew the local rumor mill would soon have all the particulars. He had to save face.

"Until you tell me who took that note into Hurricane, you' ll not live here. This is my house - I'm movin' in here, with Pauline. So far, she's been livin' with her mother, but she's my wife and your sister-wife. I just know you'll like livin' downstairs in the dugout, Hannah. Serves you right! And don't plan on startin' any of your nonsense, or you're not even stayin' in the basement. Life can only get worse for you, you know. And if you don't tell me pretty quick about the note, me and my relatives here might just have to talk with you some more. You won't like it, Hannah - maybe you can give one of 'em a call. Just dial 911!" He began to walk out.

She pleaded, "I don't *care* what you do with me! Just tell me about

Flora! I see you have a new car, a new diamond ring, so I know you've placed her with someone with money. It must be one of the brethren. Who is it, Fred?''

''You'll hear when I want to tell ya! It's for damn sure my daughter is more able to live with the tests of this here life than you, Hannah. So in the eternities, she'll be in the family, but you - hell, you'll *never* prove yourself!''

Confident that he now had the upper hand in the discussion, Fred stormed from the house with his two relatives hoping they would report that Fred Jackson knew how to handle an errant wife. Anything to the contrary would hurt his prospects for advancement in the religious leadership, a goal which was the subject of his greatest desire. He already had five wives, but he knew if he paid his dues to the brethren he could have ten or more before his siring years were done.

''If she had just had more children, perhaps she wouldn't be such a sour old bitch,'' he commented to his associates as they each climbed into their pick-up trucks and drove away to more important tasks.

Moscow, Russian Republic, Mid December, 1992

The return to Moscow from Vladivostok had been all he hoped it would be. Nieca was there, waiting for him at the airport. As Alexander walked across the tarmac toward her, he felt his steps become lighter. What a lucky man I am - I will be a devoted husband. The guilt that had plagued him, memories of his deceased wife, faded as he drew Nieca into his arms.

''I missed you so..!'' Nieca threw her arms around Alexander, looking almost like a daughter hugging her father- until they kissed.

''So, are we still on schedule for the wedding?'' Alexander just wanted to hear the positive words.

''Oh yes, while you were gone, I took vacation and planned it all. I'm so happy!'' The couple strolled through the airport, their arms linked closely, aware only of each other.

The wedding occurred a week later. It was brief and without fanfare or celebration. Nieca had packed her car and met Alexander at his apartment. Adding his suitcase to the luggage in the trunk, they drove to the Marriage Registry at the corner of Bochkova and Mira Prospect, one of seven such official offices in the city.

Both had been married once before and neither was interested in extended family and relative involvement. Although Alexander sensed the need for a religious ceremony, he had chosen not to raise the subject. He had been hesitant to discuss it with Nieca. Accordingly, a purely civil marriage was held in the presence of various official marriage registry employees as the obligatory witnesses.

Nieca had chosen an attractive blue dress to match her eyes for the occasion, and Alexander a new tie. The purchase of a suit had been out of the question. Rubles simply could not be stretched to afford such a luxury. His money would be better spent paying for the honeymoon. Nevertheless, the photographer who flashed pictures as they alighted from the doors of the official building and kissed on the steps, enthusiastically carried on as though he were photographing the wedding of the century. He captured in pictures the expression of their happiness.

Nieca owned her own automobile. It was a Volga of early 1980's vintage, but still a car that seemed to run well, had good tires and, best of all, sported a large gas tank. The car was a luxury unknown to a majority of Muscovites, including Alexander. As she explained, it had belonged to her husband before the divorce and had been maintained through the joint efforts of her mother and herself. Alexander viewed it as just another example of Nieca's remarkable resourcefulness. Not only was she beautiful, but she was also very smart.

They drove northward, out of the city to a resort on Beloye Ozero, a lake in the rolling forested hills eighty miles north of Moscow. Though Alexander was, by nature slightly reserved, Nieca's enthusiasm for their time together made the honeymoon everything they had hoped for. The resort had included a restaurant, cure baths and also excellent ice skating on the large frozen lake. The couple spent long hours walking and talking.

Much of the time, Alexander sat at one of the small tables watching Nieca glide across the ice. It was obvious to him that she could have been a professional skater or perhaps a teacher, both significant callings among the Russian people. She was a most feminine athlete. She had given up so much to take care of her ailing mother and had then entered into a marriage that, as she explained, had been earmarked for disaster resulting in great stress both prior to and after the divorce. She put forth a compelling argument that it was never wise to marry a soldier. Alexander pledged to himself that their union was bringing Nieca out of her past and into the future in the same way as she had so effectively done for him.

The accommodations at the lake side resort, near the town of Belozersk, had deteriorated since Alexander's previous visit to the area twenty years earlier. The pains of the supposed freemarket adjustment were evident as the entire facility was short on staff and barely staying open, despite the large number of guests. In earlier days, guests did not have to carry their own luggage and were treated very well, considerably different from the normal humdrum of life among the Moscow masses. The whole point of the resort was to give people an opportunity for true rest and relaxation as a sort of reward for their hard labor on behalf of the State. Now that the State was no longer the focus of one's work, rewards superior to vacations at Belozersk were filling the dreams of many Russian workers. Long lines that had been the trademark of both pre and post 1991 Coup Russia, had become the order of the day even at the resorts.

For Alexander, even standing in line, waiting to rent ice skates or to be seated at a restaurant was a pleasure, so long as Nieca was by his side. She seemed so knowledgeable and refined on a variety of subjects. To him, she was a woman of incredible instincts, timing and wit. His thoughts were filled with Nieca, and he did everything he could do to tell her through word and deed how much he loved her.

The final night of their honeymoon, they sat in the restaurant behind the large windows which overlooked the lake and the snow-covered hill country beyond. They had exchanged ideas on many subjects. Alexander had told Nieca things he had never shared with another person. This night they retreated early to their small bungalow. How wonderful it is to love and be loved, Alexander thought as he watched Nieca sleeping. How lucky I am.

Tomorrow they would return to Moscow to begin a new life together as the Family Kutuzov with Nieca continuing her job working three days a week at Toko Bank. Alexander would face the challenges of the stressful and precarious situation in which he had placed himself.

"There is one thing that bears heavily on my mind," he spoke in somber tones. Nieca's attention was immediate. "Since tomorrow we return to work, I must tell you that I am very concerned. I am worried about the bank."

"Well, what worries might you have? Alexander, you are free to tell me anything. After all, I am your wife," she said evenly.

"That you are, Nieca." He smiled and thought momentarily of the previous night before he continued on with his thought. "I learned some things in Vladivostok. They led me to make one inquiry in Moscow before our honeymoon."

"What was your inquiry, Alexander? Share your concerns with me." She seemed sincerely interested, it was another attribute that Alexander treasured.

Alexander looked at her a moment, then said, "You remember that Trans-Siberian train that was attacked last September?"

"Yes, I do. Who doesn't?"

"I was ordered by the cashier to put the money on that train. And up until ... that is, up until my trip to Vladivostok, I had no idea what else was on that train. But now, I strongly suspect there were billions and billions of rubbles in gold being shipped. I think that someone at Toko Bank, as well as the other State banks that are holding the gold reserves of the Russia Republic, authorized the placement of gold bars onto that train. I'm not alone, I think the KGB thinks the same thing."

"How can you know that?" she asked inquisitively.

"On my arrival in Vladivostok, the KGB contacted me. They questioned me as to how much gold was on the train. Of course I told them I had nothing to do with the transfer of gold. But I did know exactly what there was in currency and rubles. It was not something anyone would kill fifty-eight people over. The KGB told me very little, but I was asked to try and confirm whether or not gold was actually removed from the vaults."

"Are you really going to do that? I mean, gather information about this bank for the KGB?" she asked.

"If it's true, Nieca, your job and my job are finished anyway. These banks will not survive as they deplete their cash reserves and then allow the gold to be stolen.''

"I can't believe that the First Deputy or anyone else at the bank would be a conspirator to such a thing!'' she spoke scoldingly in a loud whisper.

"These foreign accounts of the Aviation Ministry... they are all undocumented. For all we know, the money is going into private accounts overseas. Who would ever know? Under this system, we can't check the supposed 'Dark Accounts' for top secret weapons funding. Have you heard of any new weapons lately? It's possible that the money just runs out of the country through our own Toko Bank international department. We really don't know what's going on. I can't be responsible for the country, but if there's a way that we can save the bank, then we can save our jobs. What else can I do? What would you do if the bank goes out of business?''

"Banks don't go out of business.''

"Oh, yes they do! It's just something new for us here in Russia. In the past, the government printed all the money and mined and processed all the gold that was necessary, but it can't do it anymore. We have to show a profit by making good loans that are good investments or we are out of business. There is no State Treasury or anyone else that will bail us out. You know, in America, banks fail all the time. If they don't make a profit, they go out of business and everyone who works for the bank loses his job.''

"That sounds so terrible and wrong,'' Nieca said. "It's as though nobody cares.''

Alexander interrupted, "It's just that the State is not in a position to care. It's very simple. We show a profit or we lose!''

"So, what will you do?''

"I think the KGB really wants to get to the bottom of this. The colonel I spoke with in Vladivostok was not a banker, but he was a very smart man. He viewed it as a conspiracy against the State and he has every intention of finding out if the gold is there or not. I have ways. I have some very good contacts. I believe that within the next two or three weeks, I will have an answer.''

"Are you sure you want to do this?''

"I have no choice.''

''Well, just remember that you've got me with you no matter what you do.'' Nieca was reassuring.

Alexander smiled and looked into the beautiful blue eyes of the blond Russian woman who was now his wife. ''And to me, that is the most amazing thing - you are my wife.''

CHAPTER 16

Caucus Mountains, Early January, 1993

A rare winter thaw had at first turned the southern foothills of the Transcaucus range into mud. But following another week of moderate weather, the wet earth had begun to solidify into workable dirt. For the farmers in the Svanathian Valley, it would have been time to start preparing fields for an early planting on the bet that only one or two major snow storms would hit the area again before spring. For the deep-rooted crops, the snows served as a blanket to protect the earth and allow for an accelerated sprouting and early harvest. It also served as a sort of insurance policy against the frosts of late summer and early fall that often rendered the work of spring and summer less significant.

This year was an exception. The equipment and workers in the fields were much fewer in number. Farmers had spent their winter planning not for the upcoming planting season, but for the attack against the Russian installation occupying the mountain ridges north of the valley.

Taking advantage of the change in the weather, Lado Deniken had moved more of his artillerymen to the battery he had placed on the ridge on the edge of the Kartalinian Forest. Although the better part of his command had braved the cold temperatures and extreme weather conditions for the worst part of the winter, he had chosen not to station infantrymen on the ridge under the assumption the Russians at the enemy installation would likewise be held at bay by the harsh weather. The prospects of a preemptive strike were unlikely.

With the thaw and now firm ground, he moved seven-hundred more of his Svanathian Militia into positions at various points from the base to the top of the hill on which the battery was located. He still harbored no illusions that the hill could be successfully defended against an all out attack by the elite Spetsnaz. But he also knew that it was likely that for every Spetsnaz trooper lost, the Russians would have much more difficulty making a replacement than would the Georgians. It was not a question of if, but only a question of when the base would be taken and some of the sorrow of the families in the valley finally vindicated.

Caucus Station, Early January, 1993

It was mid-day in the spacious command meeting hall adjacent to the Dacha at Caucus Station. An enormous map of the Soviet Union was displayed on the north wall showing no regard for the changes that recent events had forged across the face of the Euro-Asian land mass. Two ornate wooden desks of the finest in nineteenth century workmanship were positioned at the head of a long oak conference table at which some thirty uniformed men were seated in order of rank. In the center of the table was positioned a black marble bust of Lenin facing obligatorily to the east. The men were stern-faced and smartly dressed bearing the insignia of the Spetsnaz officer from ensign to general.

The south wall was covered almost entirely by an electronic bulletin board which allowed those sitting at the desks to write on note pads and have their words displayed on the large board for all to see. Each Spetsnaz officer had his black beret tucked securely under his bright red right shoulder board. The men did not smile nor did they talk to one another. Rather they sat motionless as ominous foreboding reminders of an empire which the better part of the world was trying hard to forget.

A high pitched tone sounded and all men in the room leaped to their feet at attention in almost Pavlovian response. A uniformed steward near a doorway in ritualistic fashion announced, ''Attention sons of the Rodina, the meeting of the STAVKA Command Council is now in session. Be prepared to respond as ordered. Long live the Union of Soviet Socialist Republics!'' The entire group responded in unison the words, ''Long live the Union of Soviet Socialist Republics!'' in perfect Hitlerian ''Zieg Heil'' form.

Two men took their position at the immaculately polished desks. To the left was Yuri Andropov. And to the right was the one viewed during his life as the epitome of the Communist man, Yuri Gagarin - the great hero himself.

It was clear from the astonished looks on the faces of many of the men in attendance that this was their first opportunity to be in the presence of the STAVKA. Some ventured a judicious, yet discreet look at Gagarin, the idol of their youth, and also at Andropov, the most feared of KGB chieftains and president of the Motherland, that is - before his supposed death. It was an indisputable confirmation for many, of the almost supernatural power of the leadership they had been trained to devoutly serve. Most had left their families and devoted their lives to the service of the Motherland. To see their leaders in person, who, according to Communist dogma, had passed on to a strata of existence availed to only the most elite of the communist world, rewarded their sacrifice and confirmed their faith in the STAVKA.

Presently, Yuri Andropov stood up and looked across the room. He fixed his gaze upon each of the uniformed soldiers. This quiet process took several minutes. He stopped periodically to stare coldly at certain persons as though he had the power to look through them and into their souls.

After a time, he put on his reading glasses, picked up a paper and began to read with strong voice, ''My dear Comrades, I have looked into each of your faces. They tell to me that some of you feel yourselves to be in a state of depression. Even as you congregate in this room, you feel that the great Rodina has somehow lost her vigor, lost her place, and lost her purpose. If the feeling exists in this room, then one might conclude that it also exists broadly throughout the land. But for that reason we bring each of you here. We address you as Comrades, as leaders of the true Soviet Union - the Soviet Union now, and as it shall be again in the very near future.

"Yes, I notice that some of you raise your eyebrows to that question. That it could happen in this room might be viewed as treason by some, but I will allow you at least for a moment to consider it a logical response until you learn the truth." He paused, looked the group over carefully, then continued, "Some of you are new. We have brought you into the highest levels of the Spetsnaz leadership so that you can hear and understand the position of the STAVKA. We speak the truth. We tell you of things that are not known to the rest of the world. The power that we possess in its immensity is the power to destroy the world with the push of a button, the power to redirect the entire configuration of Europe, the power to give nations their freedom or to take it away. We possess the power of life itself upon this planet. We possess the power of longevity beyond that which is known anywhere else in the world.

"I am now in the eighth decade of my life, I plan to live to at least one hundred and twenty-five years. If you think such a statement is mere wishful thinking or science fiction, stay close to us, and you will come to understand the truth!" He spoke with an infectious fervor that bound the audience to his every word.

"I wish to speak to you of a grand illusion. You may look at me and say it is a magic that such an old man could in reality be so young. For I have a very young heart. Some years ago, the Soviet Institute of Medical Science and the successes of STAVKA scientists granted me the opportunity and the good fortune to have the heart of a strong nineteen year old Georgian sheepherder planted within my chest. So you could say that despite my many years, my heart is only twenty-eight years of age. This makes me a very strong man. This gives me a chance to live a very long and fruitful life."

Andropov's rhetoric turned condescending, "Perhaps you are disturbed by the fact that the Eastern Bloc nations are now falling under the shadow or umbrella, if you will, of the Germans and the Americans? Or, you dwell upon the fact that there appears to be a new relationship developing between Eastern and Western nations? Perhaps you are pained by the fact that there appears to be a strong march toward Western-style democracy throughout the Soviet Union as if it were an irreversible disease? Does it appear that a supposed freemarket economy is coming about, attempting to emulate everything that the Americans and their Wall Street have to offer?

"You could ponder all of these things forever, as if they were reality, and as if the world is changing with them. However, the hard truth, my dear Comrades, is yes, there is change, but no, the change is not bad, nor does the change in any respect negate the efforts of the Revolution or the emergence of the new Communist man as the predominant benefactor of the world's wealth. For only when this earth is entirely held in the hands of the true Communist, then can it survive into the twenty-first century and beyond."

Andropov triggered the switch for the electronic blackboard and began drawing his own version of an historical diagram. "It became obvious, even before I was President of the Soviet Union that our nation was in need of a considerable influx of capital in order to launch a true Communist revolution throughout the world. This was recognized as long ago as the mid-fifties. It became clear at that time that the hand of fate, if you will, or the fortunes of history had granted to Western Europe and the United States much of the indigenous wealth of the globe. Many of us knew, as we studied economic theory in our earlier days, that despite all of our efforts as a part of the revolution in this land, we would not be able to catch up with developments in the Western World unless there was a substantial infusion of wealth, technology, and capital into the Soviet Union. So long as we lived in a world which had capital markets elsewhere, we would have had no choice but to take advantage of all that those capital markets have to offer. Thus, it was determined that at some point before the end of the twentieth century, an effort would have to be undertaken in which the substantial wealth of the capitalist world would be transferred to the Motherland. The Western World would call it a market correction. We call it the final step before 'The Second and Final Coming of the Communist Revolution.' " The men in the room were silent, their concentration riveted on their leader.

"During the late fifties and in the early sixties, many of our leaders

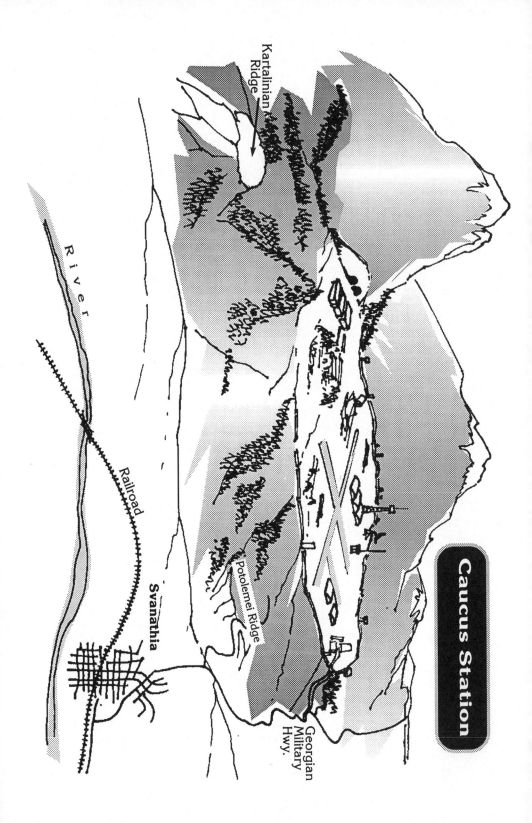

attempted to affect this transformation by way of military revolution throughout the world. This turned out to be ineffective for the reason that many of our allies such as Eastern Europe, Vietnam, and Egypt were already so destitute from an economic standpoint that they were unable to affect successful revolution against the powerful U.S. - supported industrial dictatorships of the world.

"By the end of the Second World War, it became clear to several of our key theoreticians, that the Western World was willing to engage in a very strange form of conduct. Specifically, following a victory in war, they would open up their coffers and hand out money, aid and capital to totally reconstruct the infrastructures of their former enemies. We saw West Germany arise from the ashes of war to be rebuilt with American dollars. The nation of Japan is now the second leading economy in the world, and it was largely built upon the goodwill of the United States. Thus, it was clear to us that both Germany and Japan had successfully found ways to seep the wealth out of America and into their own countries.

"The pattern seemed consistent and reached the point of being thoroughly measurable by our economists, as Third World surrogate forces of the Soviet Union would find themselves routinely losing on the battlefield only to have their own economies substantially propped up by dollars and aid from the United States. We saw this occur earlier in Egypt and more recently in Angola and Nicaragua. Our economists concluded that one of the best situations in which to find oneself would be that of the vanquished in war with the United States and its Western allies.

"It was clear to us that if we had exercised our prerogative to destroy much of the Western World and particularly the United States in a nuclear war, we would suffer in two respects. First, our country would certainly not come away unaffected and unscarred by such a war. Although we were certain we could win, the negative effects of massive nuclear detonations were unpredictable and difficult to comprehend. Secondly, if we were to destroy much of the Western World, the wealth of that world would no longer be transferable to the Soviet Union. This is a very small planet. Thus, it was concluded that the best method to pursue would be one which we could exploit the cold war to the maximum, and then feign a loss of that war. As we saw the American President, Ronald Reagan, referring to us as the 'evil empire' we knew that we had reached a point in which this plan could be implemented.

''President Reagan's zeal and relentless verbal attacks on the Soviet Union for his own political purposes played appropriately into our hands. It was most opportune that we could then lose the cold war and at the same time place ourselves in a situation in which massive wealth of the Western World would be transferred to the Soviet Union. It would allow for the transfer of technology that was heretofore off-limits due to its military application. The general improvement of living conditions in almost every segment of our society would ultimately result, and this would be accomplished mainly on the backs of the American taxpayers.

''All that we had to do to accomplish this, was simply allow the Berlin Wall to fall in front of rolling TV cameras and withdraw our forces from Eastern Europe. We also had to stand down our military readiness throughout the world - a military which has always been costly and non-productive. Finally, we needed to allow various political experiments such as Peristroika and Glasnost to ripple through the republics of the Soviet Union which would give heart to Western politicians and cause them to feel that suddenly, overnight, the Motherland has become a Western-style democracy with its arms open wide awaiting whatever gifts are sent by rail, sea or air from the West.

''Have you looked at the gifts lately?...nearly three hundred billion through the International Monetary Fund or direct from the U.S., Japan, Germany and the Saudis since the wall came down! Not bad... not bad in my book and not bad in yours! We create a little drama between Yeltsin and the Congress of Peoples' deputies, and billions flow from the Western spigot. We cause them to fret over the security of our nuclear weapons, and they pay billions just to get the chance to disarm a few old ones that we would never use. Not a bad business...eh?'' Andropov started to laugh. His supporters quickly responded to the cue and joined in.

''And so, it is all rather academic. We plan to reinstate control over the Soviet Union once the West has rebuilt it. A good Western capitalist would say it's always smart to do business with other people's money. I tend to agree.'' The laughter occurred again in a lesser volume.

''History is on our side. The time will come when the entire country and its people will fall in line like sheep, pledging allegiance to whomever controls the Kremlin. It happened in the days of the Czars, in the days of

Lenin, in the days of Yeltsin and it will happen again.

"It should be noted that we are much closer to our goals than the present condition in the Soviet Union might indicate. Although we have experienced considerable problems over the past several decades in the Motherland, it is clear that throughout the world, basic socialist principles have been largely accepted and implemented by supposed non-socialist democracies. One need only look at the morass of social programs in each of the countries of Western Europe to see that socialism is being pursued by government decree and with the approval of broad constituencies. They don't want to admit it, but it is clear that most of the systems rely on principles which fall consistently within the doctrines of Marxist-Leninist Communism.

"The adoption of such doctrines throughout the world is inevitable. It is consistent with all that we have been taught and have grown to love. Thus, with the proper infusion of capital, the Soviet Union can finally become the leading Socialist democracy of the world. The Motherland is on the verge of a renaissance and it will soon be able to control virtually the entire world."

Andropov was winding down, sensing an air of absolute consensus from his listeners. "So, in conclusion, Comrades, you should realize it is all part of a grand illusion. And each of you are playing a role in causing the illusion to come about for the good and welfare of the Soviet people. With the objective of implementing all of those goals for which we have striven over all the years of our lives, you should understand that there will be a Second Coming - of sorts.

"At the perfect moment, Comrade Gagarin and I shall come out of our hiding and retake the helm of the Soviet State. The entire world will be shocked. But as we stand firm with the dedicated Communists within the Congress of Peoples' Deputies and Communists throughout the world, it will be a moving and religious experience for the Soviet people on a scale that will shake the foundations of the entire world. A new Communism, distinctly different - distinctly smarter than its predecessor, shall be spread across the face of the earth.

"And when we appear - that is Comrade Gagarin and myself, the Russian people will be able to accept and be inspired by the greatness of the STAVKA. The time will soon come when Yeltsin has all but wrecked the country economically. The masses will surely submit to the STAVKA. Can you imagine the day when Yuri Gagarin shall suddenly appear, high on the Kremlin Wall to proclaim to the world the STAVKA's return and the emergence of a new world order? Think of the hopes, the dreams and the drive to serve the Motherland that it will inspire among our people. As we bask in the warm sun of prosperity, the Western World will be decapitating itself in the guillotine of self destruction.

"The only salvation will be to align with the Motherland in her days of renaissance and enlightenment. Yeltsin and his force of minions cannot stand in our way. The people will rally to Yuri Gagarin - their hero. They will feel safe in the restoration of a strong Supreme Soviet and Congress of Peoples' Deputies. They will not be safe with Yeltsin. He will be a lone voice among the masses when the Hero of the Soviet Union returns.

"Safety will be achieved only by looking East! It will happen sooner than you think if we all work hard to realize this important objective. But it must be exactly at the correct time! It is a very delicate balancing act. It must happen at the last possible moment. We cannot allow Yeltsin to destroy the Congress of Peoples' Deputies, but neither can we effect this Second Coming before the huge amounts of capital needed have flowed in from the West...there can be no mistakes!"

Andropov paused, looked up and studied the gathering closely. He began to clap his hands together in slow, deliberate applause. Within seconds, the entire group was standing and delivering an enthusiastic ovation to all that had been spoken. Andropov finally raised his hands to quiet the group, reached down and picked up his wine glass. Holding it high before him, he made a toast, "To Rodina, may She live forever!"

The toast was repeated in unison and they all drank in fervent agreement.

Red Rock City, Arizona, Mid January, 1993

It was 5:30 a.m. on a cold winter morning in the stark confines of Red Rock City. Hannah Jackson had been unable to sleep. She had spent much of the time watching a spider spinning a web among the floor slats on the basement ceiling. It had been a diversion of sorts. She could otherwise think of nothing but Flora. She had not seen her for almost four months.

It was 6:30 a.m. and time to start her day. She had been placed in a job by her husband making nurses' uniforms in a sewing factory located within the closed community. Hannah looked forward to the day's work because someone may have information or be willing to talk to her about Flora. She did not doubt that many of the women probably knew all of the facts and circumstances concerning the placement of her daughter in a polygamous marriage. But for anyone to breach the mandate of secrecy issued by the brethren, was tantamount to heresy and would result in unbearable scorn. In a community such as Red Rock City, scorn was something that could be turned off and on like a light bulb by the religious leadership and city fathers who were all one in the same. For any person to interfere with the marital arrangements or dictates of the leadership was simply intolerable.

The cult had small enclaves across the West from Arizona to Canada. Hannah's worst fear was that Flora may have been spirited away into a plural marriage with a man old enough to be her grandfather living a thousand miles away in the small town of Lister, near Cardston in the province of Alberta, Canada where the group had its own colony. She knew that her chances of traveling to Canada to look for her daughter were remote. Should her husband travel to Lister, she knew she would not be taken along. She was no longer the desired servant of his baser interests, particularly when he had four other wives who were considerably younger. Pauline, the fifteen year old, was her ultimate nightmare.

Hannah thought back on the moment of her own wedding. "Just place your heart on the alter and serve this man," the leader had said. "He will always be good to you. He will raise you in the gospel if you will but be obedient to his dictates." It had seemed as if there were angels in the room, as she remembered that day in the home of their leader. But somewhere, at some point, even before Fred Jackson had taken a second wife, Hannah realized that life was changing. Fred, at twenty-eight, had began spending considerable time watching the teenage girls at church. It disturbed her that a man supposedly true to concepts of virtue would spend so much time flirting and carrying on with high school girls.

It was in her eighth month of pregnancy, when a neighbor from across the street stopped to visit. The visit was brief, to the point and not cordial. The neighbor was delighted that she could be the first to tell Hannah that Fred had taken a second wife in Phoenix, Arizona. So it was in Red Rock City - a sort of continuing rumor mill, where inside knowledge of the latest exploits of the brethren relegated one to a position of power, influence and adulation.

Although the polygamist communities were spread across the western United States, most members were closely interrelated. Marriages among first cousins were frequent and second cousin marriages were routine. Yet with all the familiarity, no one had even intimated or even teased her on the subject of Flora's disappearance. She had been neither congratulated nor had she been warned. It seemed disturbing and different from conditions as they had existed in the past.

The power of the polygamist leadership had intimidated the women of Red Rock City to the point where a mother would not be expected to stand up for her daughter under any circumstances. Her attempt to send a message to the ''gentiles'' in the sheriff's department on the Utah side of the border had been futile. Of course, she thought to herself, our leaders have bragged about their control of the police, of politicians, of prosecutors, and of the welfare departments. It would only make sense that they would be the first to know when I attempted to send a note out for help.

I wonder if God really cares about women and children? Is duty and obligation really more important than love and respect? Am I just a baby machine that hasn't worked very well - am I so worn out and dilapidated that I am just thrown out for scrap? If all that the brethren tell us is true, then why is there so much hatred, so much secrecy, deception and pain within the group? Are there mothers elsewhere in this world whose daughters are taken away in the name of God, and placed as concubines of filthy old men? Are there fathers, somewhere, who love their daughters more than they love money? After I find my daughter...I will leave this place.

Caucus Mountains, Mid January, 1993

After eating a lunch of traditional Georgian meal kefir and steamed vegetables, Lado Deniken finished his tea as well as an entire quart of natural spring water. He determined to forego a bath in the cold river in favor of the excitement of the moment. Within the past hour, he had received the order to attack.

Shortly after lunch, Deniken was in his command truck, leading a column of several vehicles on the road towards his artillery on the Kartalinian Ridge. It would be the first time that he had attempted to move trucks up the hill in the middle of winter. He was still reliant on the thaw and the dry weather to keep the road clear. This was significant, for he was certain that at the appropriate time the road would be the only lifeline of retreat for those fortunate enough to escape the anticipated counterattack against the hill. He chose, for the moment, not to share such concerns with his men.

As they drove, he thought back on what had transpired over the course of the past several years. He had gone from a relatively peaceful man to one totally consumed with the need to spill the blood of the Russians at the high mountain base. His freedom of choice on the issue had long since been subordinated to focus on the mission at hand. Continually, he found himself thinking up new epithets for Russians, and slogans which would express his desire for liberty and freedom for his people.

Yet, in the back of his mind, he still wrestled with the reality that even without the use of the suitable sheepherding ground above the ridge where the Russian base was located, life had still been mostly peaceful and free in the Svanathian Valley for two years. The Russians, who had seemed to make trouble in years past as sort of conquerors from the North, had been scarcely visible in Svanathia since the transformation of the Soviet Union.

Deniken found himself driven by an innate sixth sense that told him that Russians could not maintain their bases on Georgian soil under any circumstances. In Deniken's life, he had never considered the alternatives. Things had to change. He often struggled within himself to determine the source of the supposed patriotism. In the night, often in the middle of a perplexing dream, he would find himself battling Russians hand to hand and committing atrocities of which he would never approve in a lucid state. He wondered if he would ever live to become a Dolgozhiteli, one of the centenarians of the hill-country, or if a Russian bullet would stop him first.

But the most prominent question loomed deep within the recesses of his mind as he considered his son. The Russian base had to be removed because his son had been found dead, a victim of some force which the Russians had put in motion. He often wondered, had the wolves taken his son, would he spend the rest of his life feverishly occupied with hunting the wolves of the Kartalinian Forest? But now, all that he needed was the final order from Tbilisi to open fire. Within two hours, he would be standing next to the 130 millimeter M-46 Field Gun. The round would be placed in the breech, and upon his affirmative command, for better or worse, he would become the prisoner of his own dreams.

Caucus Station, Mid January, 1993

Several key experts had made their presentations throughout the day and now Yuri Gagarin was winding up his own speech on the specifics of how control over the former Soviet Union would be implemented. "The success of the reassertion of centralized control across the broad reaches of the Soviet Union depends largely upon what information we have available at the time of the Second Coming. In this regard, the STAVKA has been gathering critical information for some ten years. Our operatives have been working with the Communists in the Russian Parliament to maintain a constant flow of information to identify our enemies across the land. Now that everyone speaks so freely, it is not hard to know who stands for and who stands against the revolution.''

He placed a chart on the electronic blackboard using the pointer to illustrate. ''Much of our earlier intelligence on internal dissent was acquired from the Seventh Chief directorate of the KGB, prior to its demise. This was done by using an extensive array of personal computers. Now, the job is even easier as we merely track Russian and Western television news reports and features on the former Soviet Union which regularly show us a host of information that will help us in the Second Coming.

''Fortunately, shortly before the KGB was compromised, through its industrial espionage group, it acquired two American-built Cray II computers. They have virtually all of the power we need to keep track of our enemies at all levels both inside and outside of the Soviet Union. The computers are currently installed at our computer center which is located to the rear of the aircraft hangars here at Caucus Station.

''Of course, all of the regular information that has existed for years in the data banks of the KGB the GRU and the Spetsnaz is likewise on our system.

''I would, however, caution you on one point further. In the event of the evacuation of Caucus Station, this information would, as of necessity, need to be removed and reinstalled at the new location. The Cray II computers are large, bulky and difficult to transport. Thus, we have engaged in backup procedures which we hope will protect this information. I cannot sufficiently stress the importance that this information is at the heart of the STAVKA plan. Without the information as to who is with us and who is against us, it would be very difficult to implement the Second Coming.

''I have spent the better part of my life in anticipation of the Second Coming of the Communist Revolution. I could have spent it basking in the glory of my achievements in space, but instead, I accepted the challenge to bring forth the greatness of the Motherland in a new day. These glorious moments are almost upon us. With all the changes that are now occurring in the world, I assure you that the new day of which I speak will be here very soon.''

Hurricane, Utah, Mid January, 1993

It was nine o'clock in the morning in Hurricane, Utah and Joe Wilson was just going on duty. Having debriefed the deputy who had worked the night shift, Joe reviewed the notes and messages to which he would need to respond during the course of the day. This led him to call the Washington County sheriff on the telephone to discuss a matter regarding a boundary dispute which had become violent the night before. One neighbor had apparently taken a shovel to another and drawn a considerable amount of blood in the process. Not only the sheriff, but several deputies had been required to respond to the problem. It had taken them almost half an hour to control the suspect and finally get him in a patrol car for the drive to St. George where he was booked for assault and resisting arrest. However, in the course of the confusion, no officer had thought to take custody of the shovel itself.

With all of this explained and instructions given to Joe by the sheriff to go to the residence and obtain the shovel, then take it to the victim at the hospital for identification, the discussion turned to other things. The conversation seemed cordial and routine until Joe asked, ''Do you remember that note that was stuck under my door last month? You know...the missing person in Red Rock City? The report has never been returned to me.''

''You know what the policy is, Joe,'' the sheriff responded strongly. ''On all matters that involve the polygs, we let their own law enforcement people take care of it. What goes on out there is none of our damn business!''

''Well, I know it's a strange place,'' Joe continued, ''but Sheriff, something just isn't right. That deal involved a missing girl, a young one. It was her mother wanting to find out where she is. It seems like that's something a mother should know.   And I feel like...well, sort of like I haven't done my duty, as if somebody has asked me to find a missing person and I haven't even tried."

"You did your duty by turning in the report.   It's been handled," the sheriff interrupted.

"Well, are you telling me that this missing person has been found?" Joe asked rhetorically.

"No, I'm not saying that," the sheriff responded.

"Sheriff, I've lived here in Hurricane all my life. I remember what it was like one night at the market when a car from Red Rock City pulled up while I was bagging groceries. A girl jumped out of the car and began to run. An old guy jumped out and started to chase her. She ran a couple of blocks down Main Street when one of those fancy pick-up trucks that the polygs drive cut off her escape. It had Arizona plates, and you could tell it was the polygs. They grabbed that girl, threw her in the truck and drove her right back up to the old bugger. I was only fourteen and didn't really know what was going on. But after I went in the store, one of the ladies said that 'it looked like another polyg marriage off to a rough start.' I mean the guy must have been in his sixties or so. She was just a little girl.

"When I was in the fifth grade. We had a girl from the polygamist group in our class. I'm still not sure why she was in our class, because she was the only one in the school. But she...you know...she started to develop and as soon as she became like a woman... I mean she was only about eleven years old, she was pulled out of school. The next year I saw her down in St. George. She was with a bunch of other women, and I could hardly believe what I saw. There she was... pregnant. Later I found out that she died trying to have the baby. The guy she was married to was seventy years old. Now, if that's what's going on with this missing person thing in Red Rock City, don't you think we should check it out?"

"Hell, Joe, bothering the polygs is not going to get us anywhere," the sheriff insisted. "They have their own ways and its nothing that we're going to change. They've been doing that polygamy thing for years and I really don't think it's any different than any guy who just has a bunch of girlfriends - at least they marry 'em. That's a lot more than I can say about most of the deadbeats around here."

"But what if this letter that we got is about a girl who doesn't want to get married to some old guy? I mean, if she's been forced against her will into a marriage and her mother hasn't approved of it, isn't that kidnapping?''

''Well, if it is kidnapping, then that's a Federal offense, and that's nothing that *you* should be worried about. They have their own way of doing things, and no matter what you do, it will be considered religious discrimination - it will be bad for the department. So, you keep the hell away from them, you understand?''

The telephone conversation ended. Joe knew that his standing with his employer had continued to worsen. But he also sensed that there was something more that he had to do. The woman behind the note - he had to talk to her.

CHAPTER 17

Caucus Station, Mid January, 1993

It was nightfall when all of the reports had been presented to the STAVKA leadership. Stewards were now in the process of serving a meal as the group continued with its work session into the evening. The most significant message had been saved for the final session. Andropov would reveal the STAVKA's most secret plan.

"I will now reveal to you the results of our many years of study." Andropov had several assistants unveil a large chart with a map next to it, with the words scrawled across the top: **FOREIGN RESIDENCE CONTINGENCY PLAN**.

He again began to speak, pointer in hand. "This plan is based upon a specific principle of fundamental Spetsnaz tactics. Always hide where you will never be sought. Accordingly, there are three underlying premises upon which the plan is based.

"One: That it may not be in the STAVKA's best interest to remain within the borders of the Soviet Union during the periods of civil strife and upheaval occasioned by the country's flirtation with freemarket capitalism and Western-style democracy.

"Two: Until the Second Coming is fully implemented, there will be local officials who could seek to seize Spetsnaz and STAVKA assets for political purposes. As we know, at this time every government official is trying to find someone to blame for the poor performance of the economy." An earsplitting crack shot through the room as he whacked the chart with the pointer.

"Point number three: The existence of the STAVKA is largely perceived as a myth throughout the greater Soviet Union. To allow our identities or our actual existence to be discovered prior to the orderly implementation of the Second Coming would obviously destroy its prospect for success. The existence of myself and Comrade Gagarin must continue to be held in strict confidence.

"With the foregoing issues in mind, it became important that we put into place a process for determining a location, should it be necessary, for the STAVKA to leave the territory of the Soviet Union. We therefore established the following criteria:

"It requires a setting similar to the one we presently have which includes facilities for our Dacha retreat and also for regular transportation by air to and from the facility.

"It must be located in an area in a remote region of the world with minimal population, yet afford the conveniences which we deem necessary for our purposes. We find the present circumstances here at Caucus Station to be somewhat unacceptable in this regard." He lifted his brows and looked at the other men in the room, searching each face for accommodation. "Being located only ten miles above Svanathia has proven to be difficult. And it is likely that more problems will arise if we do not evacuate this base at some point in the near future.

"The facility must be within ten degrees of the fortieth parallel with a fair to moderate climate which affords a continuing scientific research environment to facilitate maintenance of our Dolgozhiteli or longevity planning. Quality medical care must continue. We must have the ability to cultivate proper vegetables and to provide us with kefir and other approved dairy products. The access to a cold mountain river for treatment in connection with spring water and special herbs and teas must be available. This is particularly important inasmuch as Comrade Gagarin is now in his late fifties, the age range at which our medical experts consider him ripe to receive his transplant of a youthful nineteen year old heart. Given the current state of the medical research advancement by our experts, Gagarin should live well past his one hundred twenty-fifth year with good health and vigor.

"It is also important that we be somewhere near a heart transplant medical facility. The facility which we have used to this point in Yalta is no longer safe. Opportunities to conduct work there are becoming more remote and will certainly be beyond reach if we relocate outside of the country.

"Another requirement is one that we have studied in great detail. It is important to find a location that is safe and in which our people will not clash with other possible foreign or ethnic groups. In fact, we will make every effort to conceal our ethnicity, and for all intents, live privately and undetected. We must find a place in which a certain degree of lawlessness will be tolerated in order to facilitate the unencumbered operation of our group. We will avoid interference largely through the use of bribing public officials who will allow us to keep to ourselves."

He took several steps toward his audience and in a quieter voice said, "The last criteria deals with the subject of access to the financial markets. As you know, we have over a hundred billion dollars in gold now placed in Hong Kong and other Asian banks. Wherever we would locate, it is important to have the ability to communicate regularly with banking contacts without excessive interference that might disclose our existence.

"I suggest that most of you are wondering if such a place exists. It may sound like a sort of Shangri-La for the STAVKA. I can tell you we have worked long and hard on this issue. Accordingly we will now introduce you to the Director of what is known as the Zion Plan."

As Andropov spoke, a door opened. A portly man, his belly stretching the buttons on his blue chambray shirt, entered and took his position near the map on the wall. "I introduce you to a STAVKA operative. You may know him only by his code name 'Jim.' He has been an operative for the STAVKA for well over twenty years. He is Russian by birth, however, he was raised in New York City and has spent considerable time carrying out important missions for the STAVKA since 1972."

It was clear that many in the room were surprised and even irritated that a portly, unconditioned, nonuniformed, non-Spetsnaz person was now advising the STAVKA. Nevertheless, they paid close attention as he walked to the map of the world and placed his pointer directly on the Western Hemisphere.

Jim wasted no time and spoke in a very matter-of-fact style. "The assignment I was given had to be accomplished without having to recreate the wheel. It already had historical precedent. Specifically, following the First World War and more importantly World War II, disaffected German leaders fled to various parts of South America. In fact, if you were to travel to the countries of Uruguay, Paraguay and Southern Brazil, you would find certain communities in which the dominant language spoken is German rather than Portuguese or Spanish. Street signs are in German. The restaurants serve German food and blond-haired, blue-eyed Aryans are still to be found. The notorious Nazi death camp commander, Joseph Mengela survived in Brazil for forty-five years without interference. He even used his own name which was listed in the local telephone book." A chuckle went through the room.

"Of considerable interest is the methodology that was used. During the abandonment of the Third Reich in early 1945, the German SS began infiltrating many of its prime leaders into the South American area. Despite knowledge of this program by the British and intense naval blockades, the effort went largely uninhibited until well into the late 1940's. I am sure you are wondering how a migration could successfully take place that would be of such significance as to result in a complete change of certain parts of South America into German enclaves.

"The answer is simple. Quite literally the actual German leadership made the move. It was merely a process of stowing away men who seldom traveled in groups of more than three or four on ships and planes. A reception program was already in place in South America. As soon as the German leader was on South American soil, he was in the presence of armed SS troopers who were able to provide him all the protection that he needed.

"As a matter of necessity, an accommodation had to be reached with the local authorities. In South America, it was principally bribes and the threats of force that accomplished this. An additional factor, however, that over time has moderated the entire circumstance very effectively, is that the Germans did not bring women or children with them. They mixed with the best of the local women and began to conform comfortably into the indigenous society.

"They were able to largely maintain their confidentiality. Many of them changed their names, and almost none of them entered the country legally. All were undocumented, but the local authorities found it better to avoid conflict and contention with the group than cross swords with the Nazi SS units already stationed in the area. The overabundance of gold and money available from the Germans, likewise, was a major factor for success of the program.

"Now, almost fifty years later, the German contingent in those countries is living well. They still remain very much to themselves and distant from the indigenous ethnic groups. A certain compatibility has developed, however. Without question, it has proven to be a very successful program.

"As I undertook the assignment of finding the principal foreign Dacha for the STAVKA, I was asked to consider a short-term program in which it would be used as somewhat of a foreign safehouse affording the STAVKA the opportunity to be out of the Soviet Union for a period of time and facilitate the objectives which have been enunciated by Chairman Andropov today. So in using that model, I have found a location which is already operational and is fully acceptable to the STAVKA."

Jim took the pointer again and tapped firmly on the map of United States. A dull but definite disturbance emitted from the men in the room as they whispered.

The speaker was pleased with the sound. "I expected this sort of response. Because it is true, the new Dacha is located in the United States of America. We have found a location which meets every criterion more precisely than any other location in the world. And believe me, we have evaluated and reviewed every possible site.

"If you will note, the pointer is directed to the southwestern part of the United States and specifically to the southwestern corner of the state of Utah. I am indicating the location which has been the focus of the Zion Plan. You have all likely heard of the Zion Plan from time to time, and have assumed as do all, that it deals with some matter relating to resettlement of Soviet Jews. This is not the case.

"In 1976, in searching for the proper location, I, along with a colleague from the embassy, traveled through Texas, New Mexico, Arizona and then into Utah. The reason for evaluating the Utah site was that we had satellite photographs that showed the existence of a hard-surface, modern aircraft runway on the top of a high desert plateau in the corner of the state. This intrigued us, because we could not document the existence of any secret U.S. military installations in that location. Thus, we assumed that it could be an abandoned installation and perhaps a suitable site for the foreign Dacha.

"We attempted to prevail upon the local director of the Chamber of Commerce in the nearby city of St. George who, according to our intelligence, was a former colonel in the United States Air Force and had been assigned to the Office of the Air Force Chief of Staff at the Pentagon." Jim shrugged, "Unfortunately, he became suspicious of our actions. Within a few hours of our arrival, the FBI stopped us and we were ejected from the United States two weeks later for violating embassy travel restrictions.

"Although we were only in the area several hours, we were very impressed at the pristine beauty of the mountains and the remote desert canyons. It was clear, both in the satellite photos and from on-scene inspection, that the area was not densely populated. This afforded us the opportunity to inspect the other attributes of the area. We found an exquisite horse ranch located deep in one of the canyons not far from the airstrip on top of the desert mesa. The canyon was inaccessible from any direction with the exception of a remotely traveled public highway which passed near the front gate of the ranch. The ranch included facilities with a good potential for expansion. And, as a bonus, running directly through the pasture area was a clear mountain stream.

"Finally, after an extensive ground inspection several years later, agents confirmed that the canyon area was ideal for the construction of deep tunnels in the sandstone canyon walls, if necessary, to accommodate an underground system similar to that at this and other secret Spetsnaz installations.

"Most amazing, however, was the fact that within about ten miles of the ranch was a major autobahn, or superhighway as they call it in

America. It was somewhat of a contrast that such a prominent highway could be located so near a facility that is virtually cut off from the rest of the world.

"Incidentally, the reason we call this The Zion Plan is because this ranch property is located adjacent to Zion National Park, a government reserve for hiking and maintenance of wild animals which excludes in its entirety development in the area. We were assured that if we were able to acquire the ranch property, there would be no construction or neighbors who might locate near us and interfere with our security concerns.

"Even more interesting, are the peculiar dynamics of the community. It is an area of bizarre contrasts, all of which run to our favor. First, the largest community in the entire area has a population of only thirty thousand. That community known as St. George, is located over twenty-five miles south of the Dacha. The small village of Virgin, with a population of about eighty people is located approximately eight miles down the canyon from the ranch entrance. There are few businesses in the community. People who live there, work in the nearby cities of St. George or Cedar City.

"Cedar City is about forty miles to the north. The town of Hurricane, a strange name as I would say, is located eighteen miles from the front gate of the ranch. This town has approximately four to five thousand residents. But importantly, the road which runs past the ranch is not heavily traveled. It serves as the access road to a reservoir and the mountains for fishermen, backpackers or campers. Fortunately again, most of the area is off-limits to camping. The steep canyon walls prohibit backpackers from trespassing on the Dacha property. It is truly a unique situation." Jim seemed to be tiring a little. He paused and sipped a glass of water, stared vacantly for a moment, then continued.

"The story does not end there, however. The STAVKA's desire to fit the critical criteria that we have a secure area in which to locate where there is little governmental interference has been squarely met by this situation. Specifically, the government officials and local law enforcement groups seem to be timid and non-assertive. This is best explained by the existence of a polygamous religious cult that lives in a small community in the desert some thirty miles away to the southeast.

"These people are very authoritarian and extreme in their practices. They appear to have subjugated the women and children of their community to slavery. This is clearly exhibited by the fact that they have provided several young women for our own recreational needs. The fathers of these women seem unflinchingly eager to receive compensation for these services. In finally getting one of their men to discuss their true intent with me, he explained very simply that the young women are devoted to following the dictates of the religious leaders. In so doing, they could provide the service for us which would bring revenue and income into the community. They claim a sort of communal economic arrangement which I do not fully understand. Maybe they are the American version of Communists?'' All laughed.

"From what I can tell, the young women, after having learned the virtues and joys of life from us, will be placed in harems with some of the polygamist leaders. This will be their reward."

Jim could see the look of incredulity on the faces of the men throughout the room. He smiled. "I realize this sounds far-fetched and extreme. All I can tell you is that it must be one of those things unique to America. I know it works. I've tested it out first hand. The price was very reasonable and these little girls do exactly as they are told!"

The statement brought more laughter.

"The recreational amenities we thought we would lose if we left the Black Sea area are very readily available. Additionally, the communities seem to have a strange set of double standards. We have already found that money can buy almost anything. In observing the practices among the polygamist cult, we have noticed that they are able to construct any type of building on their property that they wish without any formal permit or government approval. We have already done the same on our property and have received only one easily diverted inquiry from the local government . We did not pay money, but explained to the inspector that we were a religious order.'' The entire group began to laugh again. The STAVKA leaders were also amused.

"As strange as it might seem, the problem was simply resolved by replacing a set of elk antlers which sat prominently on the sign across the top of the entrance gate to the ranch, with a large wooden cross. We then explained to the inspectors that we were part of a religious order and they have not come back since. We have successfully turned our foreign Dacha into what appears to the outside world to be a religious retreat. So, when you arrive, I expect you all to be as pious in appearance as possible!'' The group again enjoyed a boisterous belly laugh. Jim, seemingly bolstered by the group's response to his humor, continued.

"Now, another critical issue is that of the availability of medical resources. By coincidence, one of the foremost heart transplant teams and facilities in the world is located just three hundred miles to the north in Salt Lake City. In fact, if you will remember, years ago when the first artificial heart transplant was done on an unfortunate man named Barney Clark, it was at a hospital in Salt Lake City. The ability to continue the Dolgozhiteli program is fully available so long as some sort of quiet arrangement can be worked out with the medical researchers at that location. We have no doubt that the transplant technique used in Utah is equal or superior to that which we have used. Inasmuch as Chairman Gagarin is reaching his transition point, this facility should be ample to serve his needs.

"It is truly an interesting place. It is one which exhibits necessary contrasts which will protect you. And to the extent that anyone confronts you regarding the existence of the Dacha, or the activities there, it is important - and I reiterate important - that you be prepared to expound on the religious justification for anything that you do. The authorities literally fear the polygamists. If we are successful, they will literally fear us, also.

"We have a very unique method of legally getting our people in and out of the country. Boris Yarov has established a subsidiary of one of his companies in St. George itself. It is run by a Danish national. He is merely a young man whose wife is from southern Utah. He has no knowledge of the existence of the Dacha, and has been very helpful bringing in our people on visitor visas. The Russian subsidiary is operating as a computer company, but is also establishing a presence in the St. George area related to Russian tourism.

"As the situation develops, there will be more cause for Russian persons to be in the St. George area. Our company there will afford the opportunity for more of you to travel legally to the United States in and around the southern Utah area without suspicion.

"As you know, the American intelligence agencies and the FBI seem to be so busy with the massive influx of eastern European and Russian visitors to the United States, that they have insufficient time to even keep track of the legal visitors.

"The non-visa or illegal entrants, as many of you who make the trip will be, will have little difficulty getting in and out of the country so long as they use the sophisticated means that we have at our disposal. We fly them in from Cuba, a fairly rigorous adventure by air, but so far, it has worked very well.

"So, there you have it gentlemen," Jim beamed in conclusion. "The American Dacha is ready and waiting for you. We have constructed some accommodations in addition to the ranch facility. I might also point out there are at present, over ninety members of a Spetsnaz Alpha company from the Far Eastern Command who are now stationed at the American Dacha, or Zion Station as we call it officially." He turned to Andropov as he made his parting observations, "I have given you all the information that I have regarding Zion Station. It provides all of the comforts of the Western World. It is a very impressive facility in certainly the most beautiful location that I have ever seen in my life! I believe that you will also find it very compatible. If the security holds up, we should be able to be there for many years to come. Or, at least until you choose to return to the Soviet Union."

Chairman Andropov thanked Jim for the presentation. "As you can see, we have covered literally all aspects of this project. We are well-positioned to conduct the affairs of the STAVKA from other parts of the world. Given the extensive overseas investment in gold which we now control, we are among the strongest corporations in the world in terms of net wealth. It gives us incredible power to deal in both the freemarket, as well as control many of the aspects of Russian markets through our control of our aerospace industry. We are uniquely positioned to be a major force in the aerospace industry, and at the same time await for the opportune moment to stage the Second Coming which will allow for the return of the Soviet Union in all of its prominence."

Boom! Boom! Two percussive thuds shook the building. The electronic bulletin board slid off its wall mounts and crashed onto the floor. The chandeliers began to shake wildly in the swirling dust. The soldiers fell to the floor anticipating that the building might implode from the blast's powerful shock wave. In the next second, an incoming round was heard as it rattled through the sky, sailed over the Dacha and landed on the airfield beyond with another earthshaking concussion.

"To the shelters immediately - to the shelters *now*!" Andropov yelled to the soldiers, showing little fear or intimidation on his own part from the sudden change of circumstances.

Colonel Aniamov, the commander of the base defense for Caucus Station, had been at his post outside the meeting hall as a resource person if his opinion was needed. He immediately ran to his command car and grabbed his radio. Before he could put the telephone to his ear, he sensed another artillery round on its way. As he dove to the ground, it hit within twenty yards and shook him and the building with bone-jarring force. He saw members of the Spetsnaz and STAVKA dashing from the building in the direction of awaiting command vehicles. As men filled the cars, they peeled away, frantically one by one, making their way without lights, across the fields in the direction of the caves against the mountain cliff to the west.

"Is it the Kartalinian Ridge - tell me, is it the Kartalinian Ridge?" the Colonel yelled into his radio telephone.

He received confirmation from his security tower on the southwestern perimeter of the base that an artillery battery had opened up from the ridge amid the foothills on the edge of the Kartalinian Forest. At first count, the rounds had come in at twenty-four per minute. Now five minutes into the action, the bombardment was continuing at the same ferocious pace.

In the computer center a mile to the northeast of the Dacha and well-across the airfield, the computer programmer and the engineer were busily shutting down their equipment. Within a few minutes prior to the bombardment, they had taken a large amount of data into their system by modem transfer and were in the process of putting it on the extensive magnetic disk system in the Cray computer memory when the whole building seemed to shift.

In an urgent effort, they had shut down the support and excess memory systems, but did not want to lose the modem transfer that had just been received. As other power went out, they succeeded in engaging a battery backup system before the base power was lost altogether. With several minutes left on the memory transfer, the two technicians huddled beneath a steel desk hoping that they would complete their work and be able to evacuate without losing their equipment.

An incoming round rattled through the air and exploded on the hangar next door. Seconds later, a huge secondary explosion caused the roof in the computer room to collapse. The two technicians found themselves crawling around in the darkness, flashlight in hand, trying to assess the damage. In the dim light, they could see that the worst had not happened. Both Cray II's had avoided the steel beam that had fallen crushing everything else in the room. It was too dangerous to stay, and they began crawling to the door. In the next second, however, there was another explosion directly at the entrance of the building. Both Spetsnaz computer technicians were blown in all directions.

Kartalinian Ridge, Mid January, 1993

Stalking nervously from gun emplacement to gun emplacement, Lado Deniken patted his men on the back and shouted encouragement to them as they unloaded spent casings and slammed new rounds into the breech. The guns continued to ignite with a deafening roar causing the ordinance to sail off into the dark northeastern night.

From where Deniken stood, bright flashes could be seen on the high plateau where the secret base was located. It was clear that some targets were being hit. The spirit of the men was high and contagious. There appeared to be a heightened sense of camaraderie as the guns continued to boom away at the mountain base. To some, it even seemed easy, a sort of anticlimax to their many long months of waiting.

Deniken made his way to the battery command post located in an underground bunker some eighty feet behind the guns. To insure survivability, the post was well-underground with wooden beams covered by several feet of sandbags to serve as a bunkered ceiling.

Radio contact inside the command post with the spotters high on the mountain to the northwest was continuing. The principal target was the airfield. It was the Georgian's plan to crater the runway and disrupt communications to whatever extent possible in order to avoid reinforcement of the base's defenders from the air.

In the valley below, citizens gathered in the public square in Svanathia, and gazed into the intermittent darkness of the vast Caucus Mountains. Periodically, brilliant flashes filled the night sky followed by deafening echoes as they rolled down the river valley like a gigantic thunder storm. Even larger flashes of light, possibly announcing secondary explosions, could be seen beyond the ridge. With each such blast, a cheer arose from the people in the town square. "The time has finally come to drive the Russians out!" they shouted in an almost singular chorus. It was time to break out the vodka. With any good fortune, vodka would soon be the only purely Russian item left in Svanathia.

Deniken was cautiously optimistic. The bombardment had continued for over fifteen minutes with no response. The spotters on the mountain peaks now reported to the command post that they could see structural fires near the airfield. Deniken hoped that there was the possibility of aircraft having been hit. It also appeared that the power system on the airport had either been knocked out or had been turned off intentionally to avoid spotting of targets.

For the moment, it appeared as though the shooting was a one-way affair. The lack of response was encouraging to Deniken. At least, it bolstered his expectation that he could hold the hill until morning. By that time, the entire complement of fifteen thousand rounds of 130 millimeter high explosive ordinance would be expended.

Suddenly, in the command center on the Kartalinian Ridge, the radio crackled with an ominous cry, "This is Spotter Three...we see *aircraft* - we repeat, aircraft rising from the area on the east end of the airfield! We can see their lights, one...two...three...four...seven....eight....ten. I repeat - ten at least, helicopters now moving in your direction! They're splitting into two groups! They should be over your position within seconds!"

Immediately, Deniken ordered a ceasefire in an effort to keep the flashes of the howitzers from disclosing their exact position to the gunners in the attack helicopters. If only I had missiles, he thought desperately. At least his men were high on a ridge and as the helicopters came at them, he hoped they might fly low and expose themselves to small arms fire.

He had never been in battle before. The uncertainty of what to expect caused him to shiver, as he realized that his greatest fear was quickly materializing. Among the defenders, only a few had experience in Afghanistan. Most were World War II veterans and at least one had served under the Czar against the Kaiser. But this was different. None of them had ever fought against the Soviet equivalent of a tank assault from the sky.

Deniken crawled out of the bunker. A constant glow could be seen in the direction of the Russian base on the ridge. Fires were burning as they created flickers of light from the east. But where were the Hinds? He could hear nothing. His inexperience notwithstanding, he knew that silence was the awful lull before the storm.

"There they are!" an artilleryman near one of the big guns yelled, pointing into the eastern sky.

Another screamed, "To the south, look high up there. Far above us!"

The vibration from the rotors of the jet helicopters bounced off the mountain with a haunting insistence. The resonant thumping pulsed through the bodies of the wary artillerymen. But no lights could be seen, only slight, periodic shadows in the multishaded sky. No one could be certain as to the distance of the gunships. The incessant beating continued to intimidate and dampen the spirit of the men as they frantically looked in all directions - seeing nothing. They could only guess where the aerial death machines might be.

The Mil Mi-24 pilots and their gunners had chosen high altitude standoff positions from which they slowly descended in the darkness. There was no moonlight and they were confident that until they commenced firing, their exact positions would be undetectable by the defenders on the Kartalinian Ridge. Nevertheless, a standing order had been given that they should remain at least a one kilometer distance in order to avoid possible surface-to-air action against them.

The pilot of the smaller and faster Kamov "Hokum" attack helicopter carefully descended amid the din of the larger Mi-24's. He assumed that the noise of the large chopper would likely conceal his location and he would be able to get in for a close shot at the artillery positions using his forward-firing automatic canon and two air-to-surface rocket packs mounted on under-wing pylons. The "Hokum" had a better chance of success than the Mi-24's due to its enhanced maneuverability as well as the fact that it enjoyed the advantage of a "see in the dark" starlight scope. It provided distinct black and white images, appearing like a photographic negative in motion. Men simply appeared as bright white objects on the screen, standing erect around their gun emplacements. The Georgian militiamen looked as if they were waiting to be cut down. The pilot locked-in his automatically-controlled 30mm wire-guided rockets, then put his hand in the metal sling to the left side of his cockpit seat and applied a gentle finger pressure to the grip. In a millisecond, a rush of geometric lines streaked away from him in the dark sky causing a slight recoil.

Suddenly, sheets of steel explosives ripped up the entire area across the top of the Kartalinian Ridge. Men fell to the ground, jumping behind rocks and equipment, some shriveling up from the searing heat of the rocket explosions like ants under a blow torch. Nothing seemed to protect them. Terrifying flashes from the south erupted as the gunners on the heavy ordinance-laden Mil Mi-24 Hind "F"'s began to open up from their standoff positions.

Lado Deniken, standing near the entrance to the underground artillery bunker, jumped through the door and landed hard on the floor. The continuing explosions were so fierce that they bounced him against the rock and dirt walls of the bunker like a beach ball. Sandbags on the makeshift roof ruptured, spreading sand, dust and dirt throughout the closed-in command post with each major vibration. It's like being in the middle of a lightening storm, he thought to himself. There's nowhere I can go - nothing I can do!

He listened to the wretched screams of the men outside and could feel the searing heat as one high explosive after another ignited on top of the artillery emplacements and blasted fire hot air through the entrance to the bunker. Suddenly, a man jumped through the door and collapsed limply on the floor of the bunker. He lay motionless, apparently blown in the direction of the command post door.

There was a slight lull in the bombardment. Deniken attempted to crawl to the door of the bunker. The continuous warping thud of the helicopters could still be heard. As he peered out the door, he saw the large spotlight of one of the Russian aircraft beaming directly down on the artillery position. The Mi-24 appeared to be searching for anything that might be moving on the ridge. Deniken realized it was going to attempt a landing on top of the command post itself. He knew that within the next minute there would be Spetsnaz soldiers all over the hillside and he was not prepared to become a prisoner of the Russians at the first skirmish.

Deniken jumped out into the darkness and crawled along the edge of the bunker embankment keeping a close eye on the helicopter hovering to within seventy feet of the top of the ridge almost directly over him. He took two deep breaths and crammed a thirty-nine round clip in the magazine in his Kalashnikov rifle. He aimed it directly up at the helicopter and began to fire his weapon on full automatic.

It clanked off the rounds with almost a toy-like report. The metallic zing of the hammer seemed somehow unreal to him, a cheap toy against a multimillion dollar monster machine. The spotlight went out immediately. The helicopter churned and spinned - he could see fire. The Mi-24 started to dip and roll. A orange flame belched out from the opposite side of the aircraft. It tipped crazily to the east and in a futile attempt to work its way back to the base, it fell, crashing into the deep gorge between the remnants of his artillery battery and the southwestern perimeter of Caucus Station. A fireball plumed into the air again illuminating the entire battlefield as if it were daylight.

The remaining helicopters began to retreat. The noise was not as deafening as it had been. The few men who remained alive could discern that they were now out of danger and that at least for the moment, they had gained some respect from their highly trained enemy.

Deniken ran quickly to the artillery battery to assess the damage. Up and down the line, he saw that of the eight howitzers, none appeared to be left in working condition. He could see that they had been reduced to scrap metal by the first missile attack.

What concerned him even more were the sounds of men dying around him. The screams of pain and the terror of the moment separated his mind momentarily from the battle. He thought of Steffan. Then his military mind reengaged and he took courage in the assessment that he had accomplished his initial objective. The Russian base had been heavily bombarded. Although he had not conducted the barrage through the night as planned, the brilliant orange glow of fires on the high mountain plateau to the north clearly confirmed to him that the Svan Warriors had experienced some success.

With the artillery neutralized, it was time to evacuate the Kartalinian Ridge. He worked his way again to the command center and picked up the radio phone, communicating with his units at various positions on the battery where radios were still working and ordered a withdrawal from the hill.

CHAPTER 18

St. George, Utah, Late January, 1993

The winter flu season was in full force at the Christensen household. This resulted in Michael staying home from work for several days of what would have otherwise been a busy week. Then, as he was on the road to slow recuperation, the rest of the family took their turn at being hit by the malady.

In his absence, the Transcontinental Trading Inc. offices in St. George had continued to operate. A half-dozen Russian software programmers had been rotated into St. George as a reward for their diligence at Technoserv in Moscow. Most of them did not speak English, resulting in considerable confusion. Periodically an interpreter would be sent from the Technoserv offices in Moscow, but the interpreters were not allowed to remain in St. George for more than a few days at a time.

An additional time-consuming task had been that of dealing with the shopping and purchasing habits of the Russians. They were much like spoiled children in a candy store armed with shopping lists that extended far beyond the immediate family. They viewed it as a once-in-a-lifetime opportunity to purchase every conceivable item ever wanted or imagined they needed and which they could sell for a profit on the black market back home.

As the first group reached their rotation date from St. George, there were over a dozen boxes per man to ship back to Russia. Along with his many duties, Michael functioned as a shipping and packing clerk. Yarov required it of him.

In his spare time, Michael did what he was supposed to be doing. Successfully obtaining options on the several parcels of real estate in the downtown St. George business district had been the first major step toward bringing the Russia Center to fruition. In total, it comprised over five and a half acres strategically located in the middle of a bustling and historical part of St. George.

Meanwhile, city officials had undertaken an effort to further investigate the Russia Center prospects. To them, the idea was like manna from heaven to a town in need of a major commercial project right in the center of town. The mayor had been skeptical. However, with his exchange of letters with the mayor of Zhukovski, the Russian city adjacent to the aerospace complex at Star City, even he became a believer in the project. The respective mayors arranged for their city councils to draw up sister-city resolutions. They were also in the process of preparing reciprocal visits to announce their newfound international relationship. The Russia Center had become the talk of St. George and Michael had become a featured speaker on the luncheon circuit at the local Chamber of Commerce, Exchange Club and Rotary Club meetings.

As Michael arrived for work following his sick days, he first inspected the computerized telephone records to see the extent of the personal calls having been made by the Russians working at the office. The cost was becoming a burden. He would have to send an E-Mail message to Yarov regarding the matter.

His next task was to check the electronic mailbox. As he did so, he was surprised by what he found. A message in poor but readable English flashed on the computer screen:

> *To: Michael Christensen*
> *From: Boris Yarov*
> *Hello, Michael,*
> *I am to inform you that Technoserv will be conducting*

*a seminar in Moscow on the subject of doing business
in the computer industry in foreign countries. It will be
presented to all of the business managers of the Ministry of Aviation. We plan on at least 250 to be in attendance. We are proud of your heroic efforts as the Manager of our U.S. subsidiary and we would like you to speak
on that topic and tell them all how to be successful in America. We have already sent the visa application and invitation letter to the Russian Republic Ministry of Foreign
Affairs. Your visa will be approved this week. Please make
travel plans immediately.
Best Regards.*

Michael knew all too well the Aviation Ministry's track record with seminars. Seminars regarding private enterprise and privatization were frequent. For the most part, however, it was the case of Russian bureaucrats communicating with one another in a vacuum with equally transparent results.

More important, however, was Michael's commitment to Gina, as well as himself, that he would not return to Russia at any time in the near future. Additionally, it was now winter and he could not think of a place worse than the streets of Moscow in the winter time. Without further contemplation, Michael quickly typed a return message declining the invitation. He knew it would irritate Yarov and smack of insubordination. The new Russia Center was Yarov's "pet project." To have Michael bragging of its "heroic" attributes at the seminar would make Yarov the top captain of the industry for at least a weekend. Michael figured that sending the architect's renderings would accomplish the same result. He relished his insulation from Yarov. Going to Moscow just for Yarov's benefit was out of the question.

By late afternoon, Michael had not heard from Yarov and assumed that the rejection of the invitation had been somehow taken in stride on the other side of the globe. The receptionist buzzed,"Call from Moscow, Michael."

Here we go again! Michael realized that his plan to get out of the office before his least favorite Muscovite could ruin his day had just evaporated, " Hello, this is Michael."

"Michael, pay close attention." Yarov's voice thundered even from the other side of the world, transcontinental delay included. "You should know that you must be here at Conference on International Trade. I have told many great things of Russia Center. You, as director, must be here."

"I can send you the architect's pictures." He knew Yarov would not understand the word "renderings."

"No, Michael. Bring pictures with you, or - we get new director!"

The temptation struck Michael to resign. He could sense the anger in Yarov's voice. "You do not be loyal, you have no job!"

As Yarov' s threats rang through the earpiece of the telephone, Michael reasoned that along with the difficulty of working with Russians still came the benefit of very good money. The Russians always paid on time. He also knew that Yarov was probably sorely in need of a credible Westerner to back up his continual bluster to the Ministry of Aviation and the Moscow establishment regarding Technoserv's business ventures in America.

"So, what is it Michael - you come to Moscow or you be fired?"

Michael took a deep breath, balancing his desire to avoid another Moscow trip against the mortgage on his new home and all of the debt that he had incurred in anticpation of a good job, at least for a while, with TTI. And then there was the lingering worry about the woman Cosmonaut. The Soviets were experts at blackmail. Michael suspected that the scene at Star City and then the pass in the car in St. George had all been a setup. He racked his brain for some reason why the Russians had put Raissa in his path but couldn't think of anything that made any sense. It made Michael nervous about taking this trip. He wanted more time to decide and was about to ask for it when Yarov threw down the final gauntlet, "Okay, Michael, so you are fired now, correct?"

Deferring in favor of the financial realities, Michael interrupted, "No, Yarov, if Technoserv really needs me, I will make the trip. But I can't stay there long. I've got a lot to do here in St. George."

"Zat is good Michael, very good," Yarov seemed relieved, almost jovial. "We will treat you good. Thank you... Comr..."

Yarov had never thanked Michael for anything. Michael knew it was time for caution when a Russian like Yarov almost used the word "Comrade..." But he also knew that he could spend the rest of his waking moments trying to second guess Yarov's various agendas and still get it wrong every time.

Moscow, Russian Republic, Late January, 1993

Alexander Kutuzov had spent most of the cold Moscow night in the apartment deep in contemplation, trying to decide on his next move. He was jolted into full awareness by the shrill ring of the telephone. The message was quick and simple, "You and I have got big problems! Meet me at the loading dock."

He patted Nieca as she raised up on one elbow and tried to focus her eyes. "I must go out - Leni Artemoshkin is in trouble. I fear that something bad is happening!" He dressed quickly, taking a hasty look in the mirror, adjusted his tie and precious tie tac and rushed into the night.

Earlier than the Moscow rush hour, Alexander headed out into the early morning deep freeze in the direction of the Technoserv offices. The caller had not stated a time. Alexander knew from the sound of Leni Artimoshkin's voice, he meant immediately.

Alexander emerged onto the street from the underground metro station on the Pervomayskaya Street. He walked eastward for three blocks, and rather than entering the main entrance of Technoserv, he walked south on Parkovaya to a point where he could have a clear view of the loading dock area. It would also keep him from being within the view of people entering and exiting the main entrance of the Technoserv offices.

He turned a corner and saw Leni across the street, standing next to a light pole fidgeting with a cigarette. Leni was always jovial and smooth in his style, a sort of computer programmer with a rare personality attached. For him, lighting a cigarette was second nature. But this morning, his body language clearly dictated a different person.

Alexander whistled. Leni's head moved slightly and he briskly crossed the street. They walked together down Parkovaya south into the remote expanse of Petrovskiy Park. There was no discussion, no conversation, until they were unmistakably alone.

"They know everything, Alexander - I mean everything!" Leni blurted as if he could not wait another moment.

"Who, Leni? What are you talking about?"

"It was just like a visit from the old ... the old KGB. They came to my home. They handcuffed me in front of my children and hauled me out. They blindfolded me and drove me to some government building here in the city. It could have been Lefortovo...from the sound of the traffic in the square, I think it was Lefortovo! And then they told me...they told me I was in trouble. They told me you were the cause!"

"What do you mean, Leni? The cause of what?"

"The message was very clear, Alexander. They told me I would need to give you one message...it is that you should leave the country immediately. Or they will...?"

"Or what?"

"Or you will die!"

Alexander was suddenly chilled. He wondered why Leni would be singled out to deliver such a message to him. "Now slow down! Tell me, what exactly did they say? Who were they?"

"They didn't tell me who they were. I was blindfolded most of the time. I think it was a basement area. They pushed me down a long ramp. Inside, no one showed a badge. But they were all officials. It was just like ... like I said, the old KGB! My first comment to them got me slugged in the ribs with a baton." Leni grimaced as he placed his hand on a severe rib bruise.

"Leni, tell me once more, what exactly did they say?" It all still seemed unclear to Alexander.

"It was very simple. They said I was to stay away from you, or it would be terrible for both of us," Leni repeated.

"Did they say... did they say what they would do?"

"No, the message was that simple. The meeting lasted for not more than ...I would say, ten minutes. But they know that we are best of friends. And they know that we've been snooping on banking matters. They did say that if you persisted, I would be fired from Technoserv. My job as a computer programmer would be over, permanently!"

"But you don't know who they were? You think that...that maybe it should be reported to the police? Have you thought of going to the police?" Kutuzov asked.

"Alexander, these people *were* the police - they didn't stage it. I saw the inside of the building. There were long halls and lots of official looking people. They were serious - I mean very serious! And they had guns. I saw them...shoulder holsters like policemen have."

"Any insignias or badges? Any uniforms?"

"No, nothing. But I know they're serious," he hesitated, "and Alexander...I'm afraid! Afraid for you, for my family and I am sick in my heart...nothing has changed in Russia...nothing!"

They walked out of the park and across the Izmaylovskiy Prospeckt back in the direction of the Technoserv offices. There was no discussion for approximately two blocks. As they reached the corner where Alexander would return to the metro and Leni to Technoserv, Leni finally broke the silence. "I don't know what you have gotten yourself into, Alexander, but my wife and my children cannot pay the price. If Toko Bank fails and if the problems you are looking into are all true, I feel sorry for you and for the bank and everyone involved. But there's nothing I can do about it. From the way it sounds, there is nothing you can do either!"

Alexander was uncertain how to respond. He sensed the pain of seeing their friendship stretched to its outside limit. Kutuzov reached out his hand and placed it on his friend's shoulder. "I must talk to Nieca. And...I will do what I can to keep you out of it from now on." Then he turned and walked toward the metro.

Over his shoulder he heard the words. "Alexander, there is only one thing that you can do - leave it alone!"

Vladivostok, Far Eastern Russia, Late January, 1993

An uneasy standoff seemed to be in place as reports filtered into the KGB Headquarters in Vladivostok of Russian Marines shadowing KGB

Border Police. A standing order had been issued that KGB would be refused entrance to the FEC compound and military areas unless accompanied by an escort. Colonel Ziyetski also assumed that the constant parade of UAZ 469 Troop-carrying vehicles, the Russian equivalent of the Jeep near the KGB Headquarters, was more than just a coincidence.

Yet, despite the clear tension between the two entities, there had been no direct communication between the Far Eastern Command and the Vladivostok KGB since Ziyetski and his group successfully removed the young Trans-Siberian Railway guard from the naval hospital several weeks earlier. Communications, however, had been constant between the Russian Federation Defense Command offices, and the Federation Security Agency in Moscow.

Each day, an officer had been sent to the KGB offices to meet with General Dombrayov demanding not only the return of Sokof by the Vladivostok KGB office, but also punishment of Colonel Ziyetski to include his removal from assignment with the Far Eastern Command. Only a direct order from Dombrayov or Yeltsin himself could excise Ziyetski from the FEC. Although he was technically subordinate to the FEC in military matters, he was independent as an investigative arm of the Federal Prosecutor's Office in criminal matters.

For his part, Dombrayov had routinely rejected any such demands. He maintained that it was a police matter and if evidence existed regarding the commission of a crime, the matter would be turned over to the State Prosecutor's Office and military interference was not appropriate. Although he spoke the words, he knew they had limited force behind them. There was still no real judicial prosecutorial system in place in Russia to deal with high crimes by government officials. Other than the prosecution of the failed Putch leaders of August, 1991, which had been highly publicized and required quick public prosecution, the only method of dealing with treasonous military leaders was by removal and prosecution under the orders of the Chairman of the Communist Party. Inasmuch as the post no longer existed, and since no direct clash between the authority of the President of the Republic of Russia and any prominent military leaders had occurred, there was simply no precedent. A cautious truce seemed to be in place as the State avoided offense against the military. More time was needed to enact new laws that would address such matters.

But now, the situation was grave. Dombrayov had no doubt that Colonel Ziyetski was one of the more capable KGB Regional Commanders. He also knew that lack of loyalty on the part of the FEC had been a problem in the past, but that problems had always been somehow resolved short of direct confrontation. This time, however, Ziyetski had strong evidence that the FEC was involved in the massacre at the Ozero Khanka rail crossing. He hoped that the possibility still existed for some type of resolution. He felt that the best solution would be to require Ziyetski to establish a motive. This would allow for more time and perhaps cause the FEC to make an improvident move that would incriminate itself sufficiently to convince Yeltsin personally to take action. At this point, a political solution was preferable to a scandal. It would require more investigation and more time. He had to get Ziyetski out of Vladivostok. Dombrayov cabled:

I am sympathetic to your position. However, a motive must be clearly established. This is a very sensitive political matter. I fear this will severely damage your credibility and that of the entire Federation Security Agency. Thus, I am requesting that you pursue the investigation outside of the Eastern Front area. I am ordering that you report to the Moscow KGB Headquarters and be prepared to conduct whatever investigation you deem appropriate in Moscow relative to your suspicions regarding items of value on the train that may disclose the extent of the loss as well as a specific motive. If, however, you are unable to gain the proper evidence rather quickly, then Corporal Sokof will be returned to the FEC and the Agency will cease any further investigation relative to your present suspicions.

Moscow, Russian Republic, Early February, 1993

Michael had flown from Las Vegas to Chicago and on to Toronto. From Toronto, Michael flew by KLM Royal Dutch Airlines to Moscow with one stop in Rotterdam. As an astute business traveler, he knew the value of avoiding Aeroflot under any circumstances. The poor accommodation of passengers was legend. Flights seldom arrived on time because of constant problems with fuel shortages and poor maintenance.

There was no passenger loader direct to the terminal. Instead, the passengers walked down the steps of the airliner onto the tarmac and toward the entry gates into the building. As he walked, he looked up at the broad two story glass window. It took only a moment to spot Raissa. Technoserv had sent its token siren to pick Michael up from the airport. He started calculating an alternate route through the terminal that would allow him to avoid her altogether and take a cab into the office.

His impatience increased as the line slowed and he nervously kept one eye on getting through customs and the other on the woman in the fur coat standing nearby in the broad entry hall. She had strategically placed herself in a position Michael could not avoid as he approached the foreign visitor check-in counters.

Finally, he made it through and began walking the fifty feet to where she stood. As he approached, he could see her impassive blue eyes examining him from beneath delinquent strands of red hair that partially covered her face. They were fixed on him with a look that only reinforced his certainty that he had made the wrong decision in coming to Russia. He looked again for an escape route. But it was too late. He reached the woman. She stretched out her hands to grasp both of his in the semi-personal Russian greeting. He wanted to run away, but could not halt his forward motion. As they touched, he felt the frigid palms like a statue in wintertime, frozen in place. He sensed motion in her eyes, serving as perfect mirrors. In the next second a strong hand gripped the back of his neck while another grabbed onto his left arm. He was swung off balance and found himself looking into the ugly bloodshot eyes of a large burly man

"You are under arrest!" The surly Russian spoke in rough, fractured English.

"What?" Michael was startled and struggled to get a glimpse at Raissa, but saw only a badge as it was shoved before his eyes

"You are charged with violation of the Federation Anti-Black Market and Racketeering Act Section 2156. You will come with us." As they dragged him away from the spot of the arrest even before a crowd could gather, Michael strained to catch a glimpse of Raissa. She was not there.

He was whisked to a waiting car where his captors roughly jammed him into the back seat, blindfolded him and drove off into the grey wastes of a winter Moscow day.

Reston, Virginia, Early February, 1993

"Daddy, it worked. I'm pregnant! Can you believe it? I'm going to have a baby!"

There was silence. He heard the childish voice which, to him, belied her age.

"You are excited, aren't you, Daddy?"

Somewhat fettered in his thoughts he responded. "Oh yes, I am, sweetheart. This is wonderful."

"The doctors say it all worked out perfectly. The whole test and everything was just right. I'm so happy. I knew you'd want to know. And Jim, well, he's on cloud nine as you can expect!"

"I'm happy for you, sweetheart." Stony Chapman spoke in a subdued voice. His daughter noted his less than enthusiastic response, but in her joy and exuberance for the moment, ignored anything which could be even remotely perceived as negative.

"Well, you had to be one of the first to know, Daddy. I'll talk to you later - got to call Mom." She hung up.

Congress was in session, and for Stony Chapman to be home rather than at work at mid-morning was not only unusual, but it was something he had never done before. There had been times when he had been carted to the floor of the House of Representatives in a wheelchair in order to participate in a debate or cast his vote, despite the fact that he had been laid up by surgery. Now, his mood had swung into deep depression. He could not escape the persistant voice that spoke to him day and night repeating words that only he could understand.

At first it had come to him only in the darkness. But now he was hearing the voice in the daytime and sometimes thought he was seeing the image. The congressman hated to close his eyes. He abhorred sleep. In each visitation, the long gaunt face with tired eyes would appear again, vividly in his mind, tall above him and speaking softly, but directly. Why is it that it was so easy for me to take the bribe and withdraw sponsorship of the legislation and break my promise to the President? Why can't I just enjoy the good that has come of it? Soon, I will be a grandfather. My daughter's husband is finally out of debt and out of trouble. Yet, I dare not pay a single debt of my own with the money.

The long, mysterious face loomed large in his mind as he closed his eyes and fought to escape the prison walls within his own soul. No person ever had money enough to bribe my conscience or to stop its utterance against wrong and oppression. My conscience is my own - my creators, not man's. I shall never sink the rights of mankind to the malice - wrong or avarice of another's wishes...the words jerked him awake and out of his chair as he found himself struggling with an increasingly sorrowful spirit. The sickening sensation was enhanced as he visualized his life plunging downward with his continuing recollection of his misdeeds. He felt trapped in a hell with no escape. It was all too unfamiliar - something with which he had never reckoned in the past. He had made deals, created Pork Barrels and wielded heavy influence over the course of the many years, but never had anyone so craftily and directly purchased his services as a U.S. Congressman.

Now, he thought of the child that would soon be born. He would look into its eyes and always see a distinct and lucid memory which would cause him to forever mourn the awful reality of himself. The pain was sharp and real. He was amazed at the intensity of his despair, not having anticipated its severity.

The day he changed his position and withdrew his support of the President-elect, party regulars had rallied to his support. He received congratulation and positive messages from every direction. He endured the smiles and back slaps with a sense of pride. Then, in the darkness, like a ghost, the noble face continually stared at him as if permanently affixed to the inside of his eyelids. The man was strong and tall, with a beard, wearing a dark suit. The congressman feared that the appearance of his new friend or tormentor, dependent on how he should respond to the stranger's prompting, was the first step on the road to insanity.

Desiring sleep, but fearing the dream, Congressman Chapman, still dressed in the dirty jogging suit in which he had slept the night before, threw on an overcoat, climbed into his car and drove through the cold winter afternoon in the direction of the nation's capital.

Moscow, Russian Republic, Early February, 1993

The blindfold was removed. The green interior of the cell was the first thing Michael noted as his eyes adjusted to the new scene. A soldier in a drab grey uniform clanked the bars shut behind him. Before he could turn around to examine the remainder of his confines, he heard a voice, familiar but also different, "Michael, good to have you here."

Michael turned with a start to see Boris Yarov sitting on a wooden chair in the corner of the cell. "What the... what's going on Yarov!"

"She was a fine idea was she not?" Yarov spoke with a wry laugh.

"I've been around Russians long to avoid getting caught in that trap, Yarov," Michael was defiant.

"You don't understand, we save you from her."

"What does that mean?" Michael was irritated. What did Yarov's remark have to do with anything here?

"She will have you."

"No, she won't...now get to the point. What is *going on*, Yarov!" Michael could feel his frustration and anger rising. He couldn't believe that he had worked with these people for so long only to find himself involved in a typically Russian mess like this.

"You have trouble. You bring computers into country last summer without permit. Very bad."

"I got a permit!"

"No, you get no permit. They say you come for inspection, but you drove through... Dane have no permit, but still send money to Denmark for computers... against law."

"You paid me! It was your money!" Just as Michael's voice raised to a threatening pitch, a black-jacketed Spetsnaz trooper entered the cell. Michael kept his distance from both. "I remember distinctly going to the Ministry downtown and then to the airport to get inspected."

"No...they have photo of bribe at ministry for fifty dollars, then, at airport, you just drive through."

Michael struggled with his recollection of the tiresome day almost five months earlier. He had spent the better part of the day wheeling a huge semi around the narrow streets of Moscow in search of an import permit only to be waived through at the inspection area. His experience with Russians began to dictate his thought processes. It was becoming clear to him that Yarov had set him up according to a plan that had been hatched months earlier. The Russia Center, the woman Cosmonaut - it was all a ruse, for some strange purpose. He was more angered than afraid.

"Okay Yarov, we play the game your way. What in the hell do you want of me?"

Yarov smiled slightly then stood up, "Maybe you rot in prison."

"No, if that was true, you wouldn't be here telling me about it. You need something. If you Bolsheviks have stooped to kidnapping and ransom, you might as well forget it. My family has no money."

"I do not need money."

"Then what do you need?" Michael could hear his voice to echo down the hall of the medieval structure.

"I need help with computer, Michael."

"And you had me arrested to get me to help you with a computer. Why in the hell do you think I came to Moscow - there was a seminar on international business trade and computers, you know."

"All not so simple. You do download and prosecutor drop

charges.''

''What download...what are you talking about?''

The door to the cell opened again and Yarov's interpreter from Technoserv walked in, visibly disturbed by seeing Michael in such a beleaguered circumstance. Yarov began to talk through the simultaneous translation.

''Do you remember the Unix work stations that we acquired through your St. George offices for use here in Moscow?''

''Yes,'' Michael answered through clenched teeth.

''And the Pentiums with the two gigabyte hard drive that you sent to us three weeks ago?''

''Sure, they were the Unix servers with the Sony removable optical drives. Why do you ask?''

''I'm glad you remember. You also sent us twenty removable disks, one gigabyte each.''

''Okay, so what does it all mean? Why are we talking about this here in a prison cell - will you just level with me?''

Yarov noted Michael's sudden burst of confidence as the discussion of computers began to develop. He chose not to let it get out of hand. ''We are not negotiating a deal. This cell is where you will stay for a very long time unless you assist us with a certain project.''

''Well, what is it...I mean that would require all this?'' Michael gestured in the direction of the Spetsnaz trooper.

''We must move some data. I want you to download data off some Cray II hard drives onto the Unix server.''

Michael began to suspect the reason behind the coercion.

''I get it - so you want me to do some kind of espionage in the U.S. Crays are off-limits and you think I can get to them for you?''

''No, Michael, we have the Crays.''

''That's prohibited hardware; Russians aren't allowed access to Crays.''

''All I can tell you is that we have them and that your task will not be an easy one. They are slightly damaged and there may be additional formatting problems. We are in need of your expertise.''

''Seems to me like you've chosen a funny way to get it.''

''Regardless of your skill Michael, I assure you that it will not be an easy task." Yarov moved to the door. The trooper positioned himself between Michael and the door as Yarov and the interpreter walked out into the dark hallway.

"We will be back tomorrow. In the meantime," Yarov spoke with a flat emphasis, "enjoy your prison cell." The bars of the door clanked shut. Michael was alone.

* * *

Yarov was not finished with his day's work. He made his way across the city to keep one more appointment but stopped first at Toko Bank to pick up the First Deputy. The drive was an opportunity for another secret meeting. The uniformed Spetsnaz driver-bodyguard steering the car in the direction of the mammoth apartment building complex at Sviblovo not far from the Rostonkino Rail Station on the East side of the city could be trusted implicitly.

"We must move much more quickly than originally planned," Yarov surrendered a certain measure of anxiety as he spoke to the First Deputy.

"I've been worried, but I have seen nothing at the bank. If there is an investigation, I'm not aware," the First Deputy responded.

"It's coming from an odd quarter, Comrade. There is an inspector of the KGB who has been relentlessly pursuing the train incident."

"Who is he?" The First Deputy had been much more worried about exposure on the release of the twenty-five million dollars at the request of Yuri Gagarin than he had the hundred billion dollars in gold lost in the train massacre.

"I'm told it is the KGB Regional Director in Vladivostok, by the name of Ziyetski. They tell me he just won't stop."

"Don't ask me for more money to pay him - I'm out. The bank is about to fold."

"It's too risky to offer him a bribe. They say he wouldn't take it anyway. But it's only a matter of time before he'll be here asking questions.

We know he's already talked to Kutusov."

"That fool, we should have gotten rid of him a long time ago," the First Deputy was now sharing Yarov's concerns.

"Don't touch him. For some reason that I do not understand, the STAVKA doesn't want him harmed. But we do have to get him out of here before Ziyetski shows up from Vladivostok."

"Well, if we can't kill him...and I've already done everything I can do to isolate him at the bank, what are we going to do with him?" The First Deputy was confused.

"That's why we're headed to his apartment right now. The STAVKA has given me instructions. We've got to get him out of the country before the KGB starts listening seriously to him."

"What about me? They'll be after me in a heartbeat," the First Deputy noted the irony. His condition was continuing to worsen due to congestive heart failure. He awaited the further contact with the STAVKA that Gagarin had promised. Perhaps this was it.

"We need your help with Kutusov. If you do as I ask, you will be leaving the country within a matter of days to get the medical relief you need. A business visa in your name is already in place. In fact, I will be your traveling companion."

"Whatever you need, consider it done." The First Deputy was excited at the news and relieved that Gagarin had actually come through on his promise.

The afternoon traffic was picking up as the pair made their way to the apartment of Alexander and Nieca Kutusov for an unexpected visit, unaware of significant developments in Washington D.C. that could bear heavily upon their plans.

Washington D.C., Early February, 1993

Congressman Chapman had driven aimlessly all day around the nation's capital. His wife was at their home back in Edmond, Oklahoma unaware of his anguish. With the news of a pregnant daughter, she was attending to other things. He looked vacant and ragged, his usual self-assured animation drained away. Having failed to take his wallet with him, he ran out of gas near Potomac Park and so continued to wander on foot. Unshaven for two days, he looked like a street bum. An excruciating headache pounded relentlessly as he attempted to deal with his deep and painful thoughts. It was overwhelming - beyond anything he could handle.

After a period of time, he found himself walking up the steps to the Lincoln Memorial. He was uncertain why, but to return to the scene of the crime seemed to offer some solace. As he sat there, looking out across the mall, the beautiful view of the sunset on the Washington Monument and the Capitol Building beyond, he tried to sort out the staggering consequences of his actions.

Resolving his financial problems at the expense of peddling influence had seemed so easy at first, and now so impossible. Perhaps he would give his money to charity, or perhaps...

To avoid the chill of the eastern exposure, he walked into the monument hall, retracing his steps from the day he had met the man from China. Eventually, he found himself sitting on the bench looking up again at the north wall. Confused and exhausted, he rested his eyes. But then, the words began to come. The moving impression of the thin bony face of the man appeared again within his eyelids, and he began to read,

"Fondly do we hope, fervently do we pray, that this mighty scourge of war may speedily pass away. Yet, if God wills that it continue until all the wealth piled up by the bondsman's two hundred fifty years of unrequited toil shall be sunk, and until every drop of blood drawn with the lash shall be paid by another drawn with the sword, as was said three thousand years ago, so still must it be said, 'the judgments of the Lord are true and righteous altogether.' "

His eyes then focused on the phrase, etched in stone, of Abraham Lincoln's Second Inaugural Address: *"The Almighty has His own purposes."* The words continued, *"With malice toward none, with charity for all, with firmness in right, as God give us to see the right, let us strive to finish the work we are in; to bind up the nation's wounds..."*

The congressman got up and staggered slowly around to the front of the memorial, cocked his head back and looked up at the long, noble face of Abraham Lincoln.

This time, there was no pigeon to insult his grandeur, as the congressman saw that the man visiting him in the night had been the sixteenth President of the United States, deep eyes, sorrowful face and all. He knew that for this moment in time the words were meant for him. He stared and wondered how it was that some men could do such great things at times of immeasurable challenge, and yet men like himself could stoop to such selfish vindication in a time of plenty. He closed his eyes and turned his head, but the face, as in his dreams, was still there.

For all of his years as a public servant, he had successfully played roles in a double life, always positioning himself to have the best of all worlds. At a time when he could have been brave, he was not. When he could have been good, he was evil. He had caused a great wound to come upon the nation. His moment of truth had come, and he had failed. Realizing that both the crime and the person had merged in him, he stood before the magnificent statue of Abraham Lincoln - sitting as if in judgment of a man who had truly defiled the temple.

He sat slumped on the steps and remained still for hours. At closing time, the park police directed all tourists out of the monument and noted the scraggly street person, sitting on the steps of the monument and attempted to speak with him, but to no avail. Within minutes, the paddy wagon had arrived and Congressman Stony Chapman was hauled off to the D.C. jail to sour overnight in the drunk tank.

At early morning, the officer woke him up and asked for his name and occupation. As he repeated, "Stony Chapman, Congressman," the jailer laughed and responded, "Sure, and I'm Michael Jordan." Stony was nevertheless given the opportunity to make a phone call. He dialed 202-456-1414.

The operator at the White House switchboard answered. She listened to a person claiming, "This is Congressman Stony Chapman - I would like to speak with the President." She quickly referred the caller to the Congressional Affairs Liaison Officer who had little difficulty recognizing the voice, albeit distressed, of the eminent Stony Chapman, Congressman from Oklahoma.

Within the next minute, the Assistant to the President had been notified and shortly thereafter, the young man from a southern state, having just returned from his morning jog, picked up the telephone to receive the call from the D.C. jail.

"Mr. President, this is Stony Chapman. I have done something unforgivable to you, my party and the country. I feel that I should explain it to you first, before the world knows...and I assure you, it will."

CHAPTER 19

Moscow, Russian Republic, Early February, 1993

The loud, staccato rapping did not conern Nieca as she opened the door of the apartment on the fourteenth floor of the State-constructed high-rise. Cowering as she saw the men before her, she called, "Alexander, come in here - now!"

"Please, Mrs. Kutusov, may we come in?"

Nieca, her face white with shock, stepped back to allow the First Deputy, Yarov and the nonuniformed escort to walk into the room. At the same moment, Alexander entered from the kitchen. "Mr. First Deputy... uh," he was likewise astounded by the visitors.

"Alexander, it is urgent that I meet with you in your home today. Allow me to introduce Mr. Boris Yarov and our driver, Victor." Yarov followed the common Russian practice of not introducing the last name of a person not essential to the pending conversation. "May we sit down?"

"Certainly." Alexander moved some chairs from the kitchen to the living room to accommodate the group. He knew the name Boris Yarov from his good friend Leni Artemoshkin at Technoserv. Suspecting that Yarov was somehow connected with the treachery committed on his friend, he avoided making any reference to the common acquaintance.

"Alexander," the First Deputy began, "we have become very much aware of your effort to injure Toko Bank. Your rumor mongering has come back to us! It will not be tolerated!"

Alexander was weak on direct confrontation. "But...all I have done is try to tell the truth...what I know - that is all."

"What you know and what you think you know may be two different things. Has it occurred to you that your knowledge of banking may not extend to the monumental problems that we at the top must deal with. Our country isn't exactly overflowing in cash as you know!"

"But, Sir, my concern has been for the bank also. I cannot trace funds in certain accounts, and I have hoped that you would at least check to see what has happened."

The First Deputy interrupted, "Do you think we do not check? Do you think we do not keep careful records of every ruble in this bank?"

Alexander paused and tried to build the requisite courage, "No, I don't think you do. I think the bank's gold reserves have been substantially depleted sometime in the past year and that it has not been properly reported!"

There was brief silence as the First Deputy prepared his next fusillade, "We understand that you have been talking to the KGB! Are you at all aware of what it means to divulge company secrets to the authorities or anyone else?"

Kutusov was extremely intimidated by the First Deputy's angry attack. He could see the veins on the man's forehead beginning to bulge. Even to Alexander, it was evident that the bank's CEO was very ill.

"I don' t know exactly, Sir. The KGB, sought me out. I told them what I knew."

There was another long pause as the First Deputy stood up, walked across the room to the window and looked out at the dreary apartment complex below. "Kutusov, I don't know what kind of games you are playing. In fact, maybe I don't even know who you really are. But its clear to me that your time with the bank is over!"

Alexander looked at Nieca - he could see the terror in her eyes. Their worst fear was coming about. The First Deputy sensed the communication. "Not only are you a problem Kutusov, but your wife is likewise an irritation to us all at the bank. She is also finished!''

"What? Why are you doing this? This is...preposterous.'' Kutusov stammered.

"Well that is the way it is, so you may as well adjust to the idea!'' The First Deputy fired back.

Nieca began to cry.

Kutusov tried to comfort her while at the same time trying to figure out what to do next. Nieca hugged Alexander and as she put her head near his she whispered softly, "Try to get your position back. Do *anything* Alex - they have us trapped.''

The group stood up and made slight motion toward the door. Alexander stopped them, "Please, listen to me, I will do anything you wish to have my job. I will work motor pool - anything.'' As he pleaded, he also began to weep.

The First Deputy looked at Yarov and accepted a slight nod. Then he spoke calmly. "What if there was a job for you still?''

"I will do anything, Sir,'' Alexander was embarrassed to be begging in front of his wife.

"Well, I'm really not interested in you after what you have done, but,'' he pointed at Yarov, "Mr. Yarov might feel differently.''

Alexander looked up as the portly Russian knotted his eyebrows. "I know of a position for both of you with one of our companies in the United States.''

Nieca repeated his last words in amazement, "The United States!''

Before you assume it's some kind of holiday, let me tell you, it is a job mailing computer equipment from a place called Salt Lake City. You will have to leave immediately. I need people in the position right now.''

Alexander likewise was wondering if he was hearing correctly. Was he going to be punished by being sent to America - how wonderful, he thought.

"You will only be allowed to stay for six months. The visa will not run longer. There are no guarantees once you return - none.''

"But maybe if we do well?'' Nieca pleaded for a positive word.

"If you do well, then I will try to forget what has happened with the bank.''

Alexander and Nieca hugged each other again. For them it was at least a reprieve. "How soon do we leave?" Alexander asked as he tried to regain some of his lost pride.

"You leave tomorrow." Yarov responded. "And if you tell anyone, there will be no job. Be at Shermietovo by thirteen hundred."

"We will!" Nieca responded for both of them.

Within a few minutes they were back in the car. "You did very well Comrade First Deputy. You should get an award for your acting."

"Just let it be the heart surgery I need, and let it be soon," the First Deputy responded as he pressed his hand to his chest to deal with constant reminders of discomfort. "And by the way, when do I leave?"

"You will be off even before the family Kutusov. You should be at Shermietovo at eight in the morning.

*   *   *

"It's quite incredible," one prison guard commented to the other as the morning shift change was in progress, "the Dane has slept like a baby most of the night. They usually scream all night long the first time in."

Michael was still oblivious to the two men squinting through the observation hole in the thick iron door. But he was awakening to the rude recollection of his dilemma. The first decision in the solitude of the stark cell the night before had been to talk to the only person left who might have some knowledge of his whereabouts. He had prayed.

By mid afternoon, circumstances had changed again for Michael as he accepted Yarov's proposed data offloading task in exchange for his freedom and was immediately driven to Domodedovo Airport about one hour south of Moscow. He clutched the satchel of Sony 600 megabyte disks for use in retrieving the memory in the hard drive of the Cray II computers. He was informed that additional technical assistance would be available at the site. In the back of his mind, he hoped that it would be someone well-versed on the Cray.

The flight from Moscow to Volgograd was crowded. Women held children on their laps with older children sitting in the aisles. One woman, apparently the stewardess, but looking more like a female wrestler, barked out orders to passengers which were obeyed with fearful respect.

Until now, Michael had always been successful at avoiding flights on domestic Russian airlines, but assuming that he was being watched, he knew his only ticket out of the country and he wanted to get the job done. He was prepared for the worst, assuming that if the plane landed safely, whatever else occurred during the flight would be survivable. For the first hour, however, the plane sat motionless on the tarmac. For some reason, it had not received clearance for takeoff. By the end of the second hour, when the plane finally began to move, Michael found himself having to cover his nose with part of his coat. The woman seated next to him had brought a portable potty along for her children. Each of her two youngsters had taken their turn on the apparatus, but there was nowhere to put the container. She merely put a newspaper over the top and scrunched it beneath her legs between the seats. Michael tried to ignore the odor, but soon found himself fighting the impulse to gag.

The situation only became worse. Although he knew the domestic airline flights did not serve food, Michael had no way to prepare for the flight. Within the first hour of flight, people began opening their varied packages of food. The stewardess appeared with a metal cup and pitcher of water. She poured water into the cup and then passed it down the aisle. Passengers drank from the cup, one after another, with no apparent concern. Within an hour after the conclusion of the meals, the need for people to use the restrooms became intense. Each time the door opened at the two rear toilets, the stench would blow forward through the aircraft, causing Michael, and likely a few others, to be nauseated. It was one of the few times in Michael's life where the strong smell of cigarette smoke was actually appreciated. By the third hour, the cigarette smoke had largely overtaken the myriad of human smells. After three hours in the air and two hours on the ground, the aircraft finally made a smooth mid-evening landing at the Volgograd Airport.

Stepping out of the airplane, Michael took several deep breaths before he noticed a difference in the weather. It was cold, but not sub-zero as was normally the case this time of the year in the north. Given a little penchant for history, Michael knew that the city of Volgograd had formerly been known as Stalingrad, the sight of the epoch battle that reversed the fortunes of Hitler's Third Reich in the Second World War. As he walked down the ramp and began making his way toward the terminal, he saw a group of men, dressed like soldiers next to a vehicle similar in appearance to an American Jeep. He clutched the satchel provided by Yarov and a small suitcase. He had only enough clothing to last for three days by Western standards and at least three weeks by Russian.

As he walked past the three men they watched him closely. Over his left shoulder he heard the words, "Mr. Christensen, we would like to speak with you." Michael turned around.

"You are Mr. Christensen?" one of the uniformed men asked.

"Yes." Michael did not know whether to admit to the fact or not.

"Then you will join us. Please put your belongings in the vehicle." They could see that Michael was hesitant. "Yarov says you will come with us."

He joined the group in the small UAZ 469. Rather than driving in the direction of the terminal, the vehicle moved along the flight line off into the darkness. Michael could tell by the blue taxi lights along the runway that he was not on a road, but still in the middle of the airport runway. He became jittery when he realized the Jeep was headed for a plane parked at the end of the runway with its engines running. Several uniformed, armed guards were stationed around the aircraft. The vehicle pulled up next to the fuselage and the group climbed out - the leader beckoned Michael to join them.

Shortly, he was aboard a medium-sized jet. He was motioned to a seat and the jet raced down the runway climbing into the moonless night sky. The half-dozen military men on board the plane did not speak.

After about an hour of flight, the plane began to orbit steadily in a pattern. As they circled, he saw lights below as small villages twinkled up to the sky. Distinct flashes and streaks of light could also be seen at intervals below. It was a curious light show to Michael and tweaked his curiosity. It helped take his mind off of his empty stomach and his continuing nervousness.

The aircraft finally left its orbit, made a sharp bank and a steep dive. Michael saw a mass of darkness outside the cabin window, which he could only assume was a huge mountain. The plane bounced fiercely in the steep descent and Michael could hear the loud rush of wind storming past the fuselage with a roar. Suddenly, a bright burst of fireworks appeared above the aircraft and within Michael's view through the cabin window. The plane jerked to the left and began to shake, but continued its dive. As Michael nervously looked around he noticed that the others on the plane were showing no signs of concern. The aircraft leveled out and within seconds, he could see white and blue runway lights similar to those he had seen in Volgograd only hours earlier. As the aircraft touched down, the pilot immediately reversed its engines and the plane came to an abrupt stop. It then turned to the right and taxied at high speed. Momentarily, Michael thought perhaps the pilot was attempting another take-off, but again the plane halted. The cargo door at the tail of the aircraft was lowered.

"Come with me quickly!" ordered the English-speaking soldier. "You must hurry!"

Michael grabbed the satchel and his bag and ran down the rear ramp along with the others. As soon as he was outside the aircraft, the engines again began to rev and the hydraulic lift pulled the ramp back into the aircraft. After only moments, he felt the vortex of the aircraft blow past him as the plane taxied back out onto the field.

The group stood watching the plane as it raced down the runway. Michael was surprised that it would drop them off so quickly and take off again. His thoughts were interrupted, however, as the frightening reality of a red-orange explosion near the airplane answered his question. The aircraft lifted off the ground; the pilot quickly retracted the landing gear. Using steep angle of climb, the plane barely avoided the arching streams of light which Michael suddenly realized was tracer-fire from a large calibre machine gun somewhere on the hillside to the north. Though he had never seen such a sight before, it took only a second to know what it was.

"Where are we!" Michael demanded of his English speaking host.

"That, I can't tell you!" the man yelled over the explosions and the roar of the aircraft's straining engines.

A sense of doom struck deep into Michael's heart. He was beginning to wonder if he would ever find a way out of this nightmare. The men climbed into another vehicle and indicated that Michael should join them. They drove to an underground bunker not far from several partially destroyed airport hangars. Michael was no longer hungry, nor was he tired. He was suffering the paralysis of terror. His fellow passengers were obviously likewise preoccupied with their own survival and had little incentive to do any explaining.

Caucus Moutains, Early February, 1993

Over the past several weeks, Lado Deniken had tightened the noose on Caucus Station. His forces had swelled to over twelve thousand. They had become proficient in the use of small mortars in laying down accurate bombardment on top of any motion detected at the base. Each night, his forces had inched their way up the slopes and ever closer to the perimeter.

On the Potolemei Ridge at the sheep camp, ten of the twelve T-72 Battle Tanks were now parked under the camouflage of the thick pine trees. Behind the dugout positions, reinforcements of over five thousand men had steadily made their way up the winding sheep trail without detection and into the well-developed trench lines to bivouac. An all-out assault on the base was imminent.

In the three weeks since the Kartalinian Ridge fiasco, Deniken had decided to replace the lost artillery. In each effort, the Russian gunships came roaring out of the night sky. On the third such occasion, his forces were ready and equipped with small, but effective ZSU-24-4 Shilka self-propelled surface-to-air rocket launchers supplied by the Georgian National Guard. It had been a perfect snare, and ever since that event, the Kartalinian Ridge and battery had been free from aerial assault.

The victory at the ridge, along with the absence of snow storms, had freed movement of infantrymen through the dense Kartalinian Forest on the western approaches to Caucus Station. Accordingly, Deniken had stationed three thousand men in the forest. They successfully reached the perimeter of the mine fields and were now slowly, but surely, disengaging the land mines in a dangerous nocturnal effort. He had lost several good men in the delicate and tedious process.

* * *

The Dacha itself had been largely abandoned. The STAVKA ventured back to the large mansion only in the daytime when hostilities were at a minimum. Given the considerable intensity of the shooting and artillery barrages in the area over the past three weeks, the building was nevertheless largely still intact. At the insistence of their medical advisors, Andropov and Gagarin still slipped into the warm baths on the Dacha grounds in the early morning hours. Continuation of the Dolgozhiteli process was a necessary risk.

Preparations for evacuation were well underway. Document destruction had been a major project, as the STAVKA administrative staff had been working night and day to rid the complex of any documentary evidence which would disclose the true nature of the activities at the base. The item of greatest significance was the data compiled in the two large Cray II computers at the base computer center. The information gathered during the most intrusive periods of the Communist Party in the history of the Soviet Union could not be replicated. It would need to be readied for transit on moments notice.

"It's up to you to tell us when we absolutely have to leave, Colonel." Yuri Gagarin spoke to Colonel Anaimov, the Chief of the base defenses.

"We know that they are massing near the sheep camps for an attack. It could come today, or it could come tomorrow. In any event, we have saved the helicopters. We're not using them in battle any longer. We will be able to evacuate the STAVKA by air, or we can escape over the high mountain ridge to the north. We have kept a ground route open, but I would prefer to have you leave in the two Mi-28's."

"That would be our preference, also, Colonel," Gagarin responded. "But what about the computer problem? Where do we stand on that?"

"We have had a man retrieving the memory data off those Crays onto some type of disks since early morning. I'm not sure how long it will take, but the reports indicate that he is succeeding."

"Where did you get him?" Gagarin asked.

"His name is Christensen. He's a foreigner from Denmark or somewhere. He's the only expert Yarov could get for the job. But don't worry, Sir, he has no idea where he is or what he's doing here. Oh, by the way, Sir, he lives in America. Yarov says this individual can install all of the memory retrieval from the Cray's to our new system in the United States as well."

"How is it that this foreigner can be working down at our computer center and not have any idea what's going on there?" Gagarin was clearly irritated.

"Yarov says it was the only expert he could find under the circumstances. He assures us that there will be absolutely no security leaks. In fact, in my last conversation with him, he said he would stake his life on it."

"Well, he certainly will if there's a problem." Gagarin countered, not amused by the comment.

*　*　*

Michael was so hungry that even the military box ration that he was offered for breakfast looked good. At that point, anything would have tasted wonderfu. The conversation over the breakfast table was still sparse and uninformative. No one, it appeared, could speak English and, of course, Danish was out of the question.

Immediately after breakfast, he was taken to an above-ground location near the destroyed aircraft hangars. It was not difficult for him to recognize the two large Cray II computers amidst the wreckage of a collapsed roof. The Russians had quickly enclosed the area with tarps and plastic and were piping in warm air to the previously heated computer center. Electrical power had been quickly restored. From his initial investigation, he ascertained that the only apparent loss had been information which had been in the process of modem transmission at the time the power had been knocked out.

Working with two other men whose knowledge of computers seemed limited, he was able to engage the Cray II system and discovered that the hard drives hadn't suffered damage. The task was to transfer the entire 9.3 gigabyte hard drive data storage to the removable optical disk for easy transport. Fortunately, the Unix servers that he had sent to Technoserv from the States three weeks earlier were already in place. With brief inspection, he saw that it had been improperly installed. After a quick effort at correcting the configuration problem, Michael started formatting the Sony one gigabyte disks he had been given at the prison. He used the quick format rather than the safer system format. Given the frightening welcome upon his arrival the night before, he wanted to be prepared to leave as quickly as possible.

* * *

By early evening, ten T-72 battle tanks were on the move at the Potolemei Ridge. Infantrymen had created crossing points on the trench lines which would allow the tanks to emerge from out of the trees between the sheep camp and the Russian perimeter and then charge at full speed approximately one mile across an open field infested with a variety of anti-personnel obstacles.

Deniken noted, curiously, that the Russians still had not placed any anti-tank structures in the no-mans land area. He presumed that it was probably too late for the base's defenders to bolster their defenses further before the serious shooting started. He was willing to gamble with ten tanks and five thousand men in an attack intended to break across the southeastern perimeter of the base and place his troops in a strategic bridgehead position squarely on the eastern end of the runway. From that point, he could consolidate his position, and prevent any fixed-wing aircraft landings on the airfield. He would then prepare to launch an assault in either direction, to the east against the administrative offices, hangars and barracks areas, or to the west in the direction of the lodge, concealed along a heavily forested hillside, and the caves beyond. It would be a major undertaking and even after they had formed their bridgehead, many

Georgians would still die. But, once the perimeter was breached, he knew that a victorious end to the struggle would be within their reach.

* * *

Michael had just become accustomed to the idea that perhaps the coming evening would not be as full of terror as had been the previous night. Still, no one would respond to his questions as to his whereabouts. He only knew of one soldier capable of carrying on a seriously informative discussion in English, and Michael had not seen him since arrival at the mysterious airfield. From the shooting in the distance, he could tell that he was at some Russian installation which was under continuous attack. But from the weaponry and the rather nonchalant style of the men with whom he was working, Michael sensed that they at least viewed the situation as something less than desperate.

One of the useless technicians who had been gone for several minutes, made himself helpful as he returned with a loaf of bread. He shared it with Michael and the other technician as the process continued on its own for the moment in the computer center. Michael hoped that over the meager meal he would be able to elicit some information. But in response to each question, a wry smile and a negative nod was the only response he could get. Even sign language failed. The Russians had been clearly instructed not to talk.

Suddenly, he heard more small arms fire. The shooting was followed by thunderous booms that began to ripple across the airfield, shaking the ground. He watched the computers react, almost feeling sympathetic twinges as they bounced to the rumble which was undoubtedly interfering with the downloading of the information from the Cray onto the optical disks. For the moment, the explosions were in the distance.

Approximately two and a half miles across the airfield to the southeast, Spetsnaz troopers were dug-in in a trench line along a one mile span of the perimeter fence. They had been positioned there for the last three weeks realizing that the most vulnerable attack against the base could come at them in the form of an assault across level ground from the sheepherder camps on the Potolemei Ridge. Through their night-scoping devices, they closely watched all movement. Suddenly, the radio crackled. "Here they come - I see tanks!" A distant rumble confirmed the sighting.

The front line Spetsnaz radioman immediately contacted their own contingent of T-80 battle tanks with their 125 millimeter 2A46 smooth barrel guns carefully positioned inside the perimeter fence ready to roll quickly back and forth on the airfield's runway to afford rapid support to the infantrymen.

Suddenly, a roar of simultaneous explosions filled the air as the Georgian T-72's rolled headlong out of the trees and across the mine fields directly toward the Spetsnaz. The anti-personnel mines had no affect on the tanks, but their detonation created a clear path for infantrymen who began to carefully follow where the treads of the tanks had made deep tracks in the dirt and mud.

Deniken ordered an initial group of one thousand men to follow immediately behind the tanks. He planned to send another group in BMP tracked fighting vehicles which would ferry the infantrymen across the parts of the mine field not cleared by the tanks once a bridgehead was in place.

The noise became deafening as the Georgians laid down a barrage of artillery fire on the Spetsnaz perimeter positions just ahead of the daring charge across the open space. The Spetsnaz returned the fire - their machine guns spitting sheets of steel churning up the ground as the Georgians were attempting to advance. The human carnage common to all wars made its first notable appearance as the attackers came within range. As the two forces closed on one another, the mass of shooting and explosive clouds of fire, smoke and unfathomable din, made it difficult for a commander on either side to know what was really happening.

At the computer center, Michael disengaged another optical disk and began formatting a new one. He only had one disk left. Fortunately, he had almost downloaded the entire ten gigabytes from the Crays. As he inserted the last disk, he heard the shrill wail of sirens from various points throughout the base. The piercing sound drowned out the rumbling of the battle somewhere off in the southeast. He was alarmed and knew that if things could possibly get worse for him, they probably just did. The two technicians, in response to the sirens, jumped up and grabbed their weapons. One yelled at Michael which his limited grasp of the Russian language interpreted to mean, "Leave...now!"

With his heart pounding and stomach lurching, Michael left the Crays whirling, grabbed the satchel of downloaded data disks and ran out of the computer center into the dark, trailing the two men. He had no idea where they were going, but he did not want to be left behind.

The chase took him to the edge of one of the destroyed hangars. He slowed his pursuit when he saw the men scrambling into infantry fighting vehicles waiting to follow other vehicles rolling across the airfield in the direction of the battle. Fire clouds reached into the sky like a huge forest fire out of control. He quickly concluded that he did not want to go in that direction.

Once the soldiers had left, Michael stood on the tarmac in front of the destroyed hulk of an aircraft hangar and watched the last vehicle move off in the direction of the battle. He was alone. The scene that played out in front of him had been so unbelievable he just sat down and leaned against the wall of the steel corrugated building. For almost an hour he just sat against the wall starring into the smoke and dust of battle, attempting to put the event before him into some sort of perspective.

At first he had felt an unfamiliar, icy fascination, but the almost trance-like spell began to wear off and heart-pounding terror again took charge as an artillery round landed not more than five hundred feet from where he sat. The concussion caused him to bounce at least six inches into the air and then land hard on the ground. His ears were popping and ringing against his skull. Yet, in spite of it all, his body was cold, wanting only to find refuge from the weather.

Uncertain as to the exact location of the bunker, he wandered among the wrecked buildings. The bunker was somewhere to the rear of the aircraft hangar area, he thought. It would allow him at least a place to hide and would surely be warm. But the panic that he had suppressed while working at the computers, was rapidly attempting to assert itself. It was becoming time to accept the inexorable fact that he would never see his family again. He could run, but he had no notion of where to go. The battle was approaching. He feared that he would probably be bayoneted or shot by the attackers without being able to tell who he was or why he was there. It was time to get ready to explain the whole mess to God.

* * *

Colonel Anaimov, in command of the base's defenders, had just put the telephone back on the receiver. The seriousness of his concern was clearly discernable on his Spetsnaz-trained poker face. He made his way down the hall to Yuri Gagarin who was in the tunnel command center some six miles distant from the fighting. "Chairman, Gagarin, I believe you will need to leave sooner than planned. It is time for you and the STAVKA to evacuate. An attack is in progress from the Potolemei Ridge. It is not going well there! The Georgians have tanks and have reached our perimeter. They will be on the airfield by morning! I have sounded the evacuation siren! It applies to all STAVKA personnel. You asked me to tell you *when* - this *is* when, Sir!"

"I will report that to the others and we'll be on our way," Gagarin responded without alarm. As the first man in space, courage was built into his person. He would get the STAVKA out safely.

Within minutes, the two Mi-28 helicopters were warming their engines and taking on passengers. In one helicopter Andropov, three aids and two body guards buckled in. Gagarin was at the controls. The choppers lifted off, veering to the north dropping periodic flares behind them in an effort to divert possible heat-seeking anti-aircraft missile fire from forward positions in the Kartalinian Forest.

Watching from a two mile distance, Michael picked out the helicopters beyond the western end of the airfield as their flashing lights danced against the backdrop of the mountainside. He had no success in locating the underground bunker and had returned to the flight line area to see if he could find anyone who would help him. He searched in all directions, but he was still entirely alone. The only people he could see, were the ones he assumed were engaged in the battle to the southeast on the other side of the runway area. As for the helicopters, he could see that they were leaving the area and climbing among the mountain peaks causing him to fear even more that the base might be evacuated without him.

As the thunder of the battle grew louder and the sound of the helicopters more distant, he sat on the tarmac, hands against his knees, diligently trying to reconstruct the last few days of his life. At first he had tried to blame it all on Yarov, but with more careful introspection, he knew that he had made his own choices. Regardless of the cause, he was now in a helpless and futile predicament. He feared that those who had been charged by Yarov or whomever to protect him were already dead or dying.

As the Mi-28's lifted to the twelve thousand foot level to clear the high mountain ridge to the North, Yuri Gagarin was visited by a terrifying thought. He spoke into his microphone to his assistant. "The computer records. Do we have them?"

"No, Sir, I'm certain that we do not. They were still being recovered in the computer center as we left!" an aide responded.

"I'm going back! Without the list of all the enemies of the revolution, there will never be a Second Coming. *I can promise you that!*"

The helicopter suddenly tilted hard, made a 180 degree turn and sped back down the canyon between the snow-covered mountain peaks.

Several more rounds of artillery crashed into the buildings not far from where Michael sat. At the same moment, he heard the pulsating warping sound of a jet helicopter at the western end of the long dark runway. His vision tracked the motion causing him to conclude that it was not flying across the mountain in the direction of the area from where it had taken off, but was closing rapidly in on him. Though frightened and uncertain, he reasoned that survival required taking the chance that the occupants of the chopper were friendly. He frantically waved his hands and satchel attempting to signal the helicopter since it seemed that it was about to fly right over him.

Suddenly, the helicopter stopped in the air, hovered for a moment and then swung down for a quick but delicate landing. A man jumped from the helicopter. Michael was relieved to see that he was one wearing a uniform similar to those with whom he had been working over the past day. In the next second, however, an explosion occurred behind the building knocking Michael off his feet and causing the helicopter to lift off and touch down again like a bird trying to land on a fence post in a heavy wind.

The man was upon him. He grabbed Michael by the arm and picked up the satchel that had fallen to the concrete. They ran together, full speed, to the helicopter. The man shoved Michael on board and jumped behind him, still half-hanging out the door as the craft hovered momentarily in the air and then began ascending rapidly.

Michael lay on the floor of the helicopter trying to catch his breath and orient himself. From somewhere inside, he expected an explosion to occur at any moment and end it all. As the aircraft gained altitude and he felt the cold metal floor of the cabin pushing upward, he finally felt there might be a reasonable chance of survival after all.

After several minutes, Michael looked up as one of the pilots walked back to where a man was sitting on a cargo bench. The pilot removed his helmet and the two men, their heads huddled close together, tried to carry on a discussion among themselves shouting over the noise of the helicopter. His eyes focused on the faces which were lighted only by the red panel lights within the craft. One man, the pilot, looked strangely familiar. It was a face from the past - someone he had seen before. The other was also distinctly recognizable, but Michael was afraid to say a word. Snatches of memory flitted through his mind as he remembered the bizarre tour of the old sea captain's ship and the shrine to the *dead* Cosmonaut on the wall. His thoughts became bogged in a sort of grey haze. It had been a strenuous two days.

Michael eventually moved to one of the steel racks used as a bench. For the better part of the two hour flight, he quietly watched the two men as they conversed, both apparently confident that Yarov's foreigner could not pick out a word of Russian amid the loud din of the helicopter engine.

Michael Christensen had come face to face with the STAVKA.

CHAPTER 20

Salt Lake City, Utah, Mid February, 1993

Establishing a reputation as a member of the elite Counterespionage Unit in the Manhattan office of the Federal Bureau of Investigation had not been easy. Kenneth Swindler had spent twelve years sharpening his senses for Russian spies during the most contentious part of the Cold War. By the end of year twelve, he had reached the level of burnout. The work had become more and more inconsistent with the family life which he so much enjoyed.

The older children were now reaching the range of junior high and late grade school. He knew that when he had requested the transfer from the fast track of the Manhattan office of the FBI to the much smaller operation in Salt Lake City, it had been the right decision. For him it was like coming home, having grown up in the small town of Santequin among the sprawling fruit orchards on the south shores of Utah Lake, seventy miles South of Salt Lake City. He was a graduate of Brigham Young University where he also attended law school. After a brief flirtation with private practice in Utah, he found the work tiresome and frustrating and decided to take a chance at a career in the FBI.

Kenneth was known as a ''Russian Chaser.'' It was his group that tracked the myriad of KGB agents, operatives and slot agents across the United States and often in foreign countries. Some of the most challenging work had been maintaining surveillance of the Russians that operated out of the Soviet Mission to the United Nations. It was the assignment that everyone in the agency wanted, but few received. Yet, Kenneth had been in the middle of it all as they had played cat and mouse throughout the eighties with the well-trained, highly motivated Soviets feverishly intent on stealing U.S. military and industrial secrets under the guise of diplomatic activity.

Family life in Utah was a major improvement over New York. Being able to actually see his children on week nights before they were asleep in bed was one of the rewards of the move. But the job itself had become less interesting. With the new emphasis from the director placing large numbers of FBI agents on anti-gang task forces, Russians soon became the farthest thing from his mind. The work had turned into an intense effort to investigate and interdict the growing gang violence, primarily among Asian and Hispanic crime organizations in and around the Salt Lake City metropolitan area.

Kenneth, given his normal propensity to succeed both on the job and off, had tallied a number of early arrests of key gang members, taught Russian courses at night school at the local community college, coached little league baseball, and had fathered a new baby girl to add to his three school agers. It was not New York, but in most ways, Salt Lake City was preferable.

His blood warmed quickly as he arrived at work on the mid-January morning to see a special telex from the Office of the Director in Washington D.C. The excitement and anticipation was difficult to contain as he read the message:

SPECIAL CASE ASSIGNMENT

TO: Kenneth Swindler

FROM: The Director of the FBI

RE; Bribery of United States Congressman:
Violation 42 USC 1344
Case No. 2441-93-461

You are instructed to open a case and investigate for possible indictment individuals connected with a company known as Transcontinental Trading, Inc.
249 E. Tabernacle Street, St. George, Utah 84770.

Congressman Stony Chapman R/Oklahoma, sixth district has turned evidence to the Justice Department that he accepted a bribe on or about October 23, 1992 in the sum of two million dollars for his exercise of influence to withdraw support for the Gold for Aid legislation pending in a pre-filed bill before the United States Congress.

Contact was made in Washington D.C. at the Lincoln Memorial on the afternoon of that day by one Asian, thought to be Chinese, approximately 55 year old male from Hong Kong. Our suspect, Mr. H.I. Hui, a Hong Kong banker entered the U.S. a day before the meeting and left the country the following day.

Approximately two weeks thereafter, payment of two million was made by TTI in St. George, Utah, to a company known as Oki-Soft in Edmond, Oklahoma. The company is owned by the son-in-law of the congressman.

The company was heavily in debt, and on the verge of bankruptcy. It appears as though payments also included consideration to the congressman directly in repayment of his personal loans to the son-in-law's company.

Son-in-law is known as James D. Burrows.

Principal reason for contact to Salt Lake City Bureau is to investigate possible conspiracy to commit bribery including possible involvement of representatives of the Russian Government known to reside within the state of Utah.

Specific evidence includes the following:
1. The $2,000,000 payment to Oki-Soft was made by bank draft on the account of Transcontinental Trading, Inc. over the signature of Michael Christensen.

2. Michael Christensen is a Danish National (see visa photo attached). He resides in St. George, Utah at 4421 Gunlock Court, 84770. Telephone number 555-4878, work number at Transcontinental Trading, Inc 555-8822. All area code 801. He is 32 years old, married to U.S. citizen, Gina Wyatt, from St. George, 5 children. Christensen is Caucasian with blond hair; height-6'1".

3. According to James D. Burrows, Michael Christensen made direct contact on behalf of TTI, did not disclose that the company was owned by Russians, and made the investment of 49% of the stock on a blind purchase basis without exercising any due diligence whatsoever. To this point, actual stock certificates have not even yet been issued.

4. The company was incorporated in the State of Utah during the previous summer and shows Michael Christensen and 3 Russians, Boris Yarov and Raissa Kovac and Andre Putshkin as incorporators. Yarov is identified as a high ranking official in the Russian Ministry of Aviation and had very high level access prior to the putsch. The second person named is suspected to be a Foreign Intelligence operative. From Photo I.D. Department analysis we believe she was a member of the USSR State Sports Committee at the Goodwill Games in Seattle in 1989. To us this means KGB, Spetsnaz or worse. 5. Transcontinental Trading, Inc. is involved in the business of purchasing computers and components for use by the Russian Aviation and Aerospace Industry. Some Department of Commerce violations may have occurred. You are requested to use such violations as a pretext for contact with Christensen.

Please commence surveillance immediately.

6. Ten people have traveled to the headquarters of TTI in St. George, Utah, from Russia over the past three months including the following: Boris Yarov, Raissa Kovacs, Andre Putshkin, Andre Lianozovo, Alexander Khikov, Boris Kershnev. All are listed on their visas as computer programmers. At least three and as many as six are currently thought to be working at the facility in St. George, Utah. The most recent visa has been issued to a Victor Krovas who is believed to be the First Deputy (CEO) of a major Russian bank with strong international connections. His role with TTI is unclear.

7. The principal suspect for investigation is Michael Christensen. His visa shows extensive travel in Russia over the past 4 years.

Please report results. The director will keep you informed of additional analysis results.

"Great stuff!" Kenneth Swindler let out a jubilant holler as he irreverently declared that he was summarily off the "gang squad" for awhile. He began filling out the appropriate requests for travel and surveillance assistance in the St. George area.

His style was warm and outgoing. Many thought of him as a sort of young version of Hal Holbrook as his animated style, distinctive moustache and contagious enthusiasm seemed to put coworkers quickly at ease. He would have little difficulty assembling a team of willing agents to do the job.

For the agents, the trip to St. George would be a welcome relief from the grey deep freeze caused by the temperature inversion that had Salt Lake City in its grip for over three weeks without letup.

Arizona Strip, Mid February, 1993

Joe Wilson was on another tedious mission. The pathologist at the Utah State Medical Examiner's lab had completed his report on the two bodies that had been discovered in the cinder pit just inside the Utah border near Red Rock City, Arizona, several months earlier. A duplicate report had been sent to the Washington County sheriff's office to be filed in connection with a homicide investigation. The Medical Examiner had, however, noted that the victims had worn rings on the middle finger of their right hands. He had contacted the sheriff and requested that a search be conducted of the shallow grave to see if rings could be located.

The State Medical Examiner was hopeful that the ring would provide evidence in determining the identity of a victim. Often the style, make and composition of rings had led to positive identification. Joe Wilson was on the road again, his car pointed east on State Route 26 where he was planning to spend the better part of the morning sifting through dirt with a prospector's board.

The hot chocolate he had brought along with him helped, but did not solve the problem. The crisp, cold wind was blowing across the high desert plains of the Arizona Strip from the south. The chill factor definitely made the long morning effort more than just routine. Nevertheless, he worked his way through the area where the shallow graves had been, and by late morning had concluded that there was no ring or any other evidence of the earth's tragic use of the place.

He pondered the thought that, in many ways, the earth seemed to recycle bad experiences. Within months, or even weeks, after the discovery of the bodies, someone had already used this cinder pit as a camp site while further tearing up the hill with their off-road vehicles. It was strangely poetic that it would never occur to the campers that the place where they would put their tent was the same spot where two men, violently killed, had been laid to rest by their killers.

Making his way up the dirt road and reaching the intersection with State Highway 26, Joe could see the faint bluish haze caused by the many wood burning stoves in the town of Red Rock City some five miles to the east. He was continually nagged by his last discussion with the sheriff regarding the note from Hannah Jackson about her missing daughter. He had never trusted the polygamists and couldn't understand why the sheriff was so comfortable about treating them as if they lived on their own Indian reservation. He assumed that it had been a considerable risk on the part of the woman to send him the note. He found himself sitting in his patrol car at the Big Pine intersection with Utah Highway 26, weighing the decision whether to turn left and return to Hurricane, or right and at least make a brief inquiry of the girl's mother. After further thought, he decided to turn right.

As he negotiated the sheriff's department cruiser into the small town, he could tell by the size of the dormitory-like additions on the homes, that these people had done their best to literally multiply and replenish the earth. The problem in his mind was that they had often done so by threat, abuse or coercion.

Several years earlier, he had been to the Fred Jackson home to deliver the keys to a tractor which had been purchased from Joe's father. At that time, he had remembered young children at play and now assumed that one of them had grown up and was now the missing girl. Without this previous experience, it would have been difficult for him to locate the home since no addresses existed in Red Rock City. Joe knew the reason - to confuse bill collectors, law enforcement officials and any other "gentiles" who might venture into the area seeking a person without permission of the community leaders.

As he drove up to the home, he noted the partially finished wings and additions. Fred Jackson had taken on new wives. He went to the door and a young woman came to the door, but would not open it. "What do you want?" Joe could hear a voice through the door.

"I'm Joe Wilson, with the Washington County sheriff's department. Mrs. Jackson?" Then he remembered he was in a town where there could be five Mrs. Jackson's in the same home.

"I mean, Mrs. Hannah Jackson?"

"She doesn't live here," was the muffled response through the closed door.

His experience with polygamists in the past, convinced him that he should be persistent. Teaching followers to lie to protect identities was a tenant of the faith. It was the standard response in turning away strangers. He would try a different tack. "I know what you're trying to do, lady, but I am an officer of the law. I need you to tell me the truth. Now, where is Hannah Jackson?" He spoke loudly, making certain that his words would penetrate well into the house.

In the next moment, he heard a door creak open in what appeared to be a storage cellar which opened out from a cemented in area just off the foundation to his left below the porch.

"Hello? ....are you looking for Hannah Jackson?"

Joe looked down to see the face of a woman whose head was protruding above the concrete edge of the porch area. "Yes, that's who I'm looking for."

"Well, that is me. I'm Hannah Jackson. Please - please come down here."

Joe walked down to the cellar door below, noting that he had received no response from the person behind the door on the main floor to his more forceful demand. He was invited into an unfinished basement which had been swept clean with large throw rugs laid down in one corner. It was dimly lit with only one small window allowing the outdoor light into the room. He could see that a plastic garbage bag had been taped across the window to stop any draft. In the corner, against the grey concrete stood a propane space heater which seemed to be operating at full capacity to stem the chill of the south winds against the cold portion of the foundation above ground.

"Please sit down," the woman spoke as she pointed to a small chair near a card table.

Joe walked to the chair and watched her with interest as he detected her tentative expression. He sensed that she was suspicious of him, and there was little doubt in his mind that his passing her note on to the sheriff had only resulted in further aggravation for the poor woman.

She sat on the edge of a well-worn sofa. "Have they sent you to reason with me?" emphasizing fear and sarcasm simultaneously.

"I'm not sure what you mean, ma'am," Joe responded. "I saw your note. And...."

She quickly interrupted. "Everybody else has seen the note, too. There are copies of it all over town! Everyone is laughing at me and accusing me of unfaithfulness and everything else ungodly. Maybe they'll burn me at the stake, claiming I'm a witch for trying to just ask where my daughter's gone to!"

"I'll be honest with you ma'am," Joe was uneasy in defending his position, uncertain as to what had transpired. "I received the note from you. I passed it on to my superiors like I'm supposed to do. And that's all I've done."

"Oh, I see. So, you don't know about me? You don't know what they're saying?"

"No, I don't. And I'm not sure that it's any of my business."

"What we do here is always no one else's business on the outside. Nobody cares! They could take me out and kill me today and you would read the report in tomorrow's newspaper that it was a traffic accident. Well, I'm frightened. But before they do anything to me, I want to know where my daughter is!"

With the word daughter, she automatically looked at a photograph on the table next to her.

"That's her?" Joe asked.

"Yes, that is Flora, and she is all that I have in this life. You just don't know how awful and how lonely it has been without her. Let me tell you, young man, I grew up in all this. I believed it and I still want to believe it. But anyone who would take my daughter away without me knowing about it and probably marrying her off to some old man - it's wrong. It's from the devil! And, there is no one to turn to...no one!''

Joe barely heard her. The color photo showed a beautiful girl gazing steadily at the camera, her chestnut hair framing a perfectly heart-shaped face. Joe couldn't shake the instant impression that she was looking directly at him. He could not ignore the immediate effect. Joe knew he would think of her again and his heart ached at the thought that something really evil might be happening to her.

The hand-held radio attached to Joe's belt barked. ''One-X-Four, please come in - One-X-Four!''

Joe broke from his thoughts, quickly detached the radio and keyed the mike. ''One-X-Four, over!''

''We have a report that you are out of the car in Red Rock City, what is your situation?''

''I'm here conducting a interview.''

''You are instructed to leave the area immediately. I repeat - One-X-One says that you are to leave now!''

With this transmission, Joe knew the Red Rock City deputies on the Arizona side of the border had become aware of his visit to Mrs. Jackson and were complaining to the Washington County sheriff. He looked at Mrs. Jackson as he stood up. He could see by the droop of her shoulders that she was a severely oppressed woman.

''I'll do what I can, Mrs. Jackson. I really will. I'm sorry all this has happened. I guess I should have never passed that message on. But I just hoped that,'' Joe paused wishing he could be more reasuring, ''that the sheriff would have done something.''

''Please help me, young man!'' Hannah was pleading. ''Please, find my daughter. Someone must know where she is. In fact, I think everyone here knows, but no one will tell me. Please, for her sake - please find her, and at least let me know!''

''I'll see what I can do. I'm probably in trouble with the sheriff as it is, but I will see what I can do,'' he reassured her as he walked out and climbed into his patrol car.

As he drove up the road, he glanced in his rear view mirror only to notice the pickup trucks with several CB and radio antennas at the other end of the street observing and no doubt reporting his departure.

He left the town and drove west on the state highway back toward Hurricane. He knew what awaited - a chewing out by the sheriff.

Hurricane Mesa, Mid February, 1993

The Hurricane Mesa emerges as a towering butte neatly situated between the rugged river valleys and desert reaches flowing into the Colorado River Basin and the Red Rock Canyon country on the southern slopes of the Rocky Mountains. The city of Hurricane, Utah is ten miles due south. To the west, at a ten mile distance, is the north-south expanse of Interstate 15 as it runs through a long, deep valley on its journey from Salt Lake City to Los Angeles. Eastward, within three miles as the crow flies, the boundaries of Zions National Park maintain the remote features of the cavernous red and white rock sandstone region.

The immense natural formation is unique in its broad, flat surface area with steep, sheer, and almost vertical walls on virtually all sides. The rectangular shape of the mesa allows almost four full square miles of space on top, removed from the rest of the desert southwest by its rare configuration.

The Hurricane Mesa is not without its unique man-made features as well. Across the middle of the plateau, running north to south, is an eight thousand foot runway. At two points along the mesa's ridge are silver colored one hundred thousand gallon steel water tanks placed atop long thin towers. Near the runway, a sizeable hangar with an old house trailer is still in place which has been noted by many tourists protruding precariously over the side of a cliff on the eastern face of the plateau.

In early years, the Hurricane Mesa was known as "The Test Site" to locals who had helped construct the improvements on behalf of the United States Air Force. From the late fifties to the mid sixties, a rocket-sled situated on a high speed rail was used for the purpose of testing harnesses for parachutes and pilot seats in jet planes. By the mid seventies, the military had moved out and finding no further use for the facility and had leased it to private industry.

One such event had included the final scene of the James Bond movie, OCTOPUSSY, in which the stunt team succeeded in catapulting from the rocket-sled an aircraft, loaded with dynamite into the sky for the purpose of filming the spectacular explosive crash on the desert floor for the film's closing scene.

In the mid eighties, a company from West Germany purchased the facility for the purpose of doing additional automobile safety-related research. By 1990, it had again been largely abandoned when the German company was approached by businessmen from Hong Kong, desirous of obtaining a five year lease on the facility. The money had been reasonable, and negotiations by a man named Jim, had been concluded in tandem with the acquisition of the Sunset Canyon Ranch property, located three miles away in a deep canyon to the east adjacent to Zions National Park along the Kolob Creek.

Shortly after the completion of the negotiations, Jim and his experts had begun securing the area and installing sophisticated security and aircraft approach control devices. By early 1992, the first IL-76 aircraft from Cuba, by way of Mexico, began making periodic runs to the site.

The flights had been initially infrequent and always a risk. Normally, the secret base was reached by a discreet helicopter jump over the border and then a long trip by automobile from southwestern Arizona, up the highways paraleling the Colorado River to Las Vegas and then into southwestern Utah. Additionally, semi's and other trucks carrying equipment for the installation were routinely permitted legal admittance through the various border stations based on well-drafted, fraudulent documents. By mid-1992, most of the equipment was in place and ready for the facility to take on its new mission.

The Hurricane Mesa was an ideal location. It was the only remotely positioned airstrip that was strategically located near an equally ideal Dacha-style retreat. The Sunset Canyon Ranch provided many more amenities than had the Caucus Station as it was within easy travel to Las

Vegas and Southern California areas. It would certainly serve as an adequate safe haven from which the STAVKA could implement its plans.

All had been well-prepared by the time the IL-76 screamed out of the darkness and planted itself delicately on the Hurricane Mesa's runway on the moonless February night. The long-awaited arrival was pleasing not only to the mysterious occupants of the aircraft, but also the awaiting Spetsnaz troopers. Perhaps none were more emotionally moved than Captain Major Sarabrov as he stood near the aircraft with twelve of his men carrying out the responsibility to secure the aircraft parking vicinity. As he saw the two legendary figures alight from the aircraft, a lump welled up in his throat .

Within the next moment, they were walking towards him as Jim made the introductions, "Honored Chairman Andropov and Comrade Gagarin, this is Captain Major Sarabrov. He commands the installation defense forces at this site."

Sarabrov had always been a man able to withstand the anticipation and uncertainties of battle. Explosions, death, pain and fear of the occasion had fazed him only slightly. But now, he was standing face to face, shaking the hands of two of the greatest Russians to have ever lived - yet they were known to be dead. He was overcome by reverence for the moment. As he looked into the face of Yuri Gagarin whom he had so idealized as a teenager, he momentarily broke protocol and spoke, "Comrade Gagarin, I find this so totally incomprehensible - it is like seeing a vision! To see you - my hero as a boy and the hero of so many of us, gives us even more reason and more vigor to serve you and the other leaders."

"That is quite enough!" Jim snapped at Sarabrov. "Maintain your bearing!"

"Yes, Sir," Sarabrov responded.

"You should attend to the prisoner and avoid such small talk!" Jim continued to bark commands as troopers exited the aircraft with a blindfolded man under their control. "This is the Danish computer man. He is now in your custody. He cannot be harmed. Is the computer set up here?"

"We are still having problems, Sir, but it should be ready quite soon." Reporting anything negative in front of the great leaders was something Sarabrov had wanted to avoid.

The three leaders, together with their aides, stepped into two white Cherokee 4x4's, followed by a van confining the prisoner, Michael Christensen. They drove down the runway to the entrance on the northeast side of the mesa and from there, they commenced their journey down the steep mountain road in the direction of the Sunset Canyon Ranch or what was better known to the Russians as Zion Station.

CHAPTER 21

Moscow, Russian Republic, Mid February, 1993

Unfortunately for Muscovites, the fabled Rus, a group of powerful Scandinavian Vikings in the 9th century arrived in the middle of a beautiful summer to locate their capital city where present day Moscow stands. The Kievans say that a huge billboard was there to greet the Vikings bearing the words, **"THIS PLACE IS TOTALLY INTOLER-ABLE IN THE WINTER TIME. THE CLIMATE IS MUCH BETTER TO THE SOUTH ALONG THE DNIEPER."** The Kievans boast, further, only those that could read headed south. The rest remained in Moscow. Kievans have always considered themselves superior to their neighbors 500 miles to the frozen north.

The fourteen million-plus residents of the snowbound city were now working their way through another six months of severe hardship. Among them was a new arrival from Vladivostok, KGB Colonel Andrea Ziyetski and his team of four agents.

As he pursued his investigative efforts, he could not help but weigh one observation against another. It was his first chance to see streets of the city he had not seen since his banishment to the Far East for the supposed misdeed at Yalta during the coup of August 1991. The contrasts were many as he saw a sign of something new at almost every corner. People seemed in motion, going places or coming from somewhere. They were busier, he concluded, than they had been during his earlier times in the capital. He observed similarities between Moscow and Leningrad, something that had been previously very hard to do. But something new was certainly in the air, and despite the hardship and misery that he saw in the faces of so many in the street as they fought the winter, he sensed an absence of despair that had been a regular part of life in Moscow for as long as he could remember.

He and his driver drove to the mammoth apartment building complex at Sviblovo. It took almost half an hour, once inside the development, to locate the building. They spent another ten minutes climbing the fourteen floors to the apartment of Alexander Kutuzov.

Upon knocking, Ziyetski was surprised as the door opened and a curly dark-haired little girl about six years of age threw her arms around him, hugging him tightly about the legs. In the next moment he heard commanding words, "Get back, Erika, it is not your father - it is not!" The man reached down, pulling the child away from Ziyetski who felt the warmth of real tears having moistened the pant leg of his KGB colonel's uniform.

"Please excuse me, Sir, my niece - she is disturbed. She thought you were her father. She thinks everyone in uniform is her father. That is difficult for a child in Moscow. So many uniforms. So what is your business?"

"I am from the Federation Security Agency and seek..."

The young man interrupted, "Sir, you should understand this is my home. I have papers. We purchased it yesterday!" He continued to speak nervously. "This building is the first in Sviblovo to be privatized, and I bought the lease for ninety-nine years! We are not trespassing. I can prove it!"

"Hold up for a moment!" Ziyetski shouted He heard the doors in the stairwell area opening behind him as curious neighbors tried to hear the conversation. "I am not here to question your ownership. I seek Mr. Alexander Kutuzov. I have this as his address. Am I correct?"

The young man was thoroughly relieved, "Oh, I see. I was afraid when I saw..."

"My uniform?" Ziyetski interjected.

"Yes, I do not have visits from the KGB. It was a shock. But Kutuzov, did live here. He is gone - he abandoned it last week. In Moscow apartments don't sit vacant for even a day."

"Where did he go?" Ziyetski asked.

"I do not know," the young man responded. "But let me think." He produced a small piece of paper. "This was stuck to the message board by the door when we moved in. See, it is to Kutuzov. It says, 'Please, come see me urgently at Technoserv, L. Artimoshkin.' As far as I know, Kutuzov has never come back, or I would have given him the note."

Ziyetski thanked the man, not doubting his story, and excused himself for the inconvenience. In a parting thought, he looked at the beautiful little five year old still whimpering softly near the door. "Please tell me, what is it with the child...what has happened to her father?"

"He died three years ago. He left home in a uniform - a security guard. You may have heard of him, Dimitri Koman?"

"I am not certain that I have. I am from Vladivostok," Ziyetski was somewhat apologetic.

"He was run over by a tank the night of August 21, 1991 in the street near the Russian White House," the man responded.

"Oh yes, then of course I have heard of him." Ziyetski realized the reference was to one of the three men who had died in the streets, opposing the hardliners in the failed coup of August, 1991. He looked again at the little girl, realizing that she would throughout her childhood always be looking for her uniformed father to return.

He stooped down, held his arms out and she walked forward again, "I knew your daddy. We all knew him. He was so brave." He spoke in the best consoling words he could muster.

The child fiddled slightly with the military ribbons on the chest of his uniform. They were brightly colored and he could see that they had caught her eye. Wanting to give her something, but knowing not what else to do, he reached inside the pocket, unhitched the clasps and detached the four bars of bright ribbons from his uniform, evidencing his medals earned over many years and put them in her hand. Surprised, she looked at them and smiled shyly. In the next moment, Colonel Ziyetski was on his way down the stairs with a heavy heart.

The trip to the Technoserv offices took another hour in the dreary streets. It had snowed two nights earlier and the snow removal crews had not yet completed their jobs. Upon arrival at Technoserv, he was directed to the upstairs computer research area of Leonid Artimoshkin. As he walked through the establishment, he was certain that the director was not present because he could see, even as a computer illiterate, that no one seemed to be working. After reaching the upstairs rear computer lab area, he noticed a man sitting at a computer in deep concentration. ''Mr. Artimoshkin?''

''What do you...'' Leni turned in a start as he saw the KGB officer standing before him with an armed adjutant behind him. ''What do you want with me now? I thought we were finished. Kutuzov is gone. Isn't that what you wanted - wasn't that the deal?''

Ziyetski pulled a chair from a nearby table and sat down immediately across from Leni. ''I'm here because of Kutuzov, but tell me about this deal, what deal?''

''Well,'' Leni spoke emotionally, not sure what he should and should not say. ''You said that if Kutuzov could be convinced to stop, you would leave me alone. He's gone, I think to America, so why are you here?''

''Who made this deal that you're talking about?''

''The KGB, aren't you the KGB?''

''Are you sure it was the KGB?'' Ziyetski inquired carefully.

''Well, not really, but who else would blindfold me, haul me away into interrogation and threaten me and my family?'' Artimoshkin's voice was quivering.

''I don't know of any such incident. Did you see who did this to you?''

''Yes, I saw them in their building, but I don't know where it was. They all looked very official. They had guns and knew everything about me.''

Over the course of the next hour, the conversation continued as Leni Artimoshkin related the entire incident. He felt much more willing to talk as the KGB Colonel showed a degree of sympathy and concern. Ziyetski's assistant took notes as fast as the two men could talk. From the conversation, it became increasingly evident that Kutuzov probably had the answers that would uncover the mystery of the Trans-Siberian train attack. Ziyetski was sorely in need of a live witness. He knew that such a person would be compelling in an effort to obtain the complete support of the Federal Prosecutor's Office, as well as even more support from Dombrayov and the entire weight of the Moscow Headquarters of the Federation Security Agency.

To Ziyetski, the computer engineer's story was not improbable. Artimoshkin's treatment had been consistent with a normal KGB operation prior to the new government. That it still existed was no surprise to him. But what did Kutuzov really know - and what additional facts had he discovered as he had returned to Moscow from Vladivostok? Who forced him out of the country? Was it a group within the government?

He knew from his law enforcement work that extortion had become the weapon of the new and improved version of Moscow malefactors. Ex-KGB personnel had been recruited to stage ruthless offenses against citizens and foreign visitors alike in the semi-organized crime form of thievery. Mail was still regularly being opened before the addressee would see it, not for secrets, as had been the case during the Soviet Union, but for money. In certain parts of the city, some companies had taken down signs and blacked out windows in an effort to give the appearance of no business activity at all. In Moscow, prosperous looking businesses attracted extortionists. Colonel Ziyetski, for the first time, suspected that perhaps the Moscow extortionists should also be considered suspects in the Trans-Siberian train massacre.

By nightfall, the day's efforts had concluded and Ziyetski found himself leisurely, deep in thought, walking down a Moscow street not far from the hotel. As he rounded a corner, a poster in a store window caught his eye. The initial focus was the look on the face of a young Russian hockey player. His face bore a distinct similarity to Ziyetski's own young ten year old at home in Vladivostok which, in a slight twinge of homesickness, caused him a sense of relief. He then studied the poster more carefully to see the electrifying smile running ear to ear as the young man appeared to be jumping for joy, his Olympic gold medal around his neck and the soft Russian tri-color flag draping his body. Across the top of the poster was one simple statement **SVOBODA POBEJDAET**, a proud declaration meaning, "Freedom Wins!"

After staring at the poster and feeling an emotion that he did not fully understand, he walked off into the winter night, his heart warmed amid the slight snowfall.

* * *

Dombrayov was not happy with the results of Ziyetski's investigation in Moscow. The records of Toko Bank and all other State banks would be held closed as far as investigation of gold account losses were concerned - that is, closed until a sufficient audit and review could occur. Dombrayov shared Ziyetski's suspicion that powerful elements within the military, together with a previously unknown organized criminal group were trying to delay the inevitable truth that shipments of gold had been on the Trans-Siberian train. Ziyetski had been right all along, and as the head of the KGB, Dombrayov had to do something.

Ziyetski's report of the disappearance of his prime informant in Moscow had been equally disturbing. The audit analyst of the foreign accounts at Toko Bank, Alexander Kutuzov, had provided helpful information while in Vladivostok auditing the branch bank there. And now, Ziyetski was reporting that Kutuzov had traveled to the United States on behalf of Technoserv. The additional fact that Technoserv was a one-third owner of Toko Bank had not been lost on the KGB investigators under Ziyetski. It clearly appeared that Kutuzov had been moved out of the country to suppress information that he could otherwise have passed on to the authorities.

Following the unsuccessful attempt to contact Yarov, a similar effort had been made to locate the First Deputy at Toko Bank. It was soon discovered that both had left the country for the United States on business - to Utah in particular. A meeting was quickly initiated in Dombrayov's office. "It appears to me, Colonel Ziyetski, that everyone who could answer our questions has left the country."

"That's correct, General." Ziyetski responded.

"That puts me in a very difficult dilemma. I would like to initiate an immediate effort to determine how much gold has gone and how much remains. To do that, I must get the consent of the State Banking Committee, which is controlled by the First Deputy. To make matters worse, the First Deputy's closest supporters are in the Army High Command offices down the street, clamoring for your neck because of your insubordination in Vladivostok." Dombrayov stood and walked across the room to look out the window. He gazed nervously at the Kremlin walls which filled the expanse of his view. "I'm afraid to go to the President until we know what is really happening. If we make the wrong move, evidence will be hidden before we can prove anything. And I can tell you, that without absolute proof, Yeltsin will not confront the military. He simply will not, cannot and would not be foolish enough to do so. If he asked my advice, that's what I would tell him."

Ziyetski was disappointed at the response. He felt that he had pushed the case as far as possible and hoped that the absence of the three individuals might be sufficient evidence in and of itself. "So, what would you have me do, General?" he asked. "Should I simply return to Vladivostok and put this investigation on ice again?"

The KGB Director deliberated for a moment. He stared from his Kremlin window into the frozen Red Square below. Snow had been pushed into large mountains at various points. No funds were available in Moscow to remove it from the square. He turned from the window and looked at Ziyetski and spoke like a man afraid to jump from a burning building, but knowing that he had no choice. "You must go to the United States. Take your team and track down Yarov, the First Deputy and your informant, Kutuzov. I must have at least two of those three men back here for a taped confession so that I can show it to President Yeltsin in person. With this evidence, not even the military can keep us from arresting and prosecuting the real culprits, no matter who they might turn out to be. You have got to bring those people in so that we can get to the bottom of this. That's all there is to it."

"And how soon can we leave?" Ziyetski inquired.

"I will call the Director of the Federal Bureau of Investigation as soon as his work hours begin in Washington D.C. tomorrow. I will explain to him what you are doing and request his assistance."

He could see Ziyetski balking at the suggestion. "My Federal budget will be used to cover the trip. So, don't worry about how you're going to get there.'' Dombrayov added.

As he left Dombrayov's office, Ziyetski located his investigative team in one of the day rooms of the Federation Security Agency Headquarters. The thought of going to the United States to investigate this case had not occurred to him nor his team members. None had ever been outside of the Soviet Union. There was an air of excitement that breathed new life into the investigation of the largest murder and robbery case in the history of the Soviet Union and the Russian people.

Zion Station, Mid February, 1993

''My dear Comrade Yarov,'' Andropov spoke bemusingly, ''why in the name of Stalin, Lenin, Karl Marx, and anybody else you can think of, did we not do this years ago? Is this not the most beautiful and relaxing place you have ever seen?'' Andropov swished some water around and added crystals as he sat in the spacious outdoor jacuzzi adjacent to the clear flowing waters rippling across the red rocks in the creek at the bottom of the canyon.

''It's because of those very individuals that we haven't traveled freely, my dear Chairman.'' Yarov became more serious, ''Now that the Americans have let down their guard, we're free to travel anywhere. In fact, I plan to take in the Lido de Paris in Las Vegas next week. And for the week after that, I have tickets to the Russian National Hockey team versus the National Hockey League All Stars. Believe it or not, I will wear a ten gallon Ronald Reagan cowboy hat to the game in Los Angeles, California. This is a very good situation for us.''

''That is true. And the women, these young American girls, they know nothing, but that is very pleasing to me. Their innocence arouses me and they bring a look of fear to the activity that satisfies me. I feel a sense of conquest.'' Andropov was loosening up as well, as the combination of soothing water and vodka started to take affect.

"Americans, you know - they are such fools."

"I agree. Here we are, enjoying the finest benefits that American life has to offer. Have you watched television? Other than all the silly commercial interruptions, there seems to be much to see."

"If I didn't know better, my good Comrade, I would say that you are sounding like a gloating capitalist. Are you perhaps tempted by all this?" Andropov lightly chided.

"Not tempted," Yarov responded, "but with the problems the Parliament is having with Yeltsin back in Russia, you may have to return sooner than planned. So, I want to enjoy it while I can."

Approximately one mile away across several pastures and within a narrow but flat part of the canyon to the rear of the ranch, Yuri Gagarin had just finished a morning of knocking clay pigeons out of the sky. He was overjoyed by the knowledge that his accuracy had never been better. His partner, whom he had soundly defeated in the contest, was the chief Spetsnaz physician and medical consultant to the STAVKA. The doctor had served for years at the STAVKA compounds across Russia and had become Gagarin's closest friend and confidant.

They began walking across the field in the direction of the ranch house which they affectionately referred to as "The Dacha." As they crawled over the fence near the horse training track, their discussion of the days of youth in Russia changed to more serious matters.

"You know that your blood pressure and white blood cell count have both dropped into the conversion range, do you not, Yuri?" The doctor finally broached the subject he had sought to avoid.

"Yes, I'm aware of that," Gagarin responded.

"I was uncertain as to the exact age, but as I look at it, it has been characteristically similar to the research done at the Soviet Academy of Science and the Biological Experimentation Institute. The fact of the matter is, in your late fifties as the literature predicted, is the most appropriate time for the conversion. Plus, your blood test from yesterday is very conclusive. The time could not be more perfect."

"And what if I don't?" Gagarin asked nervously.

"Well then, you will probably still live to ripe old age of seventy-five to eighty, eighty-five perhaps even ninety. But your alertness, your ability to respond as a young man, and as a leader, will seriously deteriorate by your seventieth to seventy-fifth year. That's just the way life is. And, Andropov will outlive you by many, many years."

"Do you really think he will live past one hundred?" Gagarin asked.

"I have absolutely no doubt," the doctor responded. "His transplant ten years ago worked perfectly. The diet has consistently performed above the research expectations and the Dolgozhiteli process has continued to work exceptionally well. The human growth hormones allow the young heart to significantly rejuvenate other vital organs. As far as I'm concerned, we have a middle-aged Georgian sheepherder on our hands in Andropov. The Georgians still have men who are over one-hundred years old that run more than six miles a day, and go after the young women just like Andropov does. And with the additional enhancement that we have included, I really do think that you will live even more good years than either of them."

"It's the heart transplant that bothers me. I'm fit. Those old Georgian sheep herders, they don't have heart transplants."

"Quite true, Yuri, but you are not one of them. We will give you a serum that is created from our research on the isolation of the regulator gene. Some call it the Methuselah gene. It controls aging. But, we can't get it to control your heart. So, we've got to get you one with the longest life...and the Georgian sheep herders, their hearts just keep on ticking."

Gagarin was oblivious to the humor, "You know, in all of my years, as a Cosmonaut and a pilot, I have spent very little time in the hospital. And those tests that you and the other STAVKA doctors keep doing on me, I don't mind saying are not pleasant."

"Well, if it's any consolation to you, my dear Yuri, the doctors that will handle your transplant are much superior to those who took care of Andropov. In fact, I think you really needn't worry. If I had a chance to add forty or fifty good years to my life, then I would do it also. Maybe, by the time of the Second Coming, it will be possible for more of us. Perhaps you will be able to arrange for the hearts of many Georgian sheepherder boys to be beating in the chests of the leadership of the Motherland, as well as their key physicians, of course. You know, someone has to keep you going," the physician laughed.

"I guess I don't understand the logistics of it all. It's just that," he paused, "while we were in Russia, I had virtual control over everything. As beautiful as this land is, and as free as we seem to be, I still feel that we lack the control - the dominion. I have to admit, I feel insecure. Maybe it's these canyon walls, or perhaps I am accustomed to the view across the Svanathian River valley. That is beautiful, you know. I was there for over twenty years, and I miss it."

They walked a little further without conversation. Finally, Gagarin broke the silence. "When do you start the conversion process?"

The doctor pondered the issue for a moment and then spoke. "I would say in another week, maybe two at the most. I will prepare the injection. The Spetsnaz will take over from there."

"Well, I guess I can't complain. It's always good to rely on the most skilled people in the world, but I'm still nervous about it. Remember, I'm not a trained soldier. I haven't the cold steel nerves of a Spetsnaz trooper. I'm not really even a party leader. I'm just the test pilot who was young and foolish enough to be persuaded into climbing inside that Sputnik back in 1961."

"Don't denigrate yourself, Yuri. You can't forget that the future of the Motherland rests on your shoulders!" The doctor spoke undiplomatically, a marked departure from his exuberance and excitement at the skeet range. "The day that you emerge publicly at the Kremlin walls onto the televisions and before the masses of the people of the Soviet Union and literally everywhere, will be the greatest day in the world. It will have the significance of the reappearance of Christ to the Christians. You have been prepared for this time, and I have dedicated most of my professional life to see that you are physically able to undertake this important task. So, don't worry about the logistics. They will be taken care of. This is your destiny."

"Well, how about us taking in some major vodka before all this happens?" Gagarin spoke like a brother, his face emitting a slight smile.

"That we will do, my friend. But the women, there are no Russian women you know," the doctor observed.

"Thank goodness for that!" Gagarin responded, but have you seen what Jim has been bringing in - they are so young and also they are very nice!"

"I am sure the price is ten times what it was in Turkey."

"That's probably true. Someone is getting rich, but we are ten times more able to pay for it. Our Chinese bankers - they're financial geniuses of the first order."

Salt Lake City, Utah, Late Februry, 1993

Following a week of training and going through the administrative process of recalling his investigative team from the Domestic Gang Violence Squad, Kenneth Swindler was finally prepared to make his move into southern Utah. In addition to the extensive information which had been received on the bribery of the U.S. Congressman, a follow up investigation from the State Department had revealed over two dozen Russians on travel visas in the St. George area at the request of Mr. Michael Christensen, the president of Transcontinental Trading, Inc.

The State Department records had shown a visa issued to one Boris Yarov at the Moscow office of Technoserv. He was listed as the Chairman of the Board of TTI. He had made a trip in the previous year into the United States with Oklahoma City as his designated destination. Records showed that Yarov had again entered the country, this time with a banker known as Victor Krovas, listed as the First Deputy of Toko Bank in Moscow.

From his Russian-chasing experience, Kenneth was not overly surprised that Russian spies might still be in business in Utah. Utah possessed numerous defense industry related firms including Thiokol Industries which built the boosters for the space shuttle, and Hercules Aerospace, which built rocket engines. Hercules even had its own contingent of Russian inspectors stationed at the main gate of the massive industrial site west of Salt Lake City under the auspices of the Intermediate-Range Nuclear Forces Treaty (INF) in 1987. In addition, there were other defense department establishments including Hill Air Force Base, a major factor in the missile command of the United States Air Force, as well as Dugway Proving Grounds and the Tooele Army Depot, the largest storage depot of strategic chemical and biological warfare agents in the U.S. arsenal. The hi-tech industry throughout the Salt Lake City and the Provo area to the south had been heavily engaged in the business of serving the needs of the defense industry at various levels for many years and it was all a perfect feeding ground for a hungry spy.

In more recent times the emphasis had changed. The FBI found itself dealing with industrial espionage which, although illegal in some respects, did not always result in the type of conduct that would allow for the opening of a federal case. Well-trained agents of foreign governments, friendly and otherwise, were still in business. It was well known that former KGB and slot agents were still stationed in the United States to gather industrial and technological information for public and private concerns in their various countries.

Profit was now motivating the Russians. Yet for the FBI, it was confusing and difficult. The numbers of new Federal criminal investigations had reduced while the influx of agents was greater than ever before. It required more FBI agents at a time when politicians controlling the purse strings perceived the foreign threat to have lessened.

As Kenneth traveled south with his team, it was the first legitimate Russian-chasing operation that any of them had been on for over a year. The bribery of the congressman had been sufficient to open the case. Where it would lead, however, whether into another industrial espionage problem, or an actual foreign government intrusion into the affairs of the U.S. Congress was uncertain. The congressman had been interrogated in detail, but despite his contrition, the extent of his knowledge about a Russian connection seemed extremely limited. His son-in-law had been even less helpful.

The FBI team was made up of three pairs of agents. Each pair was assigned its own unmarked car. The agents would spend their initial days in St. George working surveillance at the downtown TTI site. Once they had photographed and determined the cast of characters, they would determine whether to move in or use it as a embarkation point for Russians who could then be tracked across the country.

A Federal Judge in Salt Lake City had already issued a search warrant for the banking records of TTI. The warrant was narrowly worded, however, allowing only access to those accounts which were used to transfer funds from TTI to Oki-Soft in connection with the alleged bribe. The agents knew it was important to conduct surveillance in the case over a period of time in order to determine the true scope of the entire project. As a more probable cause for violation was established, new search warrants requesting broader rights would be requested by the FBI.

At this point, by Kenneth's hunch, the elements of an expanded international espionage case were already in place. The bribery of a U.S. congressman by a foreigner and funds coming from a Russian-owned company spending millions of dollars in a remote part of the country were significant red flags. The presence of representatives of the Russian Aerospace and Aviation Ministries shuttling in and out of the United States in connection with the business made it even more suspicious. To Kenneth, the main questions were: Who in the Russian government was calling the shots and how high up the conspiracy?

Extensive work had been done to try to determine the scope of Michael Christensen's activity. Some in the bureau had already suggested that perhaps he had been planted as a Soviet slot agent back in 1981 when he was first sent to the United States as a Mormon missionary. It was almost impossible to analyze his background before that time. He did not appear in any FBI or CIA data banks. Swindler had, of necessity, started the Michael Christensen investigation from scratch.

His family genealogical information had been easy enough to find. The Salt Lake Bureau had simply sent one of their agents to the massive Genealogical Research Center at the headquarters of the LDS Church in Salt Lake City. Within twenty minutes, the agent had acquired a completed pedigree chart on Michael Christensen, his parents, grandparents and tracing the family all the way back into the mid-16th century. Although interesting, it was not helpful.

The team's initial analysis of the overall facts of the case continued to view Michael Christensen as the cog in the wheel for the Russian operation. The coincidence of his travel, his seemingly easy access in and out of the Soviet Aviation Ministry's computer subsidiaries prior to the East-West thaw was exceptional. Travel records obtained through Pan American Airways, which handled the direct flight from New York to Moscow prior to the company's demise, showed fourteen flights taken by Michael to the USSR in 1990 and 1991. A check with the travel agency in St. George had shown several additional flights on other carriers including the Dutch KLM Airlines into Moscow from New York as well as Copenhagen.

The Danish-Russian joint venture had seemed legitimate. However, the FBI had little opportunity to determine the full extent of the company's relationship with the Russian government. One thing was clear - several members of the joint venture board had also served in positions in the Soviet Military which had required Top Secret clearances at the highest levels. It was all enough to create deep suspicion regarding Michael Christensen. The FBI was concerned that a very capable and menacing agent had surfaced and found fertile ground to operate under a unique cover.

By the morning of the following day, each of the three FBI teams was in position. The surveillance would now begin in earnest and if Kenneth Swindler had his way, it would open the window to a massive national security problem of vital significance effectively taking him and his team out of the anti-gang business for a long time.

*   *   *

For Alexander and Nieca Kutuzov, the arrival in Salt Lake City had been none too soon. A Russian employee from the TTI office in St. George had picked them up and taken them to their small apartment in the Sugar House area on the east side of the city. After a few hours of instruction on the handling of the Federal Express shipping of the TTI computer equipment orders coming out of Salt Lake City, the TTI employee left the Kutusovs and returned to St. George, three hundred miles to the south.

On their first few days of exploration, they discovered Salt Lake City to be delightful. A small apartment had been acquired for them in the name of TTI. By American standards it was considered tiny, a small two bedroom flat. By Russian standards, however, Nieca and Alexander had found their dream home. It was far more than they expected, and it made temporary banishment from Russia more than tolerable. They struggled with the strange irony that moving them out of the country, a result obviously good for the First Deputy, could also be so good for them. But they knew it was only temporary. The return to Russia was a fearful prospect.

Within the first week, however, thoughts of Toko Bank and problems in Moscow began to fade. Their frequent trips to the supermarket and the long walks around the city remedied homesickness as well. Even the food was palatable from Alexander's standpoint. They had been informed by a letter from St. George that the first shipment through TTI had been delayed. This would give both Alexander and Nieca the freedom to spend more time exploring their new environs.

As they returned from dinner at a fast food restaurant, still overwhelmed by the number of fast food restaurants on every other street corner, Alexander tried to put things in perspective. "I'm not sure what all this means, but would it be fair to say that if Toko Bank had not been engaged in removing gold from the government treasuries, perhaps none of this would have happened?"

"What do you mean?" Nieca asked.

"We know that Russia is bankrupt. It's bankrupt because of the way we do business. If all had been going along with status quo in Russia, as it had for so many years through our lives, then we would never have come to America. We were forced to leave because we asked the right questions. In fact, I think under conditions as they existed even ten years ago, I would have been swept off the street and sent to the Gulag for suggesting that the bank might be engaged in illegal transfers of gold." His voice was upbeat, jubilant and satisfied. "This isn't the Gulag, sweetheart. No one can hurt us here. Maybe the First Deputy will like us better in six months. You never know."

Nieca put her hand over his. "By the time we go back, things might be changed at the bank. The First Deputy looked very ill when he came to us last week. I don't think he'll last much longer."

The two of them then sat down to a fresh strawberry pie they had purchased at the bakery nearby. The word "fresh" had not been part of their vocabulary as strawberries were too exotic to ever imagine on the Kutuzov table in Russia.

But now, Alexander thought to himself, here I am with everything - with my Nieca, away from my tormentors, and still alive and doing well. What more could a man expect? What more?

* * *

The University Park Hotel was about twenty blocks to the northeast of the Stringham Avenue apartment. The University Park, built in the mid-1980's to serve the regional, national and international visitors to the large number of businesses located in the research park, boasted six hundred rooms on five floors perched high on the eastern mountain bench overlooking the expanse of the Salt Lake Valley. More recently, however, due to the increased construction and expansion of the nearby University of Utah Medical Center, including the relocation of the world renown Primary Children's Medical Center to a place adjacent to the University Hospital, the University Park Hotel had also become somewhat of a hospice for families whose loved ones were being treated at the sprawling medical facilities.

On the same evening that Alexander and Nieca were eating their pie, Yuri Gagarin sat nervously in suite 427 of the hotel. He was awaiting the injection which would, over the course of twenty four hours, reduce his heart to a deteriorating and eventually damaged organ. Within days, he would be suffering from irreversible congestive heart failure as the cardiac muscle itself would begin to die. The only solution would be a transplant. The STAVKA doctors had given the assurances that there was no better place for a transplant than with the acclaimed transplant team at the University of Utah Medical Center.

Earlier the same day, Captain Major Sarabrov, together with twenty four members of the 23rd Spetsnaz Company had spent several hours clandestinely mapping and staking out the University of Utah Medical Center and its related buildings, parking lots and other support facilities. All entry ways and exits had been carefully detailed. Hallways and emergency exits had been analyzed and evaluated for suitability. The project itself had been much simplified by the existence of a large hospital map on the wall near the information desk in the Medical Center's main public entrance.

To Sarabrov, there could be no mistakes. In his mind, Yuri Gagarin was the most honored man of all of the Russian people, with as close to a God-like image as the mind of a dedicated Russian patriot would allow. Once he had realized that his hero was still alive, he had sought out every opportunity to be of assistance to him directly. An otherwise dreary, hopeless world had suddenly changed to one with an exciting, dynamic future. Now, the security of the most famous of Russians was in Sarabrov's hands. He, with his elite Spetsnaz Alpha Group would be prepared for all contingencies, the most of important of which was that Gagarin could enter the hospital, undergo his surgery and return to Zion Station without ever having been recognized.

In the event of recognition, depending on how far along in the treatment process Gagarin had progressed, a plan was in place to remove him from the hospital before formal release. It was all to be a great event that would someday figure prominently in Soviet history - and Sarabrov would be a part of it. The pride and enthusiasm was difficult to contain.

There was, however, according to the advice of the Spetsnaz medical specialist, a period of approximately five days during which they could not move the great Cosmonaut under any circumstances, even if recognition occurred. It would be the most delicate and vulnerable days in the future of the Second Coming. For this purpose, a Spetsnaz operative would be stationed at his bedside posing as a family member and in a position where he could slip strychnine to Gagarin and end the hero's life should such a drastic measure become necessary.

In conjunction with the communications ensign and input by the STAVKA medical specialists, the Alpha Group had carefully examined the names of all hospital employees. The principal fear was that a Russian ex-patriot, somehow on the hospital staff, would suddenly recognize the famous Russian, despite his emaciated and aging appearance. The risk was not considered high because the world at large had accepted the story of Gagarin's death in an airplane crash in 1968. Now, almost two and a half decades later, it was unlikely that anyone other than close friends would be able to recognize the man. Nevertheless, emergency plans were always ready in the event that the unexpected should occur.

Through the better part of the evening, Sarabrov had sat quietly in the white Jeep Cherokee parked in the long, cold, four-level parking terrace serving the University of Utah Medical Center. It was a good place, he thought, to wait with his men. The other cars could easily be seen yet kept out of sight. People coming and going from the hospital always appeared to have their own personal concerns and the possibility of suspicion was minimal. He noted the total lack of police patrol in the area. This also was to his benefit.

Finally, at 11:00 p.m., he checked with his men. He walked to another car which had several of his troopers inside, dressed in civilian clothes and looking very American. "Well, are we ready to pull the plug?" he asked his ensign.

"I think we ought to do it. It's been a long time, Sir, and I don't think that you should have to wait any longer."

Sarabrov smiled mischievously. He then looked down at his ensign and spoke again. "You're in charge here. I'll be back, and if I'm smiling, it'll be none of your business!"

He walked off to an awaiting van and climbed in. Next to him was one of his gunnery sergeants and another sergeant was sitting in the back of the van. "Are we ready?"

"We're ready, Sir," the sergeant answered.

"Then let's get going," was the command.

The sergeant put the van in gear and drove away from the University Hospital area and westward down the hill in the direction of a residential area in Salt Lake City.

Presently, the van pulled up under a street light along a quiet lane. The Captain Major eyed his watch and noted that it was 11:25 p.m. His heart began to beat rapidly. "So what do you think is going on in Moscow right now?" Sarabrov asked the sergeant behind the wheel.

"I expect my mother is wondering where I am. After all, I haven't been home for four years," the sergeant laughed. "Nor have I," Sarabrov said wryly.

"Well, some of us will get home sooner than others," the sergeant smirked.

* * *

Alexander and Nieca had long since finished the pie and were preparing for bed. Alexander was watching television.

"Would you turn it up, please, Alexander?" Nieca asked. "I don't understand English so well. Perhaps if it is louder."

Alexander turned the television volume louder, but his interests were no longer on the television. They were on Nieca. He was rewarded as she stepped from the bathroom. He watched her from the open doorway. She's a wonder. How I love her blonde hair - short like an athlete. Alexander's pulse quickened as he caught her smile as his favorite parts of her seductive young body strained against the thin fabric of her nightgown. As she moved toward him, his passion quickened. He wanted her immediately as the foreplay had been all cerebral and from the look on her face, he could tell that she felt the same way.

Alexander stood and met her smile, sensing her overpowering sensuality taking control of the moment. He looked into her deep blue, unforgettable eyes and took her in his arms. As their lips met, his fingers reached back and clumsily fumbled with the snaps on her nightgown. It was an intolerably enjoyable moment.

Suddenly, a piercing, cold excitement filled his whole being. In the next second, what had been a totally positive sensation, gave way to sharp and unbearable pain as he opened his eyes to look directly into the flaming face of the woman who was now supporting him as he sagged against her.

It took only three seconds. She worked the wide-blade Kazakhi knife from the base of his back to the top of his kidney and with perfect Spetsnaz-trained precision pulled it forward puncturing the base of his left lung and then slicing through the middle of his abdomen until the better part of his intestines began to spill out onto the floor. The tactic was designed to remove sufficient air from the lungs in order to avoid a scream. In this, she was successful as only a few words could be spoken.

"Nieca!" the horrified man whispered between gasps. "Nieca, why, what are you ..." He looked at her with his eyes wide open in disbelief as he staggered backwards, his hands uselessly clutching his abdomen.

She, in turn, backed away and replied coldly, "I'm not Nieca - my name is Yelana, you fool!"

He staggered once more and fell to the floor in a pool of blood. She walked forward and viciously yanked the tie tack with its micro transmitter from his tie. One of her tools of the trade - it would be used again. She walked to the sink, washed her hands then returned to her room and sat in the chair in front of a mirror and waited for a moment. She then opened her suitcase and pulled out a long thick red wig from the side pocket. She put it on and fumbled with the band until it was in place to her satisfaction. She combed the hair, allowing the flowing red locks to fall across her shoulders partially covering the nakedness of her night gown and almost matching the dark red blood on her body. Yelana looked at her watch. It was 11:30 p.m. In less than thirty seconds there was a slight tapping at the door.

She ran to the door, threw it open and was instantly in the arms of Captain Major Dimitri Sarabrov. Crushing her to him, he slid his hands over her body, smothering her open mouth with his kisses as the two Spetsnaz troopers entered the room to deal with the carnage. Sarabrov paused only long enough to pick up the phone and place a call to room 427 at the University Park Hotel.

"I've pulled the plug," he reported to Jim at the hotel. "Everything is in order."

He hung up the telephone, took Yelana in his arms again. Oblivious to the others, Yelana and Sarabrov began pulling at buttons on his uniform and disappeared into the bedroom.

"My beloved Yelana. How I have yearned for you all these years!" Her blood-soaked nightgown only served to heighten the perverse intensity of their unspent passions.

In the next room, the two Spetsnaz troopers dealt with the issue of Alexander Kutuzov. Within minutes, they had removed his body to the van and driven off into the night, leaving their Spetsnaz's Captain Major at the apartment. Kutuzov's remains were taken to the foothills of the nearby Wasatch Mountains and unceremoniously dumped in a ten foot deep grave.

Yelana had positioned herself to carry out the most critical phase of an important mission.

* * *

The injection took only a moment and seemed almost anti-climactic. Normally it would be done directly into the heart muscle, but the physician had to be careful not to create evidence of a syringe hole that might alarm the American cardiac surgeons. It was then time to wait and not to sleep. Through the night, in room 427 of the University Park Hotel, the Hero of the Soviet Union, Yuri Gagarin sat in a chair, physician by his side, the other aides and Spetsnaz troopers nearby. They observed the minute-by-minute deterioration of his body as the heart that had once orbited the earth was now beginning to degenerate at a rapid pace that would mean only death for its owner - that is, unless a transplant could soon be found.

CHAPTER 22

Zion Station, Late February, 1993

The stark room was less comfortable than the green-walled cell in the Moscow prison. The bed was softer and the situation more private - far too private. Michael would have preferred the gruff Russian jailers to the periodic hand that slid a tray of food through the thin horizontal slat in the door twice and sometimes three times a day. He wanted to see or talk to someone. The isolation was tearing away at his ability to think clearly. He wondered if perhaps he might be going insane.

The periodic sound of feet shuffling in the hallway told him that there were people nearby. The sounds of foot traffic were varied. To get a fix on where he might be was an exercise in sheer speculation. He had been hooded and shackled as soon as the helicopter fleeing the mysterious battle in the mountains in southern Russia had made its initial landing. From that point forward, it had been a journey of misery. He had lost track of night versus day, and sometimes even up versus down as he moved from aircraft to room and then back to aircraft again. The hood was only removed when he was in a room without windows. The rules were clear

- if he deviated in the slightest from his instructions, he would be shot. To make the point clear, a rifle barrel had been put to his head only to click without a round in the chamber. But the emphasis was made. He intended not to test the resolve of his captors.

In the darkness of the past two weeks, his expansive world of international business had been whittled down to an existence in which eating and going to the bathroom were the principal happenings of the day, and both actions still required the permission from others. But he had used the time to keep his mind busy by continued pondering of his circumstances. His imaginary map of the world was continuing to expand with sophistication. He tried to connect the many voices, strange languages, the smell of certain foods, and even the temperature of the air to places where he might have been. The varying engine sounds told him he had been on a variety of aircraft. But the motion of the plane in the air made it impossible to estimate direction.

As he attempted to reason through the purpose for his dilemma, it was becoming increasingly certain to him that he was a condemned man and that the chamber would be loaded the next time a barrel was put to his head. His reasoning stemmed from an image in his teenage years. It was spawned of his Danish ancestry by way of the indigenous fear of the peril from the east. The face he had seen in the helicopter was the same he had remembered as the dictator of the Soviet Union at a time in his past. How such a thing could be possible, he did not know. He had paid little attention to history and couldn't remember the name, but it was the face of an unmistakable menace from the past - and somehow, he had been drawn into its evil center.

The other face had become easier to place. Michael was almost certain that it belonged to the Russian Cosmonaut, Yuri Gagarin. As improbable as it might seem, the smile on the wall in old Captain Petrofski's state room was the same. But to Michael, how it all related to him was a mystery.

Reason dictated that it all had something to do with the Cray disks. Certainly, he had no hostage value. But it also made sense that he was needed for something, otherwise his captors would have already mortally removed him from their charge.

By his estimation, it had been almost three weeks since he had left

St. George for Moscow. He would soon be expected home and Gina would start to inquire. But if she called Technoserv in Moscow, surely Yarov's goons would put her off with excuses. And when he never arrived home, the final word may well be that he was last seen with a woman at the airport in Moscow. His greatest hell while still living was the devastation and disturbing memories he knew it would create for Gina and his children-something he was now powerless to stop.

There was a small set of holes in the log wall apparently intended to afford minimal ventilation. With careful effort, he could see parts of evergreens against a brown snowless ground cover. Beyond, he thought he could see the red rock of a cliff, but he was unsure. In any event, the mid-day sun allowed enough light to break through the trees and bounce off the perceived rock that at least with a good imagination, reminded him of home.

* * *

Yuri Andropov reclined in the jacuzzi as he watched an event of significant proportions unfold on Salt Lake City television. A man had arrived from Russia for business only to fall extremely ill a few days after his arrival. His wife, desperate for help had pleaded with the media for a heart donor to save her husband's life. Reporters had flocked to her assistance as the event had evolved into a sort of cause celeb for the Salt Lake media market. Even in her distressed state, the obvious physical virtues of the young Mrs. Kutusov had caused more than one male reporter to hope that the old guy would die and give the reporter a chance to make her an American citizen.

The lead-in was trite enough to even cause Andropov to snarl. "Here's a Russian story that really tugs at your heart," the anchorwoman began. The report then switched to a teary-eyed woman sobbing before reporters as she had just been told that her prayers had been answered.

**The woman, Nieca Kutuzov, just arrived in the
United States from the Soviet Union a week ago**

for a six month visit. Her husband, Alexander Kutuzov experienced extreme heart failure a few days after arrival. He was taken to the University of Utah Cardiac Care Center where he has been awaiting a transplant.

The story, however, has a happy ending. Word of her dilemma reached relatives in her native Georgia. Rothman Chemical Corporation, headquartered and based here in Salt Lake City coincidentally owns and operates a large cement processing facility in Armenia.

Nieca was informed only five minutes before this interview, that Rothman Chemical is providing one of its aircraft to transport the body of a brain-dead 19 year old Georgian man who was severely injured last night in a motorcycle accident near the Georgian city of Svanathia.

The Rothman corporate jet, which flies into Armenia several times per month, landed in Tbilisi, Georgia to pick up the sensitive cargo. Her husband's new heart will be arriving in Salt Lake City by tomorrow morning and the transplant should be well in progress by mid-afternoon.

Andropov watched, carefully relying on his KGB English training in the fifties to understand the television report as the interview continued, and the reporter posed a question:

"How do you feel about this, Mrs. Kutuzov? Did you ever think a heart would be available, let alone, one from your native land?"

Amid sobs, the woman appeared distraught, nose running, tears spread across her face in a state of emotional see-saw, as she spoke in broken English. "I love American people. They so good to me and make husband now live. I thank my family in Georgia." She continued to cry

as the camera pulled back to the reporter's signout:
"So there you have it, from Russia with love!"

The news then moved to another story.

Andropov was relieved that the most critical step of getting a donor from Georgia had gone so well. His protege now had a good chance at assuming his roll in the planned Second Coming. Much like the woman on television, Andropov reveled over the events and the seemingly unending opportunities that were continually unfolding. Similar to his Spetsnaz agent that had captured the media spotlight, he loved the Americans too. Their naivete gave him hope, and their stupidity gave him power.

* * *

The most critical moments of the open heart surgery had come and gone without incident. Captain Major Sarabrov, along with his force of twenty-four Spetsnaz troopers had maintained a constant vigilance in and around the University of Utah Medical Center complex during the entire period. They had taken great care to avoid detection. The use of radios had been entirely shelved out of fear that their transmissions might be picked up by scanners or modified shortwave radios. The area of the hospital complex was small enough that members of the two teams, working in shifts - twelve hours on and twelve hours off, were able to maintain visual contact with one another to assure communications.

The more difficult assignment went to the STAVKA medical officer whose job it was to pose as a friend of the family. He and Yelana had spent long hours masquerading in the presence of the recuperating patient known on the hospital records as "Alexander Kutuzov." Hospital personnel were extremely courteous and accommodating to the foreign visitors and the patient whose heart transplant had enjoyed such a touching, international story.

In the first few days of the transplant activity, members of the print and broadcast media had regularly checked with the supposed Mrs. Kutuzov on the progress of her husband. Other news, however, eventually claimed media attention elsewhere. That was good for the Russians who sat in for the long wait as the Hero of the Soviet Union slowly regained his strength.

By the end of the third day, Yelana was sitting in the room with Yuri Gagarin on an almost full-time basis. This provided an additional body-guard and observer as well as one who was trained to handle compromising situations as the need demanded. She sat quietly near his bed, reading magazines and relaxing as she pondered with pleasure the few hours she would spend each night at the apartment down the hill in Sugarhouse with Captain Major Sarabrov.

An additional aspect of the ruse included a careful effort to avoid any photographs being taken of the patient, Mr. Kutuzov. This was not an easy strategy because the heart transplant team routinely photographed all of its patients. The team enjoyed a world-renowned reputation, transplanting at the rate of one heart every other day, while serving a waiting list which could easily accelerate the pace to double the current output. The only problem was availability. Although specific rules and protocols were in place which prohibited selecting recipients on the basis of anything other than need and seniority from the top of the list, the touching story of the heart from Georgia in the Caucasus had been allowed to override the normal procedures. Plus, the money had been readily available without complication.

Kutuzov's relative, the Spetsnaz medical officer, who seemed to have a working knowledge of medicine, a fact recognized by several of the treating physicians, had arranged for funding through a private source which had been referred to as an anonymous benefactor. Many assumed it was the Rothman Chemical Corporation, given its broad friendship and philanthropic involvement with the peoples of southern Russia, the Ukraine and Armenia.

In truth, one week prior to the surgery, in Michael Christensen's absence from the TTI office, Spetsnaz experts had prepared a check on the TTI general account to the University of Utah Medical Center in the amount of one hundred thousand dollars. It bore the perfectly forged signature of Michael Christensen.

* * *

Despite all the good will and international brotherly love at higher levels, getting a KGB Criminal Investigation Team into the United States to investigate a mass murder case exposed the bare endings of diplomatic nerves. From the afternoon upon which Dombrayov made the telephone call to the Director of the FBI, it had taken another ten days before Ziyetski and his five assistants had finally been issued visas and welcomed in Washington, D.C.

The hurdles had been at other levels of governmental authority as well. Specifically, the CIA abjectly opposed the idea and made an issue of it with the Administration before being overridden by the President himself. Sharp differences and competition still at cold war levels existed between the CIA and many of the reformed Russian intelligence agencies. Although distrust of the decimated Communist party was no longer fashionable, intense suspicion of the more right-wing elements in the new Russian government was very much a concern. The fact that Ziyetski's team was a criminal investigation unit working principally for the Border Security Ministry of the KGB was not compelling to the CIA. Espionage and clandestine intelligence gathering was still continuing in both countries.

The matter had finally been resolved with the laying down of ground rules that allowed for Ziyetski and his group to operate, but only in the company of FBI agents trained in counterespionage operations. No weaponry more sophisticated than side arms could be brought into the United States.

For Ziyetski and his men, the administrative and technical hassles of gaining entry into the United States were subordinate to the culture shock associated with seeing the United States for the first time. With the exception of Ziyetski and his prime assistant, a lieutenant from Kiev, the KGB soldiers were from far Eastern Russia. Three of them were clearly of Mongolian and Anue descent and looked more like Eskimos in uniform than the traditional KGB soldier stereotype that the American hosts expected. The Russians were stunned as they viewed the affluent circumstances of American life in Northern Virginia between the Dulles Airport and the hotel at Tyson's Corner near the CIA center at Langley.

By the twelfth day following Dombrayov's call to the FBI Director, Ziyetski's group finally arrived by commercial airline flight in Salt Lake City, Utah. It was late January and the grey gloom hanging over the city reminded Ziyetski of a Siberian winter. Utah seemed to be in a state of deep freeze. The principal difference from the Dulles Airport was the number of people with skis and ski equipment busily coming and going through the airport.

Kenneth Swindler had returned from southern Utah with his coterie of FBI agents to meet the Russians. The obvious agent to deal with Russian visitors, Swindler quickly put his non-English speaking guests at ease by rattling off his greeting in perfect Russian. From the first moment of their meeting, it was evident that he and Ziyetski were kindred spirits. The topic of discussion quickly moved from professional to family matters. Pictures of wives and children were exchanged in the car on the way from the international airport to the FBI, Salt Lake City Bureau.

For Swindler, this was indeed a unique opportunity. The better part of his professional career had been spent chasing Russians in counterespionage operations which had taken him up and down the East Coast and periodically to Europe. The KGB had always been the enemy, yet now, with the thaw in East-West relations, he would be working with a professional who headed an entire district of the KGB's operations. He chose his words carefully in an effort not to create suspicion that he been given a parallel assignment of intelligence gathering. He assumed that his guest had the same orders.

Professional callings aside, he was intensely curious not only about Colonel Ziyetski, but also in how the KGB operations had changed since the installation of new government structures in the Eastern World. Swindler was not willing to accept the many briefings from supposed experts in Washington as the final word, especially with the opportunity to decipher the truth directly from agents of a much more open KGB.

The group drove to the Federal Building on State Street and First South in Salt Lake City, where further greetings in Russian were exchanged. The KGB agents were pleased that each of the American FBI agents spoke Russian with a degree of fluency. Presently, an agent under Swindler's supervision stepped forward to a grease board in the conference room and commenced the briefing. "Gentlemen, we have been assigned to accompany you and facilitate your investigation of the Trans-Siberian Train attack. The Bureau in Washington, D.C. has provided us a summary of your purpose for being here. We are prepared to provide you assistance.''

The FBI, was careful to only assist the KGB with it's search for Boris Yarov, the First Deputy and Alexander Kutusov. Permission had not been received to disclose the existence of their own investigation of the bribery of Congressman Stony Chapman through the Russian-owned company in St. George, Utah. The concern was simple as much of the FBI's investigation was intended to determine how high up in the Russian leadership the bribery plan had been concocted. The FBI was not willing to trust the KGB officers in this regard.

"You are seeking Alexander Kutuzov. We can provide you with the following information which we hope is helpful.'' The young FBI agent continued, trying to impress his guests with the best Russian possible. "Alexander Kutuzov will be very easy to find. He is, at this moment, lying in a bed in the University of Utah Hospital, recovering well from heart surgery. It is ten minutes from our office. I am surprised you haven't heard of his situation.''

Colonel Ziyetski felt an instant rush of excitement as he realized that perhaps part of his case could be resolved quickly.

"Boris Yarov and Victor Krovas, according to State Department visa records, have entered the United States within the past two weeks under an entry and exit visa with the intended purpose of doing business in St. George, Utah. For your information, St. George is approximately three hundred miles south of here in the desert, not far from Las Vegas, Nevada. We are not certain whether either of the men are there. St. George is under surveillance. We will take you to St. George and you can make that determination for yourselves. Our identifying information on the men is sketchy.''

In actuality, the FBI was certain of Yarov's presence in St. George. Their extensive camera work had confirmed Yarov as they compared the picture on his visa with the many hundreds of photographs taken by agents conducting surveillance at the Tabernacle Tower office building. Nevertheless, they were unwilling to share the extent of their information to avoid compromise of the ongoing bribery investigation. It would be a delicate, tenuous and somewhat sensitive effort on the part of the FBI to assist the KGB without creating problems for themselves. Hopefully, by the time the Russians located Yarov, the FBI would be in a position to raid the various TTI facilities in St. George and file formal charges through the U.S. Attorney's Office.

Prior to the arrival of the Russians, considerable debate had occurred among the group that perhaps the real purpose for the KGB was to get to Yarov before the Americans did. The conclusion that prevailed, however, was that if in fact such was the case, other clandestine agents could easily have done so and that working through formal relationships with the FBI would have been the last and most unlikely means to that end.

"Kutuzov is in the hospital?" Colonel Ziyetski asked, making certain that he had understood.

"Alexander Kutuzov is the fortunate recipient of a new heart. A heart transplant has been conducted within the past two weeks and we understand that he is doing quite well."

"That is odd," Ziyetski spoke, relaxing his Russian, realizing that the Americans understood him well. "I met with him on occasion in Vladivostok only six weeks ago. He showed no signs of ill health. In fact, he seemed to be a reasonably jovial, robust and happy fellow. He was about to be married."

"Well, it was a very celebrated public event, actually, Colonel," Kenneth Swindler interjected. "No sooner had the man arrived here in the United States from Russia, and he had a heart attack. He was put in the hospital and on the same day, his wife made an impassioned plea for help. Apparently, relatives in your country of Georgia, by coincidence, located a heart of a young shepherd boy which had been harvested after his death in a motorcycle accident. It was on all the television stations here in the United States. In fact, a prominent philanthropist here in Salt Lake City, who just happens to own a cement plant in Armenia, donated his private jet to bring the heart to Salt Lake City. Sounds like the transplant was successful."

Ziyetski was surprised by the circumstances. He wasn't exactly certain as to the genesis of his uneasiness, but something seemed a bit strange. "How soon can I see Mr. Kutuzov?"

"As soon as this meeting is over, we'll take you to the hospital. I'm sure he will be glad to see you."

"I think he probably will. Our suspicion is that he left Russia under less than favorable circumstances."

"Is he a suspect?" a younger FBI agent asked.

"No, not at all. But he is a key witness who has both banking information that we need as well as information on why he left the country in such a hurry. We suspect that those who forced him out of the country may be prime suspects in Moscow in trying to cover up evidence involving the train massacre."

The meeting lasted approximately an hour and a half. Following a brief lunch, certain members of the group, including all of the Russians and two FBI hosts, drove from the downtown area to the University of Utah Medical Center.

The elevators took the group to the Cardiac Care Ward. As they walked through the facility, the Russians again marveled at the unbelievable application of American technology. The hospital was spotless, and the machines, computer equipment, and facilities constructed to serve the hi-tech operation amazed them. Each could not help but recall his own unpleasant experience in a Russian hospital and realized that the level of health care between the two countries was literally decades apart.

They emerged from the fourth floor elevators which placed the them immediately before the nurses' station. "I am agent Swindler of the FBI." He showed the nurse his badge. "We would like to visit Mr. Alexander Kutuzov."

The nurse showed a slightly perplexed look on her face.

The agents, both American and Russian immediately noted her concern before any further words were spoken.

"Why," she explained, "Mr. Kutuzov is not here. He checked out yesterday....he's gone."

"Where did he go? Do you have an address where we can reach him?" the younger agent quickly asked.

"Yes, we were given an address." The nurse keyed her computer and began to read: " ... on Stringham Avenue."

"Do you normally release heart patients following transplant this quickly - shouldn't he still be here?"

The perplexed expression remained, "He checked out of here at the request of his personal physician. In fact, he had his physician and a group of several relatives with him. Our cardiologist spoke with his physician and was convinced that he knew what he was doing. The man with him...I mean his physician, seemed very knowledgeable. It is unusual that we would release someone so quickly, but they insisted. And with his own doctor, we allowed him to check out."

"Do you have the name of his doctor?"

Again she keyed up the computer. "No...no, I don't. It doesn't give his name. But I can tell you, he knew as much or more about heart transplant surgery than we do, and we are the experts. And he spoke Russian with the patient. Mr. Kutuzov seemed to understand everything he said - that is, as far as we could tell. We don't speak Russian here."

Swindler looked at his counterpart who was busily interpreting the nurse's comments to Colonel Ziyetski and his group.

"Get on the radio. I want an agent down at that Stringham Avenue address immediately. Tell them to hold anyone there!" The command was direct, but nervous.

"Yes, Sir!" was the response as the agent punched in numbers on his cellular telephone.

He then directed his comments back at the nurse, "I need to talk to Mr. Kutuzov's doctor immediately. Page him and get him here!"

It took twenty minutes before hospital personnel could produce a doctor who had any knowledge of Alexander Kutuzov's case. The information seemed minimal and the doctor fidgited with irritation in his rush to get on with his other duties. The conversation was briefly interrupted by the beep on the agent's telephone. The speaker was on for all to hear.

"This is Agent Crofts at the Stringham Avenue address. Let me confirm it, that's 1947 Stringham Avenue - is that correct?"

"That's it," Swindler responded.

"There's nobody here. In fact, according to the landlord, they have been out of this apartment for over a week. It was a woman and a man, but the man hasn't been seen for over two weeks. He confirmed that it was the Russian woman that has been on television...you know, regarding the heart transplant."

As the simultaneous translation continued, Colonel Ziyetski's anxiety rose. The case was taking on a new dimension that he could not understand. He did have one other question which might be appropriate for the doctor. He reached in his briefcase and pulled out a photograph from Alexander Kutuzov's KGB dossier similar to that which the KGB still had on most Russian citizens, particularly those formerly employed by the government.

"Is this Alexander Kutuzov?" Colonel Ziyetski asked through the interpretation of the FBI agent.

"That definitely is *not* the man that we had in this hospital!" the doctor responded.

At that moment the nurse joined the review of the photograph, "No, that's not him, not him at all!"

The doctor was suddenly less anxious to leave. He folded his arms and looked the FBI agent straight in the eye and with a suddenly dry throat posed the question that no one could answer. "Then *who* in the hell was our heart transplant patient - can you tell me that?"

Although the doctor's question went unanswered, the effort to discover the facts continued. Within the hour, Swindler joined Ziyetski at the studios of KSL, the CBS television affiliate located in Salt Lake's sprawling Triad Center. They gathered in a viewing room to watch tapes of the evening news some two and a half weeks earlier on a large screen television.

Not more than thirty seconds of the tape of the weeping Russian woman had run when Ziyetski signaled that he wanted to speak. The sound was turned down and the simultaneous translation began.

"I know her! There is something terrible underway, gentlemen...something terrible!"

"Please tell us, Colonel. How do you know her?" Swindler asked.

"She is the Angel of Death. Yelana is known as The Angel of Death. I have known of her work before. She is the most cunning and most capable murderer the First Chief Directorate of the KGB has ever produced. She is a legend. We were sure that with the change in government she would begin to free lance - and now we know - she has been here in your city."

"How can you be certain it is the same woman?"

"I have only met her once, and will never forget her. She is a woman that a man, though he knew nothing of her exploits, would never forget. She is patient like a cat and a master of disguise! An expert with every instrument of death - a sort of witch that must be fed!"

"Sounds like you don't give her real high marks," Swindler responded with slight levity.

The humor was lost on Ziyetski, "If Kutuzov was with her, I fear for his life - that is unless he is one of them, which I seriously doubt."

CHAPTER 23

Zion Station, Mid March, 1993

The mood was festive at the Sunset Canyon Ranch Dacha. Jim raised his wine glass in a toast to the incredibly good news. CNN had just reported that the Baychunas space shot financed through the joint Star City - Western conglomerate effort had been executed flawlessly. Aerospace, the only significant commercial enterprise of the old Soviet Union was still in the hands of the STAVKA, and making money as well. Despite the late hour, Andropov was bright-eyed and even boastful over the success of the event. The party continued into the night with a group of specially invited staff and advisers as well as Spetsnaz officers of Zion Station.

For his part, Yuri Gagarin was not up to partying. He was asleep, having been comfortably situated in a special care room of the medical facility which had been constructed according to the strict dictates of STAVKA doctors specifically for its current use. He was in the care of a different, unanticipated attendant. Yelana had been quick to reset her sights on the man designed to be the new leader of the world. Intending to be at his side and share the power, Yelana would nurse the famous

Cosmonaut back to health and take control of his new heart in a way that only she had the power to do.

Gagarin's return to Zion station had been somewhat abrupt. However, there had been no alternative as the Spetsnaz team headed by Captain Major Sarabrov had informed Jim that an inquiry had been made by the FBI at the hospital regarding Alexander Kutuzov. The decision had been to immediately remove Gagarin from the Medical Center in Salt Lake City and return him to the Dacha in southern Utah.

Although the process had not been easy, the STAVKA staff doctors considered the risk to be minimal. Other than the heart transplant surgery procedure itself and critical care recovery work, the STAVKA doctors considered themselves fully capable of providing all other attendant care. Each was well-trained in cardiology as well as having personally performed transplants on numerous occasions. With the move to Utah, the ruse to have the top American transplant team perform the procedure had been concocted. All had gone off without a hitch, with the exception of the FBI telephone call, which was in and of itself enough to prompt a quick move.

The special medication which had been prepared exclusively at the Experimental Biological Institute in Koptevo near Moscow was now feeding through the IV into Gagarin's body. His new nineteen year old heart, combined with the years of extensive medical research on isolation of the aging regulator gene were in the process of assuring him eternity - at least a longer life than any other human in modern time would likely experience. If all went well, and with the continuing human growth hormone and gene splicing research successes, Yuri Gagarin could now live for another sixty to seventy years, putting him in his prime between the years 2010 and 2030. Thus, the suffering and difficulty associated with the current transplant was merely a brief inconvenience in the life of the man earmarked by the STAVKA to bring Russia into a new age of world dominance.

The doctor again checked his patient noticing that he was sleeping soundly. He then rechecked the vitals-monitoring and telemetry equipment and left the building to walk the thirty or so yards to the meeting hall. Joining the celebration with the other two members of the STAVKA they took great pleasure in the success of the Baychunas space shot and its two hundred twenty million dollar payday.

The doctor's walk down the hall in the medical facilities building did not go unnoticed. He passed the thick oak door behind which Michael Christensen sat wondering if pet dogs considered themselves to be captives too. The thought had crossed his mind as he reasoned that just like a dog he found himself noticing every sound, no matter how slight. He had detected the sound of airliners passing high in the night sky. Even the mild rustle of the wind or a door slightly creaking somewhere in the building could not escape his attention. My senses twitch - just like a dog in the night, he thought.

As he sat, his ears were picking up the strains of music. The melodies were Russian. A party was clearly in progress somewhere, though he assumed it was probably not in his building. Periodically he would hear the drift of echoes from men yelling foreign language nonsense into the night. The metallic sounds caused him to suspect that the buildings were located in a canyon.

Concentrating on each noise helped occupy his thoughts. The only other pastime was to read old English language computer magazines that were infrequently rudely shoved under the door. His family was without a father. He wondered how they were adjusting to the condition that they had yet to know would be permanent. The futile thought terrified him. He wondered if the agony of death could be as painful as the anguish of the reality that he was now suffering.

He had measured the time by the length of his beard. Whiskers had grown into scraggly curls. There was no mirror or wash basin, but only a hole in the corner of the room near the outside wall apparently leading to a space beneath the building. A bug crawling out of the makeshift commode on one occasion had been a major event.

Michael was also hungry. Sometimes his evening meal went undelivered. He assumed that due to the apparent festivities in progress, his welfare had been ignored altogether.

Suddenly, the four inch panel in the oak door through which he had been delivered a change of clean underwear a day earlier, slid open. He saw the slender fingers of a woman steadying both sides of the tray as it slid through the space. His new dog-like intuition told him that the process of delivering the tray through the door had been done with more thought and care this time. He didn't need to rush to catch it before it fell onto the floor. This time, the tray was steadied. He accepted it and started to consume the tasty leftovers from the apparent party nearby.

But as he took the napkin to brush away food from his mouth, its coloration caught his eye. In the next second, he was reading a message which he assumed was scribbled with a makeup pencil of some kind:

"Help, I am being raped every day, I'm not one of them - Flora."

Michael did not finish the meal. For the remainder of the night he lay awake wondering how bad it must be for this "Flora," asking for help from a man who was cut off from the world and probably condemned to death.

Salt Lake City, Utah, Mid March, 1993

Three hundred miles to the north in Salt Lake City, Kenneth Swindler, likewise, was not sleeping. The cause was not celebration, but an irritating battle with his thoughts regarding the new discoveries in the Russian case. Initially, it had appeared as though the effort in hosting the KGB would be merely a pleasant, but largely innocuous diplomatic gesture. With the strange disclosures regarding the Alexander Kutuzov heart transplant, and his virtual disappearance, there were suddenly serious issues which gave new legitimacy to the Russians' effort in Utah.

The link between Ziyetski's case and the bribery case was clarifying itself. Michael Christensen, the Danish businessman had evolved as the prime suspect. The evidence showed that not only had he issued the check triggering the bribe to Congressman Stony Chapman, but he had also issued the check for one hundred thousand dollars to the University of Utah Medical Center to cover the heart transplant on someone other than Alexander Kutuzov. Both the unknown transplant recipient and Kutuzov were now missing. And, Christensen, the visa sponsor for Yarov and the

First Deputy was, according to the State Department, still in Russia.

Thus, the sleepless night for the FBI agent continued, his thoughts riveted on one other fact which only the most intense and investigative mind would consider. A few months earlier, as he had been working on the anti-gang task force, he had become privy to reports normally not circulated through FBI offices. In previous times, gang activities had been largely dealt with by state and local law enforcement officials. The FBI had been limited to Federal criminal activity. But with his recent assignment, anything remotely related to gang activity throughout the state of Utah was not only reported to local law enforcement agencies, but also to the FBI which served as a clearing house for the administration of a multi-jurisdictional gang crime task force. His thoughts were not fully developed at the moment, but he was kept awake with the lingering recollection of a report regarding the bodies of two men found in the shallow graves of a cinder pit in southern Utah some five months earlier. There had been something distinctly different in the pathology reports attached to the death certificates. It had something to do with Russians, he thought to himself, but he could not quite lift the connection from his subconscious.

Despite the early morning hours, Kenneth picked up the telephone and called the FBI control center where two agents were on duty in the Salt Lake Bureau. He quickly referred them to the gang report which referenced the bodies found in southern Utah, and requested that the State Medical Examiner's autopsy report be read to him. Initially, the agent read the entire report over the telephone to Kenneth and nothing seemed to stand out. Kenneth then directed him to the incidental comment and suspicion portion of the examiner's report.

The agent read, "Two noteworthy or coincidental aspects are apparent. Both of the deceased show indentations from rings on the middle digit of the right hand. Inventory of property, however, shows no rings present. Second, both show evidence of the Illysarov procedure having been performed on both of their legs. I find this highly unusual for the reason that the Illysarov procedure was performed on both legs of both men anywhere from five to ten years prior to death."

"Is there anything else?" Kenneth both demanded.

"No, Sir, I have read to you the entire report," the agent responded.

"Read me the part regarding the Illysarov thing...once more. I want to write it down word for word, and then give me the State Medical Examiner's home telephone number."

Within the next few minutes a sleepy and annoyed Doctor Corry Mason, the Utah State Medical Examiner, was talking in his sleep to an FBI agent. Part of Mason's benefits of having become the State Medical Examiner was to regularly experience an organized nine to five workday. His patients, always dead, had few demands during the late hours of the night, and he liked it that way.

"Now, say it again," the doctor was still trying to clear his mind enough to be communicative. "What did you say your name was?"

"This is Kenneth Swindler. I'm a Special Agent with the FBI. I want to ask you some questions regarding a pathology report which you prepared in October."

The doctor sounded clearly vexed by the inquiry. "And how do I know you are an agent with the FBI?"

"I guess you don't, but if I'm on your doorstep in ten minutes, ringing your doorbell, you'll know that I am! It would probably be easier for you to just talk to me right now so that things don't have to get so formal." Kenneth did not have time to play games. "So, are you ready to talk to me, or do you want to see my badge?"

"So what do you need Mr. ... what did you say your name was?"

"The name is Kenneth Swindler. That's special agent Kenneth Swindler, S W I N D L E R."

"That's quite a name," the doctor remarked.

Kenneth was used to the snide comment. It had been with him all his life. He didn't react.

"You know, Agent Swindler, I perform anywhere from five to ten autopsies a day, at least my staff and I do. It may be difficult for me to recall anything without having my report available."

"I've already looked at your report. I want you to tell me about a particular procedure. It's called the Illysarov procedure. Now that's a Russian term isn't it? I note in your report that you indicated how peculiar this situation was, because you autopsied two men, white males, middle-aged, upon whom the Illysarov procedure had been conducted on both knees. Now, tell me about the Illysarov procedure, everything you know."

Swindler was speaking rapidly, anxious to get to the point.

The doctor now seemed somewhat more interested in participating in the conversation. ''Yes, I do remember that particular autopsy. We talked about it several times. In fact I sent out for more information. The Illysarov procedure is, as you have already guessed, a Russian orthopedic development. Illysarov was a Russian orthopedic surgeon who perfected a process by which the leg length, just above the knee could be extended by as much as five centimeters. It allowed for obviously greater height, but also considerably improved strength about the lower extremity. And both of these guys had it done, not just on one, but both their legs. That was unusual, so I wrote it in my report.''

''Is that an accepted medical procedure here - I mean in the United States or in the Western World?'' Swindler asked.

''Oh yes, orthopedic surgeons use it quite regularly - that is, the most experienced and capable surgeons do. It's done routinely when dealing with certain types of injuries and limb-length inequalities.''

''What type of leg injuries?''

''Any major fracture of a long bone, particularly in the lower extremity where one leg is going to end up significantly shorter than the other. They use Illysarov to lengthen the short leg. But the Russians - who knows what they're doing,? I've read that in their experiments, they've made some mighty tall dwarfs using the Illysarov.''

''So what are the odds, Doctor, of both of these fellows having, say, broken both their legs and having undergone the surgery at approximately the same time?''

''I would say it's virtually impossible. But it looks to me like this was some type of attempt at an organized therapeutic or experimental application. The work was clearly done by the same physicians. I'm also rather certain that it was done at the same time. So, in answering your question, I don't think there was any other injury. In fact, if I recall my report, and I would have to look at it to be certain, there was no evidence of major leg or bone trauma on either of the men's legs, beyond that of the surgeries themselves.

The doctor's input had been helpful. It was time to test some hunches. ''Where are these guys now?''

''Well, they are certainly not out to dinner,'' the doctor commented facetiously. "I've got them here on ice, but the law only requires me to hold them for another month. Then they become cadavers. The state has an on-going murder investigation in process. But again, I don't have to hold them forever. The State Medical Examiner doesn't run a hotel."

"I'd like to get down there to look at them first thing in the morning. Would that be all right?"

"See you then. And Agent Swindler, it sounds like you could probably use some sleep," the doctor commented in a closing remark, as if counseling a patient.

* * *

Locating Colonel Ziyetski and his group the following morning had been no easy undertaking. Normally, they had been in the constant company of FBI hosts. But one of Ziyetski's boyhood friends was stationed with the Russian INF monitoring team at the Hercules Rocket Manufacturing plant in the town of Magna west of Salt Lake City. For the better part of the morning, he had been with his Russian friends at their monitoring checkpoint at the plant's front gate.

Finally, by late morning, Kenneth Swindler was able to get an agent to the plant and convey the message that Colonel Ziyetski and his entire investigative team needed to accompany their FBI host agent to the State Medical Examiners Office. It was Swindler's hope that input from Ziyetski and his people could shed some light on the questions raised in the Medical Examiner's report regarding the two dead men found in southern Utah.

The Office of the State Medical Examiner of the state of Utah was located on the east bench of Salt Lake City between the University of Utah campus and the University Medical Center where the mysterious transplant had taken place some three weeks earlier. Hospital officials had reviewed records and interviewed all medical staff and persons associated in any way with the Alexander Kutuzov transplant for any information as to where the patient had gone. In each event, investigators found themselves at a total deadend.

Dr. Mason and his associates were prepared for the visit. The corpses, normally kept in eight-foot long refrigerated drawers adjacent to the autopsy rooms, had been moved to the autopsy tables. In addition, each of the pathologists who had participated in the respective autopsies had been called to the examination room to answer any questions. The unusual bodies had been cause for considerable discussion among the group over the past several months. Accordingly, the pathologists had appointed each body a name rather than the normal case reference number used where the deceased passed through the office in the normal course and then on to the morticians.

The doctors were curiously interested as introductions were made and they discovered that Colonel Ziyetski and his men were from the Russian KGB. Visions of international intrigue flowed through their minds as each commenced his part of the presentation by repeating the procedure that was used and the conclusions that were reached.

The doctors took approximately twenty minutes. Much of the time was spent explaining the procedure by which the body gases and chemical constituency were tested through samples taken from the liver. Normally, only a small sample would be taken. However, in the case of the two unknowns from southern Utah, where overt evidence of homicide existed, the Examiner's team had been interested in trying to determine the types of food or exposure to other environmental evidence such as levels of lead, carbon monoxide, and the various toxins that could possibly reveal the origin of the victims.

The final portion of the report dealt with an inventory of clothing and other personal effects. It revealed that the clothes were largely American-made and purchased in the United States. Some items, such as socks and underwear were normal U.S. brand names. The conclusion was that generic clothing had likely been put on the victims intentionally in order to avoid identification. They wore almost identical clothes as if they had purchased the same clothes at the same time, or had someone purchase the clothes for them.

The doctors concluded their report and stated their willingness to answer questions.

"You have not told us of shoes," Colonel Ziyetski began. "Can you tell me what types of shoes were these men wearing?"

"The report shows that they were in stocking feet only and had no shoes," Doctor Mason responded while reading from the report. "Guess somebody figured they weren't going anywhere."

Ziyetski moved close to each body and examined the leathery remains, carefully touching various parts around the feet and toes. The facial parts which had been found scattered near the bodies had been kept in plastic bags and laid on the tables next to the right shoulder of each of the bodies, a gruesome testament to the effects of a shotgun blast to the back of the head at point-blank range. The cold temperatures of the Arizona Strip had slowed decomposition.

He then examined the right hand of each and measured the imprint of where a ring had existed on the middle digit of each. The skin was crusty and largely sloughed off to the bone.

Kenneth Swindler, the other FBI agents and examiners associates watched the Russian operate with keen interest. For Swindler, it was a unique opportunity to see the KGB at work. The enemy that he had always been trained to suspect, was now showing its ability, and Kenneth was impressed.

Presently, Ziyetski pulled out a small hand-held dictaphone and began dictating as he looked at various parts of the two corpses. One of his assistants also began taking notes as if responding to various words spoken by Ziyetski. Kenneth's Russian was reasonably good. However, he did not have full command of the various buzzwords used by the KGB among themselves and on their internal reports.

Concluding his review, Ziyetski looked up and began speaking to the agent asking him to interpret for him. He then addressed the entire group authoritatively stating his conclusions. "Gentlemen, I will tell you something which causes me great concern. What you have here lying on this table, are two corporal rank troopers of one of the elite Black Beret units of a Spetsnaz Alpha Group. This is my conclusion, and I am absolutely possitive it is a correct one."

Kenneth and the other FBI agents were surprised by the certainty of the statement. Kenneth wondered why the KGB Colonel would so freely disclose his findings. He had also been this way with the identity of the woman agent - simply speaking in absolutes with nothing to hide. The existence of two dead Spetsnaz troopers in a shallow grave well within the borders of the United States was truly a discovery of major international significance. Yet, in further thought, it struck him as almost a virtual impossibility which caused him to venture a question before the Colonel could continue.

"How can you be so certain, Colonel Ziyetski? How could Spetsnaz soldiers be in the United States?" Kenneth asked the second question displaying some skepticism which was immediately noted by the Colonel.

"Let me answer your second concern first. I have absolutely no idea what Soviets elite forces are doing in your country. I tell you that honestly and without reservation - although I assume that given the history of antagonism between our two countries, you may still foster suspicions at my answer.

"Answering your first question, however, I would point out to you that the Spetsnaz troopers, upon their initiation into the ranks, were made a part of a special brotherhood which was known in its time as the Order of the New Soviet Man. We are not as liberated as you and even the women Spetsnaz agents were initiated under the order of the New Soviet Man. In order to avoid any body markings as they had used in earlier times, a special ring was formed and was placed on the middle finger of the right hand. It was exactly one centimeter in width, I have measured each of these hands as you have noted, and on the middle finger a one centimeter imprint exists in both cases. The depth of the imprint is likewise important because it shows to me that at no time has either man removed the ring. The rings were obviously pried off before or after the killing."

The pathologists were amazed as they listened to the Russian's analysis of facts.

"The next point is the muscular structure that you will notice in the shoulders and across the backs of these men. This is significant given the fact that they are required to make at least four parachute jumps per year in their training and must routinely maintain their skill levels by excessive physical conditioning. I have been around the Spetsnaz many times in the past. I have trained with them and I know of their regimen. I have no doubt that as we look at these bodies, how these men have likely gained their muscular structure, which I can see, despite the affects of severe decomposition.

"Another matter, which is significant, is that which Agent Swindler detected in the first place. The procedure which caused his suspicion is, in fact, one which is used periodically among the Spetsnaz and other super secret military organizations within our country. You use the surgery to treat injuries. The Spetsnaz have used it to avoid injuries. In fact, if you were to examine the legs of the current world champion skydiving team from Russia, you would note that each of them have undergone this surgery. It is another one of the national secrets which are slowly leaking out of our country. For those of you that may wonder, it is performed at the Pirogov Medical Institute in Moscow.''

Swindler was still skeptical, finding the whole explanation interesting, but improbable. For the first time since he received word of the assignment, he began to suspect that there was at least a chance that this was some type of Russian intelligence ploy that would take some time to play itself out.

''I'm not sure I see it the same way,'' Kenneth spoke. ''What you have is two men who had rings that were identical in nature. One centimeter is probably the size of many rings. You've got men who have undergone surgery which is done in Russia and America. And they have strong muscular development which I would assume would be the case with anyone who would go so far as to have some type of radical surgery done to improve his physical abilities as you suggest. But what I am not convinced of, and the evidence does not tell me, is that in fact these two men were Spetsnaz. It seems all too improbable. The facts you have quoted still seem too circumstantial.''

Ziyetski was cool and undeterred by the doubting American. ''What I haven't told you is the most significant part of the evidence. The information I will give to you comes by way of your own FBI and its experts, and not from me.''

The comment immediately caught Swindler's attention. His eyes were riveted on Ziyetski as he walked back down to the foot of the two tables and elevated the leg of one of the corpses. ''Earlier this year after the Trans-Siberian Railroad massacre occurred, we gained the assistance of the FBI Crime Laboratory from Washington, D.C. They came with their dogs and mobile crime lab and assisted us in some of the initial investigation at the site. I think that this relationship may have been instrumental in our gaining the privilege of coming to the United States and continuing the investigation as we are now doing.

"At the scene of the massacre, we had found a boot with a foot inside it which apparently had been severed from one of the attackers. The boot was distinctly different in size, type and style from anything worn by the postal guards who were defending the train. Your compatriots from Washington D.C., through their own investigation, determined not only the source of the boot, showing that it had been manufactured in East Germany prior to the change in power there, but that the foot inside it had worn the boot for a long period of time. They specifically examined the foot and showed us the callouses and how they developed in various places caused by pressure on the foot by the special construction of the boot."

Ziyetski flipped through his brief case and pulled out a piece of paper that he had been looking at earlier when he had dictated into his dictaphone.

"Allow me to show you a copy of the FBI's diagram of the foot found at the massacre scene." He then placed the paper in his hand next to the foot elevated in his other hand as all gathered closer to compare. Each man gasped slightly in surprise as Ziyetski exhibited the computerized mapping which showed a three hundred sixty degree scan of the entire foot. He then correlated the various pressure marks to the callouses on the foot. They could see that the evidence was unmistakable - the pressure points were all identical to the feet of the corpses before them.

"As you compare, let me announce to you the other findings that the FBI gave us in connection with the boot and the Trans-Siberian Railroad incident. Specifically, the boots were manufactured at the East German manufacturing plant until 1989. They were of much better quality than anything manufactured in the Soviet Union and were only issued to the most elite of the Soviet forces, especially, the paratroopers. I can also tell you that there is no other Soviet paratroop unit which would have the ring on the middle finger of the right hand. Therefore, if there is any room for doubt, it is very remote. It is much more reasonable than not, that what you have here are two Soviet Spetsnaz troopers. That is my conclusion. Do you have further questions?"

Kenneth found himself shaking his head with amazement. His skepticism had evaporated entirely as Colonel Ziyetski had supported his final points with the FBI Crime Lab evidence. The only questions remaining, were questions which he could not ask; whether these KGB agents had been intentionally brought into the situation as a yet undefined part of a Russian intelligence or even military operation against the United States. But in his next thoughts, he began to dismiss the possibility of any intrigue on the part of the KGB because it was he, Kenneth, who had identified the suspicious points on the autopsy report in the first instance. Prior to his inquiry, it had been a mere state and local law enforcement investigative matter, and it was doubtful, if not impossible, that the KGB would have had any knowledge concerning it.

By the end of the normal work day, the FBI agents found themselves favorably impressed with the competence of their Russian counterparts. It was time to return to southern Utah and join the agents already in place performing surveillance operations and to move in, try to capture Yarov and the First Deputy, and then start asking hard questions about dead Russians in the American desert.

CHAPTER 24

Zion Station, Late March, 1993

An urgent meeting had been convened by Andropov in the Sunset Canyon Ranch. The jubilation of the previous day's success over the Baychunas space shot was now tempered by numerous problems peculiar to the new American Dacha.

Present with Andropov were Jim, Captain Major Sarabrov, Yelana - sans the wigs and now sporting her actual short bleached blond hair - and Boris Yarov. Sarabrov had been running his men through a physical training exercise near the river and was anxious to return.

Jim spoke, "We have received information through my local contacts that the FBI is on its way to St. George!"

"For what purpose?" Andropov was worried.

Jim was one to always speak frankly. Unlike the others, he harbored no fear of reprisal. "They must suspect something from the hospital. Apparently they were looking for Kutusov there. It was bound to happen. We knew they had called. That's why we left so fast."

"How much do you think FBI knows?"

"It's hard to tell. They've no one from our group in custody, and there is no way they could know about Zion Station."

Andropov was not at ease with Jim's expressions of confidence, "Then why are they coming to St. George?"

"The money for the transplant was paid by TTI. So, they'll probably go there and start asking questions."

"That worries me, Yarov interrupted. "The First Deputy is at TTI right now. If he gets pressed, he'll talk."

"How much does he know?" Andropov asked. "As I understand it, he knows nothing of Zion Station - am I correct?"

"No, but he is aware of the concept," Yarov explained. "He still expects us to take care of his heart problem. If the Americans got him, they'd promise him the care and he'd tell all he knows. He's not stable."

Yarov paused and was about to continue when Andropov cut him off. "We've got to get him out of there. Yarov, you go to St. George and get the First Deputy out of town. Take him to Las Vegas and hide him in a hotel. Don't bring him here, and whatever you do, don't get picked up by the Americans! I don't want either of you to be interrogated."

"Well, I would never talk!" Yarov feigned insult at the mild inference of a weakness in loyalty on his part.

"They have ways - don't fool yourself." Andropov was direct and of no mind to banter. "How soon can you leave?"

"I have one computer problem to deal with." Yarov responded. "It will take about twenty minutes."

"And not a second longer!" Andropov enjoined like an irritated parent. Yarov left the room.

"We have other problems as well, Sir," Jim spoke. We must deal with the low morale among our own Spetsnaz. It is very bad." He looked accusingly at Sarabrov, "They are becoming undisciplined. Many were drunk last night. I was shocked. Such was never the case at Caucus Station!"

"It is as simple as this," Sarabrov continued. "We have maintained strict rules to keep the Spetsnaz troopers on the Dacha grounds. Their only travel outside of the ranch area has been to the Hurricane Mesa. And that only occurs when we have an incoming flight. The men are getting restless and I am concerned."

Jim interrupted, "I always found that the recipe for morale-building among Spetsnaz was to provide them as many women as possible. That seemed to keep them satisfied."

Sarabrov and Yelana exchanged a knowing look.   Sarabrov proceeded, "The problem is traffic. We have several hundred men here and we simply cannot be bringing the women here in the numbers that are necessary and still avoid detection. At present, we have thirteen girls from the polygamists. Six of them are assigned exclusively to the STAVKA. They are not prostitutes, but young well-behaved girls and though they serve our purpose, they do not come here willingly."

"The supply of women was never an issue in the Caucasus," Yarov responded. "They brought girls in from Turkey, Bulgaria, Greece and practically everywhere."

"With a little bit of time I think we can solve the problem," Jim had a plan. "I propose that we acquire some property near Lake Mead in Nevada. It is only about an hour and a half away. At this place, we would set up a brothel of sorts and hire professional prostitutes from the Las Vegas area. This would keep them from envying so much the opportunities of the STAVKA and also give them a chance to escape what they call in the United States 'cabin fever' that seems to have set in here at the Dacha." Jim explained his plan.

"How soon can I share this concept with the men?" Sarabrov asked.

"Why in the hell are we talking about this!" Andropov interrupted. "The men aren't going to be here forever. They're soldiers - trained to wait! We'll likely be back in Russia within a year, or as soon as the Parliamentarians have paved the way. And these men will come back as heroes. They'll surely get all the attention they need then! I really don't think it would be wise to suggest to the men that their stay will be long-term. A brothel, well, that sounds long-term! What we need is strong discipline. That's what they're used to and that what they should get!"

"I would tend to agree," Jim spoke in support. "If we let up on the discipline there is always a chance that it will break down altogether. As you know, we've already had one big problem. Two of our troopers got out-of-hand several months before you arrived and arranged an auto accident which caused a car to go off the mountain road above the ranch.

It fell all the way to the bottom of the cliff and crashed near the gate. The two then looted the crash site using their night vision goggles. They were almost detected. In fact, we know that they were seen by a sheriff's deputy and perhaps some of the ambulance drivers. It was a total breach of discipline!"

"So, what did you do with them?" Sarabrov asked.

"They paid the price," Jim responded with total dispassion. "They did not even receive the formal firing squad. It was a simple shotgun blast to the back of their heads. We cannot tolerate any such activity among the ranks. They must understand that they conform strictly to discipline or they die. And should you desire to use this particular example with your men, feel free to do so."

"Anything else on that issue?" Sarabrov asked.

"No, Captain Major, you can return to your exercises."

At that point, Sarabrov left the room leaving Andropov, Jim and Yelana to discuss the remaining issues.

"What about the nearby towns?" Andropov asked, "Is there any suspicion developing? I am worried that we may not be as secure here as first thought. Those men who bring the girls up must have some idea."

Jim interrupted, "Sir, their only thought in the world is money. You needn't trouble yourself with them. To the leaders of the cult, it is a blessing from God. They can't tell the difference between manna from heaven and dollars from Hong Kong. As far as the other communities in the area are concerned, I've made the appropriate friendships with certain of the local authorities and they are much richer for what they don't know. And there is that cross over the front gate. It goes a long way around here-this is a religious retreat, you know." Everyone laughed.

Andropov moved to a different subject. "What about the computer information? Comrade Gagarin is still quite ill but he wants to know how soon we will be doing what he calls installing the Cray data. That's all he talks about."

"It's something that the Dane must do." Jim responded.

"Why isn't it being done?" Andropov demanded an explanation.

"Yarov is taking care of it today. His computer just arrived. He's setting up the Dane on it before leaving for St. George."

"And what do you plan to do with the Dane when he's finished?

You can't release him,'' Andropov observed.

Jim raised his eyebrows as he turned to Yelana.

''I will have him,'' the woman spoke in a sadistic tone that drove a cold spike even into the nerves of the most hardened of the men. There was no doubt in their minds that her greatest need was to kill in her own depraved way. The Dane would be a good offering to keep her satisfied for awhile.

Yelana had been spending the past several weeks recovering from her many months of Spetsnaz duty which had included long and tedious time spent with Alexander Kutuzov playing the role of Nieca. Until she left Moscow, she had been slipping away severals days per week to Star City and under Yarov's direction posing as the elusive Cosmonaut and TTI director, Raissa. Her only break from the tedium had been the trip to the TTI offices in America while Kutusov was away from Moscow at the Vladivostok branch of Toko Bank.

Using Kutusov's identity for the Yuri Gagarin heart transplant had not been easy. The plan had been laid years earlier as Alexander Kutuzov had first returned from the Foreign Service to work at Toko Bank and certain operatives of the KGB remembered his striking resemblence, even in mid-life, to the young Yuri Gagarin of the past. For the first year, it had been a contingency, but as the STAVKA evacuation plan became a reality, and it was understood that the surgery would, of necessity, be conducted by foreign doctors, a way had to be prepared for a Russian of the same age to be conveniently in place in America. As she reflected on her recent past, the work at Toko Bank had been rigorous, the assignments at Star City interesting, and the marriage to Alexander Kutuzov repulsive.

But Yelana had played her role well. It was consistent with the performance required of a well-trained KGB main-line agent who had been pulled into a Spetsnaz unit directly assigned to the STAVKA. The period of rest at the Sunset Canyon Ranch was both well-deserved and well-appreciated on her part. It gave her time to ponder her future. The famed, irresistible Angel of Death was beginning to see the need of directing her attention away from Sarabrov. He was a mere soldier. She relished the opportunity to finally be trafficking at ease among the prime leaders of the new world. To her, once the the Communists in the Russian Parliament had paved the way, the Second Coming would occur and her world prominence as well would be but one short revolution away.

She kept her eyes fixed on the powerful man that she had never known, but whom she desired to seduce as soon as his new heart could endure the ecstacy. In her mind, Yuri Gagarin was the man of destiny. Andropov on the other hand was a pathetic excuse of a man. As the only Russian woman among the STAVKA, if she handled herself carefully, power would be hers. She left the meeting to see if Yarov needed help with the Dane.

* * *

The hands again delivered food through the opening in the door. Michael looked for a note even before he started to eat. There was none. But within minutes after he started, the door was suddenly unlocked for the first time that he could remember.

In the next second, Michael was face to face with the woman Cosmonaut. The short blonde hair created no confusion. He knew her instantly. Her other attributes were still conspicuous. She struck a pose of innocence, but he had no difficulty seeing through it to the utterly evil core of her nature. He could see a gadget in her hands - a set of handcuffs with about a six-inch chain between the cuffs. "You hold hands out."

Michael clearly understood the command, but hesitated. Yelana looked back into the hall and a pair of black-shirted soldiers came forward with machine pistols drawn to emphasize her point.

"Hands out!" she again demanded.

This time Michael complied. He was then marched out of the building, fully expecting to be placed in a location where he could be shot without bleeding all over someone's floor.

Once outside, he was amazed at what he saw. The buildings were unidentifiable, but the towering sandstone cliffs reminded him of the Utah canyon country. The scent of the canyon air even conveyed the same message. It caused him to wish that home was just over the hill, but he knew that in his current predicament, if home was nearby, he might just as well be thousands of miles away.

A brief walk across the pasture to the ranch house and Michael found himself in slightly more familiar territory. The woman had him sit down at a UNIX server which had been set up as a work station in a side room just off of the gathering hall of what appeared to be a large hunting lodge - type cabin. The woman lacked diplomacy, ''You sit here - stay or you die!'' Michael got the message.

Within minutes, a familiar voice came booming through the room. Yarov spoke through his interpreter, ''Michael, how good to see you again!''

Michael had largely given up thoughts of self preservation. ''How wonderful to see you, Yarov. How about telling me what in the hell is going on? I did the little deed with the Crays. So what's happening?''

''Oh, not so quick. The job is not done.''

''You want me to reinstall the data from the optical disks right?'' It was obvious to Michael.

''How did you guess?''

''This new Pentium is a dead giveaway.'' Michael regretted the use of the word ''dead.''

''We need your help. There are still some communication problems. We assume you can fix them.''

''Maybe I can. So what if I do it. Will you let me go?''

''Well, of course, Michael. This slight detour has been an inconvenience for us all. I always keep my word.''

Yarov was lying, and Michael knew it. He decided at that moment that negotiation for his freedom was a waste of energy. He would stretch out the installation effort and try to use the time to plan an escape from the confines of Yarov's strange associates.

For Yarov's part, he had developed a degree of familiarity with Michael that caused him some discomfort as he walked out the front door to head back to the TTI offices realizing that it was the last time he would ever see his Danish joint venture associate alive.

Hurricane, Utah, Late March, 1993

''You really opened a can of worms when you sent that slug to the State Crime Lab!'' The sheriff was not happy. ''That damn report of yours has been picked up and they want a field-card done on the people that own the property closest to the accident.''

''What's the problem with that? I field-card people every day - it's no big deal.'' Joe sensed the sheriff's irritation but still had no qualms about being flippant.

''The hell it ain't. It takes man-hours and other people to cover your out-of-town time. I'm sure you don't have any inkling of concern about that!''

''I've done it before.''

''And we've had trouble in Hurricane with nobody to respond to calls.'' ''Well, I can hurry.''

''You best get up there, and don't cause no trouble with those folks. They're just like the polygs, they wanna be left alone to contemplate their navel or women or whatever religious B.S. they do up there! So just fill out the field cards and that's all. Don't make enemies, and don't make no friends, just do your damn job!''

''Are you sure you shouldn't just send someone else?''

''No, I'm not sure, but it's your part of the county. I'd send someone else if I had another body to replace you!''

''Hey, sheriff, one more thing.''

''What's that?''

''You'd better find somebody else, cause you got thirty days. I don't have to put up with this crap! Not from you... not from anybody!''

And so the conversation had gone, or at least it was how Joe had recollected his earlier verbal bout with the sheriff as he drove up the Kolob Road for the first time since the disturbing night almost seven months earlier. The sheriff's verbal attack had triggered his decision. Job or no job at the batch plant, Joe would endure only one more month with the department.

Zion Station, Late March, 1993

By mid-afternoon, the normal day's tasks at the Sunset Canyon Ranch had been completed. Sarabrov had met his goal of training his men daily in the art of horseback riding. It was one of the few skills that Spetsnaz troopers had not been taught in the course of their regular training. The horses had been groomed and returned to the stables. The men of the 23rd Spetsnaz Company were gathered in their barracks at the rear of the compound tucked away in the trees out of view of the highway.

The girls from the polygamous cult were still carrying out chores assigned by Jim. A matronly polygamist wife had free walk of the compound as she governed the young girls, making certain that they were ready and prepared for the desires of the STAVKA. The woman had little understanding of who or why these people were at the Sunset Canyon Ranch. It was not her concern. She was there to perform her duties and accept her lot in life and to further assist each of the girls, some her own nieces, to accept their circumstances as a valued test of faith. They would soon enough be moved back into the homes to serve God's anointed.

"We've got a visitor," Jim, standing in the main room of the ranch house, was on the line to the speaker box at the front gate and yelled across the room to Sarabrov. "It's a deputy sheriff. He has some type of questionnaire - says he has to talk to us."

"What's it about?"

"He says it's something to do with the car accident."

"You know about that don't you Jim?" Sarabrov asked, knowing that Jim should handle the matter. "I wasn't here when it happened. It was on your watch as I recall."

Jim disliked Sarabrov. The recrimination regarding the car wreck had never quite subsided. "Let him in." Jim was interested in seeing just what the police might know about the event. He gathered several of the STAVKA aides together in the main room of the lodge and instructed them in Russian, confident that Michael Christensen, who was working at the computer work station would not understand.

"Let me handle it. Just remember, we are a religious group, are we not? So put on your most pious faces. Get a few of the girls out here. They will leave us alone if they think we are polygamists. And keep the deputy out on the porch, I don't want him anywhere near the Dane.''

Joe Wilson watched the electronic gate latch slowly slide to the left. He drove the quarter of a mile across the open field toward the clump of trees where he remembered the ranch house to be. As he did so, he looked back across his left shoulder at the site where the car had careened off the cliff above and virtually shattered in all directions like a glass bottle. The gruesome thought of that late-night experience had been put in the back of his mind. But he could not avoid a certain chill that nagged at his memory as he passed so near to the spot.

He drove the car slowly down the dirt road and reached the small bridge which crossed a brook. The stream was lined by a rock wall which ran the length of the thicket of leafless cottonwood, aspen and dense evergreens separating the uncultivated open field from the tree-covered ranch area. He pulled into the yard, and negotiated his car around the circular driveway in the same manner that his father had done in years past as he had come to see the legendary race horses as a boy. As Joe climbed out of his car, he stood in the driveway and cautiously took in the scene. The sight of the horses grazing in the pastures to the south of the ranch house and the sound of the breeze blowing through the trees like waves of water caused a brief feeling of deja vous. In his earlier days, he would have come to the ranch for a swim after riding horses for several hours.

He walked to the door and knocked. Jim invited him to enter through a screen door and stand on the enclosed porch with shuttered windows pushed open to allow the breeze to pass through. ''How are you doing, young man?'' Jim was trying hard to sound like a local.

''I'm doing fine, Sir.''

''And what might be your business here?'' Jim asked.

''I just need to ask a few question, you know, about that car wreck last September. Didn't I see you there?'' Joe inquired, trying to break the ice.

''Yes, I heard it and walked out to it. That was really a shame. Please, sit down.'' Jim invited him to sit at a small table situated on the enclosed porch only a few feet from the front door.

''It seems like a bullet was found in one of the wheels. Do you have any idea how that could have happened - I mean did you hear anything peculiar, like a shot or something?'' Joe was struck by the look that passed between Jim and another man standing nearby.

"No, I heard no shot." The question unnerved him slightly. "Perhaps you would like a drink?'' Jim asked.

"Well, I guess I could use a Coke or something,'' Joe responded. Jim made a gesture through the door to someone, ostensibly to bring drinks to the group.

"How do you think a bullet got in that wheel, young man?'' Jim needed information.

"We're not sure. It wasn't just any bullet. It was a peculiar make from Russia or somewhere.'' Joe again sensed tension.

There was a brief pause, "We hunt sometimes. But we are a religious people. We have gathered here to enjoy the strength of one another and freely exercise our faith in God. The law protects that, you know?''

Joe felt that the man was trying to change the subject. "Do you keep any rifles here?''

Jim stuttered momentarily, "We have some hunting rifles in the lodge, maybe two or three.''

The conversation was interrupted as the door from the main part of the house opened and a young woman walked onto the enclosed porch carrying a tray with one soft drink and one alcoholic drink. She politely lowered the tray into a position to serve each of the men. At first, Joe could not see her face, as her long brown hair had fallen forward when she leaned down allowing him to reach to the tray. Then, as his hands grasped the glass of Coca-Cola, he leaned back, tilted his head slightly and caught a glimpse of the face of the young woman as she shifted her hair back to her shoulder with her hand and began to step quietly away. The recognition was instantaneous. He was certain that he had just seen Hannah's daughter, Flora Jackson. It was the memorable face in the picture. His eyes followed hers. Jim sipped his drink apparently unaware of the brief eye contact.

Joe was careful not to be too obvious, but he caught her gaze as she stepped back and walked toward the door. It was in that moment that he sensed a look of real fright. She left the room and the discussion continued. He felt certain he had seen a mute cry for help.

As she walked through the front door of the ranch house, Flora saw Michael at the computer across the room. She could see the modified handcuffs that still allowed him to work the computer keyboard. Flora nodded slight recognition as she maintained an even pace toward the hall leading to the kitchen in an effort to prevent any detection.

"I would like to suggest to you, Mr. Deputy Sheriff," Jim explained, "that perhaps it would be better, out of respect for our religious beliefs, that you not inquire as to our ownership of firearms - that is protected under the constitution you know."

"I'm not sure that your religion has anything to do with it," Joe responded. "This is simply a preliminary investigation. I have no suspects, but I do need to interview anyone who might know something."

"Well, we have two Mausers - they are German rifles. We have hunted deer with them during the season."

"Anything else?"

"No." Jim knew that his arsenal competed with that of a sizeable military base.

"I need your name, social security number, date of birth and a bunch of other stuff - is that okay?"

"Sure, no problem." Jim's false identity was well-developed. He answered all the questions without difficulty.

The door opened. The young girl stood before them again and prepared to clear the glasses from the porch table. He watched as the man's eyes moved in her direction. She looked quickly away, picked up the glasses and returned to the house, acting much as a maid and nothing more.

Joe was taking quick mental notes, but this was not the time to act. He had been warned by his boss to stay out of the polygamist's business. This was obviously a strange spin of events that he would need to flesh out clearly before acting. "I remember two other men at the accident the night I saw you there - may I talk to them also?"

"They're gone," Jim was quick to respond. "They have been transferred to another one of our retreats in Europe."

"Is there anyone else around who was here when the wreck happened?"

"I can't think of anyone. Most everyone here is a new arrival."

"Well, I think I have what I need." Joe started to put away his notebook and stood up. "If I need more, I'll be back." He walked out the screen door and down the steps to his car.

Sarabrov and Jim watched grimly as the deputy sheriff 's car completed its way out of the circle, across the one-lane wooden bridge and then out along the dirt road to the gate at the Kolob Mountain Road.

At the gate, Joe paused and thought for a moment. He was worried that his present lonely situation might have caused him to read more into a simple action than was real. But still, he paused. He got out of the car, took a piece of black electrical tape from the emergency kit in the glove box and tightly placed a strip inside the electronically controlled gate latch. He pulled onto the highway, turned left and headed down the mountain in the direction of the town of Virgin. Joe knew he would be coming back.

St. George, Utah, Late March, 1993

Surveillance of the Tabernacle Tower Building had been set up using six agents. The building was positioned deep in the middle of the city block with one road leading into the parking lot and circular drive of the four-story building. There were no other routes by which vehicles could enter or exit.

The building itself had been constructed in a rectangular shape with a long, rear fire wall bordering on the windowless wall of the Rodeway Inn Motel. Between the two buildings was an alley approximately eight feet in width in which compressors, heat pumps and other mechanical devices serving both buildings had been placed. The only windows facing the alley were on the ground floor of the Tabernacle Tower Building along the rear wall of the TTI office. The windows, however, were constructed of steel mesh within the glass as a protection against burglars who might try to enter the building from the isolated alley - they could not be easily broken.

One agent had been posted to the west of the building in the upper floors of a small apartment atop a store approximately two hundred feet from the alley itself. He had complete view of the area and would be able to see anyone who might try to escape across the open lot in his direction to the west of the building. Swindler, with Ziyetski in the passenger seat, was stationed across the street from the entry to the parking lot itself. From their position sitting in a car, they were about one hundred yards away and had a complete view of the building. They would drive the car to the front of the building, and would be the first through the door.

The third group of agents, both Russian and American, were preparing to close in on the building by working their way across the parking lot. They would be the heavy armed-response if it became necessary.

Inside the TTI office, Yarov was in a heated discussion with the First Deputy. "I don't know how soon a heart surgery can be planned. It should be soon."

"But I have no time. Going to Las Vegas will only delay the process. I am sick. I can't walk up a flight of stairs. You must take me to Gagarin!"

"That is impossible!"

"Then tell me how to get to the American Dacha. I will go myself!"

"It is not that simple, Comrade. You must have patience. The American arrangement is not going as well as planned. We must leave immediately."

The First Deputy pulled out the medal of the Hero of the Soviet Union. "He gave me this." He stretched out his hand.

Yarov was impressed, but knew his orders. "We must wait. That is all I can say."

There was an interruption at the door to the inside office as the only other person in the office, a software engineer from Kiev, burst into the room. "Yarov, we are in trouble. There are agents or police or someone getting into position around us - look!" He drew them out into the foyer. They could see the surveillance car about a hundred feet down the lane. An agent had just left his car and could be only partially seen crouched near the rear of a parked car. Yarov tried the phone. It was dead.

Yarov and the First Deputy returned to the back office that had a window facing the alley. Yarov picked up the heavy Samsung video monitor on the desk, reared back and launched it at the window. To his dismay, however, it bounced, leaving a crack, but failed to break the glass.

In another frantic move, he picked up the video monitor again, reached back and with all of his strength heaved it against the window. The monitor burst through the glass.

The size of the hole was only partial. Its jagged edges were difficult to avoid as he, followed by the First Deputy quickly crawled through the smashed window into the alley. Blood oozed from cuts on their hands and legs as each stepped across a compressor in the alley and ran eastward, between the high walls of the Tabernacle Tower Building and the Rodeway Inn Motel. The First Deputy, lagged torpidly behind.

"I see one, no...two white males going *out* the window, down the back alley - eastward!" the agent screamed into his radio from his vantage point in the apartment above the store to the west of the Tabernacle Tower.

"Crash the building! *Crash the building now!*" Swindler shouted the command into his radio and immediately started the engine of his car. The agents moved into the road in front of the Tabernacle Tower in an effort to cut off the escape.

Other agents, both FBI and KGB, ran up the fence line on the side of the parking lot, still trying to stay out of view of the TTI office windows. Upon reaching the building, they charged forward, bursting through the unlocked door, only to find one bewildered software engineer in the back room.

Swindler and Ziyetski had quickly driven around the corner rather than invade the building as had been originally planned. They turned northward heading to the intersection with St. George Boulevard, the town's main thoroughfare. As the pair reached the intersection, they saw an obese man, his business suit flapping, loping up the sidewalk directly in a line of sight off the driver's left shoulder. Swindler switched on his siren and spun the car around in the middle of the intersection, stopping traffic and almost causing an accident. He turned left, sped up the road in a westerly direction in front of the fleeing man, then pulled around on the curb to cut off his escape.

Just as they jumped from the car Yarov raised a pistol to the firing position and sent a volley into the car. Instinctively, the agents took cover. Yarov used the moment to retreat behind cars in a restaurant parking lot.

A restaurant with a large plate-glass window and a tour bus parked next to it was immediately behind Yarov. Swindler and Ziyetski had no choice but to hold their fire. The agents fell to the ground to avoid two shots which splintered through their car.

Swindler then pulled out his cellular phone and screamed into it, "Shots fired! We've got two Reds on the fly and one shooting at us!" Swindler was uncertain where the other man reported going out the window of the building might be.

The First Deputy had crouched behind a dumpster at the edge of motel parking lot. He had not run out onto the street with the Yarov. The excruciating fire in his chest that had prohibited any nimble moves was now taking over. He could not speak, but only grimace. He tried to lift his head to locate his pursuers, but the power to even straighten his back was gone. His left arm felt as if it was being torn away from his torso - the First Deputy was in cardiac arrest.

A police siren could be heard whining from somewhere in the downtown area as it closed in on the scene in response to the FBI agent's "nine-eleven" call over their open-band police radio. The message was clear, "Officers in trouble - shots fired."

Swindler and Ziyetski began moving from behind their car and along the edge of the front side of the Rodeway Inn. Their plan was to try and corner the suspect against a safe-fire backdrop. They scampered from the side of the building to the cover of the two brick columns and a large planter serving the covered entryway to the motel. In response, Yarov unloaded another volley of three more rounds from across the parking lot. The bullets shattered the windows of the motel lobby causing people inside to frantically jump for cover in all directions.

A city policeman arrived on the St. George Boulevard. Slowing his car, he saw the two agents positioned and pointing at the suspect. The officer rolled down the window on the passenger side and tried to understand Swindler shouting to him. "Control the traffic and keep the people in the restaurant!"

The policeman sped to the intersection and positioned his car, red and blue lights flashing, to block traffic from the eastbound lane. At the same time, using his radio, he called for another patrol car to do the same from a safe distance down the road.

Yarov, seeing that the two agents were now closing in on him from two different directions, abandoned his position near the restaurant and ran back in the direction of the Tabernacle Tower Building, escaping past the dumpster and around the far side of the Rodeway Inn. He backed into the alley between the two buildings only to hear a loud yell from the other end.

"Drop your weapon or I'll blow your head off! This is the FBI!"

Yarov swung around and cranked off one shot up the alley in the direction of the unexpected order. In the next second, five rounds of nine millimeter high-velocity hollow points buried themselves in his chest and stomach in rapid succession. His body flew back out of the alley towards the dumpster. He collapsed in a spread eagle heap only a few feet from the final resting place of the First Deputy of Toko Bank whose heart had ceased to function five minutes earlier.

For the next few minutes, Kenneth Swindler explained to local police officers the sanitized version of what had led to the deaths of the two men. With the KGB agents sequestered away in an FBI van, Swindler was successful in averting disclosure of the true purpose of the raid. For all the local police knew, it had been another drug battle with a group of foreign drug runners.

CHAPTER 25

St. George, Utah, Late March, 1993

By mid-afternoon of the following day, the FBI van had been packed for the trip back to Salt Lake City. The load included a considerable number of assault rifles and ammunition that had been put in place in St. George to facilitate the raid. Kenneth Swindler, two of his agents and the KGB would travel in the large Dodge van.

The failure of the plan to capture Yarov and the First Deputy alive had been a severe set back for Ziyetski. Yet, the shootout had confirmed the majority of his theory regarding the train heist and massacre. Yarov would not have run had he thought that he had any way of talking his way out of the trap. The account books at TTI had confirmed the payments to the hospital for the still unexplained heart surgery and many other expenditures on behalf of the Aviation Ministry as well as Toko Bank in the U.S. It was a wealth of evidence and would be copied to expedite investigations in Russia and the United States.

Both Swindler and Ziyetski agreed that the case would now focus on the Dane, Michael Christensen. Plans for Swindler and his team to travel to Russia for a reciprocal search for Christensen were already underway. A pair of agents had been left in St. George to keep the Christensen home under surveillance should he somehow slip undetected back into the country.

The trip to Salt Lake City would follow a slight detour. Swindler and Ziyetski were both anxious to inspect the site in the desert where the bodies of the two supposed Spetsnaz troopers had been found. They drove to the town of Hurricane where they were met by Joe Wilson, who had been assigned to guide the FBI to the remote Arizona Strip location.

For Kenneth Swindler, it was a good day. The tension of the gun battle had subsided. The FBI crime lab was now working over the TTI offices. His involvement was not necessary. The lone computer engineer who had been captured had been flown to the Federal facility in Salt Lake City for further questioning by a special counterespionage team flying in from Washington D.C. It was hoped that much more information would come to light in connection with the congressional bribery case. But with dead suspects, Swindler was uncertain where to go next. He was satisfied that at the very least, the Russian operation in St. George had been broken. Another cog in the investigation wheel was to somehow answer the question of how two Russian elite soldiers died in the desert. The TTI operation in St. George had to tie into it somehow. But in any event, this was passive work. Following a day of lethal action in St. George, the drive into the picturesque Arizona Strip country north of the Grand Canyon was a welcomed relief.

Joe Wilson had never worked with the FBI before. In his mind, the FBI was the ultimate in law enforcement. He had been asked by the sheriff to guide the FBI to the shallow grave site below the cinder pit. As he carried out the assignment, he toyed with the idea of sharing his thoughts about the supposed kidnapping of Flora Jackson with them. He knew it would probably get him in more trouble with the sheriff but he was moving on anyway. He couldn't erase the look he had seen a few days earlier in the girl's face from his mind.

Colonel Ziyetski and his agents examined the burial site. Like Ziyetski's work at the State Medical Examiner's autopsy room, the men were thorough and inquisitive as to every detail. The Russians, on hands and knees, carefully combed each section of dirt and broke up clumps of dirt clods as they searched for the slightest piece of overlooked evidence.

As they placed items in evidence bags, Kenneth Swindler curiously watched the delicate recovery effort. Taking Colonel Ziyetski aside in order to avoid any disclosure of the Russian nature of the investigation from the deputy, he asked the Colonel, in Russian, what he had found.

The Colonel smiled and spoke proudly as he held up the bag and pointed to a small brownish object, a portion of which had been rubbed clean exposing a gold sheen. ''I will bet you one American McDonald's hamburger that this is the tooth of a human being, and in particular the gold that is in it will be proven to have been put there by a Russian dentist. Our dental procedures, including the material used for fillings are archaic compared to those used in America. The experts will prove that this is the tooth of a Russian - remember, one McDonald's hamburger.''

Kenneth Swindler was amused. He was watching the standard Russian principle of compensation at work. Despite the fact that their equipment, techniques and technology were often behind the times, the personal ingenuity, creativity and astuteness of the Russian investigator overcame the technology gap. Swindler was now viewing Ziyetski as a true equal, a colleague in every respect.

At approximately 3:00 p.m. the work had been completed. Various relics had been recovered by the group. Ziyetski was certain more than ever that two Soviet Spetsnaz troopers had been killed at the burial site in southern Utah. This disclosure would be not only significant to the Americans, but also to Director Dombrayov in Moscow. How such military activities had ranged all the way into the heartland of America was indeed a mystery and one which he hoped both the KGB and the FBI could uncover jointly.

Just as the group seemed to be wrapping up, the Russians decided to hike to the top of the cinder cone. Colonel Ziyetski thought it would be a good vantage point to view with binoculars any other burial sites or disturbances on the surface which might be suspicious.

Joe Wilson and the FBI agents remained behind. As they stood near the graves, Joe continued to stew as the inner debate raged as to whether or not he should share his thoughts regarding the Flora Jackson incident with the FBI or just leave well enough alone. He didn't need another major problem with the sheriff just prior to leaving. But to sit back and blame it on the sheriff's hands-off policy, would be difficult to live with. He decided to try.

"You guys investigate kidnapping, don't you?" Joe enquired of Swindler.

"Yep, that's always been part of our business - at least since the Lindberg baby case back in the thirties. From then on, the FBI has been in the kidnapping business and I've done quite a few of them myself," Swindler responded.

"What is the technical definition of kidnapping as far as you guys are concerned - would it be right to say that when a person is taken or held against his will that is kidnapping? I mean, it can happen with adults just like kids, isn't that right?"

"Sure. Kidnapping is a case of violence, often directed against children. Seems like we normally get into kidnapping cases when it involves children or some kind of extortion. Why - you got some kind of kidnapping problem around here we should know about?" Kenneth spoke kiddingly.

Joe did not answer. His body language however, told Kenneth something was wrong. Kenneth's mood was no longer light. He read the concern and sense of reservation on Joe's face. "Now, do you have something to tell me, deputy?" he queried in a sudden change to seriousness.

Over the course of the next twenty minutes, while they awaited the return of the Russians on the cinder cone, Joe related the entire story to the FBI agent. He disclosed everything he knew, including the visit to Hannah Jackson and the strange religious cult at the Sunset Canyon Ranch.

At first, the story had seemed doubtful. But as he continued, Swindler could see that Joe Wilson was speaking primarily from an objective policeman's perspective. Encouraged by Swindlers interest, the deputy produced a copy of Hannah Jackson's letter.

By the time the Russians returned from the hill top, Kenneth Swindler had a new case to investigate prior to his return to Salt Lake City. Under normal circumstances, it would have required an official referral and staffing request, but under the present situation, with his team already in southern Utah, and since Deputy Wilson had described what appeared to be a crime in progress, it was wholly appropriate for him to take immediate action rather than to wait. In fact, the agent's oath required it. If he knew of a crime such as kidnapping or any other major federal offense in progress, he was duty-bound to intervene and halt the criminal activity at once. The deputy's story and the letter were compelling.

The proximity to the event was likewise a factor, he reasoned. It would take days to get other agents into the area to investigate the allegations. Yet, it was only forty-five minutes out of the way to make the detour up the Kolob Road to the Sunset Canyon Ranch. Swindler briefly explained his plan to Ziyetski. The Russians would go along for the ride but would have no involvement. They divided the group with one FBI agent and five Russians in the rented van. Joe Wilson, along with Kenneth Swindler and another agent rode in the deputy's cruiser.

The shadows were already casting thick and deep across the canyon floor as they arrived at the ranch turnoff. Kenneth Swindler took note of the massive wrought-iron sign arched over the entry gate announcing "Sunset Canyon Ranch" with a large white cross at the apex. The pristine beauty of the canyon, the pastures and the ranch house tucked away amid the tall aspens and cottonwoods was both impressive and distracting.

Since it was intended as an initial contact and likely a noncustodial interrogation, Kenneth suggested that the Russians remain behind at the front gate near the highway with the van. It was decided that he, his two agents and Deputy Wilson, all riding in the deputy's car, would make the visit to the ranch. The approach would consist of himself and Wilson at the front door of the ranch house and the two agents hanging back in the yard for cover. It was standard operating procedure to make such an approach and particularly under circumstances where the response was largely unknown.

As they walked, the two spoke of their intentions. "Now, you understand, Deputy Wilson, that kidnapping is a major felony. We don't just go in and accuse people lightly. So, we're free to make an inquiry. And I believe what you've said, but all we can do is talk to the girl in a non-intimidating environment. If we're convinced she's speaking freely and denies the situation, then there's nothing we can do."

"Yeah, I realize that. I'm willing to take the chance and make a fool out of myself. But I think if we ask her and she really knows that we can help her, she'll talk to us. You should've seen the look on her face. It just got to me. There's something weird going on. She was trying to tell me something. If I hadn't talked to her mother though, maybe I wouldn't have even noticed but...I don't know."

"Well, it's always better to be safe than sorry," Swindler responded.

Joe Wilson's electrical tape on the gate was still firmly in place. They were able to enter the gate and drive the car through and onto the ranch property. They drove the deputy's car in along the narrow dirt road across the open area from the gate in the direction of the rock wall along the creek. They pulled into the circular drive, then stopped the car halfway around the arch with the car pointing away from the ranch house. It was a subconscious habit to always allow an escape route.

As the four got out of the car, a congregation of men was already standing on the front porch, arms folded and obviously not inclined to welcome visitors. Joe Wilson recognized Jim as he and Kenneth Swindler walked forward to the steps leading up to the enclosed porch area. "Jim," Joe spoke loudly, "I'm sorry to come back and disturb you again, but we need to talk about something!"

"I gave you your interview - what else do you want?" Jim shot back tersely.

"Well, it's the girl. You know, the young lady who served drinks to us two days ago. We want to talk to her."

The men on the porch reacted only slightly and Kenneth Swindler read their mannerisms. He could see that Joe's request had struck a sensitive nerve. He knew something was definitely wrong.

Inside, Michael Christensen was sitting at the computer. A guard was posted nearby. The raised voices of the men outside was the first real English language he had heard in almost a month.

"Why do you want to talk to her?" Jim inquired.

"It's part of an investigation. I would like you to bring her out here." Joe responded.

"Well, I really don't think that's possible," Jim yelled back. "She is a member of our religious order, you know."

"I think you heard me, Jim! Let's not have any trouble here!" Joe tried not to sound nervous in the presence of experienced FBI men.

"And if I refuse, then what?" Jim asked belligerently.

Joe paused, noting that agent Swindler still had not spoken and was leaving the lead up to him. "You need to meet these guys, Jim. This is agent Kenneth Swindler of the Federal Bureau of Investigation. He is helping me in this investigation of a possible felony. It involves the girl. So just have her come out here and talk to us, okay? Don't make us come in and get her."

At that point, Sarabrov came out the door and joined the group. Swindler inspected him immediately from a distance and noted the ear plug with the wire disappearing into his bulky shirt, obviously leading down his back to a receiver. It was not a good sign. It meant that someone else was talking to him, possibly from another vantage point. Swindler started searching the roof lines and upper windows with his peripheral vision, trying to avoid being too conspicuous. The men on the porch talked momentarily and then Jim spoke again. "All right, we'll bring the girl out here. But what is it you want to ask her?"

"Like I said, that's our business. Just get her out here!" Joe said curtly.

Suddenly, from over Joe's right shoulder, a powerful and authoritative voice boomed in sharp unequivocating terms. "The young lady had better appear in two minutes, or this whole matter is going to become a Federal case of interfering with the investigation of a felony by Federal agents. Regardless of what the girl says, you're all going to be under arrest!" Kenneth Swindler's words were crisp. Joe was relieved to hear them as they echoed through the canyon.

At that moment, the man with the earplug walked inside. Jim remained on the steps with his two counterparts who did not speak English. At the same time, Kenneth was nagged by a premonition. As he watched the two men standing silently in front of him on the porch, he was disturbed by their appearance. It was a demeanor he had seen before and had represented the essence to him, of evil.

Inside, at full pitch, a heated whispered discussion in Russian was taking place in total disregard of the fact that Michael Christensen was sitting nearby. "I'm not sure what's going on here," Jim spoke to Captain Major Sarabrov. "This is total lunacy. I think these agents really are here to pick up the girl. They don't know who we are!"

"No, that's impossible. They are just clever," Sarabrov responded.

"Well, if they're so clever, my dear Captain Major, what are they doing here with only three agents and that clumsy kid from the sheriff's office? We can take these guys out in a minute and bury them in our own backyard."

He was suddenly distracted. A message was coming over the ear piece, and then he spoke, "Apparently, there are six more out at the front gate. But it is still strange. Our lookouts say they are not deployed. They're just milling around."

Yelana who had just joined the group, having arrived from the back hall, listened to the discussion and interrupted, "If they're not here for us, then I don't know what all the fuss is about. Those little girls, are just robots. They have no personality - they don't show emotion unless you beat them. Then they just cry. That old bitch - you know, the old lady that runs those girls, get her out there with the girl. Then there won't be any problems."

Sarabrov rattled off a command to one of his aides, sending for the young girl whom they referred to as "Brownie" because of the color of her hair. Her real name was of no consequence to him.

Jim then inquired of Sarabrov, "Are we deployed?"

"Certainly, the two ready platoons are in position. That's twenty-eight men, and I've got another fifty or so in reserve at the barracks. They should be ready in five minutes."

"I don't know if you're going to need them," Jim spoke. "But something is strange here. Can we really assume that all they want to do is talk to the girl?"

"We're ready for anything, so let's just see what happens," Sarabrov responded, his sense of a possible military solution starting to control his thoughts and give him courage.

Two minutes later, the door to the porch opened and a matronly-looking woman in a long dress appeared with Flora Jackson, similarly dressed, following close behind.

Joe recognized Flora immediately, but he noted that as soon as she stepped onto the porch, she looked down at the ground.

The FBI agent standing at the back of the driveway near the rock wall noticed movement in the high yellow grass amid the cottonwoods some fifty yards to his right. He became uneasy. The agent was certain that he had glimpsed someone moving - perhaps crawling - in the grass and he was certain it was *not* an animal.

"What do you want of our little girl?" The old woman spoke noticeably proud and defiant.

Joe glanced at Kenneth, and seeing that Kenneth was still leaving the matter largely in his hands, softly said, "Flora - Flora Jackson! That's your name, isn't it?" The girl continued to stare at the ground like a frozen statue. "Flora, I have talked to your mother. I know your mother, Hannah Jackson. Your mother is Hannah Jackson isn't she?" he asked, his voice pleading for a response.

The girl remained silent. Kenneth Swindler then noticed several men walking onto the porch from the door behind Flora. From their stance, he knew they were not religious fundamentalists. They appeared far from having any sectarian appearance about them, nor were they Southern Utah cowboy types. But the odor caught his attention. It was that strong combination of moldy damp body odor and stale vodka. He'd smelled it before. There was only a slight breeze but Swindler recognized that smell even at some twenty paces. It was distinctly that of the Russians he had spent so many years tracking through the streets of New York City.

"Flora, your mother has told me that you were kidnapped. That you were taken away from her, against your will and without her permission! Now tell me, Flora, is that what happened? Is your mother right?" Joe continued his interrogation.

The girl continued to stare at the ground. She stood motionless.

"Why doesn't she speak? Tell me, lady, *why* isn't she talking to me?" He leaned toward the older woman.

"This girl has some special problems!" The woman put her arm around Flora's shoulders and spoke with inbred piety. "We are hopeful that her stay here will allow her to recover from her illness. That is what we do here. We are a religious people and we do not understand why you are bothering us."

Jim interrupted. "That's right, we understand that we are entitled to the protection of the great and heroic principles of the Constitution of the United States! We do not understand why you would be here interfering!"

As soon as the word "heroic" registered in his ears, Kenneth Swindler felt a cold chill race down his spine. He knew, now, exactly who he was facing. The stocky, well-built men were Russians. And not just any Russians. They were KGB, Spetsnaz or GRU. His dread accelerated to mild panic as he wondered if Ziyetski had trapped him here on purpose. But then he remembered it had been the deputy who had brought them to the ranch. Ziyetski had no way of knowing.

The sweat began to bead on Kenneth's face. He knew his suspicions would soon be noticed by the highly-trained adversaries before him. It was now all *too* real, the two dead Spetsnaz troopers, the TTI office, Michael Christensen and the shootout with the Russians the day before. The events converged in Kenneth Swindler's head. Fear gripped his entire being and he forced himself to concentrate on breathing steadily - one breath in, then one breath out. There was no doubt that he and his men had unwittingly walked into the center of a potentially lethal situation.

"Your mother told me to come find you, Flora Jackson!" Joe spoke in a loud voice to be sure he was heard. "She told me I could take you home to her. That is, if you want to go. Flora, are you here because you want to be? Is someone holding you against your will?"

Swindler stood behind Joe, gripped his arm and whispered urgently, "We need to get out of here - we need to do it now, deputy. Just back off. Trust me on this one. We're in deeper than you know!"

Joe Wilson, oblivious to the perilous situation continued to plead with Flora, but noted that agent Swindler was beginning to move back toward the car. "I've seen your mother's picture of you. She's really feeling bad. Thinks you didn't want to leave, Flora. Why don't you just tell me?" he spoke, almost shouting. "Just tell me what the hell's going on here! Does someone have some kind of control so you just can't talk?" Joe was becoming frustrated, his voice getting louder.

At that moment, Swindler noticed men gathering near the fence-line of the corral approximately forty yards away. "It's time to leave, Deputy Wilson, *come on!*" He no longer cared if his alarm was detected by the men on the porch. "We're leaving now, Deputy!" Swindler said. "She doesn't look to me like she's here against her will!" Swindler spoke loud enough for all to hear.

Joe Wilson was irritated by the comment and surprised that the FBI agents had given up so easily. But taking the lead from the experience of Agent Swindler, he turned to walk across the gravel driveway in the direction of the car.

The men on the porch wandered back through the door of the house confident that the matter had been resolved. The young girl and the old woman disappeared into the foyer area behind the door.

Inside, at the computer, Michael, with his newly-heightened senses, had distinctly heard the entire exchange. The commotion had distracted his guard. The fact that he had only one chance to make a move to escape was confirmed by the look of terror on the face of the girl as she moved back through the door. Without further thought, he lunged across the room, approaching the men who were still looking toward the outside and wrapped his handcuffed arms around the girl as he reached the doorway. In the next second before anyone in the room could sense the unusual motion from behind, he wrenched her through the open door.

"Are you satisfied?" Jim yelled, as the visitors moved to withdraw.

Joe turned around, "I'm not..." At that moment Michael and Flora burst through the door and jumped across the porch, headlong into the air, skipping all three steps before crashing onto the gravel driveway. As they landed, they separated.

Instantly, Jim jumped off the steps to grab the girl. Michael could not get to his feet and tried rolling toward the car. Closest to the girl, Joe sprang forward and smashed his fist into the side of Jim's head. Jim fell backward into a row of low bushes.

"Help me - help me, please!" Flora screamed as she grabbed Joe.

He backed up and pulled her away from the house, his arms supporting her small frame. Flora was sobbing out of control. They reached the door of the patrol car. Michael, who had just made it to the rear door, dove into the back seat.

As people again gathered on the front porch of the house, Joe looked over at Kenneth Swindler. The FBI agent was pointing his .357 magnum autoload pistol in the direction of the house. He appeared frozen like a cold iron statue. Joe realized that the look on Swindler's face was one of pure fear.

" Get her in the car and get the hell out of here!" Swindler barked loudly.

Joe moved Flora around the car to the driver's side. His arms were shaking. Flora sobbed quietly as he shoved her into the car. His own fear was taking over. Once she was in, he looked over the top of the car, his eyes on the other two agents. One was backing up in the direction of the rock wall holding his nine MM. machine pistol at waist level. He waived impatiently for Joe to get the car across the bridge.

An eerie silence governed the moment as the car careened around the circle near the house, across the small bridge and onto the dirt road. The agent on the right continued to back up. The agent on Kenneth's left had already climbed over the wall and assumed a crouching position behind it. Others joined the group on the porch. It was as though some unwritten rule was allowing time for the two sides to measure the extent of the other's resolve to deal with the tense standoff.

The crouching agent again noticed motion in the brush in the cottonwood grotto between himself and the horse corrals. He took careful aim. The car had stopped on the other side of the bridge. Joe was waiting for the agents to climb in.

Kenneth Swindler and the agent nearest him were now on the same side of the wall as the creek, but still ten or more paces from the idling car. Kenneth weighed the prospects of providing sufficient cover-fire to allow the car to get away and at the same time protect the lives of himself and the other agents. He concluded if they attempted to get in the car, it would make them all one easy target.

Suddenly a volley of shots rang out from a point of concealment where the wall ran along the south end of the creek. The agent who had been crouching behind the wall sprawled backwards into the creek, his body adding the thick stain of blood to the trickling water. Kenneth screamed at Joe, "Get her out of here!" He then cranked off five rounds at the ranch house scattering the men on the porch, and dove behind the rock wall near the bridge. Joe gunned the engine. Gravel and dust flew from the wheels, creating a dust screen as he fishtailed up the road. Kenneth Swindler and the remaining agent began picking targets near the house, firing rapidly.

In a matter of seconds, the ranch house was converted into a fortress. Gunners on the roof, windows of the house and behind fences and outbuildings were concentrating fire on the rock wall area where the two FBI agents concealed themselves. They could not move.

At the halfway point on the road across the open field, the sheriff deputy's car was bouncing wildly on the rock and gravel road as he fled with Flora Jackson and Michael Christensen in the direction of the gate. Suddenly, the front of the car lifted up and the car twisted sideways and stopped as an RPG free-flight anti-tank missile, fired from somewhere along the south end of the creek, bounced off the front left tire and exploded only a few feet away. Joe quickly swung his door open, reached over and grabbed Flora, pulling her out of the car. Michael rolled out the rear door, and scrambled to his feet. As the car rocked from automatic rifle fire, the three made a dash toward the gate. Seconds later, another RPG scored a fiery direct hit on the car, a massive explosion knocking them off their feet. They recovered quickly and continued to run.

Colonel Ziyetski, at the first sound of gunfire had gathered his men into position along the fence line near the gate. The toy-like metallic clatter of gunfire from the ranch area four hundred yards away revealed the first evidence of the shocking truth. "Those are Kalashnikovs! I am certain. I think we've found our Spetsnaz!" he yelled.

The Russians, however, could only crouch low. The handguns they were allowed to bring into the United States were useless at such a distance. The FBI agents had the cellular phones. The first phone was rendered useless by the dead agent in the creek along the south wall. The other phone was in the hands of Kenneth Swindler who was busy using all of his strength and FBI training to stay alive as he hugged the rock wall. He knew that he was out-gunned, but hoped that Deputy Wilson could radio for help.

Ziyetski, confirming a hunch, ran to the van and ripped open the wooden crate below the middle seat. There he found five rifles - two Armolite AR18 rifles, two M-16's and a mini M-16 amid boxes of ammunition. He immediately tossed the weapons to his men, who without hesitation, began concentrating their fire on the grotto of trees along the south side of the rock wall. Spetsnaz gunners were now attempting to pick off the sheriff's deputy, the young woman and Michael as they ran the last one hundred yards toward the gate.

Amid the noise of the battle, Kenneth Swindler had not seen the explosion of the sheriff deputy's car. As he turned to see if the deputy, the girl and the stranger who exited the ranch house had safely made it across the open field, his vision was drawn to the burning hulk of the patrol car with its police-band radio two hundred yards beyond his position. This translated the one clear signal he did not want to receive - no help was on the way. He yelled down to the agent behind the wall to the north, "We've got to make a break, Matt - there's no other way!"

At that point, the younger agent began running north along the creek, parallel to the wall, using it for cover. As he did so, however, to generate any speed he was required to run somewhat erect. After twenty yards, the Spetsnaz gunfire caught up with him and he, like the first agent to be hit, sprawled fatally into the ditch.

Sarabrov, from the roof of the ranch house, could see gunfire now being directed at the house from the vicinity of the gate approximately a quarter of a mile across the open field. He carefully calculated the continually changing situation. He was hopeful that the only radio communication available to the attackers had been destroyed in the sheriff deputy's car. He knew, however, that the group positioned near the front gate of the ranch would still need to be neutralized as quickly as possible. If the girl and the Dane escaped, Zion Station would be doomed.

His decision was quick. There was no time to waste. He picked up his radio and barked an order, "All troopers in the building will rush the agent at the wall and troopers mounting vehicles should move as fast as possible to the front gate and kill, I repeat, kill, every person there. Except the Dane. Capture him if you can!"

With the appropriate acknowledgments over the radio responding with quick consecutive dispatch, the twelve members of the Spetsnaz tactical team inside the home poured out the front door charging across the driveway and front yard directly at Kenneth Swindler's position behind the wall. Through his field glasses, Ziyetski could see the deadly attack unfold. "They are Spetsnaz...I can see them clearly now. They are Spetsnaz, absolutely and for certain!" he yelled to the others. From a quarter of a mile distance, he ordered his men to direct their fire toward the front porch area of the house in an effort to try and protect Kenneth Swindler.

Hearing the front door fly open and slam against the side of the building, Swindler looked up and saw them coming. With one clip in the gun and his last clip in his free hand, he took careful aim allowing only his head to be exposed. He began squeezing, popping away rounds as quickly as the .357 would fire. For a moment, it appeared as though his accuracy and the distant cover fire from Colonel Ziyetski and his KGB men at the gate would stall the attack.

Attempting to reload interrupted Kenneth Swindler's awareness of his attackers. In the same moment, he sensed a slight relief as he realized the carnage on the porch being wrought by the Ziyestski's group despite the considerable distance. But the respite was overcome by a fierce charge. While he was still trying to engage the reload clip in the handle of his automatic pistol, the fanatical rage of seven Spetsnaz troopers carried over the wall, guns blazing and bayonets tearing at point blank range. Trying helplessly to fend off his attackers, Swindler fell in the creek bed, but then stood up and attempted to make his way across to the other side. At that point, his assailants attacked him with bayonets to finish the job in crude medieval style.

At the same moment that the Spetsnaz troopers were upon Swindler, four jeep Cherokees rushed around the ranch house, across the bridge and over the creek in another charge, Russian military-style, against the defenders of unknown identity at the Sunset Canyon Ranch gate.

With automatic weapons fire from the ranch now finding its range, Colonel Ziyetski could see that this was not the time to confront a fully-armed Spetsnaz Alpha Group. Unable to communicate with Joe, he grabbed him by the arm and pulled him to the van signifying with his hands that Joe should drive. Ordering the others in Russian, they quickly jumped inside. Joe Wilson swung the van onto the asphalt and sped down the Kolob Mountain Road with his cargo of Russians, Michael Christensen, and Flora Jackson next to him in the passenger seat.

Darkness was already moving in on the shadowed parts of the canyon. The reflection of multiple headlights off the canyon walls not more than a half mile behind them confirmed the fear that their pursuers were not satisfied with merely having run them off the ranch property. Ziyetski had already begun to deal with the thought of how he would communicate to his superiors the nature of this discovery of a lair of Spetsnaz forces hidden away on a ranch in a remote part of the United States. Momentarily he struggled with his concern of loyalty. Until recently they were both part of the same armed forces - were they still?

They were Russians, and he was Russian. But he had seen them murder the FBI agents. It was reasonable to assume that he, his men and the three Americans would be the next victims long before any questions were asked or answered. Curiously, the Spetsnaz had killed far more Russians than Americans.

His thoughts were quickly redirected to the issue at hand as two of his agents smashed out the back window of the van with the butt of their rifles. They knelt against the back seat, rifles aimed to deal with the reality of the pursuers, who, though still at a distance, were closing slowly.

Michael was thoroughly confused as he listened to the Russian-speaking men shout instructions back and forth. He had been taken captive by Russians, and now he was fleeing his captors with another group of Russians. It made little sense. But he was alive, and he was no longer in an isolated cell. While the terror level increased for all others in the van, he sensed an incredible feeling of deliverance upon seeing a Utah state highway road sign and then a sign advertising the distance to Zion National Park. It meant he was not far from home. Even amid the dread of the moment, it was euphoric for Michael.

The KGB agents looked somehow calm, despite the tension, as they peered out the rear window of the van. Again, after a long straightaway, they could see the parade of lights making the turn onto the main road running between I-15 and Zion National Park at the town of Virgin. There were at least five vehicles in pursuit.

As they sped along the wider and straighter part of the road, Joe noted police lights, red and blue flashing on the road, approximately one mile ahead. He yelled to the Russians, who did not understand his English, "I can't believe it! The U.S. Cavalry - we're saved!"

Michael understood and sensed immediate relief.

From the smiles on the faces of the Russians, Joe knew they understood. He continued to speed toward the flashing lights to be rescued from the unbelievable predicament.

Suddenly, Joe was bothered at what he saw Under the flashing lights less than a quarter of a mile in front of him against the backdrop of a near-darkened sky, he saw only the sheriff's cruiser. A premonition slowed his enthusiasm. Something appeared wrong. Slowing the vehicle to within two hundred yards, he squinted and carefully inspected the scene in front of him. He brought the van to a stop. "There's something wrong here. My gut tells me we aren't being saved by this guy!" Joe shouted to no one in particular.

Without warning, the front window shattered as a bullet carried through the van, splattering glass over Flora and back onto the others. His hunch had been accurate. It now all made perfect sense. The sheriff was somehow in league with the men at the ranch. The plan was to stop the van long enough for the men from the Sunset Canyon Ranch to catch up. The bullet through the window was meant to drive them back into the hands of their pursuers.

Joe swung the van around facing the oncoming mass of headlights. Colonel Ziyetski began to yell some of the only English words he knew, "Why - why?" Joe was wondering the same thing himself. Michael said nothing.

As he closed at high speed with his pursuers, not more than a quarter of a mile between them, he slowed and made a sudden sharp turn to the left, and accelerated again. The road was narrow. To Ziyetski, it seemed to disappear off into the black shadow of an ominous mountain that loomed ahead of them.

Joe continued speeding in a northerly direction along the straight-away but slowed to negotiate the steep switchbacks that followed. In the rear view mirror, he could see some confusion as the pursuing vehicles appeared to momentarily congregate as they reached the intersection. Some drove straight ahead while others made the turn.

It was a road he had known as a young boy, but had never patrolled as a deputy sheriff. The road soon became steep with a sheer drop off on its right side. Joe hugged the inside of the road assuming that there would be no oncoming traffic. They came to the top of the plateau and Joe stopped the van as he reached a high chainlink fence with a sign across the front: **HURRICANE MESA TEST SITE. NO TRESPASSING.**

With little pause, he gunned the engine and smashed the van through the gate snapping the steel posts from their foundations. He veered out onto the runway, driving full speed in the direction of a group of buildings, one of which was a medium-sized hangar. He was astonished to see men under lights near the hangar, with rifles, taking aim. Almost before he could react, bullets were again zinging through the vehicle. A sudden groan came from one of the Russians as a bullet grazed the side of his neck.

Joe veered the van away from the hangar. Having no other plan of escape, he raced down the runway to the west, realizing it would soon come to an end at a sheer drop-off on the edge of the mesa.

Once at the runway's end, he was still able to navigate the vehicle onto the gravel where he then reached the edge of the Hurricane Mesa itself - a sheer eight hundred foot cliff. It was the dead end of the escape attempt. He turned around, held up his arms and simply said, "I don't know, I just don't know what the hell to do next!" As his options evaporated, fear of death was now foremost in his thoughts.

Colonel Ziyetski slid the door open and took charge. He quickly directed his men out of the vehicle as they assisted the wounded comrade. He grabbed a small backpack and after a frantic surveillance of the area, started running in the direction of a rock formation at the edge of the cliff. It was situated above the plateau's flat surface by some twenty to thirty feet. Joe and Flora followed the KGB troopers who, along with the handcuffed Michael, were dragging all of the equipment and ammunition boxes in the van with them.

Within minutes, they had all covered the rugged terrain to the outcropping approximately three hundred feet from the van. Immediately, Ziyetski began setting up defensive positions, barking orders in Russian to his four men armed with the assault rifles. The boxes of ammunition from the FBI van were cracked open and they began packing extra clips. Michael was uncertain what to do realizing that there were five rifles and seven men. His speculation ended as Ziyetski approached him, shoved an automatic pistol into Michael's hand and generated a phrase in broken English, "Don't waste."

Joe found a wide ledge along the cliff that was on the opposite side of the outcropping. Although precariously perched above the sheer precipice, it would be a good place for Flora to hide. He hoped it would shield her from gunfire coming from the airfield. He then returned to Ziyetski who motioned to him, pointing out the position behind a boulder that he should take in the defense of the rock pile.

They watched a long parade of headlights pass through the broken gate onto the airfield and stopped near the aircraft hangar. It was evident that the Spetsnaz were orienting themselves, uncertain as to exactly where the van's occupants had fled. Colonel Ziyetski assumed the Spetsnaz could not see the rock outcrop in the dark without a more elaborate reconnaissance of the area. This would give him time to dig in, and possibly look for an escape route down the cliff.

Michael was venting his disgust in a struggle with the handcuffs. Joe Wilson pulled a pair of mini-pliers from his service belt and worked to loosen the chains. Neither said a word. Throats were far too dry to manufacture words. The intensity of the fright and apprehension of the moment caused them to merely await the next order from the Russian officer whose words they did not understand, but who appeared to be actively making plans for something. He was clearly in command.

Some twenty minutes later, the headlights began working their way along the runway to the abandoned van. Soon, even more commotion could be seen near the van. Ziyetski had no doubts that the Spetsnaz would quickly discover where he and his people had gone. To run for the high ground was an elementary tactical decision.

Troopers were creeping forward slowly under the cover of darkness. Suddenly, with the shrill blast of an ensign's whistle, the standard Soviet frontal attack commenced. Thirty Spetsnaz troopers attempted to storm the hill. On Ziyetski's signal the defenders opened fire. After suffering heavy losses in the first minute of the attack, the Spetsnaz unit withdrew to plan a new approach. The Spetsnaz now knew how the hill would be defended. In the judgement of Captain Major Sarabrov who had arrived to coordinate the attack, the critical intelligence was worth a few casualties. He would have sharp shooters using starlight scopes snipe at the hill until a more effective and less hazardous plan of attack could be devised.

Over the course of the next hour the defenders found themselves under a heavy barrage of sniper fire. The slightest movement would invite a ricocheting bullet. To reduce the danger, they peered carefully through the cracks in the rocks. Fortunately, the moon was working its way into the eastern sky above the high ridges of Zion National Park. With the added light, it was not difficult to detect an attacker within a hundred yards of the rocks.

For the next two hours, the battle was reduced to periodic rifle shots from ten to fifteen per minute. Ziyetski checked the rear of his position near Flora's hiding place, searching for an escape route. All he could see was a huge cliff dropping nearly a thousand feet to the desert floor. It provided sobering reality. He realized there was no chance of retreat or escape. But by the same token, there was assurance that no attack from the rear could be made. It was a good position and also a poor position, depending on how the course of the battle would go.

Ziyetski returned to the firing line. His peripheral vision caught the motion of a figure crouched in a shadow approximately one hundred-fifty feet directly ahead of his position. He carefully laid an M-16 on a rock, took aim and cranked off two rounds into the shadow. The scream in the darkness confirmed that another Spetsnaz trooper had lost his opportunity to serve the Rodina.

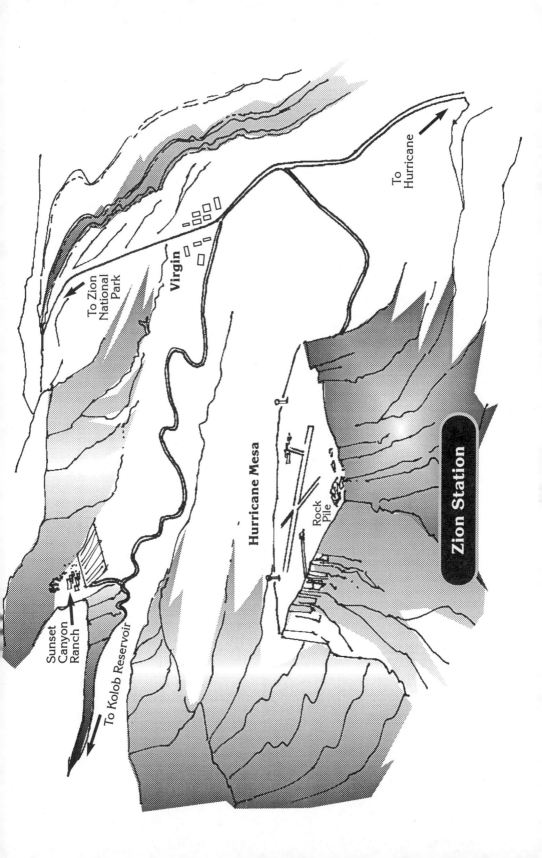

To Hurricane

To Zion National Park

Virgin

Hurricane Mesa

Rock Pile

Zion Station

Sunset Canyon Ranch

To Kolob Reservoir

CHAPTER 26

Hurricane Mesa, Late March, 1993

The moonlight began to fade. It was near midnight. Colonel Ziyetski was certain that as the moon set, and well before sunrise, there would be a period of darkness in which the Spetsnaz were sure to attack. As he awaited the advent of the darkest point of the night, he busied himself with the one piece of communications equipment that he had been allowed to bring into the United States and which had been standard issue for KGB agents operating outside of the country over the past two decades. He needed a flat surface on the ground at least sixteen feet square. The jagged rocky outcropping in which they were positioned made it difficult. But still, he laid the delicate foil-coated copper wires across the smoothest rocks he could find in order to keep the entire contraption as flat as possible. He knew that the effort was dangerous as he was likely exposing himself to night vision scopes of the Spetsnaz snipers by periodically standing up near the top of the outcropping to do his work. He operated quickly and methodically to get the job done. Finally, he pulled out a long pencil-shaped object that took on the appearance of a twelve-inch tire gauge. He extended it as each part slid out in telescopic form until it produced an antenna six feet in height but only one-half inch in diameter at the widest point. He then screwed the antenna into the console on the compact eight-inch square box which he had laid on the sandstone next to Flora on the south, unexposed side of the rock pile.

The next move was to attach the wiring running from the box with the long antenna back to the makeshift horizontal wire dish laying flat on the rocks near the top of the rock pile. Once all was attached, he returned to the ledge. Using a small pen-size flashlight and crouching over his work to avoid any disclosure of his position, he engaged the operating switch of the low power SPK-341 Satellite Up-Link.

It was a well known device, having been used for years by secret agents spying on the United States and the Western world. In its time it had been an expedient, cheap and clandestine method of passing information back to the headquarters of the KGB, GRU or Soviet Military Intelligence. Some of the West's most precious secrets had been compromised as successful spies had passed their newly discovered information back to their superiors in the Motherland for the purpose of advancing the interests of world wide Communism. But now, in an ironical twist of fate, the world had changed and the battery-powered SPK-341 was transmitting a signal to a hoped-for spy satellite, beaming the message in Morse code: **"COLONEL ZIYETSKI/KGB/SITUATION DESPERATE/UNDER ATTACK BY RENEGADE SPETSNAZ."**

Following the message, an emergency-locator signal then continued to transmit. The Colonel knew that he had limited power in that transmitting words and phrases by Morse code, rather than merely activating the longer-life emergency locator beeper only. The coded message would quickly deplete the power, but under the circumstances it was likely that the life of the battery could well outlast his own.

His greater concern was whether or not any spy satellites of the former Soviet Union still remained in place where his message could be received. Much had changed with the supposed demilitarization of the Motherland. He feared that with the reforms and cutbacks in the military, and with the standdown of the strategic nuclear forces, that perhaps there was no one left to monitor satellite data. Maybe the spy satellites were merely whirling around the earth with no further purpose.

To the KGB Colonel, the nature of the turn of events was as

unbelievable and it was absurd. A man, born deep in the heart of Russia, having been raised to hate and despise Americans was now desperately trapped in the heartland of his former adversary, hoping, and even praying, that military satellites spying on America could now save him and his men from the most bestial remnants of the Motherland's military machine. As the frenzy of sniper fire intensified, he knew that another attack was imminent and that the prospects for rescue were remote and probably non-existent.

The bullets began ricocheting off rocks. Each of the men braced themselves for the next onslaught. One of the KGB agents, an Anue from near Vladivostok, had been bleeding from the neck through the night. Each of his comrades had tried his hand at packing the wound, but the neck was a difficult spot to treat. Life was slipping away as the cold night air sent his body into an irreversible chill. Ziyetski had assisted him in assuming a prone position from which he could lay on the ground and fire his weapon through a small crevice in the rocks.

The defenders could see the darkened figures moving forward again from their rallying point near the runway. Ammunition supplies were depleting, and the orders were for no area fire, but only direct targeting. This meant that every bullet had to count. Michael would only use the revolver if their attackers were close enough to overrun the position.

* * *

Despite the early morning hour, the Sunset Canyon Ranch had become a very busy place, operating like a rear logistics support facility for a major battle. Trucks were rapidly entering and exiting the compound. The medical clinic was already being pushed to its maximum.

The STAVKA was meeting in a war council to decide how to handle the unanticipated situation. The debate had been strenuous on all, particularly Yuri Gagarin, as he had come in a wheelchair to help make the important decision.

"So what have you done with those dead FBI agents?" Andropov queried.

"Their bodies have been disposed of," Sarabrov, having returned from the Hurricane Mesa responded. "We buried them far back in the canyon near the caves. No one will ever find them."

"Why is it that you cannot dislodge a mere seven men and a girl from that defensive position up on the mesa?" Andropov fired the question at Sarabrov. He was loud and demanding. Sarabrov could see that his entire future rested on this battle. "I find it odd that you can successfully attack a well-armed train with over fifty defenders and get away with billions of dollars in gold, but you can't knock out this little group of policemen on the ridge by our airport!"

"We've got some severe limitations," Sarabrov responded. "We do not have gas or chemical weapons which we would normally use in this situation."

"And why not?" Andropov shouted.

"We have none in our stock piles. There are some supplies we simply have not been able to get into Zion Station."

"But you have hundreds, and they, only a few!"

"They are set in a very effective defensive position," Sarabrov explained. "It's almost as if they were inside a tank without a cannon. They're behind large rocks which are elevated above the ground. Our only approach is across a narrow open space that serves as an effective kill zone. And there's no way we can attack them from the rear."

"And why is that?" Andropov demanded.

Sarabrov realized that the lay of the land was still lost on the esteemed Russian leader. "There is a one thousand foot cliff behind them. It is impossible to scale that cliff, at least without proper equipment. And if we tried, one person could probably defend that position against all attackers with success."

"Well, you simply have to destroy them, and do it quickly! I suggest that you find a way to attack them from all directions, and get up that cliff!" Andropov yelled in a rage. "I just can't believe that a company of elite Spetsnaz cannot oust a ragtag bunch of American policemen, who have been out all night in the freezing temperatures. Don't you fear that they are calling in forces to back them up? You know you have to kill them before they can talk! I assume all this has occurred to you, Captain Major?" He continued to scream, his face turning red as he uttered one

Russian profanity after another.

Sarabrov had been uneasy about telling the truth regarding the men that were trapped on the Hurricane Mesa plateau. "They're not American policemen. They're not FBI."

"Then who in the hell are they?"

" What we are dealing with, is a well trained Border KGB strike team!"

His words caused immediate silence around the room as he stood looking at the other men sitting in the chairs in various stages of surprise at his disclosure. Andropov stood up and Gagarin strained against his wheelchair, himself attempting to stand. Jim sat stone cold, wondering if the words he had just heard were accurate.

"What in the name of the Rodina is a KGB team doing here? And why are you even shooting at them?"

"We believe," Sarabrov's voice was dry and nervous, "that they were sent here to find us - that they are not with us. They are against us."

"Do you know that for sure?" Jim shouted.

"We do not, but they were with the FBI. We think it was some cooperative effort with the Americans. In the deputy sheriff's car, we found the deputy's day log in the wreckage. It survived the fire. His last assignment says, 'Escort KGB and FBI investigators to Big Pines, see Colonel Ziyetski and Kenneth Swindler.' From the battle they are giving us, we can only assume we are facing well-trained Russian soldiers and not mere American policemen."

"Well, can you talk to those people? Get a bull horn out there and see what you can do!" Andropov shouted.

"We have considered that. But we don't know how much they really know about us. If we could at least get the Dane back, maybe we could strike a deal."

"Yes, we need the Dane. The records must be completed!" Gagarin demanded nervously.

"That doesn't really matter now," Andropov spoke, overriding Gagarin's concern to get Christensen alive. "Because they're all going to be dead! Whatever they know won't hurt us. That is, unless they do have the ability to communicate before we kill them."

"We feel that they do not. The FBI agents each had cellular

telephones. The sheriff's car had a radio in it, but we destroyed that vehicle. There was no radio antenna on the van. And as far as we know, the KGB cannot mount a radio net in this part of the world. Unless they had American equipment, they could not work the local frequencies. Thus, we think that they were likely only relying on their American hosts for communications. This may be a very good development for us," Sarabrov advised.

"Well, for your sake, Captain Major," Andropov threatened, "I hope you are correct. But for our sake, until the situation settles down, I would suggest that we leave Zion Station, and that we do it now!"

"One more thing Captain Major," Andropov continued, "the explosions up on the Mesa must be discernable from those cities to the south. They may be ten to twenty miles away, but an explosion at night will cause commotion. And all we don't need is a bunch of fire trucks coming up the road!"

"You needn't worry about that," Sarabrov responded. "We are not using incendiaries. That is another reason why the situation is difficult. We have avoided the use of mortars or RPG's for the reason that it would appear as a fireworks show from a distance."

"Well, let me tell you, Captain Major," Andropov continued, "you go back up the plateau and see if you can talk to those people. We have no choice but to leave this area until the whole situation cools down. Perhaps it is still under control, but if it is not, our entire cause is in jeopardy!"

Sarabrov exited the room immediately, passing Yelana in the hall as she was arriving late. It disturbed him that she, as a mere Spetsnaz Lieutenant had been invited at all. But as they met, a rush of fear caused him to think he would never see her again. He put his arms around her, drew her to him and kissed her. Her cold response caused him, without hesitation, to shove her away and storm out the door to an awaiting vehicle.

* * *

The third attack of the night had just been repulsed. The Spetsnaz strategy of forcing the defenders to exhaust their ammunition, however, was beginning to work. As Colonel Ziyetski moved from man to man reviewing each individual's situation, he figured that each was down to not more than three dozen rounds. In one more pitched defense of their position, the ammunition would be used up. But he also knew that from the slight orange hue in the eastern sky, that morning was approaching and that daylight would be to their advantage as they could perhaps get a better view of their targets. He hoped that they still had more bullets than the other side had attackers.

Joe Wilson had been distracted by a continuing fear. He crawled over the rock pile to the ledge. The view off the cliff was terrifying. He had always had a fear of heights. But even more fearful was the premonition. He could not see Flora - she was gone and there was only one way to leave the ledge.

He climbed down to look over the side, but could see nothing but darkness below. As he began to accept that fact that she may have only been the first to make the inevitable choice, he heard a sound, much like a chipmunk in its burrow deep in the rocks. He turned to see the face from the picture looking out at him from a narrow crevice which appeared to be so narrow it was beyond human access. He crawled to her and reached for her hand, feeling an overwhelming sense of relief that at least for the moment, she was still live. He felt her shaking from hypothermia and pulled her to him. She at first resisted, but as Joe removed his jacket and put it around her small frame, she burrowed against him to gather the warmth.

She said no words. But Joe knew, as he sat gently stroking the hair of the girl whose plight had obsessed him for so long, that he had found something that filled his heart far more than any of the youthful phases that had caused him so much confusion. If it was time to die, at least he had tried to save someone he thought he could love, and for him, if life was to end in the next few hours, it would be enough. She fell asleep. He rejoined the others in their defensive line on the other side of the rocks.

Colonel Ziyetski's optimism turned to dread as he crawled to the position being defended by the wounded Anue KGB trooper. Michael Christensen was shivering in the cold, having placed his light jacket over the young Russian in hopes of keeping him warm. Ziyetski looked closely, examined the man and simply shook his head and waved his hand. He took the jacket off of the trooper and handed it back to Michael. He then handed Michael the man's rifle and Michael returned the Colonel's pistol. The young Russian had died.

As the Colonel crawled back around the defensive positions, he quickly scurried back up toward the top of the rock pile, a move which invited two bullets ricocheting off the rocks near him. Once back in a position of concealment, he could see that the foil-covered wires of the SPK-341 Satellite Up-Link had been wrecked and shredded by thousands of bullets impacting the rocks at the top of their position. This meant the transmissions had stopped, perhaps as early as during the first attack after it had been set up.

Suddenly, out of the faint early morning light, from somewhere near a gathering of trucks at the end of the runway, an announcement in Russian began from a loud speaker. "Friends, attention please! This is all a mistake. We should not be fighting one another. Again, this is a terrible mistake! We are Russians, and we are with you! We do not know why you are shooting at us! It is a mistake, we thought you were bandits, but have now discovered that you are our brothers in arms! Please stop now! Please walk out of your positions, and we will give you food and all will be well!" The message droned on for about a quarter of an hour. The dawn in the eastern sky was spreading.

Ziyetski spoke to his men. They were all positioned close enough to one another that even a loud whisper could communicate to the entire group. "Don't anybody move. You don't want to end up like those railway guards. These are Spetsnaz and they are going to kill us all!"

"My name is Captain Major Dimitri Sarabrov of the armed forces of the Soviet Union. We would like to come forward and talk to you and explain to you that this is all nonsense. You need to talk to me before this mistake continues. It is not right that you should all die!" He chose his words carefully, realizing that all but the Dane would be killed. "I am coming forward, unarmed. You will see me with my hands raised high in the air and I would like to speak with you. Please do not shoot me. Consider this an expression of our desire to avoid more bloodshed!"

Momentarily, Colonel Ziyetski could see one individual walking forward from the runway area toward his position in the mid-dawn light. And as he reached a point approximately thirty yards away, Ziyetski loudly yelled, "Halt, if you come any closer, you will be shot!" Ziyetski was determined that the Spetsnaz Colonel should not get a close look at the defensive positions, nor the condition of his men.

"Again, I am Commander of a Spetsnaz company of the Union of Soviet Socialists Republics. I sincerely want to avoid more bloodshed. There is no reason for one Russian soldier to be killing another."

Ziyetski was bothered by his use of certain outmoded terms. "It is clear to me, Captain Major, that you are living in the past. I am a Colonel with the Federation Security Agency. I am a citizen of the Republic of Russia. The Union of Soviet Socialist Republics is dead!"

"No, you are mistaken, Colonel!" Sarabrov was quick to respond. "The Soviet Union is very much alive. All that you have seen in the past few years is an illusion. The Soviets are in control. The world is not as you think it is. Much has changed. But much has stayed the same. You are fighting against an unstoppable force, and for no reason!"

A cluster of additional headlights could be seen on the runway as daylight was still approaching. A black Mercedes made its way to the end of the runway where it stopped and two men in business suits climbed out of rear doors of the car on either side. They began to step forward in the direction of the Captain Major. Michael thought he recognized the car. He had rented it before for Yarov. One of the other agents, having his binoculars trained on the subject, could only gasp and then yelled across the twenty yards of open ground between the protection of the rock pile and to spot where the Colonel stood. "You will not believe this, Sir. You simply will not!" Ziyetski examined the two beings as they approached. He suddenly felt his heart drop to the pit of his stomach. Shivers traveled down his spine and sweat began to gather in droplets, trickling down his backbone to gather in a frost-frozen reservoir where his belt gathered at his waist.

He squinted - he blinked. He tried to clear his vision as if his brain was no longer in sync with his eyes. Ziyetski could see the unmistakable face of his former boss, the man who he had served for the first ten years of his career. It was none other than Yuri Andropov, the former President of the Soviet Union and Chief Director of the KGB, walking across the open field in the direction of the Captain Major. He was alive. But the other man - it was even more incredible. It was the face - the smooth boyish countenance, the likeness from a thousand posters, banners, newspapers, newsreels. The image, replica and portrait of the New Communist Man which Ziyetski from his youth had been taught to emulate. It was Yuri Gagarin, and not the cold nor the tension of the terrible night just past could dim Colonel Ziyestski's realization that he was now standing not more than thirty meters from the greatest hero of the Soviet Union. In the humility of the moment, it was hallowed ground. He was feeling helpless.

Suddenly his stomach growled. A slight pang of hunger shot through his otherwise immobilized system. In a fleeting return to reality, Ziyetski knew it was not possible. According to him and the rest of the world, Andropov died in 1984. Gagarin, everyone knew, had long since passed away. His funeral - Ziyestski recalled the event and even the month of official mourning, and years of unofficial bereavement that had followed.

He shook his head, rubbed his eyes and looked again. There stood the great Cosmonaut next to the man, who next to Beria during Stalin's reign of terror, was the most powerful leader of the KGB in the history of Russia. He was the man who had led the KGB through the Cold War years and effectively captured the most significant secrets of the West in protection of the Motherland. What have they done, he thought to himself. Am I seeing a resurrected beings? He knew it was Andropov. He had seen him before on numerous occasions. It was the Chairman. And, Gagarin - the hope and pride of the Motherland had been wrapped together in this man. It was him. Ziyetski was certain.

As Andropov, with Gagarin walking slowly behind, stepped boldly forward, past the spot where Captain Major Sarabrov had halted, Ziyetski gathered strength and spoke again. This time, his voice was noticeably distressed, uneven and shaken by the perilous events of the moment. Yet, standing his ground, his voice engineered a clear command, "If you come any closer, you will be shot!"

"I doubt that very seriously, Colonel Ziyetski. I really do doubt that!" The former Russian President spoke with confidence as he continued to walk.

At that point, Ziyetski raised his M-16 and took careful aim at the man's forehead, wondering if he could shoot a ghost.

With that motion, Andropov stopped and cleared his throat as if about to address a banquet, "Colonel Ziyetski, the greatness of the revolution is before you. You are a mere man, pointing your rifle at beings who are living in eternity. It is a gift of the revolution, something that you and your men should be a part of and enjoy as this world changes.''

Ziyetski stood stiff and frozen, his warm right cheek pasted to the ice cold butt of his rifle.

''Colonel. You will not shoot. I order you! But you *will* think. I order you to use your brain for a moment and think.''

Ziyetski did not change his position nor respond.

''One thing is for certain, nothing ever stays the same. You are fighting against a power that you have known since you were a very young boy was destined to control this world for the betterment of mankind. All of this liberalization - these changes, Perstroika, Glasnost, Detente, Democratization - all these changes, we have allowed in the Motherland and we have them well under control. Thus, you are fighting against nothing but yourself. It makes no sense to me that you and your men would commit suicide out on this hill in the land of our enemies.''

Gagarin had said nothing. He took a step forward, but quickly stopped with the sudden jerk of the rifle previously trained on Andropov now pointing at him. Andropov's boldness had disturbed him. He began, ''Colonel, I gave up the very best years of my life so I could be saved to come forward in the day when I could help redeem the Motherland. Well, this is that day. I will soon return, and it will be glorious. I have sacrificed much so that you and your children can have a homeland. It has not been easy. How I wish that I could have been like you and just lived a normal life, but there are reasons, and very good reasons. Now you must give. You must be understanding and sacrifice. We want you to stop this fight. We want you to be a brother to us, as you are a servant of the Motherland. Please give up your position and join us in our cause. You will return to Moscow a hero. Join us please.'' Gagarin then stepped gingerly a few paces back toward the car as if he had said his piece and made his expected contribution to the exchange.

Both men waited for a response. But there was none. Andropov was irritated. He broke the silence, ''So, you have your choice. You will either join us or you will die. You have made a great and heroic accounting of yourselves and we are in need of men like you. But you must understand that the New Communist Man is emerging, perhaps with a different look, but emerging all the same. He is destined to control this world within a very complex system which will take considerable time for you to fully understand. Will you be one of us, or will you not?''

Colonel Ziyetski began struggling for words. His mouth was dry. He hoped he had not telegraphed his vulnerability. He knew that his next utterance would surely seal his fate.

He sensed the pain of nervous hunger and the sting of the frost-bitten air of the cool morning. The frigid temperature had long since numbed his toes, causing him to balance back on his heels to assure stable contact with the ground. But still looming large in his mind was the wretched anguish he had endured as he watched one of his men bleed to death in the night. Equally powerful in his thoughts, were the images of the two Gods of the Soviet world that now stood before him. It was awkward. He sensed that the incredulity of it all prompted twinges of slightly pleasing relief. As he measured the words of the Chairman with the face of the statesman he had served for so many years and the words of the great Cosmonaut he and all Russians had adored, it occurred to him that any force from Russia that could freely operate as the Spetsnaz was now doing within the United States must be of awesome power. Perhaps it was true. The Chairman's words made sense. The return of the hardliners in a sort of natural evolution of Russian-style power grabbing had always seemed only a thought away from the status quo in the minds of all Russians. It was the paramount fear, and a lingering certainty that it was not a matter of "if," but only, "when."

Ziyetski remembered the week in August of 1991 as he had attempted to wrest Gorbachev's freedom amid a confused and uncertain situation. It had all seemed like such a fraud at that time, a much less certain outcome - the perfect success of the darker powers of the revolution than he was now facing. The banishment to the Far East, the accusations against him - had it all been a ruse? It is no wonder that men with the power to live far beyond their own public deaths would also have power to orchestrate the deception of the people of the Motherland. He tried to speak, "What of Russia? If you control Her, why are you here?" Ziyetski asked, his voice cracking. He could not muster enough oxygen to fill his words.

Andropov was relieved to hear the Colonel speak. "We go where we wish. We control what we will. The reforms in the Motherland and many events in this country occur only at the pleasure of the STAVKA. Now, Colonel, please join us. It is the wise thing to do."

"What of the Americans? What will you do with them?" Ziyetski asked, showing his first sign of compromise.

"They will be taken to a safe place by us, of course."

"And how will we leave this country?" Ziyetski asked.

"We have our own Air Force. One of our aircraft sits in the hangar!" Andropov pointed. "And think, Colonel, you can be home to your family by tomorrow. It is that simple. Just lay down your arms!"

The Colonel surveyed the scene of carnage and death across the kill zone before him. He looked at his men and the two Americans some thirty meters to his right, and began to consider the best terms of a negotiated surrender. He lowered the rifle from its aimed position.

Andropov capitalized on the nonverbal sign, " That's it, Colonel, join us." He stood still. He wanted his victim to make the first capitulative move.

The Colonel was lightheaded. It seemed as if he was atop a great swaying tree. The mental forces of self-preservation were starting to take control. "The Gods are right," he whispered to himself, "there is only surrender now."

"Will you become great with us now?" Andropov importuned. This would be a victory and the American Dacha, and the Second Coming as well would be safe.

Ziyetski did not respond. He only stood in silence. But his eyes were busy. As they followed from man to man among the defenders, he suddenly focused upon the still body of the young Anue KGB Sergeant from Vladivostok. The sight caused his mind to wander, and despite its fatigued condition, he found himself on the streets of Moscow observing the tough, but hopeful faces of the Russian people. Suddenly he saw the eyes of the beautiful child looking desperately for her father in every uniform - a fate that would likely befall his own children, depending upon the decision he was now pressed to make. He remembered the eager face of the child's uncle as he had announced with pride, his ownership of his apartment and his willingness to stand up, even to the KGB, in his defense of his home.

The minutes of silence continued, disturbed only by the chilling morning breeze. Together with the confusion of the moment, sleep deprivation had taken control of Ziyetski and he was imprisoned in an alien stupor of thought. The bewitching faces from the familiar overpowering beings of the past were now closing on him. Andropov walked forward.

"Give me your rifle, Colonel Ziyetski," the former President of Russia spoke in his most tender voice.

The streets of Moscow still loomed vividly in Ziyetski's daydream as he failed to note Andropov's approach. The poster in the store window as the snow fell lightly - he could see it - he could see it clearly. The face of the young hockey player wrapped in the tri-color red white and blue flag of the Russian Republic. And what were the words? He struggled with his memory. What were the words? Andropov was now only ten paces away, "That's right, give me your rifle, Colonel," his words were hypnotic.

The words were coming, hope, optimism, faith, freedom. "That's it - Svoboda Pobejdaet!" he spoke quietly, and then with increased intensity he declared loudly, **"SVOBODA POBEJDAET! FREEDOM WINS!!"** His words echoed into the morning air.

Andropov stopped in his tracks. Gagarin was startled and stood still. Ziyetski, emerging from the confinement of his thoughts, screamed like a crazed fanatic, "That's my answer, you sons-of-bitches! Freedom Wins!"

Andropov, sensing the sudden change of circumstances began to step back. Gagarin, still weak from his surgery, moved even faster. "Your position is hopeless, Colonel Ziyetski!" the Chairman pleaded in his retreat. "As an intelligent member of the KGB that I trained, I would assume that you would recognize your dilemma and realize what has to be done! To die on this pitiful hill of rocks in America makes no sense! It is not befitting of a Colonel in the KGB!"

There was a short pause. "You should understand, Sir, that I understand what's really at stake here!" Ziyetski's voice had gained strength. It was direct and powerful. He felt a sense of pride and defiance well up inside him as he spoke his final words.

"If it's all an illusion as you say, then *it is an illusion worth dying for!* If you continue your attack against us, as far as I'm concerned, you are attacking the Motherland, and She needs defending whether it is here on this pile of rocks in America, or wherever the new spirit of our land might take a stand! Svoboda Pobejdaet! *Freedom Wins!"*

Ziyetski repeatedly screamed his new battle cry into the morning air with a sense of rejuvenation that frightened even Andropov. Michael and Joe watched the drama from the safety of their rifle pits, not understanding a word, but clearly sensing Ziyetski's spirited defiance.

"In your ignorance, Colonel Ziyetski, you shall die! You have gone mad - you are not worth saving!" The old man turned around and walked briskly away, catching up with Gagarin who had reached the black Mercedes. As they reached the point where Captain Major Sarabrov was standing, Andropov said flatly, "Shoot the bastard - kill him now!"

Ziyetski's peripheral vision anticipated Sarabrov's right elbow raising to shoulder his Kalashnikov. In the last half of the same second, Ziyetski raised his M-16 and cranked off one round, not at Sarabrov, but directly at the body of the dark figure of Russia past. Assured that Sarabrov's bullet was already tumbling in his direction at seven hundred meters per second, Ziyetski pulled the trigger again at the Hero of the Soviet Union. He felt an enormous explosion in his head. As he fell backwards, and hit the ground, he grabbed his head - his left ear was gone. As he touched the gaping hole in the side of his head, his last conscious thought was the certainty and satisfaction of two black-suited demons dropping like mere range targets.

Gunfire erupted from both sides. Joe and the Russians carefully picked their targets. Michael, less able with a rifle, was momentarily frozen. He looked at the young Russian soldier next to him, firing forward while anxiously looking off to his left as well, at the body of his leader, Colonel Ziyetski for signs of life.

As the soldier continued to fire, Michael took up the macabre watch, and within seconds saw the Colonel move a leg and try to stand before collapsing to the ground. As if drawn by the moment, and with no pause for common sense to control his actions, Michael bounded from the protection of the fire pits and lunged headlong, running, rolling and tumbling across the open ground to where Ziyetski was laying. Bullets whizzed and kicked up small dirt explosions all around him. He heard a groan from the Colonel as he worked the M-16 loose from the wounded man's grip.   Michael reared up, sent a burst of automatic fire in the direction of the black Mercedes, then did his best to hoist the Russian whom he had never formally met over his shoulder.   They stumbled clumsily toward the rock pile.

The Russians as well as Joe, following Michael's efforts, laid down a heavy barrage of cover-fire. Within seconds, Michael crashed to the ground inside the protection of the rocks, landing on the Colonel. Michael hoped that he had not injured him even worse. At almost the same moment, there was a commotion near the black Mercedes. In his exhaustion, Michael raised his head carefully from behind a rock to see the Spetsnaz backing off and the black Mercedes heading down the runway at a frantic speed in the direction of the hangar.

CHAPTER 27

Hurricane Mesa, Late March, 1993

As the morning light became more prominent, the defenders of the small rock pile were able to survey the havoc they had wreaked upon the attackers through the night. Bodies were strewn across the field before them as the Spetsnaz had attempted several direct charges up the hill, each time, without success.

But now, the situation had changed drastically. Yelana had learned the extent of the change as the Mercedes raced in the side utility entrance to the hanger which housed the Ilyusin and served as the Spetsnaz staging area for the attack on the rock pile. The driver was wailing like a grieving mother. Sarabrov climbed from the passenger seat and opened the rear door to expose transformation of the power of the SATVKA to two lifeless men whose imposter hearts had each served as the bull's eye for one of the better marksmen of the Border KGB.

Yelana was stoic as usual. She took Sarabrov by the hand and led him into a side room. ''Now what is your plan, Sarabrov?'' She demanded as if she was his superior and entitled to an immediate answer.

Sarabrov was not impressed. He grabbed her by the waist and pulled her to him. In the next second, his mouth was awkwardly covering hers in what he intended to be a powerful passionate kiss. He grabbed at her clothing, and felt the primal satisfaction as she begin to submit. The sensation drove his passions into higher gear, but in the next second, the agonizing but certain feeling of cold steel was driving its way through his kidney and into his vital parts.

Mother Russia was taking her victims wherever she could find them. Sarabrov collapsed dead on the floor.

Within minutes, she had returned to the main hangar area and had, along with Jim, the brilliant and powerful architect of the American experience, taken charge of the battle. It would be absolutely necessary to rid the Mesa of any witnesses. The defenders on the rock pile had to be finished off without further delay. She had opposed any negotiated trickery in the first place. Only men would be so stupid as to think it really could have worked.

She was prepared to use heavier weaponry. Pyrotechnics in the night sky might have attracted attention, but now the day was breaking. She could start using small caliber rocket-propelled grenades. Within a matter of one or two more attacks, the position would be overrun and the affair of the unexpected KGB agents resolved in its entirety.

* * *

As they waited, a pronounced lull in the action intimidated the defenders. At the same time, however, the first rays of the sun moved into the rock area where shadows had preserved the frost. The warmth, ever so slight, reminded Joe Wilson that he was still alive. The gunfire now pinned him down. He could not raise his head, let alone climb over the rock pile to check on Flora. As he watched dozens of soldiers walk from the hangar area across the airstrip in his direction, he realized that all could be over soon, despite the good fortune of their survival through the night.

New activity could be seen from the rock pile as a squad of Spetsnaz troopers began creeping forward with long thin tubes on their backs. They carried rocket-propelled grenades, RPG 10D's, which if fired within range, could detonate high explosives all across their defensive position.

Michael Christensen was still shivering, more from terror than the cold. With no military experience, he had exhausted his remaining nerves and energy in the dash to recover Ziyetski. It was nonetheless clear to him that the enemy had regrouped and would now employ a more effective method to deal death to him and his odd group of allies. He wondered what Gina might be thinking at the moment. He castigated himself a thousand times over for having returned to Moscow. He had fashioned himself as an expert on Russians. But trusting Yarov had been a fatal mistake, one that could very well make Gina a young widow and leave his five children fatherless. How long would she wait for his return from Russia? What would the frantic, futile search for him in Russia do to her? What lies would Yarov and the others at Technoserv tell to cover up the secret of his death, when, in reality he was fewer than twenty miles from his home?

Michael hugged the cold steel of the rifle he had pulled from Ziytski's grasp. At the same time, he looked at the young KGB trooper attending to his fallen commander. The young man hugged the Colonel to keep him warm, until he heard Joe yell out the words that he understood perfectly despite no knowledge of English, "Here they come!"

Michael response was immediate. His earlier fear began to flare into anger. A primal desire to kill washed over him. He knew he could die as well, but was determined now to see some of his bullets strike down the enemy before his own fatal moment arrived.

Suddenly, a pop followed by a whining sound with a distinct buzzing broke the brief morning silence. An object streaked over their position leaving a small vapor trail. Seconds later, an explosion was heard on the desert floor below the mesa. The rocket-propelled grenade had missed its target. The young Russian, in spite of his inexperience, still knew that the Spetsnaz troopers were only calculating their range. The troopers, hidden some four hundred yards away near the edge of the runway, would soon be laying down murderous fire and high explosives directly onto the rock pile itself.

Again they heard a pop, then a second, and a third, each one followed with the whirling and buzzing sound. Joe Wilson flattened himself against the ground as he saw the KGB agents doing the same. The next second, the ground shook. Rocks fragments flew in all directions and Joe heard blood curdling screams coming from one of the Russians on his right. Smoke engulfed the rock pile - the smell of fire was everywhere. Suddenly, he felt a sharp pain in his left foot. He looked down - his own boot was on fire as a phosphorous fragment wedged itself in the instep. There was no chance to stand up and run. All he could do was grab his boot and kick it off as the acid-like phosphorous burned through the leather and continued to devour the boot without producing a flame.

Joe was terrified as he watched the boot disintegrate before his eyes. He turned to his right again to see the young KGB agent with the Native American-like face, screaming and rolling around on his back and onto his stomach again as he tried to put out the phosphorous shrapnel which was embedded themselves in his body.

The other KGB agent could not move. He knew that marksmen were waiting for the slightest motion and that to jump to the rescue of the young agent would only cause the phosphorous to spread onto him, also. With no means to smother or stop the burn, the Russian was left to die a slow and most agonizing death.

The ground attack was on again. Joe Wilson yelled to the others as they saw a frontal assault - a wave of several dozen steel-helmeted soldiers charging up the hill, bayonets fixed. The burning phosphorous still clouded the view and only through breaks in the smoke could they see the attackers. The remaining Russian, Michael and Joe began firing at indistinct targets through the thick smoke.

Suddenly, the Russian agent, reacting violently to the phosphorous burns, pulled himself up and jack-knifed over the rocks with his rifle at the ready as he charged into the oncoming attackers, leaving a bluish-gray trail of smoke from burning flesh and clothes behind him as he ran. With his weapon firing on automatic, he had been hit almost as soon as he stood up, but in his charge down the hill, the forward motion of the Spetnaz was confused and momentarily halted by the surprise one-man counterattack. As the young Russian disappeared into the smoke, blood curdling screams could be heard, not only from him, but from his victims as he moved forward into the fray.

The remaining defenders used the diversion to more carefully pick their targets. As they fired, they saw the attack slowing in intensity, but still nearing their position. Men were falling on the bodies of others who had succumbed earlier to the deadly volleys from the rock pile.

But this time, the situation had changed dramatically. As the smoke cleared, Michael realized that he had one nineteen-round clip remaining. Joe was out of rifle ammunition and only had nine rounds for his service revolver. He realized with a dreadful certainty that his little group could not survive another attack. Joe motioned to the other Russians, trying to get some idea of their supply of ammunition, and in each case sign language from the remaining Russians conveyed a bleak message.

Joe attempted to count the dead on the field before him. To the best of his observation, he could see no fewer than fifty-eight men lying on the field. Realizing that the end was near, Joe leaned in the direction of Michael. He whispered, ''Save the last bullet for yourself.''

The sun was now high in the mid-morning sky. Again, the Spetsnaz troopers began moving forward. But this time, several vehicles joined in the attack. Two of the American Jeep Cherokees had been rigged with steel shields across the front, in a slanting back position which would deflect gunfire and allow the vehicles to make their way to the edge of the defensive perimeter at the rock pile. Joe calculated the number of Spetsnaz troopers that would come pouring out when the makeshift personnel carriers stopped at the base of the hill. He doubted that his group had enough bullets among themselves to stop the attack even if every bullet struck its mark. It would be impossible to stop the attackers as they charge up the twelve foot hill to fight at close range.

The ''jury-rigged'' armored personnel carriers were now making their way across the runway and would soon start working their way around the rocks and brush in a slow, but certain journey to the base of the hill. Joe Wilson and Michael Christensen needed no translation to know that the end had come. Although neither had understood the words the Russians had spoken, each began wondering just how he should die. Michael found himself laying prone, his head against the ground and imagining the deep, awful pain of a bullet blasting through his back at short range. He quietly began speaking the names of his wife and children, saying the special words of farewell for one last time. Joe considered a dash to the ledge from which he and Flora could jump together, but he knew that he would attract a bullet before he could even stand. The effort would be futile.

For her part, Yelana was confident that she had finally concocted a plan that the men in their stupidity had overlooked. As the vehicles with the steel plates moved forward, she ordered the riflemen to open fire to provide cover once the trucks closed in on the hill. Yelana herself followed in another truck only one hundred meters or so behind the armored vehicles.

Joe whispered to Michael and the Russians to not open fire until the vehicles reached a point approximately twenty yards below the hill where they could go no further and where the Spetsnaz troopers would unload for the attack. It was now time for fateful decisions. Joe determined that if he was to follow through with his plan to get to Flora before the Spetsnaz, it would have to happen now, before the Spetsnaz could stop him. He then looked down the hill and realized the vehicles were closing much more rapidly than he had anticipated.

The assault commenced with the now-familiar pop and the whine of the RPG's. Explosions were impacting the rock pile, first one, then two, then half a dozen. Michael gasped in pain as a ricocheting bullet tore into the calf of his left leg. In the next second, Joe saw a vehicle come to a halt. Spetsnaz troopers poured out of the side and rear doors and bolted for the base of the hill. He opened fire. As he fired, he felt a searing, burning sensation in his shoulder. He tried to rip his shirt off as it sizzled from a hot fragment of an RPG explosion that had ricocheted down from the rocks above him.

Suddenly, above all the noise and commotion he heard Flora's shrill, blood-curdling scream from the other side of the rock pile. Joe's only thought was that the Spetsnaz must have found a way to scale the cliff and their position would soon be over-run from all sides.

In the next moment, the air vibrated with a deep, rhythmic, pulsating sound that gave way to a strong thumping. The ominous noise caused his heart to race at the realization that a horrific death was truly imminent. The earth shook, dislodging boulders from the outcropping, the dust and debris adding to the confusion.

Rising over the crest of the rocks, Michael saw the rotors, followed by the hulking giant insect-like form of a battlefield helicopter ascending steadily to a hovering position directly over the outcropping. Instinctively, he took cover frantically jamming his body against a large boulder. There were no other choices. Joe Wilson did likewise, lying face down and burying his head in his hands as his final choice of death. Michael was huddled against a boulder, grabbing at his leg to try and ease the tremendous pain.

A powerful whooshing sound pulsated above the din of the rotor blades. Smoke, dirt and sand kicked up in all directions. The loud, metallic rumble of a large millimeter automatic cannon shook the ground, raining rocks on the helpless men.

Joe tried to raise his head and somehow reckon with the terrifying events of the moment. To his left, he saw an awkward shadow lifting up over the rear edge of the mesa. It was another helicopter, rockets launching, with a chain gun blasting away, creating such a clamor that he thought his eardrums would explode. As he awaited death, he imagined momentarily that the target for destruction might not be his position. He cleared away some of the debris and glimpsed over the rock between himself and the enemy in time to see the makeshift armored vehicle blown almost forty feet. His heart pounded as he saw through intermittent breaks in the clouds of fire and smoke, what looked like Spetsnaz troopers fleeing from their position and being shot down in the process. The helicopters, not just two, but now at least a half a dozen, were sweeping up and over the ridges and moving out onto the mesa in the direction of the airfield.

Michael gaped in amazement at the inexplicable scene. It was still too uncertain. Nevertheless, beneath the noise, the confusion, the dust and smoke, a sense of relief was beginning to overcome him. He was still alive and his pursuers, once at the bottom of the hill within twenty yards of him, were now either dead or on the run. Michael looked up to see still more of the contraptions pouring across the ridge directing their fire at the retreating Spetsnaz force.

Suddenly, one of the helicopters tilted sideways and plummeted to the ground, exploding in a terrifying fireball. Though it was almost two hundred feet away, they felt the searing heat, reminding the defenders that it was still a very dangerous place to be.

Within minutes, some of the helicopters began to land. Michael was not familiar with the unique appearance of the Apache helicopters.

They were followed by Black Hawk helicopters which landed, deplaning riflemen who immediately formed an unbroken line along the edge of the runway. The insignias on the side of the helicopters, however, were clear. Michael could see the black words, U.S. ARMY against the dark green color and realized that salvation, for at least some of them, had come.

As the fight continued to carry on across the plateau, it became evident that the Spetsnaz were going to make a stand around the aircraft hangar area on the east side of the plateau. As they did so, Michael, Joe and the two KGB agents watched the AH-64 Apache Battlefield helicopters, the flying tanks of the American armed forces, hover at a distance and rocket the Spetsnaz positions. The American troopers on the ground remained static, not attempting the kind of high casualty assault tactics the Spetsnaz had used against the rock pile.

A stand-off battle in reverse was developing as the Spetsnaz forces were holding the vicinity around the buildings along the tarmac to the runway, when he heard a different sound in the distance. Michael turned to his right just in time to see the form of a black aircraft with a thick fuselage, an American A-10 Thunderbolt, also known as a "Warthog." The battlefield support jet came in almost at stall speed from the south, churning up the building area with its powerful thirty millimeter tank-killing cannon. Suddenly, the jet jerked sharply up, and peeled away from its course allowing a cluster of bomblets to leap from its wings toward the ground. In seconds, all of the buildings along the tarmac erupted into flame, pitching huge fire balls and billowing black smoke high into the desert sky.

Now realizing the miracle of their rescue, they took further heart as a helicopter bearing the large red cross on a square white background landed at the edge of the airport runway. Similarly, a smaller Cobra-type attack helicopter, which they had seen orbiting above the battlefield, landed at the base of the rock pile not far from the burning hulk of one of the makeshift armored vehicles. Two men alighted from the Cobra and began to run up the hill toward the survivors. As they approached, one was clearly a military officer and the other was wearing a dark blue cap with the gold letters across the front - FBI. As the two men climbed the embankment and finally reached the large rocks behind which the defenders had made their stand, they surveyed the situation and one spoke in perfect Russian to the two KGB agents, "Colonel Ziyetski?" They pointed to the Colonel lying on the ground surrounded by three corpsmen. He noticed the dead and injured defenders among the rocks. "It looks like we made it in time for some - but not all."

"Where is Ken Swindler and his people?" the FBI agent asked. Michael related the gruesome details of the past eighteen hours.

As the men spoke, Joe Wilson backed away from the discussion and quietly stared eastward toward the massive napalm fire in progress where the airport buildings had once stood. Numb and terrified by the events, he could not stop shaking. As another discussion nearby continued in Russian, Joe realized that he had, somehow over the last day, become accustomed to the words and tone of the language even though he did not understand it. He had grown close to the men who had died near him, and he hoped they had a better appreciation for what was at stake than did he.

He was abruptly drawn by another thought. He moved away from the group to the top of the rock pile, continuing past remains of Ziyetski's SPK-341 Up-Link transmitter, and around to the other side where he found Flora Jackson. She was huddled on the ledge, her arms wrapped tightly around her knees, but apparently unhurt.

Flora looked up and saw Joe's anxious face. Drawing herself to her feet, she gazed searchingly at him, then stepped the two paces across the ledge and folded herself into the safety of his arms. He held her as her control broke and she cried in racking sobs. Joe felt the silkiness of her chestnut-brown hair against his cheeks and looked down to see his own tears disappearing ino the rich depths of her hair. *Freedom* for her had come at a very high cost.

* * *

In the World Wide Command and Control Center at the Pentagon, Vice-Admiral Richard Moody and his staff were on full alert and working overtime. The call had come in the early morning hours from the Federal Security Agency of the Republic of Russia in Moscow. Director Dombrayov had requested urgent assistance regarding a message that had been received, not by a Soviet spy satellite, but by two Cosmonauts in the orbiting Mir Space Station as they were conducting routine experiments. During a pass over North America, the space station's up-link receiver had appeared to malfunction as it had received a weak signal impulse normally reserved for passes over or near the borders of the former Soviet Union. The Cosmonauts had noted the words, **"COLONEL ZIYETSKI/KGB/ SITUATION DESPERATE/UNDER ATTACK BY RENEGADE SPETSNAZ,"** they had attempted to immediately pinpoint the location of the emergency locator signal. The impulse was detectable only for a few minutes and when the space station continued on its northern trajectory, it was no longer in position to receive the message.

The Cosmonauts had immediately referred the emergency locator message to the Aerospace Center at Star City near of Moscow. Technicians there had dutifully passed the information on to the KGB headquarters in Moscow. As Dombrayov himself became aware of the situation, he contacted his American counterpart, the Director of the FBI.

A training detachment of the U.S. Army's Delta Force regularly stationed at Fort Bragg, North Carolina had been on special training at Fort Irwin in the California desert near Barstow. The group had been dispatched, as soon as it could be assembled, in a northeasterly direction across the Nevada Desert in the direction of St. George, Utah. In addition, a Ranger company of the 82nd Airborne Division from Fort Benning, Georgia had likewise been training at the Desert Warfare Training Center at Fort Irwin. It had been hastily mustered into helicopters and followed toward southern Utah as well.

In the meantime, the scope of the battle and the need for substantial fire power on site had been determined by an aging RF-4C Phantom reconnaissance aircraft of the Idaho National Guard which had been scrambled from Mountain Home Air Force Base near Boise, Idaho. It had positioned itself in a circular pattern thirty-seven thousand feet above the spot of the emergency locator signal and began transmitting video and still photos to the Pentagon as early as 6:00 a.m., some eight hours after the Mir Space Station had picked up Ziyetski's message.

Vice-Admiral Moody had continued his review of video transmissions from the scene which showed an array of forces on the ground attacking a position on the edge of the plateau. To the Vice-Admiral's amazement, the pinpoint aerial photography confirmed that mainline elite Spetsnaz troopers were conducting a substantial military operation on American soil. As he prepared his report for the President, he hoped that intelligence would produce prisoners who could later confirm his analysis of the situation. Based upon the video and still photographs, he had ordered an attack on the forces conducting the siege against the defenders cornered on the edge of the mesa.

Through the course of the day following the rescue, however, there were no reports of prisoners being taken. The Spetsnaz troopers who had not been killed in the action had injected themselves with deadly poison consistent with the requirements of their training. It was feared that others had escaped off into the wilderness of southern Utah and that it might be days before any sort of successful roundup, if at all, could be affected.

The battle at Hurricane Mesa was over.

CHAPTER 28

From the scene of the battle, Colonel Ziyetski had been flown to the hospital at Nellis Air Force Base in Las Vegas, Nevada. His hospital wing had been placed under heavy guard by a group of nonuniformed agents from an elite cross-services military unit flown in from Washington D.C. He was allowed no visitors, other than a continual parade of American governmental officials from the intelligence community. He recited the Andropov and Gagarin confrontation time after time. Yet, it was clear to him, by the questions that were asked, that the Americans were skeptical.

Before his return to Russia, Ziyetski had hoped to attend the memorial service for the fallen FBI agents. Contrary to the efforts of the Spetsnaz, the bodies of Kenneth Swindler and two agents had been recovered by FBI teams as they scoured the Sunset Canyon Ranch inch by inch for evidence. But as with any other request involving contact with the outside world, Colonel Ziyetski was denied the opportunity to meet the family of Kenneth Swindler, the man for whom he had developed great admiration and friendship over such a short period.

Colonel Ziyetski would return to his native land bearing terrible disfigurement and injury that would leave him in great pain for the shortened remainder of his life. The head injury had been severe. His vision, hearing and use of the left side of his face had been largely compromised.

In Moscow he would present extensive evidence regarding his suspicions. His story of the shootout in St. George, and the night of terror locked in battle with the Spetsnaz would be followed-up closely by investigators at the highest levels. But the morning encounter with none other than Yuri Andropov, the former President of the Soviet Union and Director of the KGB, and the sighting of Yuri Gagarin, even with the corroboration of his two surviving agents, would be no more successful than his recitation of the same to the Americans. The Russian doctors would follow orders and write it off as the consequences of severe battle fatigue. How many times had the image of Lenin made its appearance on the front to inspire the Red Army against the Germans during World War Two? Such visions were common among Russians.

At last, he would be able to return to Vladivostok to his home and the family he often feared he would never see again. Tension would still exist between the local KGB and the Far Eastern Command as it would for years to come. The investigation of the Trans-Siberian Train robbery and mass murder would remain open.

In the United States, a major political event was in progress - the bribery scandal and indictment of Congressman Stony Chapman. His career was at an end. But one reality was irreversible. His daughter was soon to give birth to a child. Although the prosecutors would seize the millions of dollars of the bribery money from Oki-Soft and all of the Congressman's assets in punishment, they could not reverse the greatest benefit of all - the new grandchild he was soon to meet.

A deep silence pervaded the investigation by the FBI at the Sunset Canyon Ranch. They had listened intently to Joe Wilson. He had made certain that the FBI listened to Flora. It would result in Hannah Jackson's reunification with her daughter Flora and ultimate removal from the Red Rock City area under the close supervision and protection of armed government agents. In time, the wounds would hopefully heal, at least sufficiently for Joe Wilson and Flora Jackson to have a life together.

It took a very short meeting for the President and his National Security Council to conclude that the disclosure of the mythical STAVKA's existence, the killing of the great Soviet hero Yuri Gagarin and a former President of the Soviet Union in a battle on American soil would likely spur a major backlash from the Russian masses. It could be akin to that of a nuclear attack on heart of the Motherland itself. The lighting of an irreversible fuse on the already explosive potential of militant Russian nationalism which could refuel a possible reemergence of Soviet Communism as well was the last thing the planet needed.

Under confidential executive order, the entire event would become a national security secret. All government participants would be pledged to secrecy, with the appropriate disinformation tactics applied by the government to deflect inquiries. The abuses of the children at the ranch, other than facilitating the exit of Hannah and Flora from the cult, would be ignored. The indictment of Stony Chapman would be carefully sanitized to not go beyond the bribe.

The moderate winter that had allowed time for war had given way to the harsh freezing winds that preempted spring in the Caucuses. The frigid conditions had not subsided as Colonel Anaimov and his Spetsnaz defenders finally evacuated Caucus Station and made good their escape into Russia over the precarious high mountain ridge to the northwest. Lado Deniken's first duty had been to thoroughly inspect the sprawling captured base. On the first day of the inspection, he made his way to the caves on the western end of the installation, not far from the perimeter bordering the Kartalinian Forest.

Within minutes of his arrival, he was taken deep inside a cave to a medical complex where a special surgery facility was located, well-stocked in readiness for operations. As he and his experts examined the area, Deniken suddenly found himself confronting the gruesome nightmare of his destiny. The purpose of the surgery suite was confirmed as they examined the equipment and the undestroyed medical history logs. His son, Steffan, had lost his heart in that room.

As the sickening reality sliced into Lado Deniken with the force of a dagger, he left the base he had conquered, his own heart broken, pledging never to return to Caucus Station. He would relinquish his command of the Svanathian Militia. The hero of the Svan Warriors would shun notoriety and return to the fields of his father-in-law, never to fight again.

It was afternoon as the unmarked FBI sedan pulled up to the modest three bedroom home on Gunlock Court in St. George, Utah. It took only the appearance of the car to ignite the age-old words of treasure, "Daddy's home!" Five blonde-haired little girls of various ages and sizes bounded from the house to meet their father as he was assisted out of the car and onto crutches with the help of an agent. Amid all the questions, sympathetic hugs and loves, Michael was about halfway to the front door when Gina appeared.

Running across the yard, she threw her arms around her husband, savoring the reality of his presence. They managed the last steps to the house with Gina steadying Michael's balance as if there were no possibility that he could make it to the door without her help. "What happened, Michael - tell me what has happened!"

Michael leaned on her, warming to the feel of her body near him at last. Tears streamed down his face as his children gathered at each arm, taking great care to avoid his bandaged leg. He had a remarkable second chance at life, and Michael knew it. "I'm not sure where I've been... but I'm home, and I love you. I really, truly love you."

The young family, huddled together, squeezed in unison through the entryway of their home. The door closed softly behind them.

* * *

The flashes of light in the winter night high on Hurricane Mesa had blended into local lore - another strange, inexplicable event wide open to rumor and conjecture on the streets in Hurricane, Utah. On the other side of the world, equal uncertainty existed among the defenders of the Communist faith in the Russian Parliament. They had awaited word from the STAVKA.

Unable to wait any longer, the anti-Yeltsin Parliamentarians, forsaken and confused, would go it alone against the forces of Yeltsin in the celebrated siege of the Russian White House. Calling for help, and hoping desperately that the STAVKA would somehow see their plight and save them at the last moment, they iniated the historic battle that raged for several days in full view of the television cameras of the world, an event that would be etched in Russian history as the The Coup of Bloody October, 1993.

But the STAVKA had perished on a remote red rock mesa in southwestern Utah. The urgent cries from Moscow for rescue were never heard. And the last extreme vestiges of one of the most treacherous and menacing forces the world had ever known - Soviet Communism, were eliminated, hopefully and prayerfully - forever.

The dark secret of Hurricane Mesa would be safely kept.

THE END